MONTCLAIRE SCOWLED

"You find my company less pleasing than Walter's because he's smaller? Why? Do I crush you?"

"Nay, milord." Mackenna sighed. She had meant only that Walter wasn't such a huge presence in her life.

"Do I block the sunlight from your sky?" Montclaire opened arms that encompassed the world, and knocked over a candlestick.

"Not often, milord." Mackenna pinched off the flame before it could set fire to the stack of parchment.

"Have I gone to fat since becoming the lord of Fellhaven?"

"Nay, milord, I've not seen a dram of fat anywhere on you." She stumbled over the memory of a huge, naked warrior lowering himself into a steaming tub of water.

"Must I travel on my knees to gain your favor?"

She paused and stared. "Do you seek my favor, milord?"

Her aspect was so direct, he huffed and blustered, "Hell, no!"

FOR MY LADY'S KISS

LINDA NEEDHAM

AVON BOOKS ◆ NEW YORK

FOR MY LADY'S KISS is an original publication of Avon Books. This work has never before appeared in book form. This work is a novel. Any similarity to actual persons or events is purely coincidental.

AVON BOOKS
A division of
The Hearst Corporation
1350 Avenue of the Americas
New York, New York 10019

First Avon Books Printing: February 1997

AVON TRADEMARK REG. U.S. PAT. OFF. AND IN OTHER COUNTRIES, MARCA REGISTRADA, HECHO EN U.S.A.

Printed in the U.S.A.

RA 10 9 8 7 6 5 4 3 2 1

For my husband, Brad,
and all the roads less traveled by.

And for my son, James,
truly a hero-in-training.

Chapter 1

Northwestern England
Late September, 1292

"**C**hoose *me*, Mackenna Hughes! I'll make you happy, lass!"

Mackenna was sure the bellowing voice belonged to Robbie. 'Twas a blessing she was blindfolded and couldn't see the rutting boar and his frothing scarlet hair; she'd laugh for certain and damage his brittle male pride.

"Don't go choosing Robbie, Mackenna. He has nary a whisker to show for all his twenty years—should make you wonder what else he's yet to grow! 'Tis me you ought to be choosing."

Garvey, the braggart. A bit raw, but she could at least trust him to do a full day's labor—

"Just three steps more, Mackenna, and I'm all yours. I'll work hard for you, sweet lass; plow my furrows by day, and yours by night."

Mackenna cringed. Poor Kyle must be deep in his cups; he was usually a pious man without a ribald thought in his head. Aye, a good man, but—Nay, she shouldn't be listening to any of them! She didn't want to know. . . .

"Damn it, Mackenna. You'll come here, if you know what's bloody good for you. I'm standing right in front of you."

1

Owyn. The blacksmith had the nature of a hedgehog: prickly, dull-witted, and quick to anger. A man to avoid.

"Over here, Mackenna! To the right a little more, then straight on into my arms! No, no, my girl, to *your* right. . . ."

Lucas.

"I love you, 'Kenna!"

And Cody.

And then all the others began caterwauling as one, angering her to the core. This wasn't some silly Michaelmas game to pass the time till the dancing began. This was her future! And now, these unfeeling louts had ruined everything! She knew each voice as well as she knew her own, and now she knew exactly where each man was standing in the surrounding circle. Blessed Lady, if she weren't such a coward she'd rip the blindfold off and just choose.

Aye, but this *was* a coward's way to choose a husband.

"What are you waiting for, Mackenna? They're none of 'em gettin' any prettier."

She rounded on Meg Bavitts's voice. "If you think you can do better, Meg dear, choose one of the sluggards for yourself. I'll be glad to pick from the leavings."

Laughter rose up around her, carried aloft by too much Michaelmas ale. The minstrels launched into a lively tune and the market square exploded with singing. Even blindfolded, Mackenna felt the circle surge inward impatiently. Evening was near upon them, the air was sweet and unusually warm, and the dancing was soon to begin in earnest—gladsome dancing that would surely greet a rose-soft dawn.

And why should it not? The harvest had been bountiful this summer; hard work and good planning had paid off as never before in the four years since she'd become the reeve. The hogs were fattening on acorns in the forest, most of the winter plowing was done, and the grain stores were safely hidden in the abandoned castle, where no one outside the village would think to look.

The castle—forsaken and overwhelming as it threatened from its precipice—was a bitter reminder that the king would one day send an overlord to reclaim the fortress, to enslave the village as Lord Gilvane had done, to plunder and starve and destroy.

Strong fingers suddenly claimed her elbow. "You must end this blasphemy, Mackenna."

She might have known: Father Berton and his confessional voice, raised now to compete with the tumult around them.

"'Tis not blasphemy, Father," she said through clenched teeth.

"A stranger wandering into our fair village would think you a practicing pagan. You must remove this blindfold."

"I'm choosing a husband, not a rooster for my hens. Shall I have them strut through the market square so I might pick the one with the best display of tail feathers and the largest comb?"

Oh, but how could she choose *any* of them? Though most were pleasing in some way, none had made her heart quicken, nor caused her to wonder if his kiss would be as sweet as May wine.

"'Tis unworthy of you, Mackenna."

"I admit it, Father; I'm cowardly to the marrow, unable to choose from among my suitors in the ordinary way."

"So a game of chance is your answer? 'Tis unnatural."

McKenna yanked off the blindfold and glared into Father Berton's ice-blue eyes. "I'll not be blaming myself for something I'm being forced to do. Suppose I choose wrong? How do I live with myself? I'd make the poor man miserable, and myself as well. Better that my eyes are closed and I have naught to blame but chance."

The small priest hunched his shoulders to enfold their private words. "Wait on it, Mackenna. You needn't take a husband today."

"I've got four elder brothers, one married, one soon to be, and two others with marriage on their minds. 'Tis long past time I should have found a husband and a home of my own."

"For the love of God, then, spare yourself a bit of

dignity, Mackenna, and decide within the privacy of your own family."

"Aye, we did just that, Father," Galen grumbled suddenly from behind her, "but our sister refused to marry the man! 'Tis a disgrace."

Mackenna whirled and glared at her eldest brother. "I don't need your help, Galen." He'd broken through the perimeter, trailing Cadell, Bryce, and Addis right behind him. She loved her brothers, but lately she'd begun to think she had far too many.

"We tried to stop her," Galen continued.

"You threatened to tie me to a tree—"

"That never worked when we were children," Bryce said, grinning as he tugged gently on a length of her hair. "You always escaped."

"Well, she's not going to escape this time. Bloody blazes, Mackenna. Choose a husband immediately, or we'll do it for you." A vein throbbed in Galen's forehead.

"You'll name my husband over my dead and bleeding body."

"*That* we could manage right well," Galen shouted.

The circle of bridegrooms had once been twenty paces across; now it was less than ten, and getting smaller with every passing oath as everyone in Fellhaven pressed in closer for a better look at another Hughes family debate.

"Now, choose, Mackenna!" A familiar tic animated the corner of Galen's right eye. Cadell pushed him aside.

"Ah, leave off your bellowing, Galen." Cadell settled his arm across Mackenna's shoulder, his brow so sincerely furrowed she wanted to slap him. "Look, sweeting, Owyn told me he was willing to take you to wife." He gestured toward Owyn, who looked as if he'd eaten burning coals for supper.

Mackenna grabbed Cadell's tunic at the neck and dragged his face down to hers. "Owyn will just have to take his chances along with the rest of them. And if I hear his name escape your mouth one more time before the moon has set on this night of horrors, I shall give you scars you'll remember each time you and Willa think about having children."

Cadell cringed and straightened when she let go of his tunic. "As you say, love."

The circle pressed in closer—a great, gangling, many-legged entity, breathing in concert, moving as one, smelling of meat pies, ale and spices. If she stomped on one toe, every throat in Fellhaven would cry out in pain.

"Whatever you do, Mackenna, my love, do quickly," Addis said. "You've got a near riot on your hands. Your prospective grooms are champing at the bit, frightening the children. Look at them!"

Young Robbie nodded at her like a grinning, freckled duck worrying the silt in a puddle. Kyle was rubbing his palms together and arching his beetle brows, casting her a slanting smile that left little to her imagination. Richard had already apologized to her for being old enough to be her father. What an enchanting lot! Oh, to melt into the hard-packed earth. . . .

"They won't marry until you're unavailable," Addis said under his breath. "You know as well as I that there hasn't been a wedding in the village since you began your search for a husband."

Mackenna might have been flattered and fooled into thinking she was a beauty. But she knew better: her unruly hair was a peculiar mix of copper and flax, her eyes were the dark rust of cinnamon bark, and her lips were too full, too arching. Aye, her bridegrooms were waiting all right, but they were waiting to wed the reeve, a woman whose dowry included the grist mill and a cartwright shop. She couldn't hope to marry for love. Waiting for it hadn't worked, and hoping for it hurt more and more with each passing season. Marriage was the best thing she could do for the village and for her family. It would settle things.

"All right, all right," she shouted, suddenly full up with the delay. "Stand back! All of you! Give me room to breathe." She thrust her arms out in front of her and rounded the circle, dodging the grasping hands and the suggestive sniggering, until the circle was again more than twenty paces across.

"A warning to my prospective bridegrooms: if any of you call out to me, or identify yourself in any way before I've removed my blindfold, you'll be immediately disqualified." She didn't want to know who her husband would be until the last possible moment.

"I'll be waiting for you right over here, Mackenna darlin'!" Kyle tottered on his heels and threw her a wobbly kiss.

"Don't listen to him, Mackenna. Kyle's plow is small and liable to break! Mine is sturdy and plows a deep furrow!"

It was easy to ignore the bawdy comments, but the circle tightened a step with the rising wave of laughter.

Father Berton raised his arms to his flock and they gave him their attention. "Do keep a decent thought in your hollow heads. And Mackenna," he said just for her, "God keep you and your choice." With one final glare, he stepped out of the circle.

She could delay no longer. Less than a minute from now, she'd know for certain whom God had planned to join her to for the rest of her days. She hoped He wouldn't inflict His inscrutable sense of humor on her to teach her another unfathomable lesson.

She strode to the center of the circle, took a deep breath, then pulled the scratchy wool blindfold over her eyes.

Blessedly dark.

The village grew silent, save for an occasional cough, a shifting of feet, the stir of clothing.

And a faraway rumbling. Thunder? Nay, it wasn't thunder. The late afternoon sky had been clear, the sun ready to set over the sharp crags of Mickelfell. It was an eerie sound from under the mountain, and hinted at a long-ago sorrow.

But she was stalling again.

And now her memory was too good. She needed to cloud her sense of direction; she'd make herself good and dizzy. She began to pivot on one foot, spinning slowly at first. As she picked up speed, she lifted her arms and the ground seemed to drop away from her feet. The minstrels struck up a bright melody, and someone started to clap to the beat of the tabor. Soon everyone was clapping and stomping in a rhythm that shook the market square. The dizziness stayed with her as she slowed, and kept her spinning while she tried to recover her balance. When she finally stopped, she was lost inside the circle.

Blessedly lost.

The music had evaporated, and the clapping too. No voices, no coughing, not even a breeze to tell her the direction of the lake. But there was something . . .

She squared her shoulders and tamped down the unaccountable fear that her plan was about to go horribly, inexorably wrong. Just a few moments and it would be over. *Now.*

Lifting her chin, Mackenna took five long, confident steps forward and crashed into a towering, immovable wall.

The barrier might have been a horse, except that her nose had buried itself into soft woolen cloth that smelled of cloves and dust and leather. She tried desperately to recall which man in Fellhaven was that tall, that massive, and which would have had the consideration to scent himself with cloves. She'd have to thank him sometime. Thank him? Blessed Lady, this man was to be her husband!

She put her hand where her nose had just been. Her palm settled against hard, shifting muscles and a searing heat cloaked beneath the wool. Heaven be praised! But which of the tall men in the circle had she seen in the fields with his tunic off, clad only in his long braies, and sporting a chest of rippling wonder? She was certain these muscles were as bronze as the bell in the church tower. No matter his identity, at least she would always have this magnificent sense-memory of her husband, one she could conjure in the dark while he was bedding her.

She wondered again why everyone was so still. Given

the near-riot of a few moments ago, she hadn't expected her high-spirited friends and her impatient family to keep her plea for silence past her first step. She knew they were nearby, that she wasn't alone with this man. There was a crackling in the air, the kind that came after a lightning storm had swept the valley and disappeared over the next ridge.

Mackenna smiled to herself. All of Fellhaven was caught up in the anticipation. Well, she was ready to face the face—almost. She ran her hand upward over his finely woven tunic, over a diagonal strap of leather that crossed high on his chest. My, his shoulders were wide! Undaunted, shamelessly eager to discover who this delicious man was, and wondering how he'd hidden his better qualities for so many years, she followed the ridges and hollows across his collarbone. The man beneath all this splendor straightened some, became taller, broader. And did she hear him take in a deep breath?

She stopped again when his long hair brushed her fingers. What color would it be? And who among her eligible bridegrooms had managed to grow his hair to his shoulders in the last two minutes? She must not be remembering right; distances were deceiving behind the blindfold.

Wonder kept her hand moving up his corded neck, found his pulse pounding beneath her fingertips. Would she know him by touching his chin, his brow, the bridge of his nose? She reached up, put both hands to his face, and her heart stopped.

A beard. A lush and silky, well-trimmed beard.

But that couldn't be. Excepting Kyle's drooping moustache and Richard's thin one, all the men in the circle had clean-shaved their faces that day to within an inch of their lives.

Then a bell pealed in her head. Bloody hell—they'd deceived her! Her vile brothers had slipped a different man into the circle. Some miscreant, mean-spirited miser who'd bargained best for her dowry, a man from another village. No wonder they had pressed her to hurry!

Suddenly blazing with blistering words for her brothers and for this black-hearted interloper, Mackenna stepped back and ripped the blindfold off her eyes.

Merciful Mary!

Her fury failed her. Stark fear staked her words against her tongue, and her feet to the ground.

This was no man! He was half the sky; hell's black shadow cast against the blood-red setting sun. The crucible-gleam where human eyes ought to have been was just a narrow, feral glint.

She prayed for the strength to run. Nay. He would overtake her before she gained a step. Surely he wouldn't dare hurt her here in a public market.

Then the beast bent to her. He claimed the column of her neck with his fingers and his calloused palm, tipped her chin to meet his measure with the end of his thumb. The closer he came, the more he drew her into his dark eyes, the better she could discern the superb definition of his mouth, the sculpted ridge of his lips as they parted.

"I don't know your game, girl," he whispered in Norman French against her temple, "but I do fancy the way you play it."

Chapter 2

Sweet blazes, the girl was beautiful!

He hadn't expected her eyes to rival the splendor of the sunrise, nor her bountiful mouth to want such a kissing. The blindfold had hidden treasures beyond his imagining.

He'd managed to lay siege to his baser instincts, standing fast against the girl's eccentric fondling. Yet now that the blindfold was no more, he'd breached his good intentions and fitted her violet-scented softness against the length of him. He'd been too long without a woman, and although he kept his stirrings in check, his flesh undeniably desired this one.

Her pulse raced beneath the heel of his hand where he'd claimed her exquisite neck. But it was cold fear, not passion, that stirred her. The blindfold had made her his equal, had given her leave to approach him with ease and abandon in her village game. But one look at him had transformed her pliable warmth into granite. Was his face so disagreeable to her that she should react as if he were the devil incarnate? Granted, she must have expected to find a village man who understood her pagan dance; she'd found instead an admiring stranger. Still, he wasn't deserving of her terror. He'd only meant to play along with the village game.

The village. He'd forgotten entirely. Indeed, he'd forgotten the reason he'd come. 'Twas certainly not to sport with the local lasses, no matter how enchanting the invitation. He rarely lost his sense of direction; his men would never let him hear the end of this little diversion.

The crowd shifted behind him and a familiar voice came to roost near his ear. "Thomas?"

Thomas Montclaire straightened and glared at his second-in-command. "You've come to rescue me, Walter?"

"I wouldn't, even if I could." Walter couldn't help grinning down at the startled young woman in Thomas's arms. She looked as if she'd been caught in a rabbit snare.

"Your pardon, mistress," Thomas said, trying to resurrect some decorum as he set her from him. But he'd managed to catch a lock of her hair in the buckle of his chest strap, and now she was frowning up at him. When he reached across to disentangle the mess, she slapped at his hands.

"Let me!" she snapped. The gaze so recently dark with terror had become a brittle and tenacious glare. She quickly worked the strand of hair free and then shoved herself away from him. "Now, sir, go back to the dark place you came from. You're not wanted here."

It was a simple statement of her position, one he could appreciate for its honesty.

"Sorry, my dear, but your wants don't concern me." He chucked her under the chin and dismissed her. "Let's be about it, Walter." As Walter followed him to the center of the oddly silent crowd, Thomas couldn't help but look back at the girl while four of his knights stepped past her to stand behind him. Parnel was the last, lingering too long, all but standing on his head to gain her attention. Thomas felt an oddly possessive satisfaction that she seemed disinclined to unlock her fierce gaze from his own.

"Not bad, Thomas," Walter said, his amusement obvious in his slanting smile.

"Aye, she's more than that, Walter. You weren't standing where I was. Eyes of purest cinnamon."

"I meant the village, Thomas."

"Aye, that's not bad either." He laughed and took careful measure of the buildings set back from the market square, a wide, imprecise intersection of five roads that met in front of the small, stone church. Great torches had been lit against the advancing night, and Thomas approved of what he could see.

He'd been told to expect disrepair and neglect, especially in the village, but he was happily surprised to find abundant evidence of careful and deliberate industry. With few exceptions the buildings stood plumb and freshly whitewashed, thatched roofs fortified against the storms that constantly rolled through these deep valleys. He'd seen sturdy fences and unbroken hedges, streams and ditches running freely. The market square had even improved on the axle-breaking ruts of most village centers, and was surfaced with stone chips. He'd been told the castle was in far better repair than the village. This pleased him even more.

But then there were the villagers themselves. He'd met only one. He assumed she was scarcely typical. The rest seemed a strangely dull-eyed and silent lot.

Thomas turned to address the crowded market square in the same commanding voice he used on the battlefield, surprised that his nerves jangled some. He'd never before faced this kind of enemy, and had no idea what to expect.

"I am Baron Thomas Montclaire," he said, "vassal to Edward, King of England. This village and yon castle now belong to me."

The king's demon lord! Mackenna realized. He'd come, and she wasn't ready for him. There were sheep in the near-meadows and grain unthrashed. This couldn't happen yet; the wounds were only just beginning to heal. She scanned the faces in the crowd: family faces, dear friends, sweet children. She knew that their fears were as deep and as paralyzing as hers.

But she was the reeve, her father's daughter. She'd be strong for all of them as she'd always been, as her father

had always been. She would battle the devil's bastard—
and this time, she'd win.

Thomas had expected at least a murmur of acknowledgment from the crowd, but the annoying silence only
deepened—a belligerent, rebellious silence.

"You've a way with words, Thomas," Walter muttered. "Your one and only acquaintance doesn't seem to
be taking your news very well. She looks as friendly as a
Welsh mountain lion."

"Had I known the risk, I'd have kept a safer distance."

"You could have lost a hand, your lordship."

"Or worse," Thomas said, hiding a smile. The girl was
scowling at him. A bit of anger was good for the spirit,
and it had pinked her cheeks and brow marvelously
well.

Beyond the girl, beyond the densely packed crowd of
villagers, his column of knights and men-at-arms, masons and household retainers stretched along the road
until the deepening evening swallowed them up. They
would be tired and grumbling after the long ride, and
itching to settle into their new quarters in Fellhaven
Castle. He would hurry this last duty.

Mackenna followed Montclaire's gaze and her courage faltered. Soldiers. Knights. They must have come
while she was blindfolded. Then she remembered the
rolling thunder. Not thunder, but devil's hooves, defiling the ground. There seemed to be hundreds of men,
the column twisting like a poisonous viper through her
defenseless village. Montclaire's banner was an unearthly amalgam of dragon and lion, ablaze in colors of
coal black, bile yellow, and blood red—a horrific beast
that had come striding out of her grimmest nightmares.

His voice lashed the evening air like a storm.

"I bring you Kind Edward's good wishes and a
garrison of soldiers to protect you." Thomas assumed he
would earn some enthusiasm over the renewed interest
from the Crown, given the years of neglect. He scanned
the crowd. Still nothing. He didn't tolerate insolence
among his soldiers, he damn well wasn't going to allow

it among his villeins. He tried again. "Like it or not, good people of Fellhaven, I am your lord—"

"I like it *not!*" Mackenna heard the challenge escape her mouth before she could stop it.

Thomas ignored the girl's barb, as he would a pebble tossed at him in full battle armor. "No doubt the years without an overlord have spoiled Fellhaven to the idea of authority—"

"Haven't you divined it yet, Montclaire?" Mackenna shouted. "They don't understand your filthy Norman tongue!"

The Montclaire devil turned his dark glare on her. "But I see that *you* do."

Mackenna stuck her chin in the air, the very chin she used on her brothers when they were being opinionated beyond their simple grasp of the world. "I make it a point to stay one step ahead of the devil," she said.

"Do you? Then you will translate for me."

"Translate?"

"You will translate between my filthy Norman tongue and your limited English one."

Mackenna felt as if her knee joints had slipped. She'd expected anger, and had braced for a blow from one of the knights standing nearby. But the lot of them were grinning at her now, a loathsome knot of arrogance, each man nearly as tall and brutish as their commander. From this distance, Montclaire's eyes looked blacker than slate, and his mouth was an unreadable line. Aye, he was Norman French, fresh off the continent, and lacking even a single word of English.

'Twas a perfect chance to aid the village. She had blundered blindly into his trap, but now she'd use it against him.

Thomas took a long step toward her, cupped his hands around his mouth and asked loudly, "Shall . . . I . . . speak . . . slower . . . for . . . you?" As he'd hoped, the firebrand blazed.

"I understand you too well, Montclaire. Go on. Speak and I shall translate."

"Come here." Thomas pointed to the ground a few

feet from him. When her scowl deepened, he held out his hand and invited her into the circle to stand where she might. That seemed to work. She approached with her chin tilted to him and her arms locked across her chest. A few sprigs of bright, curling copper framed her face; the rest of her unruly hair cascaded to her slender hips, near reaching the low-slung belt. She had a brazen swagger that proved a delight to watch. He wondered if she knew its effect. Nay, he was sure she thought it spoke self-assurance alone. Perhaps he would correct her notion one day.

He nodded to her as she settled a few feet from him, then he gestured to include the crowd. "Tell them who I am."

Mackenna smiled up at the grinning beast and nodded. She turned to the village and spoke quickly in English. "This malodorous ogre's name is Baron Thomas Montclaire. He says he is vassal to our own *good* King Edward. Fellhaven now belongs to him—every crock, ring, and ewe."

As she expected, a roar rose up, like the fury of enraged bees fleeing an underground hive. She glanced up at Montclaire, fully expecting to see him red-faced with anger. Instead she found nothing, no discernable expression at all. Just those black, flame-fed eyes boring into her.

Mother Mary, what if he knew English after all? What if he was only reeling out enough rope for her to slip around her neck? If he caught her, he'd surely make an example of her to smother rebellion among his villeins.

With any luck, his dark silence meant he was just ignoring Fellhaven's reaction to the news that they were once again to be pressed under the thumb of a despicable baron and his evil horde.

Still, she ought to test him to be sure. If she said something utterly outrageous to him in English, he would surely react if he understood.

She remembered a stray thought she'd had while he was clutching her in his contemptible embrace. A wayward thought, hardly thinkable now. And untrue to its depths. Not wanting to be overheard by anyone but the beast, she spoke softly but exceedingly clearly in English.

"I wish you had kissed me, Montclaire."

"In French, please."

Not a flicker. Mackenna smiled.

"What else do you wish me to say, Montclaire?" she asked politely in his Norman French.

He took a disquietingly deliberate step toward her. "I wish . . . hmmm." He stared down at her from that vulture's perch of his and actually flashed a smile of a sort. "Ah, yes. I wish you to refer to me as *Lord* Montclaire. Or 'Your Lordship.' A simple 'sir' would do just as well."

So, that's what he was thinking! She would play his game—arrogance drove great holes through a man's intelligence. "Yes, *milord*." She added a curtsey to make him think her amenable to his title, purposely not choosing an address on his list.

Thomas wasn't fooled by her sudden deference. She had far too much audacious courage and clearly not enough sense.

"Milord, what shall I tell them next?" she asked.

"Next, you may tell them that my soldiers will garrison the castle and protect the village from the Scots." Thomas thought her smile looked a bit too false. "Go on, tell them."

"Yes, milord." She turned to the crowd and pointed to Montclaire's string of soldiers. "We're to expect that fetid rabble stinking up our road to protect us from the raiding Scots. Shall I ask him who will protect us from our protectors?"

The village growled as a body, and Mackenna turned back to Montclaire, patiently awaiting his next announcement. A crimson flame seemed to flare in the shadow of his black eyes. He was obviously expecting a better reception.

"Tell them that manor court convenes Thursday next."

"Manor court?" Mackenna tamped down the sudden

fear before it could strangle her. "But why, milord?" She
tried not to stammer.

"You needn't know why. Only that I command it."

"We settle all disputes in our bylaw, the most recent
but a week ago. There are no cases pending between any
parties."

"Have you records of these bylaw cases?"

"Very good records." Pride had made her answer too
quickly.

"Sir Walter, my steward here, will use the records as
evidence for actions taken in the name of the lord's
holding."

"But, milord, what you ask is—"

"—quickly done," he finished. "Tell them. Now."

"Yes, milord." Mackenna turned away from him, the
sudden heat on her cheeks burning a path toward her
ears. She calmed herself and tucked her outrage back
into her stomach. "The beast will convene manor court
next Thursday. He'll use the bylaw record as evidence.
Bryce, the records must be burned, tonight."

"Thomas." It was the other man, Montclaire's steward. "I shall need time to study these bylaw records
before the court convenes. What say you?"

Mackenna looked quickly between the two men,
praying Montclaire wouldn't agree to it.

"Who knows where these records are kept?" he
asked.

"I do, milord," Mackenna said slowly, trying to guess
what the beast might do with the information. If he sent
her to retrieve them, she'd make sure they found their
way into a well.

"Anyone else?"

"My brother, Bryce." She didn't want to involve her
family in Montclaire's game, yet she could trust no one
but Bryce.

"Send him to fetch the records. Parnel, you and
Hagan accompany the man." Thomas clapped his steward on the back. "Excellent idea, Walter."

Mackenna watched them smile at each other. Disturbed by their silent communication, she turned back

to the crowd and found her brothers standing together in a solemn clump. "Bryce, go with these two men and bring back the bylaw records."

"Tell him to be quick about it," Montclaire said evenly, his dark eyes never blinking.

"And, Bryce, throw the records into the well if you get the chance," she shouted after them. Mackenna watched Montclaire for any sign that he'd understood. Nothing. His gaze was steady, and black as the night. She must have gotten away with her ruse, else he'd surely have brought his judgement down upon her long before this. "Have you any other proclamations, milord?"

"I do. Tomorrow, my steward will collect rents and taxes owed to the Crown these four years past."

"Nay, you can't!" There was no extra money in the village. Every silver penny had been used to rebuild from Lord Gilvane's devastation.

"Tell them," he said evenly.

"I . . . I can't. They won't understand."

"Taxes and rents are quite easy to understand: once incurred, they are owed until they are paid."

"But no one came to collect. . . . We didn't expect. . . ."

"You didn't expect what?" He seemed to know that her answer would be feeble and condemning.

"Never mind." She'd deal with it later. 'Twas better not to make the beast more suspicious than he already was. She turned away from him, this harbinger of sorrow and death.

"The beast and his king are demanding back taxes and rents. Tomorrow he sends forth his demons to do their mischief. Tonight, we must bury anything of value: plate, jewelry, coins. Cover your wells, board up your windows, else they be taxed. You must send your best animals to the upper fields. Council members meet me here after the dancing, and we'll—"

"Is English such a cumbersome language?" Montclaire asked.

"What?" Mackenna instantly flushed to her toes. He caught her gaze as she flicked it across his stony face, and seemed loath to let it go. She'd never stood so close to danger, had never felt so exposed. "What do you mean . . . milord?"

"I spoke not nearly that long," he said flatly.

"I was merely trying to soften the blow, milord." She wanted to look away but couldn't. "These are my friends."

He nodded. "Go on, then," he said, almost gently.

She'd better not press her luck. "I've finished, milord."

He looked at her for the longest time. He seemed to be measuring her by every means. Her ears began to burn.

"Anything else, milord?"

"Nay. You've done quite enough," Thomas said. She was a woman whose insolence would lead her to ruin. He thought it damned odd that none of the men of the village, not even the girl's brother, had stepped forward to engage him. Perhaps the true leaders were in hiding. No matter. He'd discover the truth in time and apportion his justice accordingly. He watched the still-grumbling crowd part as Hagan and Parnel returned with a small, leather-bound chest.

"The records are in here?" he asked.

Mackenna caught Bryce's look of despair. Montclaire's men had been conscientious. "Aye, milord," she said.

"Are they written in English?"

"Along with your Norman legal terms, milord."

"Then you will translate when Sir Walter requires."

She wanted to shout out a refusal, but quickly thought better of it. The closer she could stay to the business between the village and the beast, the better she could deflect harm. If she couldn't destroy the records completely, then she could at least lead the steward astray.

"Aye, milord." Mackenna hated hearing the respectful words coming out of her mouth. "I'll help when I can spare the time."

"Since your time and mine coincide exactly, you shall have plenty to spare." Montclaire's eyes flashed a warning as he turned away from her. He allowed his knights to precede him out of the circle, and turned back to Mackenna just before entering the throng. "Enjoy your Michaelmas night, my dear." He left her with a mock salute and an arrogant half-smile.

"And may your night be long and miserable among the ruins of Fellhaven Castle." She didn't wait until he was through the crowd before she spoke her plans. "We must celebrate until the locusts are well flown from the village."

The village came back to life, but now the music was forced and the dancing wary. The laughter verged on panic. So much to do, and only a single night in which to do it.

Mackenna turned to leave the circle and ran into Galen.

He snorted. "You have the devil's luck, Mackenna. If I didn't know better, I'd think you were in league with Montclaire just to thwart me. You escaped again without a husband."

"Nay, Galen," Addis said gravely, "Mackenna chose his lordship. It's Lady Montclaire, she'll be soon!"

"You've lost your mind, Addis. I chose no one!" But she *had* touched Montclaire first, sure as the sun would rise tomorrow. Her palms still burned with the memory of the heat of his chest.

"You touched him, girl," Cadell said. "He's yours."

Mackenna tried to scrub the heat from her cheeks. "Nay, Cadell. The rules changed the moment that beast entered our village and declared war."

"Changed how?" he asked, as if he didn't really know her answer. She appreciated a good jest, but Cadell sometimes went too far.

"Montclaire was not among the agreed-upon twelve. He's an outsider, a thief, not to mention a demon from hell. The choosing will have to wait. We've more important matters to consider now. Montclaire's plans to rob us blind, for one—"

Bryce draped his arm over Mackenna's shoulder. "She's right, as usual. Until we know where we stand, it's best we mount an unbreachable defense against Montclaire."

Mackenna smiled, grateful for Bryce's support, and looked around for more. "Are we together on this?"

Galen muttered and then nodded. "But you've gained only a reprieve, Mackenna. Remember that."

She reached up and planted a kiss on his sullen cheek. "I'll take a husband as soon as this business with Montclaire is ended, as soon as there is peace."

"You promise this?" he asked.

"You have my word on it, Galen. I'll marry and be gone; then you and Tilda can have your baby and your home. In the meantime, the two new carts must leave tonight for Furness—"

"Tonight?" Bryce whined.

"Tonight. Else Montclaire will seize them and we'll never see a penny of their worth. But if we don't stop grousing none of it will come to pass, because dawn will arrive and we'll find the devil standing here beside us making his own plans."

Chapter 3

❧❧

"**G**o quickly, Nabon. Take the south-facing trail and use the sally port at the base of the castle." Mackenna hurried into the dusty gloom of the stable with Nabon hanging fast to her heels.

"Aye, Mackenna. I pray we're in time."

"You will be. You'll find 373 barrels of grain hidden on the castle grounds. Move them into the sally port passage; we'll bring them to the village later."

"I'll take four men with me." Nabon's eyes glistened in the near-dark of the stable. "I'll not have another Gilvane leave my family to starve. We'll finish before the moon sets, 'Kenna." He slammed his cap onto his head and rushed away, nearly knocking over Father Berton.

"More deception, Mackenna?"

She grunted at the priest, then dug the shovel blade an inch into the hard-packed dirt. "Deception is the only thing the devil understands, Father. The grain in the castle belongs to us, not to Montclaire. 'Tis ours, earned by sweat and sorrow! He'll not profit from a single grain."

Father Berton sighed one of the great, meaningful sighs that always preceded his unasked-for advice. "Fellhaven would have perished four years ago without you, Mackenna."

"Please, Father. I've no time to—"

"Nay, I'll say this. You have courage and cunning beyond your years. You fought off Lord Gilvane's fam-

ine, you forced the villagers out into the fields by your
example, you kept warm clothes on the backs of the
cotters—"

"I am reeve, as my father was. 'Tis my job." The
ground resisted the shovel. She tapped the earth until
she found a softer place and jammed the blade into the
dirt.

"Mackenna, I often pray for the Lord to grant me the
gift to guide my flock with the same wisdom that you
guide the village."

" 'Tis a faulty prayer."

"Aye, and I'll not be offering it tonight. Don't you see
what you're doing? Montclaire has the means to raze the
village. He needs only a reason. For God's sake, don't
give him one."

She lifted a blade of dirt from the stable floor and
dumped it alongside the hole. "So, do we just give him
everything we've worked for, and then wait for the
winter to kill us all?" She continued her digging, the
sharp sound of the shovel scraping against her nerves,
her efforts made easier for her anger.

"You could try to meet him halfway."

"Halfway to starvation? Montclaire is a thief, Father, a
ruthless nobleman. As it was to Gilvane, Fellhaven will
be his lordship's private store, a bottomless coffer. Will
he be surprised, do you think, when he finds his coffer
empty?"

"He'll make the village pay for your foolishness."

"I suggest you bury the golden rood and the silver
chalice, Father. Hide them well from the good nobleman, else they will be his. Gilvane has returned. Not in
his form, but cast from the same evil. I cannot stand by
and watch it happen again."

"And you cannot right the entire world, not in one
night."

"I won't let Montclaire bring back the suffering."
Mackenna lifted out the last shovelful of dirt, and picked
up a fistful of small cloth bags filled with village
wedding rings and brooches. The bags clanked together
as she dropped them into the hole. She could feel the

priest's scowling eyes boring into her back as she kicked the pungent earth back into the hole. He would never understand.

"May the Lord have mercy on us in your vengeance, Mackenna."

"'Tis not vengeance." She looked up as he stormed away, his robes fluttering behind him. He was too trusting. She would bury the church's precious reliquaries herself. She stamped down the earth and scattered straw convincingly over the area, then hurried outside.

The market square, so recently alive with music and dancing, now seemed ghostly as silent shadows and silhouettes floated between the crofts and lanes. Mackenna stared through the thickness of the night in the direction of the castle and shook off a familiar and haunting chill.

Mother Mary, why now? The children were apple-cheeked, and laughter was the norm, not the exception. These were hard times, but they were fruitful and joyous.

She hung back in the gloom of the stable wall, sensing the coming terror, feeling its pulse thrumming through the soles of her shoes. Sometimes the burdens of her office threatened to pull her under. Whenever weeks of soaking rains ruined the rye fields, when murrain felled a quarter of the village sheep, when snow collapsed the roof of the tithe barn, the villagers looked to her. Even the day her father was killed and Lord Gilvane abandoned the castle, they sought her advice, as if Randolph Hughes' spirit had fled his body and come to rest in his daughter. They had accepted her advice as if from the mouth of Hughes himself, the champion reeve who had tried to save them from Gilvane, and had lost his life in the struggle. Four years later, she had more responsibilities than her father could have imagined. What would he have done with this Montclaire baron?

Frantic footsteps rounded the corner of the stable. "Mackenna!" The girl's screeching made Mackenna's heart thud against her chest. "My father—"

"Rose! What is it? Has Claeg been hurt?"

"Nay, Mackenna," Rose said in surprise. "Father just wants to know which of the upper fields he's to take his sheep to."

Mackenna recovered her pulse and swabbed the beading sweat from her forehead. "Rose, you must stop screeching. You're fifteen now, and should know better."

"Fifteen and to be married in three weeks." Rose bounced up and down on her toes. "Edwin asked me tonight!"

"My best to you, Rose." Mackenna wanted to give the girl a good kick in the shins for reminding her of Montclaire and her own humiliating attempt to choose a husband. "I'm glad you'll be marrying Edwin."

"And it seems *you'll* be marryin' the baron."

"I'll be doing no such thing. And don't you go saying such to anyone. Montclaire isn't one of us, nor will he ever be. As to the matter at hand, tell your father to take the sheep to the top of Mickelfell and over the ridge to the stone-circle field."

Rose sucked in a deep breath. "But that's a faerie field! 'Tis haunted after the sun goes down. Nymphs and pixies dance among the stones. I've seen 'em!"

Mackenna groaned. "Rose, I've told the faeries they couldn't dance tonight. They're busy hiding mushrooms and acorns from the new lord."

"Good. Well, I can't stand here and pass idle time with you, Mackenna. I've got to get back to father, and Edwin." As the last of Rose's words trailed into the night, Cody's voice sidled up beside Mackenna. "I've hidden the spindles of yarn in the rafters and covered them over with straw."

"Excellent, Cody. Now if you could see that Father Berton buries the church treasures, I'd appreciate it." She started away, but he caught her by the sleeve.

"Aye, 'Kenna. Uh . . . will you be choosin' another husband someday? Or will you be takin' the baron?"

"The baron?" Mackenna felt Cody's forehead for a

fever. "Have you gone mad? Has everyone? The choosing is void! How could you think otherwise?"

"I was just hoping for another chance." Cody smiled shyly and galloped away as two of the jurymen pressed her for word of the bylaw records.

"I'll do what I can," she promised. "Montclaire's at my mercy for the translation. I'll see that no harm comes."

She answered a dozen more questions as she made her way toward the cart shop. She helped finish the packing and quickly secured the last knot. The carts were loaded with dried fruits, pottery, iron pots, utensils, leather goods: all the best that Fellhaven had to offer to the market towns on the road to Furness. Their first attempt to reach beyond the village.

"Don't let anyone cheat you, Galen. And have a care with your speed. Watch the road for ruts and bandits, and don't come back without orders for at least six more carts."

"Yes, Mackenna," Galen said, overburdened with patience.

"Take an extra day or two and show the carts at St. Bees and Egremond." She kissed Galen and straightened his tunic. "And don't forget Ravensglass and Whidback—"

"And Milham," Addis interrupted. "Yes, yes, your ladyship, we've committed your orders to memory."

Mackenna grabbed his ear and pulled him down to eye level. "Don't ever taint my good name with that appellation, or I'll twist off your ear and make you eat it for supper."

"'Twould be a damn sight more tasty than your cooking." As soon as Mackenna let go of his ear, he gave her a hug. "Behave yourself, girl. We'll be back in three weeks."

Mackenna hurried alongside the carts for a quarter mile beyond the village, until the road narrowed and crossed over the new stone bridge. She waved farewell, and watched until the carts became only the dry com-

plaint from the axles. Their first trip to market; their first
trip away from home. She prayed they'd return with all
their limbs, and some money to the good. Chiding
herself for wasting time, she started back down the road
toward the village and the mill. She carried no lamp, but
the half-moon silvered and shadowed both sides of the
familiar road well enough to see. She had worries
enough to keep her company.

She quickened her pace, and wondered where Montclaire was at the moment. Aethel had reported the
wagons starting the climb up the axle-snapping road to
the castle. She prayed they would roll off the edge into
the deep, dark waters of Lake Dunmere and sleep forever at its rocky bottom.

As she neared the path that broke off toward the mill,
a shadow moved against the trunk of an ancient oak.
Not a fallen branch, not a sleeping ghost, but a man.
And there was only one man she knew who could rival
the might of an oak.

Montclaire. A current of fear eddied around her,
slowing her steps. How long had he been standing
there? Had he seen the carts go past him? Nay, he
couldn't have. She would have seen him, would have
sensed him. And he'd have stopped them on the spot.
She wanted to break and run into the forest cover. But if
she bolted, the beast would sense her guilt like an open,
pulsing vein and then go for the kill. Unwilling to cross
his path, she stopped a dozen feet from him.

"Milord," she said, forcing the counterfeit pleasantry
from between her teeth. "Enjoying a walk in the moonlight?"

"Nay," he answered too easily, "and you?"

"I had a bit too much ale and dancing; I thought to
clear my head."

His laughter rumbled along the roadbed. "I doubt
there's a more clear head in all of Fellhaven. Especially
tonight."

Mackenna suffered a chill as his specter separated
from the oak's and came toward her in his seven-league

stride. Like an ill-proportioned dream, his shadow lengthened ever more dramatically until it reclaimed the sky above her.

He seemed in his element, limned by the moon and studying her as if studying his prey. Leather creaked, and metal clanked against metal until he settled like a mill wheel come to rest.

"The wind has risen," he said finally. He put his head up and sniffed the air like the great beast he was. " 'Tis a sweet smell. It comes off the lake."

Mackenna resented his observation and said nothing.

"May I accompany you to the village?" He offered his elbow as if he were a suitor planning to escort her home.

"You needn't, milord; I'm going to the mill." She moved to step around him, but he shifted slightly and blocked her way.

"Nay, my dear, we're going to the village."

"Why?" Her question rose on the night wind, and hung there unanswered. "So, I have no choice, milord?"

"We have a choice in most matters, my dear. The difficulty arises in the rightness of our choosing. You never told me your name," he said, crossing his arms over his chest.

That wasn't the statement she had expected from him. But it seemed his way. Distract and destroy; she must remember his tactics. "You never asked it, milord."

"Aye, that's true." His forbidding gallantry remained undimmed; he gestured grandly down the road. "This is the way to the village, if I'm not mistaken."

Mackenna clasped her hands behind her back: not the penitent, but the condemned. Her knees wobbled with her first steps; the familiar road became unreliably rugged. An image of her village loomed in her imagination—houses and barns set ablaze by Montclaire's soldiers while she was selfishly sending her brothers off with a shipment of market goods. Mother Mary—men and women put to the sword, children impaled on pikes . . . !

"What have you done to my village?"

" 'Tis *my* village," he said smoothly.

So that was it; the village was his, so he could do as he pleased. She stumbled along faster, but Montclaire's pace was too deliberate for her to run ahead, his silence a frightening and brutal accusation. He knew about the carts, she was certain of it. She could endure an exploding, blue-black rage, but this unspoken kind of anger terrified her. Aye, he was an unchartable, treacherous enemy.

And what the devil was he doing here on the village road?

"Did you lose your way to the castle, milord?"

"I've not seen it yet. Will I like it?" he asked amiably.

Mackenna wasn't about to tell him the answer to that particular question. "Why aren't you there with your soldiers?"

"Why aren't you at home with your father?"

"Go to bloody hell, milord."

Montclaire grabbed her by the hand and started off the road. She dug her heels into the bracken.

"Where are you taking me?" She tried to pry his hand from around her wrist, but she might as well have been trying to open a walnut with a rose petal. She seldom panicked, but she was helpless against his strength and quite certain that the beast meant to do her vile mischief in the woods.

"I'm taking you to the village." Montclaire gave a tug, and her feet tore loose of their anchors.

"This is not the direction, you simpleton!" She recovered her balance in time to slam into Montclaire's back, which was every bit as massive and unyielding as his chest had been.

"You'll ride with me," he said quietly.

An enormous horse nickered softly as Montclaire approached. He gathered the reins from a branch and lifted himself easily into the saddle, his hand still wrapped around her wrist.

"I'd rather not ride, milord."

"What you'd 'rather' counts as naught to me. If you

haven't guessed already, girl, this night has just begun."
The sudden, chilly stiffness in his voice finally betrayed
his anger.

She had no time to form another thought. He lurched
sideways and captured her waist in a band of iron.
Between blinks she was dropped onto his lap. He took
up the lion's share of the saddle, leaving her backside
perched on his hips, and her thighs pressed against his
as if she were his concubine.

"This is unseemly, milord. I'll walk." She slid sideways, but Montclaire dropped his hand to her thigh and
held fast.

"You will ride. And whilst you sit here, you will think
of a good reason why I shouldn't throw you into
Fellhaven's dungeon and toss away the key."

"It doesn't have one."

"The dungeon has no key?"

"Fellhaven has no dungeon."

"It will," he said, as deliberately as two words had
ever been spoken together.

As his horse entered the road, shadows broke away
from shadows and became monstrous knights on horse-
back. She caught herself seeking his shelter, and stiffened.

"You've nothing to fear from them. They belong to
me."

"You're a possessive beast, aren't you?" she murmured.

"Aye. 'Tis best you learned that early."

She was trembling, but wasn't sure why—maybe her
unspent rage, or her fear for her brothers, or the
scorching heat pouring off Montclaire made the night
wind feel cold by contrast. Whatever the reason, she
found it impossible to keep from quaking like a spindly
larch.

Without a flutter of warning, an immense dragon's
wing swooped down and enfolded her in its startling
strength, a shield against the cold. Her fanciful moment
vaporized as she realized that Montclaire had imprisoned her inside his cloak.

She tried to push away from him and knocked the top of her head against his chin. "You needn't strangle me."

He ignored her and tucked the end of the cloak between them, then anchored his arm around her waist. Anyone looking on would assume she was allowing him the freedom of her chemise. She wasn't, but they would think that, and her cheeks burned.

"Milord, I repeat: this is unseemly—"

"So is deception. Have you thought up your reason?"

"First you must tell me what sin I've committed, to merit you constructing an entire dungeon in my honor."

His laughter wasn't loud, yet it was potent enough to penetrate her back, and settle low in her stomach. He stored a heat as intense as that of a smithy's forge. She was warm to the tips of her ears, nay, to the ends of her hair.

"Don't flatter yourself. My dungeon isn't just for you."

The thought of Galen and Addis manacled together in a dank cell made her stomach hurt.

She heard the frenzied clanging of the church bell and thought at first it sounded only inside her head. Then she looked toward the village, and her heart went cold. Fiendish fire shadows grappled with ghastly orange fingers along the line of treetops.

Fire!

"Devil's spawn!" she spat as she swung her leg over the pommel. Both feet touched the ground before he caught her and hauled her across his lap like a felled doe. Her nose bent when it hit his knee, sending stars to sting her eyes. Undaunted by the near-blinding pain, she rose on her elbows and glared up at him. "Damn you, Montclaire! Let me go!"

Triumph rolled across his brow as he glowered at the flames. He cast his black gaze down on her; his scowl deepened and his eyes narrowed to red-gold glints.

"Your debts will be paid in full for this, girl! Mark me!"

He gave spur to his mount, and she clutched his leather-clad knee to keep from pitching headfirst over the side of the horse. She needn't have bothered; he grabbed a fistful of skirts at her waist and locked her between his lap and the pommel.

"Let me go, Montclaire! I need to help them!"

"They're well beyond your help now, rebel. And the fault lies with *you!*"

Chapter 4

Mackenna fought and cursed Montclaire all the way into the square. The village blurred in yellow and orange as he wheeled the beast in a circle. People scattered as the brutish horse pranced sideways and finally came abreast of the market cross.

"Damn you for a devil, Montclaire!" Mackenna still lay flopped across the demon lord's lap, her backside in the air, a hank of her skirts bound up in his fist. She rose up on her hands and scanned the carnage. Torches burned everywhere, but the blaze was thankfully confined to a single croft.

Naught remained of Richard Beason's roof but a skeleton of hissing black and flickering embers. Montclaire's soldiers were entwined with her villagers in the plaited fire line, each man straining as arduously as the next to quench the flames. One of his officers had taken charge, riding back and forth between fire and well.

The cottage looked as if a giant had plucked the roof off just to see what was inside. Aye, a witless, snooping giant—which made her remember Montclaire and the undignified position she was presenting to the village.

"Will you seat me, milord?" Her demand hadn't died on her lips before she found herself seated on his lap, humiliation heating her skin as she forced her skirts to cover her legs.

Montclaire growled, snapping the reins against his

gauntlet. " 'Tis fortunate for you the fire didn't spread, rebel."

"Your plan to burn the village failed, Montclaire."

"*My* plan?" He clutched her shoulder and turned her. " 'Tis your doing, rebel!"

"You think *I* ordered this fire!" She sent an elbow into his ribs and found leather and wool and solid flesh. "Let me off this beast so I can tend my village."

"This isn't your village, it's mine. A point which you seem unable to understand."

"Mark me, Montclaire, I understand more than—Richard!" she shouted across the square. "I must go to him, Montclaire! 'Tis his house that burned." She laid her heels to the horse, but the animal didn't respond until Montclaire willed it.

"This man's sacrifice to your defiance was unnecessary."

"Sacrifice?" She snorted at his ignorance.

Richard met them amid the chaos, his face sooted and shiny. His hands shook; his eyes were red-rimmed and watery.

"Darlin', are you all right up there? I mean—" He flicked his eyes toward Montclaire. "You know . . . with his lordship?"

"I'm fine, Richard." She answered him in English, grateful for the privacy. "Was it the soldiers? What happened?"

"It was horrible." Richard swabbed at his face, slanting the soot streaks across his cheeks. "His lordship's men rode into the square and spread through the village. I ran to the garden to bury Letha's mother's silver ladle. My little Sara thought to help by hiding the candlestick under the bed."

Mackenna groaned. "And the candle was lit. . . ."

"Aye. One of the soldiers tried to douse the fire, but it had spread by then. He carried my Sara down from the loft; he saved her life. Says he has a girl just her age at home."

"Aye, Richard, and he has a dozen more children scattered across the countryside." She cast her accusa-

tion toward Montclaire, though he couldn't have understood it. He looked the sort to populate a county. "You'll
need a place to sleep until your roof is repaired; you're
welcome to use the millhouse."

"Thank you, girl." He touched her hand. "Will you be
choosin' again soon, 'Kenna?"

Her heart took off like a jackrabbit. "Aye, Richard,
when these troubles end."

His eyes got even redder and wetter. "We love ya,
lass."

Montclaire cleared his throat and drew her upright
against his chest. "Did he tell you how the fire was
started?"

"The fire wouldn't have happened if your soldiers
hadn't raided the village."

"How did the fire start?" he asked deliberately.

He would learn the truth sooner or later. Honesty
would have to serve the moment. But if the man made a
move toward Sara, it would be his last.

"That's your arsonist," she said. "There by the well;
the little girl huddling between her two brothers. She
was helping to save the family's meager treasures from
your pillaging. A candle caught a bed on fire."

Sara's curling hair was as wild as her eyes were large.
Her pale cheeks were streaked with sooty tears, and she
had fit two fingers into a frowning pout.

Suspecting Montclaire's silence, Mackenna glanced
up at him. He was looking past her, his mouth locked in
an unreadable line as he studied Sara. Mother Mary,
surely he wouldn't punish the child—

"Sara's only five, milord. An innocent. She didn't
know what she was doing."

He grunted. "And were you as innocent at five years
old?"

The beast was taunting her, trying his best to pierce
her calm. Well, let him try. She would disarm his taunts
with the truth and switch the blame from Sara to
herself. She stuck her chin into the air. "Aye, milord, I
was. But I've learned."

"I'm sure you have," he murmured. His eyes had

grown smoky and she was quite sure a smile had briefly nicked the corners of his mouth before disappearing beneath his moustache.

She bent down to Richard. "Go to Sara. She looks terrified. Tell her that I think she's a very brave girl."

"Aye, lass, I will!" He started to leave, then turned back. "If it pleases his lordship?"

It galled Mackenna to see Richard look to Montclaire for permission. He didn't deserve Richard's deference.

"May he leave to comfort his children, milord?" she asked between her teeth.

"Of course," Montclaire said without pause.

Mackenna rejected the illusion of humanity. She'd met stone statues with more compassion. The man's gaze gripped like cold iron. She pulled herself away from it.

"Aye, Richard, you can go. Please don't worry."

Richard kissed the back of her hand and ran to the well. He lifted Sara onto his shoulder, and hobbled off toward his roofless house with his two young sons clamped around his legs.

At least she'd been able to help the Beasons.

But chaos had overtaken Fellhaven. The fire still smoldered, dispatching its damp smoke to wander a few feet above the ground. A billy goat feasted on Father Berton's roses; the Merrils' milk cow bawled between two overturned feast tables. Men shouted curses at each other; boys used the confusion to chase and brawl. Mothers called to their scattered broods. And Montclaire's soldiers stood at every corner, squelching any opportunity to carry on a decent rebellion.

Mackenna felt like a traitor. She ought to be standing on village soil, not sitting on the lord's lap. She tried again to slide off the horse, but Montclaire's iron hand clamped down on her thigh.

"Take your hand off my leg. Everyone is looking at us."

"You will stay here with me," he said, his hand firmly establishing his command over her freedom. "How you appear to others while you do so is a matter of your own choice."

"You've no right to hold me without warrant, milord. Or am I your prisoner?"

"I'm building a dungeon, remember." A thick growl lifted out of his chest. "Damnation!"

The horse suddenly surged forward as if it understood the man's thoughts. The momentum threw her backward against the fierce human wall. As Montclaire tightened his grip around her waist, she struggled to sit upright, only to have the horse prance to an abrupt halt, snapping her head forward.

"Stay here, rebel," Montclaire commanded. He lifted himself from the saddle and was on his feet running toward the low churchyard wall a half-breath later. The giant nimbly cleared the stone hurdle in a single, smooth leap and landed at a dead run in the near dark. She ought to have vaulted from the horse and run in the opposite direction, but she had to know what had caught his attention. She told herself that it was because she might have to put to rights his next evil deed, but knew it was nothing but her damnable curiosity—that, and the two knights who had suddenly come from nowhere to guard her.

Montclaire disappeared around the rectory wall and emerged a moment later dragging one of his soldiers by the scruff of the neck. The hulking soldier looked terrified. The beast shoved him over the wall and followed like a black, seething cloud.

The soldier willingly presented his wrists to a mounted knight. Montclaire held up an ale crock, all the while keeping his thunderous gaze directed toward the cowering soldier.

"You understand what this means" was all she heard him say to the soldier. The condemned man hung his head.

Montclaire dashed the crock against the wall, then strode back toward her. He was in the saddle and levitating her backside onto his lap with his broad hands before she had a chance to object.

"There," he said with a sudden growl. "You'll not be alone in my dungeon."

She didn't know which insult to protest first, his search for a suitable prison companion for her, or his growing familiarity with her posterior. "How dare you?"

"How dare I what? Discipline my own soldiers?"

"That's not what I—"

"I do not countenance looting—"

"You keep your bloody hands off—"

"Or arson. Anarchy serves no one. I brook no drinking among my men, unless they are on leave and prepared to pay the consequences for their excesses. Do you object to that?"

"Nay. But I—Next time you . . ."

"Next time I . . . what?" He straightened.

He was looking down at her with a completely blank expression, his fingers spread and gripping his own thighs for a change. The beast hadn't even noticed that he'd fondled her backside. She had certainly noticed. Her face must be once again as red as a ripe currant.

She puffed herself up and turned away from him. "Next time choose someone else's village to plunder."

The beast must have thought the idea tremendously funny, because he threw his head back and laughed hard enough to cause his murderous horse to snort and dance.

"Lord Montclaire." A young knight presented himself at Montclaire's boot. "We found them. Not a mile from the village. Just where you said they'd be."

"Galen, Addis. . . . no!" Mackenna whispered before her throat closed off. They looked disheveled and dismal, dragging their feet as they were led into the square.

"You bastard! Let me go to them, damn you! They need me."

"They look to be grown men, fully capable of taking care of themselves," Montclaire said evenly.

"Please don't hurt them, milord. They aren't to blame. It was my fault."

"Who are these men to you?" His voice had taken on

an even more impatient growl. His chin touched the side of her head.

"My brothers. Let me go to them!"

"I see. And just where were these carts bound, rebel?"

A lie perched on her tongue, anxious to mislead him. But she couldn't risk losing her brothers.

"The carts were to be delivered to Furness Abbey."

"Were you so eager to deliver these carts that you sent them off in the dead of night, at the risk of bandits?"

"Better to lose the carts to unknown bandits than to lose them to the bandits who have just overrun our village."

"We'll see, won't we?"

The horse strutted and stamped, his great hooves scattering stone chips as Montclaire threaded his horse through the crowd.

Mackenna dreaded meeting their eyes, but had no choice when Galen looked up and found her sitting on the enemy's lap. The fear and loathing in his face recast themselves into anger and a boldness that seemed to surprise even him.

"Get your filthy hands off my sister, Montclaire!"

Montclaire shifted his weight and Mackenna flinched, expecting a blow. But he ignored Galen's taunt and called out to the knight who'd led her brothers into the market square.

"Stephen, are the carts repacked and roadworthy?"

"Aye, my lord. We've taken an inventory. Market items for the most part. The men are shaken, but unharmed."

"Good. Then they are to continue their journey."

Mackenna whirled around to face Montclaire. "You're letting them go?" Galen and Addis weren't to be punished. But that made no sense. They'd been caught with honey on their fingers; she'd admitted her duplicity. "What's your game, Montclaire?"

"Game?" he asked.

Had the beast been possessed of a heart, she'd have thought him injured by her accusation. But his shard of laughter left no doubt of his heartlessness.

"My reasons should be most obvious, rebel. Until rents and back taxes are paid in full, the carts and the goods are mine. The profits from the sale will be credited against your debts—"

"You're a bloody thief, Montclaire!"

"Your family operates the mill?"

"Yes, but—"

"Then your fees and taxes are far higher than most. Have you paid any in the last four years?"

"How could we? There was no one to—"

"Nay. And have you the money?"

"Nay."

"Then I suggest you accept my proposal."

"Yours is no proposal. A proposal presumes the right to refuse. Have I that right?"

"Nay."

"Then you are a thief."

He bent to her, tucked her hair behind her ear, and whispered, "And so, my little rebel, are you."

Her throat went dry. Her skin burned where his finger brushed the nape of her neck. She wanted to speak or breathe, but she couldn't. He had the most damnable way of laying his words against her ear so they tumbled down her neck to the soles of her feet.

"What's he saying to you?" Addis shouted, yanking at his bonds.

Mackenna swallowed and righted her senses. "His lordship is letting you go to Furness. You're to take the carts tomorrow—"

"Damn the carts!" Galen dragged his captor forward a step. "Are you his prisoner?"

"Hostage," Montclaire said sharply.

Ice shot through Mackenna's veins and her heart skidded to a stop. The beast had answered Galen in English. English!

"Hostage, milord?" She straightened, expecting to be dragged away and put in shackles. He had understood everything she'd said to the village: all her curses, the orders to bury their treasures! No wonder he'd sent out his raiding party.

"Aye, rebel. Tell them I will hold you hostage until this village learns that *I* am lord here, and not you." Montclaire's Norman French had returned in all its deep, dark tones.

Hostage was a bloody Norman word! The beast hadn't spoken English at all. Her relief was as warm as her fear had been chilling.

"Are you his hostage? Is that what he said?" Galen asked.

"Aye. The man has naught but sawdust between his ears."

"Enough, hostage," Montclaire said suddenly.

The fiendish horse reacted to the intonations in his master's command, tossed his huge, black head, and danced toward a knot of soldiers.

"Secure the village, Hagan," Montclaire said. "Post guards. No one is to leave their homes until morning. 'Tis past time we leave for the castle."

"The castle?" Mackenna hadn't thought beyond the moment. Fear took hold of her limbs. Old nightmares curled around her throat as she struggled to raise up her courage against them.

"I will not go to the castle, Montclaire."

"You're my hostage, rebel. You'll go with me to hell, if it pleases me."

The demon lord laughed, and his fiendish horse shook his black mane and bolted from the village.

If Thomas could have ridden away from the girl's distracting influence he'd have done so; if he could have kept her under guard in the village he'd have done that. But cunning ran swift and deep in her veins and he had no wish to confront her again in the midst of her rebellion. She had courage enough for the entire valley, the kind of courage that bordered on recklessness and treason. Nothing would be safe from her vengeance.

Her temper had dampened some when the road left the valley floor, replaced by a sullen fear that seemed to have settled over her like a cold blanket. He'd come to believe that her arrogance made her incapable of any fear beyond her coddling concern over her undeserving brothers and that village of cowards. He was gratified to learn there was a chink in her spiny-plated armor.

The condition of the village pleased him mightily; he'd expected crippling poverty, and had found instead an insolent kind of prosperity. Foolishly, he'd allowed himself to hope as much for the castle. But the steep track beneath them was overgrown with brush and bracken, slashed through and undercut by wind and rain, and falling away to nothing in places.

Yet the rutted road was no less treacherous than the young woman perched upon his thighs. She sat bolt upright, clutching the pommel, fighting the force of the incline, and unwilling to lean against him for support. He wondered for an unsettling and altogether out-of-place moment if he had carried off another man's wife.

"You're trembling, hostage. Are you cold?"

She twisted round, a grinding movement against his hips that rattled his composure.

"Nay, my lord devil. How could I be cold with the heat of brimstone so close at my back?"

He wished the girl's eyes weren't snapping with such marvelous indignation. They rivaled the sunset even in the moonlight—moonlight that lay stark across her fretted brow and silvered the bridge of her nose.

"As you please, hostage. But my cloak is available for your comfort if you don't mind scorching your backside."

"Leave my backside out of this, Montclaire!" She tilted her chin and turned away, muttering, "You know what I mean."

Aye, he knew her meaning very well. After he'd apprehended the soldier in the churchyard and returned to the saddle, he'd meant only to seat the girl again on his lap where he could keep track of her. That's all he'd meant. Yet his hands burned even now with the memory of her ripe, rounded perfection. Bloody hell, his palms were still sweating.

She'd been squirming on his lap for the past hour, calling down invectives upon his head, shouting orders to the villagers. She had fondled him in public, opposed him, baited him, and tried to cheat him. Aye, she was a distraction he would subdue as soon as possible.

The outline of the castle came into view as the horses made a bend in the track. He was encouraged to see tiny smudges of light moving along the parapets.

"What will I find at the castle, hostage? Have you and your village of thieves left anything standing?"

The girl snorted and it vexed him. She'd made quite a commotion about coming with him. It was plain that she feared his reaction when he found the castle dismantled to its foundation and carted off.

"Did you hear me, girl?"

"I don't know what you'll find, milord." The words seemed to rush from her. "I've not been there since the night the castle was abandoned."

He took hold of her shoulders and twisted her toward him. He earned a frown. "And I'm to believe that?"

She shrugged. "Believe what you will, milord."

The flatness in her voice puzzled him; its impassioned huskiness was gone, and with it the spellbinding resonance that curled around him like an intoxicating fragrance.

"I would believe you're frightened."

"And wouldn't I be a fool if I weren't, Montclaire?" The dazzling anger had returned to her voice, but not to her eyes. He smoothed a bent finger across her silky cheek.

"Aye, you would be, hostage."

Her eyes flashed then narrowed, and she pulled away from him. Her trembling increased with her anger. Rebel or not, she was his villein and he was bound to keep her healthy. He slipped his cloak around her and pulled her to his chest.

To his surprise, she settled against him and tucked the top of her head beneath his chin.

"I'm only borrowing your heat, Montclaire, because the wind has come up."

"Borrowing my heat?" he asked, his mouth straying close to her ear. "Do you mean to return it one day?"

"I—" She gasped, then her breathing stopped. "Was that a kiss, Montclaire?"

His heart thumped against his ribs. He'd buried his words so deeply in her violet-scented hair that his lips had brushed the ridge of her ear. He hoped to sound undisturbed.

"Not a kiss, hostage, a mistake. Had I actually kissed you, you'd not have had to ask the question."

"Welcome, my lord Thomas! We're nearly across."

The end of the road was well marked by a bank of torches. Men and wagons waited in a staging area to cross a great chasm. The span had been overlaid with hastily bound planks that served as a bridge to the guard towers on the opposite side. Beyond the chasm, torchlight burned meager holes of brilliance into the massive darkness of the castle itself.

"'Tis a blessed miracle, I think," Thomas growled. Leaving the girl with his cloak, he followed the lad to the edge and looked down into the deep gorge. It dropped off into utter blackness. He suffered the raw feeling that this drawbridge would soon become the very least of his troubles. He studied the two squat towers flanking the gate. The night was too dark to see much detail, but rubble was rubble. First the ravaged road, then the shattered drawbridge, now the ruined guard house.

"Damnation!" Thomas breathed. "This is your doing, hostage!" He spared a glance at the girl, prepared for a lacerating denial, but she was staring up at the castle, spellbound, silent. Torchlight flicked shadows across her fine features, but couldn't warm her ghost-given expression.

"Come!" He plucked her off the saddle and set her on her feet. "Did you or any of your apprentices destroy this drawbridge?"

"Nay, milord." She seemed impatient with his question.

"Don't tell me it was the wind."

"I wouldn't dare, milord. I don't know what happened to your bloody drawbridge, milord."

Thomas took hold of her hand and started across the unsteady, makeshift bridge, the echo of his footsteps falling into the darkness below. Halfway across the expanse, he realized he was dragging the girl behind him, feet first, her knees bent, her resistance slowing them considerably. He stopped and turned on her.

"In case you haven't noticed, my dear, this is not the best place to exhibit your muleheadedness."

As he watched in disbelief, she crumpled to her knees. He shifted his stance to counter her sudden frantic struggle to free herself.

"I can't go with you, milord!" Mackenna tried to deny her panic even as she pushed at the beast's hands, but his fingers were manacles.

Blessed Mary, she thought, four years were gone, and the terror was as strong tonight as it had been then. She had been little more than a child, and ill-prepared for the horror awaiting her behind these unyielding walls.

A sharp gust of cold wind shot up from the chasm, blinding Thomas for a moment. A half-foot to the left and they would plunge off the edge.

"Bloody hell, girl, you're going to kill us both!"

Her chest felt hollow and packed with dry leaves. Until this moment she had believed she could walk through the castle gates and survive the onslaught of memories. But she couldn't. Not even the beast could make her go any farther.

"Nay, Montclaire. Please. I can't—"

"Aye, you can. Because I command it."

He hauled her over his shoulder, and stomped across the planks to the guard towers.

Chapter 5

Montclaire finally set her on her feet, then pulled her along after him. She clenched her teeth together to keep them from chattering. She wouldn't give in to the clawing terror. She wouldn't—not in front of the beast and his minions. Instead, she damned his long strides, and her panic, and the quick steps required to keep up with him. She closed her eyes as he towed her through the passage between the crumbling towers. When she opened them again she was in the shadowy chaos of the outer bailey. Wagons, soldiers, and torch fire.

"You've made it, Thomas!" Sir Walter rode toward them, dismounting while his horse was still in motion. "An impassable mess, isn't it?"

"Aye, it is that and more. But you brought the wagons through. Trust you, Walter, to manage a miracle. We'll need another by the looks of the bailey."

Thomas looked up at the immense foundation of a tower that grew out of the heart of the mountain. The size was impressive, but the sight gave him little cheer. The base of the wall was littered with fallen stones and timbers. He could only guess at the condition of the walls above.

"Miracles do happen, Thomas." Walter nodded toward Mackenna. "Your prisoner? Or is she to be . . . ?" His eyebrows rose in implication.

"Hostage," Mackenna and Thomas said together. She

46

scowled at both men. Walter laughed and Thomas
scowled back at her.

"What's her name?" Walter asked.

"I don't know," Thomas said, scanning the bailey
with pointed disinterest.

"Don't know? She refused to tell you?"

"I haven't asked. Lead on, Walter. We've a busy night
ahead of us."

Since Montclaire still had a lock on her wrist, he
merely started forward in his emphatic stride and she
followed for fear of falling on her face.

The outer bailey rose to match the steep terrain as the
fortress stair-stepped up the mountainside toward the
main guard towers, a quarter distance around. Montclaire and his men discussed every fallen stone block
and damaged shed that they passed. They dodged men
and wagons and horses straining to gain purchase on
the rock-strewn bailey floor.

She found a peculiar sense of security in keeping her
eyes fixed to Montclaire's face. During the course of the
hellish night, she'd seen him only in shifting shadows,
and as an eclipse against the setting sun. But now and
then as he stopped to confer with his knights, torchlight
would flare across his features and the shadows would
fall away. The beast looked halfway human in the light.
His hair was dark as coal; it glistened and curled softly
over his forehead. His beard was a shade lighter and
salted with strands of gray near his temples. He re-
garded his men with eyes that were steady and intense;
she begrudged him the humor he seemed to find and
share.

It wasn't until he turned around to stare at her that
Mackenna realized he'd led her through the main guard
towers into the bailey.

"Welcome to Fellhaven Castle, hostage."

The girl flinched as if he'd struck her. Her eyes flicked
up at the shattered walls, at the keep, at the roofless
great hall. Her face paled in the torchlight. She was
plotting, he was certain, and not at all ashamed of the
damage she had already done.

"There's not an intact roof anywhere in the fortress, Thomas," Walter said. "I shall pray for cloudless skies. Tonight, as you see, your men are making do."

The bailey looked more like a hastily pitched military camp healing its wounds in the aftermath of a three-day battle, than a garrison of healthy soldiers laying claim to a mighty fortress.

Thomas smiled at Walter and clasped him by the forearm. "My thanks, Walter. Now, tell me, the great hall, is it functional?"

Walter laughed. "Come see for yourself."

Thomas led his hostage around wagons and camp-fires. He looked back to gauge her mood, but found her face averted, turned from him toward the gate towers. She would bolt if she could, and race back to her village—to *his* village, damn it.

Thomas skirted a sagging scaffolding. He hadn't taken two steps beyond it when the girl stopped dead in her tracks again.

Mackenna had always believed that the mountain would have tired of the insult and swallowed the hellish device long years ago, that it had been shattered by lightning, or devoured by the worms. But there it stood, catching fire shadows and casting them about in that same dancing, blood-red light.

"What is it, hostage?"

Montclaire stood behind her, his broad hands imprisoning her shoulders. The interest in his voice did more damage to her composure than had all his threats.

Sorrow soured her stomach. Hatred prickled her skin.

"Take your hands off me." She wrenched out of his grasp and hurried off toward the keep.

Walter had stopped to wait for them, but the girl stalked past him and ran up the broad stone steps. He bolted after her, afraid she would run headlong into the debris littering the corridor.

Mackenna stopped beneath the arching entrance and clutched at the towering door that hung askew on its hinges. She gasped for every breath as if she'd run all

the way from the village. Aye, but she had, and it had
taken her four long years. But maybe the worst of the
memories was over. She had come this far without
yielding to the tears that clogged her throat. She had
survived the demon's apparatus that lurked in the
bailey; she would survive the rest of them. Especially
Montclaire.

"Mistress, are you ill?" Sir Walter's voice was kindly
and appeasing, his smile coaxing. He placed a gentle
hand on her shoulder. His sandy hair fell into his eyes as
he cocked his head to peer down at her.

Thomas took the steps in pairs and snatched the girl's
hand as he passed her, refusing to examine the spark of
unrest that he felt when he saw Walter bending down to
her.

"Are you coming, Walter?" he asked, finally stopping
in the center of the corridor.

Walter nodded but kept his smile to himself. The girl
was a beauty. Aye, and this time Thomas had noticed.
He didn't usually. Hell, his friend had taught himself
not to notice.

"I took the liberty of setting up your headquarters
here in the hall, Thomas. One fireplace works, the other
belches smoke like a wheezy old dragon. I'll see that it's
fixed in short order." Walter shoved aside a fallen rafter
and thumped a free-standing wooden pillar. "I won't
know for certain until daybreak, but these seem sturdy
enough."

"Good. I should like to meet with my engineers and
the master mason first thing in the morning."

Walter led them toward the blazing hearth. A large
table had been fashioned of a charred door panel
balanced across four barrels. "I sent the cook to make
sense of the buttery."

The buttery. Nabon. Mackenna suddenly remembered the dangerous mission she'd sent him on. In her
selfish misery, she had forgotten about him. She
pledged herself again to her campaign against Montclaire and his thieves.

And at the moment the most prominent item among the books and rolls of parchment on the table was the chest that contained Fellhaven's bylaw records.

"Lord Thomas!" A soldier came too fast into the hall and stumbled into a hillock of rubble. He gave a curse and continued toward them. "Your pardon, my lord, but a disagreement has broken out between your chief engineer and the master mason. We pulled them off each other, but the peace won't last."

"I'll go," Walter said.

"Nay, Sir Walter, they need you both to settle this."

"Very well," Thomas said. He pulled the girl with him as he shoved a small cask next to the pillar closest to the hearth. "Sit here."

She did. Anything to hurry the man out of the hall. Her own shadow didn't cleave to her as closely as he had in the past few hours.

"Bring me a lash, Walter."

"A lash!" Mackenna jumped to her feet. "You're going to beat me?"

Montclaire's glare was fierce and low as he pushed her back down onto the barrel. "I'll do more than that if you don't sit."

Blessed Mary, he wouldn't dare! Aye, but he was lord here. If he wished to hitch her to a spit and roast her in the hearth, there wasn't a man within these walls who would try to stop him.

"Thomas, she's but a woman!"

"Nay, Walter. Her bones are forged of steel, her flesh of mail, and I do believe a stone lives 'neath her breast where her heart ought to be. Lean back, hostage." Thomas flattened his palm against her chest, causing her straight spine to meet the pillar. When he looked up from the alarm in her enormous eyes, Walter was frowning at him, his fists stuck to his hips.

"You needn't do this, Thomas. I have guards to spare."

"Trust me, Walter, you haven't half enough guards to hold her. The lash, if you please."

"I don't please at all." Muttering his disapproval, Walter unwound a slender length of leather from around an account roll and slapped it into Thomas's palm.

Thomas grunted and stuck the tether between his teeth. He drew the girl's arms behind her and around the pillar, taking care not to hurt her when he crossed her wrists. Her hands were fisted and trembling. He was thoroughly disgusted with himself; Walter's condemnation seethed round him like a hornet. But he had an unrelenting suspicion that if he let his hostage out of his sight, she would vanish into the mists shrouding the shale mountains. Why that loss should trouble him, he couldn't fathom. A thorn removed from his side, a burr from his backside; the opportunity to be rid of her should please him, but it didn't.

Relief loosened her limbs. Montclaire wasn't going to beat her; he only wanted to keep her from escaping. She rested her head against the pillar, feeling quite superior. Midnight and a thousand stars showed through the scorched rafters above.

"You have a lovely castle, Lord Montclaire," she said, testing her mettle against his patience as he knelt behind her and wound the tether around her wrists. " 'Tis so . . . airy."

"Then I'm right glad it pleases you, girl. This may be your home for a very long time."

She found defiance enough to laugh. "You cannot keep me here forever, Montclaire."

"My father's uncle entered Shrewsbury Castle a hostage in the sweet blush of youth and was ancient, withered, and gray when he was carried home to die. Don't tell me what I cannot do."

The girl drew air through her teeth and dropped her head forward. Thomas thought he'd scored a victory with his tale, but he glanced down at her wrists and found her soft flesh puckered and whitening against the leather bands.

Swearing under his breath, he fumbled with the tether until the binding was looser and the welts subsided. Damnation, he'd never treated a woman with such callous disregard. He rose and took a conciliatory stance in front of her.

"Are you comfortable?" he asked. Her head was bowed, her burnished hair tumbled forward over her shoulders to pool in her lap. Glints of firelight danced along the wildly curling tangle. He tilted her chin to bring her eyes up to meet his, hoping for . . . a treaty?

"Am I comfortable, my lord?" she asked.

The girl started laughing, a throaty, sumptuous sound that matched the resilience of her voice. He saw nothing humorous in the question.

"Bloody hell, Walter, bring me your two best guards."

"As you command, my lord."

Walter stalked out of the hall as Thomas knelt down in front of the girl. His patience was scraped raw and scorching his throat. He was beginning to think the girl was a little mad.

"I shouldn't have laughed, milord. It's just that . . ." Her brows dipped, but her grave and solemn eyes trapped his as she searched for some scattered thought. "I found your question absurd."

"Absurd? Devil take it, girl. I was asking after your—"

"My comfort, aye! 'Tis absurd. I'll have no comfort until you and your bloody soldiers leave our valley for good."

"Damnation!" No matter what he did, what he said, or how he said it, she didn't seem to understand how profound her offense was. He was lord here and she was his hostage.

Firelight gilded the tips of her lashes, skimmed the bridge of her nose. He took her chin between his fingers for no other reason than he was drawn to touch her. He lingered on the bright spot of hearth light shimmering on her bottom lip, wanting to taste the perfect arcs that bowed her mouth. Her eyes had grown large and defenseless again, flame caught up in cinnamon and put to shame.

"Thomas, do you suppose two guards will be enough?" Walter was standing over them. "Or shall I fetch your archers?"

"Two guards will probably not suffice, but I can't waste any more time here." Thomas got to his feet. "Keep your eyes on her, men." Then he realized that the pair of guards was already doing a fine job of staring at her without his direction. "Nothing more than your eyes."

The guards straightened to attention. One man averted his eyes to the absent ceiling, and the other found something of extreme interest in the hearth fire.

Thomas leveled a finger at the girl. "A warning, hostage: stay put."

Mackenna watched him stride away with Walter, pleased to see his hands fisted and clasped behind him, much like her own were at the moment. She had work to do before Montclaire returned.

"Now, you sit right there and behave yourself, young woman." The guard waggled a long finger at Mackenna as he drew up a cask and sat down in front of her. "You don't want his lordship angry with you. He's got a wicked, wicked temper."

"Aye, me!" Mackenna heaved a heavy sigh and slumped as far forward as her bound hands allowed her. "What will Mother say?"

"Now, look what you've done, Francis! Aw, don't be frightened, girl. You've nothing to fear from Lord Montclaire. I've never known him to speak ill of a woman."

"Nor heard him raise his voice to a woman, let alone inflict injury." Francis was on his feet again, bending over her.

"Nor has he . . . pardon me for speaking bluntly, miss, but I've never heard of his lordship forcing a woman to give him . . . ease, if you know what I mean."

Mackenna wailed, letting her hair shroud her face.

"Give him ease!" Francis smacked him in the shoulder. "Now you've gone and done it, Philip."

"Me? You scared her first."

"I didn't!" Francis began to cluck over her. "Don't mind Philip, here. And please don't cry. Do you need a blanket maybe, or something to drink?"

Mackenna turned glistening eyes on the man and whispered hoarsely, "A sip of water would be a blessing, kind sir." She coughed delicately. "My throat is fair parched."

Francis fanned a fistful of fingers at his comrade. "Go! Go get the poor girl some water, Philip."

She needed to get rid of Francis. She had begun to loosen the tether the very moment Montclaire had left the hall, and now she was nearly free. The skill lay in the preparation: she'd kept the insides of her wrists apart by bending them slightly, kept her fists tightly balled, and resisted Montclaire to the point where he'd actually loosened the tether.

"Don't you worry yourself, mistress. Philip will be back with your water shortly," Francis said. "Though he might have to wait for the engineers to finish. Last I saw, they were dropping long lines down into the wells."

"Oh, dear! I hope the wells haven't been poisoned."

"Poisoned!" He chuckled and grinned indulgently. "Why would anyone poison the wells?"

"Good sir, before Lord Gilvane abandoned the castle he set fire to anything that would burn. He plundered the village, murdered innocent men. Poisoning the wells would have been such a simple revenge on good King Edward, don't you think?"

"By heavens, girl, I should warn someone!" His confusion was pitifully comical as he danced from one foot to the other. He needed only a gentle nudge to send him flying out into the bailey.

"I hope the horses haven't been watered." Mackenna smiled as she watched Francis's long, lean legs clear a heap of dirty rushes on his route toward the door.

The tether fell away from her hands. Taking no chances, she dropped to the floor and crawled across the cold stones to a shadowy corner where she could stand and observe. Not a soul but herself in the hall. She headed for the fire-scorched screens.

The buttery was empty; no barrels of grain, no
Nabon. With any luck, he and his crew were finished
and on their way home. She hurried past the kitchen
doorway, and descended the stairs into cold, darkness.
She found Nabon in the antechamber of the sally port,
alone and struggling with a barrel.

"Nabon!" she whispered.

The slender man jumped behind the barrel, then
collapsed in relief when he saw Mackenna.

"Dear Lord, girl." He flopped across the top of the
barrel like an unstrung puppet. "You startled me out of a
year's life."

"Sorry, Nabon." She wished there was a panel in the
doorway to close. The rush-lamp flame was dim, but its
glow spilled out into the corridor. "Are these the last of
the barrels?"

"Aye. The rest are in the sally port."

"Fine work, Nabon. I'll give you a hand." She helped
him roll the barrel toward the passage. The whining
wind blowing up from below was crisp and fresh,
entwined among the sweet, sultry perfumes of the
valley.

"Did you have any trouble? Did you see anyone at
all?"

"Nary a soul. Heard 'em though, skittering around on
the floor above."

"Like rats. How fitting. Are you ready to move the last
one?" But his attention was cast over her shoulder
toward the open doorway. "Don't just stand there,
Nabon. We must hurry. Just this barrel and then you
can . . . Nabon?"

Nabon's mouth and eyebrows drooped into a woeful
frown. "Sweet Jesus!" he whispered.

Mackenna didn't need to turn around to know that
Nabon's lord and savior wasn't standing in the doorway.
The scent of cloves and the pulsing energy that poured
into the long narrow room were enough to tell her that
Montclaire had found her.

"Convince me, madam, that there are two of you.
Convince me that your sinister twin is at this moment

tied to a post in the great hall and that you are her opposite, the sweet-natured creature of my dreams."

"Nay, milord, I am a creature from your very worst nightmare." She whispered, "Run, Nabon," then whirled around and threw herself at Montclaire, making a suicidal attempt to push past him while Nabon sped toward the sally port and freedom.

"You're a great fool, hostage." Montclaire crushed her against him with his arm. His voice roared up from his chest as he shouted into the hallway for his guards.

"You'll never catch him, milord," Mackenna said, tossing back her head so she could glare up at him.

"I don't need him, girl. I have you."

He hadn't looked quite so dangerous since she'd first taken off her blindfold. The brutish barbarian had returned. His dark hair seemed wilder, his eyes blacker.

"I won't tell you where he's gone," she said.

"Good, then I needn't listen to any more of your lies."

Two sets of frantic footsteps clattered toward them. Mackenna's guards, waving torches over their heads.

"My lord—" Francis sputtered, skidding to a stop.

"We can expl—" Philip tried.

"Philip, Francis! Boys!" Thomas shouted, gaining great pleasure at the portrait of horror on their gray moon faces. He spun the girl around to face them. "See what I have found down here! My hostage has a twin! Can you conceive of two so fair?"

Philip was the first to find his tongue, but must have thought it someone else's when it started blathering. "Guh, uhm . . . your lordship . . . I . . . we . . ." Philip ticked his finger back and forth between himself and Francis. "A twin, you say?"

"Of course, she is a twin! How else could my hostage still be tied up in the great hall, and this woman, who looks remarkably—nay, *exactly*—like her, be down here? How else," and he paused, "gentlemen?"

Philip's face melted.

"She tricked us both!" Francis confessed, his voice a full octave higher than it had been in the great hall. "I don't know how she managed it, Lord Thomas. We left

her alone for just a moment and then she disappeared!"
Francis narrowed his eyes at Mackenna. "I'm sorely
disappointed in you, girl."

Mackenna threw his frown back at him and he
lurched backward as if she'd taken a swing at him.

"She tricked you?" Montclaire asked. "How?"

Philip's head sunk to his ears between his shoulders.
"She said she was thirsty."

"She told me the well was poisoned," Francis added
feebly.

"Which of these men unbound your hands, hostage?"
Montclaire demanded, his eyes fixed on the guards.

"Not me!" Philip scowled at Francis, daring him to
deny it.

"I didn't either!" Francis insisted.

"I freed myself, milord."

Francis turned on Philip. "As I told you! She was still
trussed up like a lamb when I left her."

"Don't blame them, milord. I played soft upon their
mercy."

"And the rain and sun will play hard upon their heads
while they spend a week in the stockade. Gentlemen,
turn yourselves over to Parnel, immediately." Thomas
grabbed the torch out of Philip's hand. "Leave now,
before you cannot."

They did, disappearing so quickly, Mackenna thought
they had vanished down a hole in the stone floor. She
suddenly wanted very much to change places with
them.

Montclaire ducked through the doorway and set the
torch into a bracket. He had to be seething, yet the
confounding man said nothing. He planted his foot on a
crate and lifted her hands to the light. He turned first
one hand and then the other.

"You won't find any chafing burns, Montclaire, or a
nick from a knife point."

"You untied your hands while they were bound
behind you?"

"Like your character, milord, your knots lack integ-
rity."

He stared down at her. "Nay, my good sense was lacking. It won't happen again. I don't think you understand your position as my hostage. I am holding you instead of imprisoning your brothers, and the skinny man who just left us, and all the rest of the fools in my village. Would you have me hold these rebels instead of you?"

"Nay, milord."

"I didn't think so." Thomas grabbed the torch and pulled her along after him into the corridor. How could such treachery be costumed in such innocent beauty?

Walter was sitting at the table in the great hall, bent over a scroll. He looked up as Thomas approached. "Not fled to the fells, then?"

"I found her in the antechamber of the south-facing sally port. Find the entrance and post guards. The passage is filled with barrels, hundreds of them. Grain, I presume."

"The devil take you, Montclaire," Mackenna spat. "We worked hard for our harvest. The barrels belong to the village—"

"And therefore they belong to *me*. Walter, see to an inventory and report to me in the morning. Until then I shall be in my chamber."

"What about her?" Walter nodded toward Mackenna as if she were a flagon of malmsey.

"She'll be with me."

Walter scowled. "Your chamber is unsuitable for a lady. It's been swept and your chests are there, but it hasn't a roof."

"I don't need a roof, Walter, I need privacy. And so will my hostage. Post four men to stand guard outside my chamber. Give strict orders that the girl isn't to leave the room unless I am awake and alert and standing at her side."

"Nay, Montclaire! I don't need your kind of privacy."

"You will, hostage. You will."

Chapter 6

Mackenna watched as Montclaire set the heavy door into the frame and pushed a large chest in front of it. Locked in. She didn't know what to expect from him next. His moods were unpredictable, and this particular mood was as opaque as any before it. He opened the lid of the chest and pulled out a limp mattress. It raised a cloud of dust when he flopped it down on the floor. He followed the mattress with a linen sheet.

"Make it up, hostage," he said, turning back to the chest.

The wind blew in through the skeletal rafters and swirled around the room, tearing at the flaming torch as it sputtered near the casement window. Stray leaves skittered in a tiny whirlwind trapped in the corner. The scent of cloves soothed the bitterness of old char.

"Haven't you a chambermaid to do these things?" She meant only to stall him so she might learn his intentions and make plans against him.

"Madam, I am a soldier. You can imagine the trouble I'd have in my ranks if we carted along chambermaids to serve us."

"Aye, I can well imagine your usual method is to steal girls from the farms and towns that you plunder."

"Imagine what you will." He threw a stack of blankets to the floor near her feet. "Make up our bed."

"This isn't *our* bed, Montclaire." She was embarrassed beyond blinking, but refused to let him know it.

"It will be." He set a pillow on the lid of the chest and glowered at her.

Aware that his foremost intention was to intimidate her, she stuck out her chin and knelt to the business of making *his* bed. She wouldn't bow to that ferocious scowl. Nor would she allow him to find any pleasure in humiliating her. But she did watch him out of the corner of her eye.

He grabbed the torch and went to the cold hearth. He built a stalwart fire using wood from a neat stack of fallen beams. By the time he turned from the blaze, she made certain she was standing with her arms crossed over her chest, waiting.

"What now, milord? Do your boots need polishing?"

"Take off your clothes."

"My—?" Her heart clogged her throat until she swallowed it. She'd not let intimidation weaken her. "Thank you, milord, but I prefer to sleep in my clothes tonight. 'Tis chilly."

"You'll be less inclined to escape my chamber and work your mischief if you're hampered by modesty—and by the night air."

"I wouldn't—"

"Aye, you would, girl, in the blink of an eye. Remove your clothes." He took a step toward her, his boot heel scraping sharply on the rushless stone floor. "Or shall I do it for you?"

"You're serious." She clutched at the neck of her gown and took a cowardly step backward.

"You give me no choice, hostage. I can't trust you, bind you, or frighten you. I've no dungeon to confine you—"

"So you think you can humiliate me? Well, milord, you'll find you can't do that, either!" She grabbed the hem of her gown and yanked it off over her head. She hoped she'd have the courage to remove her chemise with as much shameless ease.

"Skin is skin," she continued bravely. " 'Tis no matter

whether it's viewed on my hands or my face or my . . . foot." She couldn't very well continue her list with the beast looking at her with one of his bold, black eyebrows raised into his hairline.

He gave no reply, and made no move to stop her. He hadn't an ounce of decency in his shriveled, putrid heart. Well, then, she'd made her statement; she'd have to endure its consequence. Having lived her life in a house full of brothers, she'd never been afforded much privacy. She took her baths at the hearth, and after a sweltering harvest day she often stripped to her skin and cooled off in the mill race. But Montclaire wasn't a brother; he was a stranger, a barbaric Norman warrior, with a gaze that never darted.

"I'll not wait all night," he said, crossing his arms against his broad chest.

Damn the man! But she was too proud to let him see her cower for want of her clothes. She bent down and removed her slippers. When she looked up, his eyes were still fixed to her, but now his brows had merged into a single fierce promontory.

"Will you at least turn your back, Montclaire?"

"Turn my back on *you?*" His laughter was sharp, yet only chipped at the corners of his frown. "That would be incautious, given our history." He leaned with lordly ease against the chest that blocked the door. "However, I'll not take offense should you turn your back to me."

"And have you attack me while my attention is turned?"

"I won't," he said evenly. "You have my promise."

"Your promise, and a kick by a mule will leave me bruised. Pardon me if I don't believe you."

"As you wish." He shrugged.

The wicked beast left her no choice at all. Braving his gaze, she pulled her chemise up over her head. She was blind and panicky for a moment inside the folds of fabric. Once free, she clutched the length of gown to her, steeling herself to confront Montclaire's leering grin. It wasn't there. *He* wasn't there. He'd turned his back and was rummaging through the chest, leaving a swirl of clove on the chilly air. He pulled out a fair-sized linen towel and held it out to her.

"Am I to bathe in front of you as well?" she said, forcing her teeth not to chatter, though her backside was bared to the cold wind at the unshuttered, unglazed casement window.

"Not tonight. 'Tis only a measure of privacy, not enough to cover you if you should choose to wander the castle."

"I'd say thank you, milord, but I wouldn't mean it." She grabbed the towel.

He held fast to the other end. "A simple trade," he said, taking hold of her gown but not pulling at it.

"Beast." Mackenna dropped her modesty along with the gown and quickly wrapped the towel around herself, tucking the end into the folds that crossed her bosom. She raised her eyes, again expecting nothing less than the devil's leer, but the beast was gone again, striding past her with her chemise balled in his hand. He scooped up her gown and slippers and, without a care or a glance, he tossed them out the window into the bailey below.

"Montclaire, no!" She leaped onto the casement, bracing herself between him and the window, clutching tightly to the towel. "Those are my very best, my only . . . Oh, no!"

Far below the tall window slit three soldiers were staring up at her from the bailey. Her chemise was draped over one man's shoulder, fluttering in the wind. When he pointed up at her, she stepped down from the casement and away from Montclaire.

"Have you no shame, milord?"

"None at all." He leaned out the window and shouted, "Shaughnessy, is that you?"

"Aye, my lord. Will your lady be needing her clothes again tonight?"

"Not tonight. See that they're returned on the morrow."

"Aye, sir—milord. As you wish, Lord Thomas."

There was no mistaking the admiration or the laughter in the soldier's voice. Her blush ripened and spread. Montclaire stepped off the casement and turned to her. His scowl was deep.

"Now plait your hair."

"Plait my . . ." Another of his perverse notions. "Why?"

"Never mind my reasons. Plait your hair." He sat down on the casement seat and pulled off his boot.

She couldn't imagine what kind of sport he was planning now. Keeping her eye on him, she gathered her hair behind her back. The towel loosened and nearly sprung off. Glaring at Montclaire, she secured the linen, then carefully split her hair into three sections, while she watched him yank off his other boot. His well-fitted woolen chausses gave sinewy definition to his calves: warrior-crafted, like his arms and his shoulders and the cords in his neck. When she remembered to breathe, the towel pulled loose again, her hair forgotten and unplaited.

"This isn't going to work," she said. "If you want my hair plaited, milord, you'll have to do it yourself." She doubted he could. His hands were too big.

"Come." Thomas guided her to the hearth and turned her to face the heat of the fire. He caught up her hair and drew the opulence over her shoulders to cascade down her back. There was so much of it. It smelled of violets, a cloud of bright summer and meadow grass; and suddenly her heart-searing face grinned above him in that same meadow, her mouth ready to share its sweetness with him, her hair a canopy of cinnamon, brushing his bare chest, trailing across his neck, the silky tendrils trapped beneath him.

He blinked and banished the image. He had denied himself the pleasures of the flesh for a very long time. Now he was in mortal danger of breaking his vow of abstinence with this girl.

Fortunately he couldn't imagine how or when. She had sworn her hatred for him and demonstrated it in more ways than he could count. He would never take her by force. In the wild days of his youth, he had learned that a woman was more apt to warm his bed and delight his senses if he employed an excess of charm and a little honest flattery in his courting. He had no time for this woman, not now or ever. He would see to it that she remained his devoted enemy, and he would suppress his desires with the tedious process of rehabilitating the castle.

A noble strategy, but he'd buried his fingers in her cloud of silken hair, and he wasn't sure he could remain dispassionate while he plaited it. He forced himself to imagine the burnished ropes were merely straps for his battle gear, but soon gave up the falsehood. He tucked and plaited, taking care not to skim her flesh with his fingers. She held herself straight and proud. The cares of her small world rested hard on her delicate shoulders. But she was not the kind to bend, not until she broke. He tied off the plait with the same thong that had earlier bound her hands, and dropped the braid as if it burned.

"There," he said, striding across to his trunk.

Mackenna watched with dawning horror as the beast unbuckled his brace of straps and shucked his thick woolen hauberk and chausses, leaving him standing in his long-tailed shirt.

"Milord, you're not going to remove your clothing!"

His laughter was rich and deep. "Now wouldn't we be a fine pair: me, a distinguished commander in the king's army, chasing you, my skinny hostage, through the great hall and out into the bailey, the both of us stark, staring naked." He smiled suddenly and took a slow step toward her. "Nay, I'll be keeping my clothes on. Just in case."

Mackenna laughed. She hadn't meant to, but the image was so clear and comical, and his smile so genuine, she couldn't help herself.

"Besides," he whispered with a sudden intensity, reaching down to cup the back of her head with his broad hand, "you do tempt me, girl. Breath-stealing beauty and imprudent courage all bound up in insolent

pride. You can't know how much I . . . Aye, 'tis well that
I haven't time for you."

His fingers were warm where they nestled in her hair.
She wondered stupidly if his beard would tickle if she
kissed him, if it was really as silky as it had seemed
when she was blindfolded and fondling it.

"You haven't time?" she asked.

"Nay." He sighed. "And for that I am sorry."

She didn't know how to take his confession. Of
course, she was joyously relieved that he would leave
her be, but . . .

"You haven't time tonight, you mean?" She bit down
on her tongue when she realized she'd spoken aloud.
Her thoughts had been drifting dangerously through a
field of sweet-scented wildflowers ever since he'd begun
to plait her hair. Of course, she could hardly be held
accountable for anything she uttered with the beastly
lord hovering like a gargoyle.

"Won't your husband wonder where you are?" he
asked, ringing a stray curl around his finger.

"No husband," she murmured, his clove-scented
breath breaking warm against her temple.

"Never married?" he asked, stirred by the way her
eyes flitted from his mouth to his cheek to his brow.

"Never." She'd never felt so thoroughly confused.
She hated Montclaire without reservation, yet she
couldn't think of a single reason to stop him from toying
with the hair at the back of her neck, nor why she didn't
turn from the soft, sweet touch of his breath against her
cheek.

"Then the men of Fellhaven must all be blind," he
said, following the smooth line of her jaw with his
thumb.

"I wish you'd leave here," she whispered, her balance
and her breathing seriously diminished by his magic.

"Take care what you wish for, my dear."

"Why is that, milord?" she asked, fascinated by the
way his lips caressed his words.

"Because some day it may come true."

It wasn't until his mouth brushed hers that Mackenna

realized Montclaire had been speaking in flawless, un-accented English.

"English," she whispered against his mouth. Though she couldn't for the life of her recall why that word should interest her, when his lips were so smooth, so cool. . . .

Thomas told himself that he had meant only to demonstrate her treachery, her crime of mistranslating his pronouncements. But this was no ordinary sensation; her feathery sigh against his mouth had nearly felled him. Their lips had barely touched; he'd hardly have called it a kiss, except that it left him reeling, and wanting more.

"You were saying, hostage?" he asked, peering down at the tempting bewilderment in her eyes. Aye, if he dared another kiss, he would stay longer. But he braced himself for the full force of the girl's fury, already regretting the end of their truce. It was about to erupt in monumental waves of outrage.

Mackenna touched her tongue to her lips where the splendid taste of him still lingered, cloves and closeness, the soft graze of his moustache. She'd been about to say something. . . .

"I know you've not lost your tongue, hostage; I felt it too near my own."

"Too near," Mackenna sighed. Then the delicious fog burnt away, leaving only the acrid stench of her hatred. She shoved at his chest with both hands. The wall didn't budge.

"You foul-dealing fiend! You speak English!"

"Aye, and Latin, and the Scots' brand of Gaelic. Why should you think otherwise?"

"You—you're Norman."

"Nay. My grandfather was."

"Liar! You're a . . . a bloody liar and a stinking thief." The beast was grinning like a fox. "You tricked me!"

"*I* tricked *you?*"

"You allowed me to think that you didn't under-stand."

"Damned unsporting of me." He lifted the end of her plait. "But I never told you I didn't speak English. You assumed—"

"I assumed you were a degenerate, deceitful savage. And I was right! You took advantage of me."

"I thought only to level the battlefield, and learn what I could about my village." He furrowed his brow and lifted the corners of his mouth. "I learned that you don't like me much."

"Don't like you much? I hate you." Her neck ached from craning to see him.

"And I learned that your bylaw records most probably contain accounts of treachery and theft; that you've buried the riches of Fellhaven; that you sent my best livestock up into the forest."

"*Our* best livestock—"

" 'Tis mine. Every crock, bale, and ewe, as you said before."

"The devil take you back to his fold and skin you! May this unholy castle fall down around your ears!" She pulled away, but he had a studied grip on the end of her plait.

"Don't run, hostage. I've grown fond of your long tresses. I should hate to see your head plucked bald."

"Let go! I'm not a hound to be leashed." She grabbed the other end of her plait and gave a tug. Montclaire held fast.

"Agreed. You are no hound," he said, with a steady grin. "A hound is trusting, and loyal, and dotes on its master."

"You'll never be my master, Montclaire. And I shall never, *ever* trust you. Loyalty is earned by deeds alone. And as for doting on you . . . Why the devil did you kiss me?"

His lopsided grin was answer enough.

"You wished for it, hostage. Or don't you remember?" The arc of pink rising across the girl's cheeks told him how well she did remember. " 'Twas a wanton request you made of me while I addressed the village. At the time, I found it a nearly irresistible invitation. But I waited to satisfy your entreaty, and my curiosity, in private."

"I was testing your grasp of English, Montclaire, not wishing upon yonder stars!" She threw her bare arm toward the roofless sky and nearly lost the towel. "I also wished that you would leave on the next breeze. Do you grant me that, as well?"

"Nay, my dear, not just yet. I've work to do here. And it begins tonight—upon this mattress." He scooped her into his arms and carried her to the pallet.

"I should have known you'd break your word to me." She couldn't struggle, or she'd lose the towel and the tattered remains of her dignity.

"I've broken nothing, hostage." Montclaire dropped with her to the mattress and tucked her against him as if she were his favorite bedroll. Even here in his open-air chamber, the beast blocked her view of the stars as he hovered over her. He grabbed her plaited hair and wound the thick rope twice around his hand.

She snagged his fist. "What are you doing?"

"Insuring that you don't leave this pallet without waking me." The next winding laced her fingers between his.

She raised up on an elbow and glared at him. "You've made escape impossible, milord. You've posted four guards at the door, we're fifty feet above the cobbled floor of the bailey, and I am, as you said before, stark, staring naked."

"You needn't remind me, girl. I'm not made of stone." He was too well aware of his humanity; the base of her breasts cushioned and warmed his bare forearm, and he thought he might explode if she should take another lingering breath. "My word of honor is dear to me: do not entice me to break it. I hope you understand my meaning."

"Oh, I do, milord, as a salmon understands a bear." She yanked her hand free and fell back against the hard mattress.

"Good. Now, sleep." Thomas pulled the blankets over them. He'd managed less than two hours of sleep the night before. If he was to function through the morrow, he needed sleep tonight. Yet there was little chance of that; the girl was too silken, too pliant, and far too vibrant. There ought to be thick, frigid stone walls between them. But the only way he could be sure she wouldn't escape and raise her village to riot was to pin her beside him. He threw his leg over hers, crooked his spare arm beneath his head, and lay on his side facing his hostage. The sweet scent of violets tinted the air between them.

Mackenna lay still. The beast's heart was thumping against her shoulder as if he'd just run a mile. She wondered if his heart pained him, if it would do her any good to hope that it would seize up and cause him to drop dead sometime in the next week. Not bloody likely. The man was as hale and mighty as his incorrigible horse.

Mother Mary, she was lying nearly naked beneath a monstrous Norman warlord, gazing up into a black sky framed by the roofless walls of her prison. Galen and Addis were as much prisoners as she was, and would be gone for weeks. Her village was overrun by soldiers, her family and friends were helpless and frightened. What next? How could she plan her tomorrow when today seemed so preposterous?

"Damnation," she whispered.

"Quiet."

"May the devil take you in your sleep." There. She'd said it. It didn't help.

At least she was warm, although the warmth belonged to Montclaire. And, all right, she was comfortable. And she had the most unreasonable feeling that she was safe—even with the beast's hoary chin nuzzled against the top of her head. She expected him to try to kiss her ear again, since he seemed so fond of it. The new lord of Fellhaven was rather free with his roving mouth. The man had kissed her! And she had just stood there like an enraptured bawd.

His breathing had eased, now that his heart had settled back into a steady rhythm. He must be drifting off to sleep. The man better not snore; she had a pointed elbow for him if he did.

"Hostage?" Montclaire asked quietly.

"What?" She didn't dare look at him for fear he'd be looking back at her with those coal-dark devil's eyes.

"Why didn't your father come for you?"

It was a painful, crushing question. She swallowed and set her throat so that he wouldn't hear any weakness. "He's dead."

"I thought as much." He was silent for a while, then the clove-tinted air left his lungs in a rush. His returning voice was etched in a growl. "Had I a daughter or a sister such as you, I'd not have let her go without a grievous fight."

She didn't know what to say. He pulled her closer; the gesture seemed almost unconscious.

"Hostage?"

"Aye, milord?"

" 'Tis past time. Tell me your name."

"Mackenna Hughes, milord."

"Ah." He shifted his weight to trap more of her shoulder, then quieted. "Good night, Mackenna Hughes." His mouth brushed her ear again and his heart took long minutes to settle down.

Hers didn't settle at all, and her thoughts raced alongside it. They had spent hours in the saddle that night, stuck together like a pair of soup ladles; it mattered little that they were now lying together on a pallet, covered with a blanket. Except that now she lacked clothes. And they were entirely alone. And he harbored the iniquitous impression that he was her lord and master. Aye, it mattered vastly how they lay together. Married people slept like this; her parents had. The image stopped her cold. Married? To his lordship?

She sheltered a giggle, and then another. She struggled to hide it from him, but the absurdity shook her to her bones.

Damnation! Thomas rose up on an elbow. He'd finally caused her to weep. He hadn't thought it possible in one so stoic. Feeling guilty as hell, he pushed her shoulders to the mattress and peered down at her. Her hands shielded her face; her shoulders shuddered with every indrawn breath.

"There's no need to be frightened, girl. I've given my word: I'm not going to hurt you."

She peeked at him through a fan of fingers. "I'm not—" Mackenna gasped and drew her knees up to her chest. She'd set out across that circle to find a husband. A simple man with a pleasant smile would have served. And now she was sharing a bed in a dilapidated castle with the evil lord of Fellhaven! God's sense of humor astounded her, and she laughed even harder.

The girl was laughing! Thomas was insulted to the core. "You're a strange one, Mackenna Hughes. What's so damned funny?"

Mackenna shook her head, then laughed until tears gathered in the corners of her eyes and slid down into her ears.

Thoroughly confused, he let her roll back onto her side, then settled next to her and reclaimed her slender waist. Extraordinary. She finally calmed down and began to breathe more regularly. An occasional fit of giggles returned, then finally disappeared altogether.

"Mackenna is a man's name," he said, adding a grunt that puffed warm air across her temple.

"'Tis an honorable name, milord. My grandfather's family."

"And who were these Mackennas?"

"Fellhaven belonged to the Mackennas long before the bloody Normans overran it."

Thomas grunted again. Land. He didn't understand the appeal. Crops failed, sheep died, tenants took advantage, knight's fees, taxes to the king, tithes to the church. And someone else was always waiting to steal your holding. "'Tis done, Mackenna. History. There's nothing for it but tomorrow."

"Speaking of tomorrow, I want to be at the village when Sir Walter conducts his audit."

"There will be no audit, at least not soon."

"Why not? Have you stolen everything?"

He laughed. "As good as. Now, sleep."

Wretched nobleman. He didn't care; caring required a heart. She yawned and bent her knees until the backs of her legs found his. Warm again. His shirt was a soft wool. His upper arm was her pillow, thick and solid, but better than nothing. Warmer than feathers or straw. Her last thought before slipping into an untroubled dream was that if a drenching rain should fall tonight, Montclaire's huge body would shield her from the drops.

Chapter 7

"'Tis time you're awake, hostage. Dawn is near."

Mackenna opened her eyes and found Montclaire staring down at her, buckling his sword belt. He was huge and menacing, and the sight of him made her instantly aware of all that had transpired the evening before: every misspoken word, every betrayal, every misspent plan.

She sat up and drew the blanket around her. The air was cold and the sky tinged with pink.

"And what am I to wear? My plait?" She flicked the burnished rope at him, but dropped it in disgust when he smiled and tossed the bundle of clothes at her feet.

"Delivered this morning," he said.

She snarled and unwrapped her clothes. Modesty was a virtue lost on the man. Still seated, she slipped into her chemise.

"Having never been a hostage, Montclaire, I don't know the rules." She dropped her gown over her head and stood up.

"There is only one rule, and that is to obey me in all things." He studied her for a moment. "Put on your slippers."

Mackenna considered ignoring his order, but he'd probably throw her slippers out the window again and force her to walk around in her bare feet. He opened a small chest and handed her a comb. It was beautiful and as smooth as ice.

"Mother of pearl," he said. "I acquired it in Italy."

"Plunder, of course."

He laughed. "Of course."

She glowered as she unwrapped the thong from the end of her plait. The smooth teeth of the comb, so unlike the voracious teeth of her own wooden comb, slid through her tangled hair as if it were silk.

She dumped her hair back over her shoulders and stood by the open door panel. Montclaire stuck his dagger into its sheath, then led her down the stairs into the great hall.

Thomas scanned the snare of charred rafters and cursed Mackenna Hughes, her company of vandals, and King Edward all in the same breath. Most of the thick joists would have to be replaced, costing precious time and equipment. The rest of the hall had fared little better. Fire had peeled plaster to bare stone; the soaring windows were empty of glass and panes.

Walter's workmen had been busy through the night clearing the rubble. The stone floors had been swept clean, and the document chests stacked near the blazing hearth. Another table had been created from planks and barrels, the additional space overlaid with rolls of parchment and ink works.

Walter was standing over a scroll, chewing happily on a chunk of bread. "Fresh baked," he said, pointing to three fat loaves sitting in a wooden bowl at the end of the table. "Best I've ever tasted. Good morning, hostage."

"Good morning, Sir Walter."

"Fresh?" Thomas asked, willing to celebrate any victory at the moment. "Then the castle ovens have been repaired?"

"Nay, not yet. These loaves are from the village oven."

"Halry Bavitts's oven," Mackenna interrupted, unwilling to let a single village product escape comment.

"*My* oven," Montclaire said without pause. "Bring me a chunk of bread, hostage."

Mackenna smiled through her teeth. "Milord."

She sauntered to the bowl, trying to talk herself out of pelting the beast with a loaf. She turned the bread in her hand; it felt heavier than usual. Sticking a finger into the underside, she realized why. She tore the loaf in half and carried it back to Montclaire. "Milord," she said, smiling.

"You'll find it delicious, Thomas," Walter said, shoving another piece into his mouth. He bit down, let out a howl, then spit out the bread. Holding his jaw, the furious knight stared down at the splattered mess on the floor. "A rock!"

Montclaire trapped her gaze as he broke apart his own piece of bread and found the chunk of shale imbedded in the center.

"A Fellhaven specialty." She smiled and went to Walter. "Did you break a tooth, sir?"

"Nay." He clutched at his jaw. His eyes were hot-rimmed.

"Let me see." Mackenna took his elbow.

"Nay! You'll pluck my tongue out by the roots." Walter turned away from her like an obstinate child.

"I warned you, Walter," Montclaire said, flipping the rock into the hearth.

"Damnation!" Walter moaned and plunked down on a bench.

"Let me see." Mackenna held open his jaw as she would a recalcitrant hound. "Nothing cracked, probably only bruised. I'll have Willa make you a poultice—"

"A poison, more like. No thank you."

"Let me know if the pain increases. My quarrel is with your lord, not with you, good sir." She patted his shoulder.

"Aye, Thomas, you warned me fair."

Thomas was still laughing as one of his squires hurried toward him. "What is it, Daniel?"

"A priest, my lord Thomas. Come from the village."

"Father Berton?" Mackenna asked. "What does he want?"

Thomas stared her down as he repeated the question.

"He said only that he wished to speak to you, Lord Thomas."

"Good. Bring him."

Father Berton entered the hall almost immediately. "Lord Montclaire," he said, lifting his long-fingered hand from its cuffed enclosure. "Your pardon for this intrusion, but—"

"You were inquiring into the well-being of one of your lambs," Thomas said, inclining his head toward Mackenna as he shook the priest's hand.

"I'm not a lamb, Montclaire." Mackenna hurried toward Father Berton and took hold of his sleeves. "How much more damage have the soldiers done to the village, Father?"

"None, Mackenna. The village seemed quite peaceful this morning. And you look unharmed." He turned her once in place, giving her a stern-lipped inspection, then shot Montclaire a hard stare. "I understand you've taken Mistress Hughes hostage."

"I'm holding her against the good behavior of my village."

"Where did she sleep last night?"

Thomas had never been asked such a direct question by a priest. He could hardly tell a lie. "In my chamber, Father."

"He didn't—" Mackenna began.

"I committed no sin with her," Thomas said, though the truth ran deeper. "She slept beside me, on my pallet, for reasons of security. The woman is an eel."

"Mackenna?" Father Berton cast his gaze at her. "The truth, girl. Has he harmed you?"

Mackenna caught her embarrassment before it blossomed red as she thought of Montclaire's arm wrapped around her through the night, of his breath dancing against her temple, of his kiss that caused her reason to slip and her heart to flutter.

"Nay, Father. Though his lordship is the devil's own,

begat from the nobility, he's not forced himself upon me."

"How long does she stay?" he asked Montclaire.

"'Tis an answer that lies in her behavior and in the good will of the village. I'm a fair man and ask only cooperation."

"See that he gets it, Mackenna," Father Berton demanded. He turned to Montclaire. "Please call on me, my lord, if your soul should need confession." He drew Thomas down to his level with a crooked finger and a lowered voice. "Or if you should find yourself tempted by that woman. Mark me, she is difficult to deny. Not that I have ever . . . 'tis just that . . . She does get under the skin."

The suddenly blushing priest seemed to have a personal knowledge of the stunning subject who stood apart from them with her arms locked across her chest.

"Aye, Father, I give my word on it." Thomas straightened. "Will you say mass tomorrow here in the hall?"

"I would be delighted to, my lord." Father Berton smiled grandly. "'Til tomorrow then." He gave Mackenna another of his reproachful once-overs, then left the hall.

"He seems one of God's finer servants," Thomas said.

"He's an old woman," Mackenna said with a sniff.

Thomas laughed. "Sit," he said, motioning to the bench beside him. When she sat down obediently, he tagged the gesture with suspicion. Mackenna Hughes surrendered nothing that she wasn't planning to gain back by any means possible.

Mackenna watched as Montclaire spread his large, capable hands over a scroll and dropped a lead weight onto each corner.

She'd never seen such drawings. "What is this?" she asked.

He gave her a sideways glance. "A plan of the castle."

"This castle? Fellhaven?" She traced the irregular lines. "These are the curtain walls, but what are these dots?"

"Well sites."

"Ah, yes. And these?" she asked, tapping the half-dozen spines leading away from the curtain walls. "Wait, don't tell me. These are sally ports. . . ."

"Correct," Montclaire said. "Now, sit quietly, hostage."

"Aye, milord." She listened as the two men pointed to various places on the plan and plotted the day's inspection.

Montclaire grabbed a quill, then abandoned it with an impatient grunt. "We need a scribe, Walter. Cubbins will have to spare one of his."

"I'll do it," Mackenna heard herself say.

Both men looked at her. Montclaire's expression was far less readable than Sir Walter's frown of open distrust.

"Do you prefer English, Latin, or French?" she asked, moving around to the portfolio of parchment and the pots of ink on the opposite side of the table. She sat down on the bench and inspected the tip of a quill. Satisfied with its shape, she drew the tip across her tongue, then looked up at the men and smiled.

Neither had moved.

"Well?" she prompted, "Go on, I'm ready."

Thomas rested his folded arms on the table and hunched forward to study her. The devil's scheming lived in the heart of her offer, but he was hugely curious.

"Make it Latin, hostage," Thomas said, watching her draw the tip of the quill across her tongue once more. 'Twas enough to cause his pulse to pound in his neck.

"A wise choice, milord, as Latin is the language of your diagram." Mackenna tapped the feathered end of her quill on the top of his parchment. "Will you be dividing the diagram into quadrants? Eight or twelve would be the best, I should think. 'Twould be the simplest method of referencing the areas that need work. Then we can—"

Montclaire lowered an eyebrow at her. "You're a scribe, Mackenna. A scribe listens and writes; she doesn't comment."

"Aye, milord."

Mackenna covered her smile with the quill. Feint, then thrust. Montclaire was clay; Walter was thistledown. She'd be cooperative today, and lay her plans in the quiet of the night.

The castle had always been a shadow to her. Lord Gilvane welcomed only knights and barons, never his tenants and villeins. She'd been to the castle only once: the night her father died.

Now she had the map to its black heart.

By the time the master mason, the chief carpenter, and the other tradesmen had all arrived for the meeting, she had memorized every scrap of information on the parchment.

Sir Walter paced the distance between Montclaire and the craftsmen, doling out time to speak and hushing the assembly when it became unruly. Each craftsman fluttered lists of materials and growled angry words.

"Gentlemen, your grievances are mine," Montclaire said. "But I have not yet seen the castle in its entirety. I will tour the grounds with each of you. We'll note the discrepancies between the exchequer's reports and the truth. Meantime, our first order is to repair the road. Without such work, we don't need a drawbridge. All available men will be assigned to road construction, whether they be archers or carpenters or clerks."

Mackenna recorded every complaint and protest, and couldn't resist adding her own suggestions to those offered by the assembly. She alternated quills to keep the ink fresh and easily caught most every word. Setting aside a finished parchment, she glanced up and found Montclaire casting down a quarrelsome look. She kept writing. He took up the parchment and studied her script. With nary a word or another glance, he returned it to the table and reentered the discussion.

Walter dismissed each man in turn, until the hall was finally empty of the craftsmen.

"Where did you learn your script, hostage?" Montclaire hovered behind her. "And your use of French and Latin?"

"From my lessons with Father Halford."

"When was this?"

"I began when I was five. My brothers wouldn't go to their lessons, so I went in their stead."

"At five years old?" Walter asked.

"I am a quick study." She thought better of telling them that Father Halford claimed she was either gifted by God or cursed by the devil with a memory for words and numbers that had caused even her own father no end of trouble.

Walter frowned at the parchment in his hand. "We were speaking French and English, and yet she put it all down in Latin. Thomas, she's copied the entire hour onto four leaves."

"Aye, I know." But what to do with her, Thomas wondered. He couldn't very well leave her behind in the hall or in his chamber, not without a guarantee that she would sleep for a few hours. Only a sleeping draught or a clout on the head with a morning star would put her out. Accompanying him on his inspection of the castle grounds might humble her. With his soldiers and craftsmen swarming over the battlements, she might come to understand that she was outnumbered in her rebellion.

"Stand up, hostage." Thomas slipped the thick straps of a portable scribe's desk over her narrow shoulders and fastened the strap across her willowy back. "Is it too heavy?" he asked.

"Nay, milord." It was, but she wasn't about to confess it. She wanted to be with him, to study and catalog his deviltry.

"Then you'll serve me as a scribe today."

He pulled the ink horn from the storage below the slanted table, and fit it into the leather loop at the side of the desk. Walter filled the horn with ink and handed her a set of quills.

"You're certain it isn't too heavy for you?" Thomas asked.

"Milord, I've pulled a plow when we hadn't an ox. You'll hear no complaint from me."

She was obviously weighed down by the cumbersome

desk. A smear of indigo stained the knuckle of her middle finger. She could have been any scribe flogging her trade in London, but she was his, his vassal. He wasn't fooled by her offer to scribe for him. She was plotting.

"Write only what I or Walter ask of you."

"Aye, milord."

"None of your comments, unless I request them. No maledictions, or dissensions."

"None, milord."

"Now, I would see what you have carted away to the village."

"We've not stolen a single stone from your rubble. I forbade its evil from becoming any part of the village."

"A fine speech, hostage. 'Tis a pity there's not a whisper of truth in it." When she gave no answer but a too-patient smile, he tucked his diagrams and her notes under his arm.

"Bring her, Walter." Thomas stalked out of the great hall.

Montclaire traversed the battlements like a great hawk, peering and pointing, comparing his diagram against his castle. The freshening breezes whipped at his black hair. His face was bronzed, the brand of a warrior's life. Thin spokes of pink radiated from the corners of his eyes and etched his temples, disappearing when he laughed at something Walter said. He had a nose like that of St. Andrew, or at least like the statue of the saint that stood in the niche near the doors of the village church: long, straight, resolute.

And he stuck that nose into every gap and cranny, from the storage rooms and the ancient cesspits to the remains of the stables. He conversed with every man who hadn't been put on road duty. He sometimes barked an item for her list, but more often, he watched her write his words as he dictated.

The straps of the desk cut into her shoulders, and her arms ached from trying to relieve the burden. The beast had asked more than once about the weight of the desk, but she had denied her discomfort and always ventured a smile. Whether he believed her or not, it was important that she stay with him, no matter the pain.

Thomas was certain she plotted as she took her precise notes. She'd been suspiciously obedient, and silent except to answer his questions. She had an amazing memory, and wielded her quill like an indictment against his very existence.

Thomas took them in a circuit along the castle wall-walk, over displaced stone blocks, under canting arches that surely tempted fate, and finally, as the morning lengthened, into the tallest of the guard towers at the main gate. He led his hostage up a narrow stone staircase that girdled the turret room and emptied out onto the roof. There he relieved her of the burdensome desk and set it on a block toppled from the crenelation. A hundred feet below, the outer bailey sloped away and slid into the foot of the curtain wall.

There was something curiously fragile and appealing in the sight of his village and his valley, cradled between the gruff-peaked, forest-footed mountains.

The late morning sun cut sharp shadows across the long valley, carving the finger lake into two ragged shards of diamonds and darkness. The village piers and its tiny boats stitched the waters to the western shoreline. Fields were dark with turned earth, and striped golden with the stubble of shorn wheat. The rich, loamy scent of the plowing rode the breezes from the valley and mingled with the cool breath of dew-dampened pine.

"'Tis beautiful," Thomas heard himself admitting. "Truly a home to defend."

"Aye, milord, to defend with my life."

"And mine, hostage." He spared her a glance and found her eyes misted and distant, and sunlight caught up in her curls.

"Here it is, Thomas," Walter said, approaching them from the steps below. He wrested an iron pole from a long leather case. The upper half of the pole was bundled in black fabric, held in place by his fist, and topped by a silvered ball.

Montclaire took the pole and stepped up onto an embrasure, and then up onto one of the merlons. Mackenna's heart began to pound in perverse fear for the man. He was so carelessly near the edge; a willful gust of wind could send even a man of his great size toppling over the battlements.

"Have a care—" she said, stepping forward. She was halted mid-sentence by Walter's outstretched arm and his stinging glare.

"I'll not have you push him over the edge, mistress."

"I don't want him dead, Sir Walter. I just want him gone from here."

Montclaire jammed the pole into an iron fitting in the stone work at his feet; then he let go of the fabric.

A sudden breeze snatched the black cloth. It rasped and popped, then Montclaire's banner unfurled against the clear sky above Fellhaven.

Yellow claw and red fang snapped in the sunshine. Mackenna's face went hot.

A roar rose up from far below the battlements, a multitude of voices carried upward on the morning air to mix with sunshine. The road to the castle was snaked with men waving shovels and picks above their heads. Montclaire vaulted the distance to the next merlon, and waved his arms back and forth in a grand salute. The roar grew and tumbled upward on the breeze.

The beast laughed as he leaped off the merlon and landed on his feet in front of Mackenna. He extended his battle-sinewed arms against the pristine, azure sky.

"Can I make it plainer, hostage? 'Tis mine."

"Aye, milord," she said, glaring up at his sunlit face. "The resemblance in tooth and claw is extraordinary."

He stared at her for a time, forming some thought in his stone-dense head.

"Would you like to see your brother?"

"My—?"

Without waiting for her answer, Montclaire snagged

her hand and took her down the stairs into the turret room.

"Which brother? Are you taking me to the village?"

But he sped down another set of stairs, and another, until they were standing among a startled group of guards who shot to their feet at the first sight of their lord.

"Bring the man Hughes," Montclaire demanded.

"Aye, my lord Thomas. He's in the holding room."

Mackenna yanked on Montclaire's sleeve. "You've imprisoned one of my brothers? You said you wouldn't, but you had no intention of keeping your promise."

"And your promise holds water like a sieve. But your brother came on his own, and can leave whenever he wishes."

"Ha!" was all she could say. She wondered which brother had come. Bryce should be milling today. A single holy day like Michaelmas always put the mill two days behind schedule. This better be Cadell; he could be spared from the cartwright shop—

"Bryce!" She groaned. "What the devil are you doing here?"

Bryce stopped short and split his stare between Mackenna and the new lord of Fellhaven. "Has he hurt you?" He shrugged off his escort and took Mackenna by the upper arms.

"Where'd you get that?" She spread her fingers over the bruise on her brother's forehead.

"Ouch! Leave it be. I had a bit of an argument with one of his lordship's guards."

She turned a glare on Montclaire, then pulled Bryce's face down to hers. The bruise was minor. "'Tis a good thing that your head is hard, Bryce. Where is Cadell?"

"I don't know." Bryce glanced up at Montclaire. "I've been waiting here since before dawn. I was told his lordship had taken you hostage. Where does he keep you, Mackenna?"

Mackenna scowled at her brother. "In the castle, Bryce."

"In chains?"

"Do you see chains? I am well, and fed. Now, it's home with you. There's milling to be done."

"Without you? The schedule is locked inside your head."

Mackenna sighed. "Barley, seventy rings. But not before you replace the fins in the pinion gear. Do you understand me, Bryce?"

"Aye, Mackenna. The fins."

"There's thrashing to be done; give the work to Eldon. His family's in sore need of the bushel of rye he'll be paid."

"Mackenna, I've Galen's eel traps to fix and set."

"Then fix them tonight and set them tomorrow. And tell Nabon I need to speak with him about finishing the winter planting. I'll send him to you with a schedule for the mill."

"How long does the bastard aim to keep you here?"

"I don't know, Bryce." She heard Montclaire stir behind her. Mother Mary, the old ways were so easy to wear. Here she stood in the bowels of the beast's castle, throwing orders at men he claimed were his. She glanced in his direction, but didn't meet his gaze. "Take care, Bryce, he speaks English."

"Send your sister's wardrobe, Master Hughes."

Bryce swallowed noisily. "How long does she stay?"

"Good day, Hughes." Montclaire nodded toward the main gate.

"Mackenna! What about—! Hey, let go! Mackenna, I need to talk to you about—Damn you!" Bryce was escorted through the gates, sputtering in outrage.

Mackenna sighed and shook her head. "They rarely know what's best for them, do they?"

"Nay, hostage, they rarely do." The girl was a lone eagle, flying against impossible currents. She plotted and schemed to keep her brood tucked safely beneath her wings. She fed them, kept them warm, but she'd forgotten to teach them how to fly.

Walter nudged him. "Cook will throw the meal to the dogs if we don't soon eat it, Thomas."

The hall tables were set for a soldier's meal: salted

meats, clotted gravy, dried apples, unfiltered wine. The food tasted of soot and iron, with a bit of horse thrown into the pot for the full effect of a battlefield. No trenchers, only bowls to pass from one hand to the next. Montclaire had tucked her next to him and shared his flagon with her. His knights were noisy and good-humored, and deferential to their lord. They seemed remarkably comfortable with him, almost brotherly.

In the midst of the short meal, a workman nearly fell from the rafters where he was inspecting a joist. He dangled high above the stone floor until a blanket could be found and stretched beneath him. The daft group of knights caught him as he dropped to safety, then tossed him into the air a half-dozen times. Soon each man wanted his turn in the sling. Montclaire allowed them their fun until Walter turned to Mackenna, his hand extended. She caught herself grinning up at the hand-some knight.

"Care to fly, mistress?" he asked.

Montclaire stood abruptly. "I think not, Walter. Given enough of the sky, our bird is liable to fly away."

Mackenna spent the rest of the day trailing Montclaire and his craftsmen around the castle. She took notes and did her best not to interfere, but her own ideas stacked up in her head like sheaves on a hayrick. "If this were my castle, I'd—"

"You'd what, hostage?" Montclaire and his master carpenter fixed her with twin frowns. They were stand-ing in front of a tall, stone granary, peering up at the charred roof.

"I'd . . ." she began again. There were banks of reeds going to seed along the shore of Lake Dunmere. The village didn't need them this year. They ought to be harvested and set to drying today for use as roof-ing thatch before the rains came. There were—She stopped her next thought and wondered why she was suddenly so beset with helping Montclaire. "Never mind, milord."

"Thank you." He nodded stiffly at her, his expression shaded by the brilliant afternoon sun.

He was welcome to his misery.

Gilvane had insured that the king would spend his treasury rebuilding Fellhaven. Door hinges, latches, hooks, and rings: all things metal were either missing or broken. Whole walls had been torn down, hallways collapsed. And if it was made of wood, it had been split, splintered, or burned.

All except the gallows where Gilvane had hanged her father.

Each time Mackenna entered the bailey, the structure taunted her. She had shunned the site. But now, as the sun slid behind Mickelfell, it dashed red and orange across the courtyard.

Red and orange, and tangled shadows.

Like so very long ago.

The castle had glowed darkly that night, a fiery gash in the top of the world, as if all the demons of hell were holding court with the devil. She'd seen the flames from the village; she'd rung the church bell. But there hadn't been enough time, not nearly enough time.

" 'Tis strange that this structure didn't burn with the rest of it, Lord Montclaire." Carson stepped up onto the platform and stomped his heel against the planks.

"And lucky for us," Thomas said, "if the wood is usable."

"Plenty good enough for doors and shutters. 'Twill aid our dwindling supplies, my lord. We need so much more."

"As you've shown me only too plainly."

"I'll have the structure dismantled in the morning, sir."

"Fine. Have you set that to your list, hostage?" Thomas turned to his scribe, but the cloud-striped sunset held her. Her rigidly plumb back yielded almost imperceptibly under the weight of the desk. He looked over her shoulder and grunted.

"Mackenna, you've written nothing here about the platform."

"It's to be razed." She touched the quill tip to the side of the ink horn. "I know that."

"Dismantled," he said, "and the pieces used. Write it, Mackenna, then you'll be done with it."

"Aye, Montclaire. I'll soon be done with it."

Chapter 8

A door had been constructed for Montclaire's chamber, and now hung on sturdy iron hinges. The roof was reduced to nothing but the center beam. Most fascinating of all was the tall wooden tub steaming in front of the blazing hearth.

"'Tis yours, hostage," Montclaire said, indicating the bath as he lifted the desk from her shoulders.

"Mine?" She thought she sounded groveling and too eager. "And you will be where, milord, if I accept your offer?"

"Here." Thomas dropped onto a bench at the trestle table. He was bone weary and in need of sleep. His bed had been assembled and placed in the corner of the room; the first frame bed he'd owned in his life. He'd never needed one before. Beds and feather mattresses were for mush-muscled, hearth-bound old men, not for a soldier. It was King Edward's gift to him. A curse more like. Yet tonight the sturdy wooden framework and the comfort of down drew him nearly as strongly as the promise of a steaming bath. But none drew him so completely as Mackenna Hughes. Even now she almost slept, her eyes half-lidded, battling the faded night and an exhausting day.

"You needn't worry, hostage. I have neither the stamina nor the inclination to ravish you. I shall turn my back 'til the count of twenty," he said, not bothering to stifle a yawn. He rubbed the heels of his hands against

89

his eyes and swung his knees under the table. "After that I will either hear you splashing in the tub, or I shall tie you to the chair and use the water myself. One . . . two . . ."

Her shoes hit the floor first.

Thomas smiled to himself and continued his slow count toward twenty as she dragged a chair into place between them. He listened to the rustling of her clothes, to her unguarded sigh, and the unsubtle rippling of water as she lowered herself into the bath.

Mackenna made it with one count to spare, and sank to her chin in the deepest tub she'd ever been in. As soothing as the water was, she still kept an eye on Montclaire over the top of her make-do screen. The chairback was too low and her robe not nearly thick enough, but it was better than no screen at all. He was a strange man, with scruples of a sort that she didn't dare trust. She watched him light a candle and hunch over his bloody diagram. The flame danced in one of the fickle night breezes that teased around in the roofless chamber.

She soaped every inch of her sore body, then dunked her head beneath the surface and swirled her hair with her fingers to rid it of the suds. When she broke through the surface, she leaned back against the edge of the tub and whimpered with pleasure.

"Leave off the sighing, hostage, or you'll have me in there with you."

"You wouldn't fit, milord."

Thomas had every assurance that he would fit, that she would be snug and sultry. He'd lied to her; he had strength enough, and more than an inclination, to seize her, wet and dripping from the tub, and ravish the daylights out of her. He'd not been able to focus on the diagram long enough to make sense of the words. His bones ached. His flesh ached. And all he could hear was the steaming bath water shaping seductive waves against her lissome shoreline.

He cleared his throat, hoping to clear his mind. "The village has no bailiff, or beadle?"

"None, milord."

"Or reeve?"

"I am the reeve, milord."

"I see." A woman reeve? Thomas wasn't the best authority on village life, but he'd never heard of a village of men allowing any office but ale taster to be filled by a woman. What power did this Mackenna hold over them? Those men she had danced for . . .

"I appreciate you letting me see Bryce today, milord, though he shouldn't have come. With Addis gone, and me held hostage, and with the added burden of two hundred soldiers, not to mention masons and carpenters, and your household staff, there's more work to be done at the mill and fewer people to do it. That Bryce cannot see this gives me no end of headaches."

Thomas turned his head and smiled. She had draped her robe across a chair and stuck it between them to shield his gaze. He could only see the top of her head—unless he sat up straight or shifted slightly. The foot of the tub was fully exposed. He'd best leave her to her fantasy.

"Your brother was concerned for you, Mackenna." He watched her toes creep out of the water and up the wall of the tub, exposing the fine bones of her ankle and a small, slender foot.

"A wasted effort, milord. The winter store of grain you stole from us needs milling. Add that to the normal run, and the grindstones need to be turning day and night." Her toes disappeared with a splash.

"I brought some stores with me, having been mistakenly informed that the village was long ago reduced to subsistence."

"To starvation, milord, but we've recovered some. We needed no lord overseer then, and need no one now."

"Undoubtedly. But he needs you."

Montclaire's bench was only three generous paces from her. She folded her arms across her breasts, certain that his beastly gaze could penetrate the chair, her robe, and the soap-hazy water. The top of her head was cold from the roofless breeze, but her earlobes were on fire.

"Aye, you need us, milord, as a master needs his slaves."

"We are lord and tenant. 'Tis business, Mackenna."

"We produce, you plunder. You've got the right of it."

" 'Tis unfortunate you see it that way. And 'tis time you get out of there, hostage. You'll catch your death."

"Why should you concern yourself with my health? You'd be better off if I died."

He was suddenly towering over her, his fists stuck against his hips. "And how do you figure that, Mackenna?"

"Heriot, milord. Death duty." She yanked a towel into the water to hide herself from his gaze. "The mill would then be yours."

He snorted. " 'Tis already mine."

"Aye, but you could then resell the milling rights, and increase the rent."

"I shall be content with my tithe of your milling fees."

"Is that so, milord?" Her arms came easily out of the tub and languidly circled the edge, allowing the towel to float free. He averted his eyes from her shadows.

"A fair take, I warrant. 'Tis all I want."

"Oh, and does that practice stand for the past years' profits as well? You want a tithe, a full tenth of my profits?"

"I do," he said, wondering why she'd suddenly taken on the studied movements of a cat about to pounce on a plump rat. He had the distinct feeling he'd been out-maneuvered by the bit of charm lounging in the milky tub. He frowned down at her.

"Then, milord, my milling account is paid in full. I've not taken a single grain of profit in all those years. The village could not afford it. A tenth of nothing is nothing, milord. We are even, you and I. May I please have another towel?"

"We are far from even, hostage." Thomas held his smile as he retrieved a towel from an iron peg anchored in the stone wall. The girl was mighty good at twisting his words. As he walked back to the tub, a gust of cold wind dropped down off the battlements and brought with it a muffling of laughter. He looked up, past the single beam, and caught sight of a half-dozen moon-pale faces peering down from the knee wall high above the roof line. The faces blinked out as if by magic. Bastards.

He stepped into the corridor, sent a guard on an errand, then returned to the chamber.

"The water is getting cold, milord. Might I have the towel, please?" She stuck out a slender arm and wiggled her fingers.

Montclaire held out the towel for her to step into.

"I'll not look," he said when she hesitated.

The beast was either polite, or exceedingly monkish. She couldn't conceive of either in a warrior as immense and overwhelmingly masculine as Montclaire. Yet, so far he'd ventured no more than the brush of his lips against hers and a few devastating assaults on her ear, and that had been fully a night ago. Today he had been the model of chivalry. Why that should disappoint her, she couldn't fathom.

"Hurry yourself, hostage." Thomas looked skyward as she stepped toward him into the outstretched towel. He bundled her to the neck, then planted her between himself and the fire.

"May I sleep in my chemise, milord?" she asked, lifting her cascade of sopping hair from the towel.

He grunted and left her long enough to find and drop the grain sack full of clothes at her feet. He stood silent guard with his back to her while she looked for a clean chemise. Bryce had stuffed her clothes into the sack so tightly that everything had tangled. She gave a yank and all the clothing burst from the sack. A knife clattered to the floor at the same time.

Montclaire turned toward the sound and she clutched her chemise to her. He glared at her and picked up the knife.

"Resourceful, isn't he?" Mackenna said. Her backside was getting overwarm from the blazing fire.

"Dress yourself." She donned the chemise, then by some witchery, loosened the towel beneath and stepped out of it. The gauzy gown cast a dreamlike haze over her silhouette. Delicate angles and shaded curves . . .

"To bed with you, hostage. Go on."

She leaped under the blanket as a knock sounded at the door.

"Come," he said, opening the chamber door to three of his squires who transferred Mackenna's bathwater to the garderobe, then refilled the tub with steaming bath water. Thomas watched in silence, wedging a shiny, green apple with his dagger.

"Stay abed, hostage," he said, after closing the door behind the men. "If you cause me to leave my bath to chase you through the bailey, I cannot warrant my mood when I catch you. And I will catch you."

Montclaire dropped three slices of apple on the blanket in front of her. She didn't want to spy on his undressing, but her eyes quickly tired of being yanked between the window and the tub. The naked beast that stepped into the bath was only the silhouette and deeper shadows of his corded back and muscled legs. But her imagination floated on a wildly unsuitable fantasy. She shouldn't be looking . . .

Thomas forced himself to believe she wasn't watching him. He presented his backside to her to hide his arousal. He'd spent half of the day denying the damnable animation in his loins. The sweep of her hair had caused it; the way she bit her bottom lip to keep from making comment on his policies had caused it; her steadfast hand at scripting had caused it, her sable lashes, the arc of her lips, and the juice of an apple glistening there. He must stop this imagining or burst with it. The steaming water claimed his weariness. Blessed, blessed bliss.

"Leave off the groaning, Montclaire, else your guards will think I have run you through."

"Aye, but you have." He groaned again.

"What have I done to you, milord?"

Montclaire's head was pitched back against the edge

of the tub, his eyes closed. He looked asleep, but she knew better.

"Were it not for you and your resistance," he said with a sigh, "I would be but a simple overlord with a simple commission from my king. Now I am a politician. God forgive me my sins."

"I have done this, milord? I think not. You ascribe me too much power. I have none. I am a mindless village maid."

"And I have a huge headache that thrums with the name Mackenna." Thomas wearily picked up the castle diagram. Nay, he was too tired for this. "Let us strike a bargain, hostage."

"What kind of a bargain, devil? My soul is not for sale."

Thomas made the mistake of glancing over at her. The girl was fashioned for his bed. She lay on her stomach crosswise, her chin resting on her hands, her face peeking out from under a halo of drying copper. Her knee was bent, and one dancing foot swayed beneath the tented blanket. She poked the last bit of apple into her mouth, then flashed him a smile of utter defiance.

"I don't ask for your soul, hostage. Your cooperation will do. I need timber. The village has the men to do the felling and carting, and I have the writ of the king to use his forests."

"So you want my villagers to fell and cart your timber."

"*My* villagers. Yes."

"'Tis nothing more than week-work," she said with a dismissive sigh.

"What is this 'week-work'?"

"What is—?" Mackenna saw the genuine puzzlement on his usually fearsome brow. Was this another test? "Week-work, milord, is the work owed to you by your villeins."

"Ah, yes." Thomas wanted to ask other questions regarding this work owed to him, but he feared he would reveal more of his ignorance to her. "How many days are the custom in Fellhaven?"

"Two or three a week between Michaelmas and August, three to five days during the harvest."

"I see. This is my offer then: the village fells and carts enough timber, and I will return your winter stores to you."

Mackenna's heart began to pound with the nearness of this unexpected boon. She didn't want to give away her position. "Not such a bargain, lord thief. You pay us with our own goods?"

"*My* goods, Mackenna."

"I'll never concede that, Montclaire, but I offer a codicil." She hoped she wasn't pushing him too far. "The price is not only the grain, but the branches from the felled trees."

Thomas almost laughed at the idea. What the devil did he care about deadfall? He needed solid timber. "I accept," he said, quite pleased with himself.

"Then *I* accept." Mackenna was pleased beyond measure. The wood was precious to the village, and would make the difference between comfort and suffering through the winter. In one brief effort she had regained well-being and plenty for her people.

"Good. The felling will begin tomorrow," he said.

"Aye, milord, it will."

Thomas dunked his head into the water and set about scrubbing off two days of road dust. He lounged until the water had chilled, then rose with the towel as cover. He wrapped the towel around his waist, then dried his hair by the fire. He hoped she was asleep. She'd moved to the far side of the bed, but was lost to him in the tangle of blanket. When he got into bed she was staring up at the sky.

Mackenna remembered looking down off the battlements into Montclaire's chamber early that morning. From there it had looked stark and stony. 'Twas a ridiculous excuse for a chamber, with its night sky and blanket of stars for a roof. A ladder leaned against the wall, reaching beyond the natural limit of the ceiling almost to the edge of the wall-walk.

"Montclaire!" She sat up and pointed to the battlements. "There's a man up there!"

He didn't move. "A man on watch, Mackenna."

"Watching what? Watching me bathe?"

"I can assure you that this man did not watch you at your bath. He's only just been stationed there."

"And the man before him?"

"Sleep, Mackenna. You must be as weary as I."

She was, but she couldn't sleep now. The ladder beckoned to her, left in place by some workman, unnoticed by Montclaire. The chamber door was well guarded, but the roof was not. She might never have a better chance.

The beast seemed soothed by her snuggling and he smelled like a fresh mountain stream, so she made herself comfortable beside him. She tried to concentrate on her plan, but it was quickly conceived and soon bored her, leaving her to dwell on her private battle with Montclaire. Thoughts of him standing at his bath kept her alert far beyond the time she first realized he was asleep. His great mass pressed deeply into the mattress. The muscles of his arm were relaxed and as pliant as a band of iron could ever be. His brow softened in his dreams, a bit of pleasure hinting at his too-lush mouth. He looked nearly harmless. Aye, and a mountain lion looked like a tabby cat.

She slipped from his bed when the hearth had died to embers. He stirred, and then his breathing recovered its steady rhythm. He must be very tired, else he was wide awake and waiting for her next move. He'd probably beat her if he caught her.

She padded across the stone floor, scooped up her cloak, and fastened it around her shoulders. She didn't know where her shoes had gotten to, and could neither risk the noise nor spare the time to find them. Besides, her tread was quieter without her shoes.

The bottom rung of the ladder creaked with her first step. She shot a glance back at Montclaire. He didn't move. Settling her weight evenly over the rungs, she started up the ladder and made the top of the chamber wall without another sound. She listened for the guard's footfalls on the walk above her; the man soon passed her by in the direction of the main gate. She continued up the ladder, stretched the last few feet to the top of the stone, then hoisted herself onto the knee-wall. She was alone on the stone walk between the two towers.

She hurried down the nearest stairs into the empty bailey. Tonight a single small fire burned near the main gate. Most of the wagons had been unloaded and moved into the outer bailey, and now the soldiers slept in corridors and in the great hall.

But the gallows endured. She must take care of it tonight, or the wood would soon be part of the fabric of the castle and she'd never be able to destroy it all. Nothing must remain of Gilvane's evil.

Mackenna gathered an armload of ancient rushes and carried them to the gallows. She stuffed them under the platform and gathered more until the wooden foundation bristled. Careful not to alert a guard, she found a torch guttering in a bracket just inside the keep and carried it down the stone steps.

A face shimmered in the shadows—her father's dear face, with that great white-toothed grin of his, peering down at her, his golden eyes luminescent with the love that sheltered not only his family, but everyone in the village. Randolph Hughes had been everything good in her world.

Her father's beloved face lost its gilded glow; it darkened to gray and canted sharply, unnaturally, to the side. Lifeless eyes stared at nothing and would laugh no more. The thick, twisted noose bunched gray rolls of skin against the base of his jaw. The utter stillness of his body hanging there, untouched by the ever-present winds, haunted her even more than the sight of his distended face, his features distorted and rendered unfamiliar by the violence of his death.

She passed the torchlight in front of the dead face, and the chill vanished.

"Burn, fire," she prayed to the ancient gods of the elements. "Forgive me, Blessed Mary," she whispered.

Thomas awoke when the first splash of orange washed the ramparts above him. Another fire!

"Mackenna!" He reached for his hostage, but her side of his bed was empty, and cold. He wasted no time looking for her: she would be at the heart of the fire. He donned his hauberk and stepped into his boots. When he threw open the door, he found two surprised guards staring back at him.

"You let her go!" he shouted.

"Who, my lord?"

"My hostage. She's not here. The door was locked. Now there's a fire blazing in the bailey. . . ."

He cast a glance backward into the room. Outrage suddenly filled his lungs until he could no longer speak. The bloody ladder! Give the girl an inch and—

He pushed past his guards and found himself on the stone steps outside the keep without knowing how he got there. His men were standing as close to the blaze as they dared. The heat was tremendous. The light it cast was oily, and its shadows hellish.

His hostage stood closest of all, watching it burn, ignoring his constable.

Geoffrey saw him and broke away. "My Lord Thomas, 'tis your hostage's doing. By the time the first guard got here, there was no hope of saving any of it."

The infuriating woman's chin was tilted toward the bonfire in prideful defiance of their recent attempt at an alliance. She stood close enough that the fire wind ruffled the folds of her cloak and twisted her hair around her like snakes.

Enough. He descended the steps and took her by the arm. "You've thwarted me this last time, hostage."

"Thomas!" Walter hurried up the sloping bailey from the main gate. "What the hell's happened?"

"You'll have to ask my hostage. But whatever she says, do not believe her. Take her from here, Geoffrey. Put her where I don't have to look at her. Put her in a barrel and nail it shut. I don't much care what you do with her. But, mark my words well: 'tis the gallows for any man that lets her escape." Thomas leveled a finger at the assembly then stalked out of the bailey.

"Where shall I take her, Sir Walter?" Geoffrey asked.

Walter looked down at the girl and could only wonder if she understood the extent of the damage she had done to her cause. "I leave it to you, Geoffrey. Just remember she's a woman."

"But not an ordinary one. I've heard the stories, sir. Lord Thomas ordered Francis and Philip to the stockades."

"Aye, and had he a stockade, he'd have put them there." His curiosity running wild, Walter strode with Geoffrey to Mackenna's side where the heat lashed at him. "Why did you do it, girl? 'Tis lumber we could have used."

"It was rotten," she murmured. "No good for building."

"Defying his lordship will not advance your cause. Come."

"Let me stay until the last of the flame dies. After that, I don't care where you take me or what you do to me."

"Have you a passion for the flames, then?"

"This is the only flame I've a passion for, Sir Walter. After this one, there is no other for me."

"You've done well, Geoffrey," Thomas said, looking out over the training ground. The late afternoon was clear of clouds, and his head was blessedly clear of its recent distraction.

"Thank you, my lord. The quintains will be in place by sunset. Training can commence at first light."

"Excellent." Thomas thumped Walter on the back. "This has been a fine and peaceful day, Walter. Gives me great hope. Mayhaps there is something to this lord business, after all."

"Thomas, there is the matter of the girl," Walter began.

Thomas started across the lists, with Walter and Geoffrey on his heels. "Which girl is that?"

"Your hostage, Thomas. What do you plan to do with her?"

"Hmmm. I haven't decided."

Walter bristled. "You can't leave her down there, Thomas. Sixteen hours is punishment enough."

"Oh, 'tis not nearly enough. Sixteen *weeks*, mayhaps!"

"Damn it, Thomas, confining a woman to a cold, dark room goes against the grain."

"Cold and dark and *damp*," Geoffrey added proudly.

"Seems a right proper dungeon to me," Thomas said, stopping in front of the quintain. He gave the bar a spin and stepped lightly out of the way of the heavy leather ball that followed.

"She must have spent a miserable night," Walter said, turning his scalding gaze on Thomas.

"And I slept like a babe returned to my mother's bosom; God rest the good woman." Thomas hadn't really slept more than a nod at a time, but it felt so good to say that it almost seemed as if he had. Blast the girl.

"Thomas, she burned a few sticks of old timber and a pile of stinking rushes. Did you ask her reason?"

"No possible reason would satisfy. We settled a contract to supply the castle with timber, then she burns a load of perfectly good lumber. Her logic surpasses me. Leave her to rot."

Walter placed himself between Thomas and the door to the armorer's shed. "If I thought you meant that, Thomas—"

"I do mean it, Walter. She needs no champion."

Walter turned his back on his lord. "Exactly where did you put the girl, Geoffrey?" he asked.

"'Tis a stone cellar of some sort," Geoffrey answered, casting a shrug at Walter, "under the northeast tower."

"With no door, I presume," Thomas said. Each time he'd thought of her during the day—and he'd thought about her with every breath, like a stitch in his side— he'd pictured her sitting on satin cushions in a sun-drenched casement window, sipping mulled wine and writing scathing letters to him in that daring hand of hers. With Geoffrey's mention of cold and damp, the image had shifted to the dungeons he'd seen in the Holy Land.

"There's no light, my lord," Geoffrey amended. "'Tis more like a pit. The floor above is solid stone, except for a trap door that's been barred against her escape—"

Shaking off a sudden chill, Thomas said, "Show me."

Chapter 9

The darkness was so deep, Mackenna might as well have been stone blind. The guards had bound her hands and ankles, and then for good measure, had even bound those together so that she had to lie on her side with her knees drawn up to her chest.

She had listened for hours to the steady murmur of voices in the room above her. She'd been fed two meals and was allowed a few minutes of privacy to relieve herself in a chamber pot whenever she asked for it. Fortunately, her anger and outrage kept her from despair, and her skill with the ropes kept her free most of the time.

She was standing again, flexing her arms and legs, still shoeless and shivering. Her muscles had cramped like an old woman's and her shoulders ached where the desk straps had bruised them. She could only guess at how long the beast planned to keep her here. 'Twas an utter waste of time. He wanted unequivocal obedience, but that was impossible. She wouldn't obey his orders unless they served the village. As for the gallows, she'd had no choice but to burn the evil to the ground. Now it was done; her father was at rest. Time to get on with the interests of the village. She had promised Montclaire timber for his roofing. How the devil was she to manage the contract from inside his pit?

The air stunk of a moldering dampness, but it was freshened by a strangely misplaced breeze that had its source in the valley. Fresh air entering the bowels of the fortress.

"Coming from where?" she wondered aloud. "Don't know, Mackenna," she answered herself, "why don't you look around instead of standing there like a demented prisoner."

Frowning at her own feeble jest, she felt her way along the floor toward the movement of air. The stones were drier as she got closer to the wall. She ran her hand along the seam where the walls met in the corner, then moved her palms across the face to the center. Little streams of air filtered around the mortarless stones. Definitely a breeze drawn up from the valley and mixed with the chill found in a passage of native rock.

"Strange, indeed."

When she pushed gently on one of the blocks, it moved; only slightly, but it moved. Her heart pounded at the possibilities. Was it a forgotten sally port? Had the passage been sealed off by Gilvane? But why then put a trap door as an exit? 'Twas a strange room and an even stranger mystery.

It wanted exploring, but not now. If her stomach had any sense of the time, another meal would soon be carried down into the pit and she didn't want to be caught without her ropes properly tied. If Montclaire thought he could subdue her with his punishments, then let him think he had.

She'd finished retying a convincing set of knots only a few moments before Montclaire's voice thundered above her. Bits of dirt rained down. The wooden door rattled, then a light poured down on her. The meager brightness burned the back of her eyes.

"I do hope you're enjoying your lodgings, hostage." Thomas stepped to the edge of the pit and peered down. When he dropped to his knees for a better look, his blood ran cold.

"Mackenna?"

"Is she there?" Walter peered into the hole.

"Mackenna?" Thomas called again. She lay on her side, dwarfed by her cloak, her knees tucked up under her. When she turned her head to look up at him, her cloud of hair tumbled away from her face. Her eyes were dark hollows set in pallid white.

"Pardon me for not standing, milord—" Her voice cracked and faded. When she tried to sit upright the cloak fell away, exposing the leather bonds.

"God's bones!" Thomas dropped the eight feet to the floor of the pit. "Who tied you like this?"

"I don't know his name, milord, but his knots were a far greater challenge than yours. You should take lessons." She flinched as he drew his dagger. He dropped on a knee beside her and muttered curses as he cut the lashings.

"Have I served my time, milord?" she asked in his silence.

Thomas sliced through the thong at her wrists and yanked her to her feet. Anger was the only emotion he could summon that would keep him from drawing her into his arms and apologizing for her mistreatment. He couldn't do that.

"Hear me well, Mackenna Hughes, for it is the last time I will explain our relationship." He pointed a finger at her as she rubbed her wrists and stared up at him. "By the grace of God and King Edward, I am lord here and you are my hostage. You will eat when I say, you will sleep when I say. You, your family, and my village will respect and obey my edicts."

"I—"

"Silence," he hissed.

Mackenna backed away from him, her bravado routed.

"The very next time you breach one of my edicts, one of your brothers will be brought to this pit and left here until I need him at next year's harvest."

Mackenna opened her mouth to rail at him, but his upper lip curled and exposed gleaming white teeth. She thought better of objecting and closed her mouth.

"For every breach thereafter, I shall incarcerate another of your brothers until this pit is filled to bursting with the Hughes family. Then will come the other villagers.

Children will lose their fathers, wives their husbands, and so on until the castle is stinking with the unwashed bodies of your precious village men. Next will come the women—"

"You wouldn't—"

"I will." He bore down on her and caught her wrists when she stumbled backward toward the stone wall. "I will level the village before I concede my authority to anyone. And know you now, Mackenna, that a breach may be anything that displeases me. It may be the way you hold your quill, or the volume of your voice, or the way you eat an apple. I shall strike firmly and without warning. Do you understand?"

"Aye, milord."

"Liar." She hadn't heard a thing, of this he was certain. He growled and pulled her to the center of the pit. "Here she comes, Walter." Thomas grabbed her around the hips, set her on his shoulder, then hoisted her into Walter's waiting arms. Once she was safely up, Walter helped him out of the pit.

"I sent Geoffrey away until your temper cools, Thomas."

"'Tis a good thing, for my first thought is to kill the fool." Thomas looked around for Mackenna. "Now where the hell has she gotten to?"

Not waiting for an answer, he threw out a curse and hurried into the corridor. She was just turning a corner, her cloak barely caught in the light.

"Stop where you are, hostage!"

She waited for him to catch up with her.

"Yes, milord?" Her bare foot tapped on the stone floor. Her hair looked as if it had suffered an explosion.

"Where do you think you're going?" he asked, yanking the front of her cloak over her chemise. "And close this."

She grabbed the handful of wool. "I'm to the garderobe, milord. Your accommodations lack a few basic amenities. You must talk to your mason."

Thomas scowled at her. "In my chamber."

"Aye, milord, then we shall continue our commerce.

You've wasted enough time with your inspiring display of power. 'Tis nearly evening, and I've done nothing all the day long. Were any trees felled today?" She snorted when he only scowled. "I didn't think so." She stalked off, trying not to favor her leg.

Thomas had hoped she'd gained a small measure of humility. But sixteen hours in dead-dark isolation hadn't fazed her.

"She doesn't seem to have suffered any ill effects," Walter said, matching his stride to Thomas' as they followed her from the tower. "Seems madder than an impoverished king."

"She's limping, Walter. I told you to confine her. I didn't want her tortured."

"You suggested nailing her into a barrel. Geoffrey took your threat seriously. The gallows loomed."

"She was given no pallet, no brazier. The bastard—"

"Nay, Thomas. Geoffrey is a fine constable, 'though a bit green. But he's a soldier, not a nursemaid."

"Nor am I."

Mackenna stopped in front of the heap of charred rubble. It stank of sulfur. The flames had done their job reducing evil to ash. Aye, ashes to ashes. She sighed. 'Twas done at last. She was only sorry it had taken these four years. At least now she could cross the bailey without the grieving blackness clouding her vision and stuffing her chest with bitter feathers. She had rid herself of the gallows; when spring came she would plant pink roses and golden yarrow and periwinkle in its place.

"Admiring your handiwork, hostage?"

Mackenna didn't bother to look at him, but continued toward the keep. "'Twas the devil's work, Montclaire, not mine."

He was waiting for her when she emerged from the garderobe. He was frowning and fierce and nearly handsome in his tunic of forest green and all those straps and buckles. Her heart stumbled, then took off like a red fox. Needing a quick refuge from his disturbing regard, she glanced up at the rafters and found only a half-roof's worth of evening stars, the half closest to the wall-walk. A fine sprinkling of new thatch covered every surface in the chamber.

"A goodly progress, milord." She nodded toward the roof. Montclaire took a long, deliberate, heel-grating step toward her.

"Merely the guarantee against another escape."

She sighed as if explaining to a child. "I wasn't trying to escape, milord. If I had been, I'd've been long gone before now. I'm a hostage, remember: my freedom for that of my village."

"If you weren't trying to escape, why not leave through the chamber door rather than through the bloody roof like a thief?"

She carried her cloak to the wall peg. "It had nothing to do with you personally." When she turned around, Montclaire was leaning against the wall beside her, peering down at her like a dragon. She ought to be afraid of him, but she wasn't at all.

"You set fire to my bailey and I'm not to take it personally?"

"Not the whole bailey, Montclaire." She slipped her arms into the sleeves of her woolen robe. "Just rotten wood."

"Is that the way you consummate a contract, hostage, by burning my supplies? Do you scheme next to sell me my own stone blocks, then crush them to powder?"

Mackenna shrugged and sighed. "You've found me out, milord. Which brother shall I send for?"

"Damn your eyes, Mackenna. What follows is an edict and carries the full punishment: you will not leave my side again without my permission."

" 'Tis a bloody waste of time."

His eyes widened and flashed. "Meaning?"

"Meaning that I've a village to take care of and you have a castle to rebuild." She thought he looked oddly defenseless with his fists balled and his shoulders hunched like a starved raven. "How can that happen, milord, if I must follow on your heels like an unweaned

pup?" She stepped around him and walked to the
hearth, tying her belt around her hips.

"Aye, a pup who chews my boots whene'er my back is
turned."

"Better your boots than the seat of your braies," she
muttered, fingers fanned against her hips. "You have no
choice but to trust me, milord."

"Do go on. I'm fascinated."

"You need timber and I have the means to provide it. I
know where to find fish when Dunmere freezes over,
and where to quarry the finest shale. And where the
reed marshes are, and who the best thatchers are. I
know everything." She sat down at the table and patted
the bench beside her. "Take a seat, milord. You can't
survive without me, and I can't without you."

"Is that so?" When he raised his eyebrows, she
frowned and pulled a clean sheet of parchment from the
folio.

"Cooperation, Montclaire. 'Tis the only way. Best you
learn it now before winter settles in." She dipped the
quill into an ink pot and began a list of the best men
suited for felling and carting his lordship's trees.

Thomas shook his head and poured himself a cup of
wine. He ought still to be blazing mad at her, this
impudent village maid. She took his own words, heated
them, twisted them, then forged them into new and
unintended meanings. Cooperation. Aye, the girl would
cooperate only as it suited her course. Time would tell
how many village men he would have lounging in his
pit.

"Have you a woodward?" she asked.

"A what?" he asked in an unguarded instant. He
knew not the nature of a woodward: man, beast, or
kitchen spoon. He'd let her tell him, then he'd search
out the truth of it later.

"A woodward, milord, a man to manage your forest."
She turned her cinnamon gaze on him. A blot of ink
blackened the end of her nose.

He took a step and wiped a finger across the smudge.
"Ink," he said, displaying it for her.

She rubbed the end of her nose. "It's always clung to me."

"Like trouble?" He burnished the tips of his fingers with the smudge. "This woodward, is he usually a man of the village?"

He watched the truth gambol across her tongue-moistened lips before she answered.

"He can be of the castle or the village, milord."

"Then choose a village man. One who knows the woods." He straddled the bench beside her and tried to read her thoughts.

"That would be Garvey, milord." She added the name to her list and noted the new office.

"I expect you've been stealing wood for years."

"Being a nobleman, you would think it stealing, but it isn't. Unless the finder is caught within ten feet of the source, the wood belongs to the finder."

"Rather like a game of cat and mouse." He lifted a coil of her hair and brushed it back over her shoulder.

Mackenna stopped breathing and looked up at him. There was color in his eyes, after all: the inexpressible blue that hangs in the night sky just before it isn't blue anymore. A pulse played beneath a heavy cord in his neck. The same pulse she'd felt beneath her fingertips that first night in the circle. This wouldn't do at all. She struggled to reclaim control of the negotiations for the village.

"Was the road finished in my absence, milord?"

"It's been made passable. Though the drawbridge still needs chains. But, should the Scots attack, we will merely send it over the side of the mountain."

"The Scots!" Mackenna gave an unladylike hoot. "They're at peace with the English."

"But at war with themselves, my dear. The Scottish leaders have asked our King Edward to mediate. It seems they cannot decide which among them is to be king. Edward sees an opportunity to take his advantage."

"Of course he does. He is of a noble line, Montclaire, and born to stir up trouble. Just like you."

Thomas set aside her opinion. "If Edward can help the Scots choose a sovereign who is friendly to the English, then both countries will benefit. And Fellhaven will remain at peace."

"And now I can add the Scots to my list of devils to thank for your coming here?"

He looked suddenly as if he were considering a very grave matter. His brows locked together. His almost-midnight gaze shifted from her eyes, lingered on her mouth like a phantom caress, then slid back to her eyes. He lifted a lock of her hair and curled it around his finger, his gaze never wavering.

"It would have been someone else, Mackenna, if it hadn't been me. 'Twas only a matter of time."

She felt her cheeks flame. A sheen of dampness broke out across the nape of her neck. She disjoined her gaze from his and lifted the weighty curtain of hair off her shoulders, parting the mass and pulling each side to the front to cool herself.

"What is *this*?" he bellowed without a warning. He slid her gown and chemise off her shoulder nearly to her elbow.

"Have you gone completely mad?" She slapped at his hand, but he was too strong and too focused on something behind her.

He looked furious again. "Not until you tell me who did this to you."

"Who did what to me? I can't see anything."

He lifted her off the bench, forced her to kneel in front of the fire, then knelt beside her on the hearth.

"You've been beaten, Mackenna!" He brushed aside her hair. "Was it Geoffrey? I'll bury the man alive."

Mackenna could only see the bruise she'd gotten from the desk. It had darkened and spread along the path of the straps on both sides of her shoulder.

"Tell me who did this, Mackenna, and I shall have his hide."

She frowned at his misplaced fury. "You have it already."

"I have it? I have what?" he shouted.

"You have his hide. You live in it every day, milord."

"I'll abide none of your riddles, girl. Who caused this?"

"You did, milord."

"I did?"

"You and your bloody desk."

She rubbed her bare shoulder and sat back on her heels. "I have a matching bruise on the other side. See." She grabbed a segment of her hair in each hand and dropped her chin.

He tugged gently at the other sleeve of her chemise and it slipped down, leaving her back bare to her shoulder blades.

"Well, milord?" she asked when he said nothing.

"Damnation." Thomas swallowed hard. The discoloration was extensive and deep. "I'll not believe you, Mackenna, the next time you tell me the desk is no trouble. Does it hurt?" he asked, feeling stupid and cruel.

"Aye, it does. Like rolling thunder, milord. The dampness of your dungeon helped not at all."

"The cold and dark . . . aye." Glancing down at his palms, he wondered if they could give impartial comfort when his starving flesh wanted to feast. "Mackenna, if I might touch you.—"

He didn't wait for her permission. He slid his thumbs upward along her supple spine, digging into the warm muscles from her shoulder blades to the nape of her neck. His palms ached. He wasn't breathing. He'd slept beside her, wrapped his arms around her, kissed her, but he hadn't really *touched* her, hadn't lingered.

A shameless moan broke from Mackenna before she could prevent it. Exquisite pain. Dreadful comfort. Wherever his sun-soaked, unrelenting fingers persuaded, her shrieking muscles released their tenacious grip.

"That brings you ease?" he asked. She moaned again and arched against him until the back of her head touched his chest. Her eyes were closed and sable fringed, her brows winged. An elusive smile danced at the corners of her mouth. God, he wanted to kiss her. Wanted her.

"Do carry on, if it pleases you, milord."

Thomas was nearly undone. His knees were spread and her slender hips were wedged snugly between his thighs. She fit to him as if she'd been conceived for his delight. His arousal strained at his braies. Sweat sheeted his back.

"Aye, it pleases me, Mackenna." He sought to harness his threadbare breathing. He drew his fingers along the ridge of her collarbone, not entirely sure of his own intentions even as he untied the lacing of her chemise at the base of her throat.

Mackenna wrapped her hand around his fingers to stay his breath-stealing presumption. "Where is it you go, milord?" His battle-hardened hand was trembling. She'd have thought him chilled but for the heat pouring off him.

"I mean only to free your gown, that I might reach the full length of your back. If I may," he said against the tumbled crown of curls at the top of her head.

His singular gentleness bewildered her. He was leather and heat and rare spices, rising above her and close behind, enveloping her like a doeskin gauntlet. There wasn't a place on her whole body that didn't beg for his touch, this arrogant lord whose very nearness she ought to revile, this too-gentle beast.

When she nodded and freed his hand, Thomas slid her robe and chemise off her shoulders, letting them collect at her waist and catch up at her elbows and throat.

"Do stop me if I should hurt you, Mackenna," he said. As if to prove his charitable intentions to himself as well as to her, he gently tilted her chin forward and spread his hands across her lower back. He worked her ribs with his fingers and thumbs, trying to focus his thoughts on the dark bruises that had brought them to this intimacy.

He marveled at the depth of his own pretense.

Mackenna let her protest die on her lips and issued forth a most unladylike groan.

"Ohhh . . . that's wonderful . . ." She bent forward with the force of his powerful hands as they rode slowly, deliciously, up her back. His touch was as sympathetic as it was severe, dispensing relief and dangerously blissful pleasure in equal measure. She moaned again and arched upright, resting the back of her head against his shoulder, her temple too-near his mouth.

"Milord!"

Thomas's control faltered. His hand had strayed; his fingers cradled the gently sloping base of her breast. He hesitated there while temptation rode him like a wave. Three days with this woman and he was ready to spend his scrupulously hoarded passion like a green soldier on leave. She was soft and vastly beautiful, would taste sweet beyond dreaming.

"It wouldn't do, milord," Mackenna whispered, promising to scold herself later for waiting so long to speak. Aye, it had taken too long for her reason to demand that her senses move aside and let it through. His searing, rough-grained hand nestled where it shouldn't be. But she wasn't at all sure what she meant when she said, "Please, milord." Or what he would make of her sigh.

Her throaty appeal nearly eclipsed his reason. Three days, indeed. His desire to bed her had stalked him since the first moment he'd seen her, blindfolded and fearless and dancing toward him. She had touched him, caressed him, and then she'd brazenly rejected him. He closed his eyes against her softness.

"Nay," he said, through a voice thick with denial. "It wouldn't do at all." He expelled a steadying breath and confined his hands to the breadth of her back.

He growled and grunted as he massaged muscle against rib. The woman wriggled and writhed beneath his hands, yet he resisted magnificently, sweating as if in the midst of battle, at high noon, clad in full armor. He avoided her indicting bruises and worked studiously on each arm.

Sinew turned to butter, and Mackenna was soon humming and swaying on her knees. "You've unstrung me," she whispered, gripping his forearms as he drew her to her unsteady feet.

"To bed with you, hostage." He looked quite fierce again, surely watching for another breach of his orders as he cinched her chemise over her shoulders. "Tomorrow you must be at your best to defend your village accounts to Walter."

"Will you knead the rest of me in the same way you did my back? I know I shall sleep well then, milord."

"And I would not sleep at all, hostage." He carried her to the bed. "My well-intended kneading would swiftly become an unquenchable needing, then all would be lost."

"Lost?" Nay, found. In all her weary days on earth, she had never been so thoroughly relaxed, nor so thoroughly aware of her senses. Sun-warmed honey sluiced through her veins. His scent of cloves intoxicated her. She'd never before let a man be so free with her body. She shouldn't have allowed it. But muscles that had been clenched for years had broken free, melted and reformed to fit his hands.

And when he had paused at her breast she had secretly encouraged his boldness, yearned for him to lead her astray, if only for a solitary, sweet moment. Disappointment had flushed her crimson when he acquired a sense of honor: disappointment in herself for wanting his touch, and utter disappointment that she hadn't welcomed his ravishing, quaking hand against her breast.

He was still her greatest enemy, even more dangerous now because he had gained the ability to cloud her reason. And despite his bloody edicts against breaching his orders, she still had splendid and far-reaching plans to insure that he kept his hands off her village.

How was it then that she felt so wondrously safe with his hands on her?

Chapter 10

"A s I calculate it, Mistress Hughes, you stole one hundred twenty-five sheep from Lord Gilvane, hence, from Lord Montclaire, hence, from His Highness, King Edward."

Walter's account books sprawled out over one end of the massive table that had been set along the length of the great hall. He hunched over the parchment looking uncomfortable, a rugged warrior turned tight-belted steward.

"And as I calculate it, Gilvane left the sheep in an upper field. No one came, so we kept them, fed them, sheltered them—"

"And?"

"And they made more sheep, gave us fleece and milk. 'Tis what sheep do here. What do they do at court, Sir Walter, sing and play the lute?"

"Those sheep belong to Lord Thomas. He wants them back."

"Well, he can't have them." Mackenna regretted every glob of ink she'd ever set to parchment. The evidence was impossible to hide from a dogged man like Walter, who seemed to know English and Latin and French every bit as well as Montclaire did. She prayed that neither had read all the way through the records.

"He'll have those sheep, and the lambs born of the flock, and the profits from the milk, the fleece, the skin—"

"He'll not even get the manure!" Mackenna stood up in defiance of Montclaire and his belligerent knight-steward.

Walter rose up off the bench, trying to keep control of the situation. All morning, her logic had been precise and difficult to counter. He'd struggled to debate her facts against his, and more than once had resorted to issuing blanket edicts.

"Tell me where the sheep are," he demanded, planting his palms on the table top.

"Not without compensation for four years of husbandry—"

"Hell and the Irish Sea will freeze solid before that day. Neither I nor Lord Thomas negotiate with thieves."

Mackenna slammed her palms down and leaned up into Walter's anger-mottled face. "If we had allowed the beasts to die, his lordship would now have 125 piles of bleached bones instead of a healthy flock of 780."

"Ballocks!"

"I'm right, and you know it. I can see it in your eyes."

Walter had braced himself for this session with her. He had watched her carve into Thomas's steel-forged resolve as no seasoned soldier had ever done. But face to face, she was impossible to disarm. Four blessed hours with her and his spine had turned to clotted cream. She smelled like springtime, her unfettered laughter bound him in song, her intelligence challenged and changed him.

"Sheep got your tongue, Sir Walter?" she asked.

She wanted him to barter; all he wanted was to shorten the distance between them and land his mouth on hers.

"No compromises," he managed, his voice a tattered rag.

"No sheep, Walter," she whispered.

Mackenna was so absorbed in winning her argument she didn't see Montclaire until his hand dropped onto Walter's shoulder. Her heart fluttered absurdly.

"My hostage giving you trouble, Walter?" Thomas

had recognized Walter's besotted gaze from across the hall. 'Twas an old story with his friend, and the last thing he and Walter needed between them. Those days were long past.

"Mistress Mackenna has hidden a flock of sheep, Thomas."

"And you refuse to return them?"

"Aye, until the village is credited for the husbandry." Mackenna sat down and threw her tumbled braid over her shoulder.

"You'll give my sheep back, hostage, and be grateful for any credit I give you. Is that clear?" He straddled the bench beside her, speaking as a father to an unruly lass.

"Thomas, you'd best understand—" Walter began.

"I can handle this, Walter."

"Very well," Walter said, knowing the man would soon have his braies snatched from his flanks and never notice until a brisk winter wind inflated his tunic.

"Return my sheep, hostage," Thomas said, succinctly.

"Is this an edict, milord?" Mackenna asked, caught between two men whom she could easily baffle as individuals. Together, they presented a challenge.

"It is, Mackenna."

"Very well, milord, you may have your sheep." She yanked a paper from under Walter's elbows and started writing.

"Of course I may. See, Walter." But Walter only rolled his eyes and sat down across from Mackenna.

"Lord Montclaire!" A freckle-splotched squire hurried over to the table, his straight, strawberry hair flapping on top of his head like a bird's wing. "Your lordship, there's another of those village persons at the main gate. A man named Hock. He's wantin' to speak with the mistress. Says it's urgent."

Mackenna stood up to leave, then remembered where she was and who was sitting next to her. "I must see him, milord. We've had trouble with the fish smoker."

He studied her for a moment then nodded. "Bring him." The squire hurried away. "This brings to five the petitioners who've come to see you this morning,

Mackenna. I think I shall have a throne fashioned so that you may hold court."

Mackenna huddled over her writing. "'Twould be simpler to allow me to go to the village for a half-day."

"Ha. I'd never see you again." He picked up one of the bylaw records and thumbed through it.

Mackenna snagged his gaze, hoping to dissuade him from his snooping. "Would that not please you, milord?"

His eyes narrowed. "I wouldn't like it at all."

She raised her brows in extravagant wonder. "Have you grown so fond of me, then?"

He thumped his elbow on the table and leaned forward. "I've grown fond of my supplies, my buildings, and I've always been fond of my soldiers. I haven't time to spend swatting at the annoyance you would become if you fled into the hills to rob me."

"When can I visit the village?"

His eyes charted her face. "When you earn it."

Walter cleared his throat. "I need something to eat." Let Thomas fight over the accounts. The woman made his bones ache. He hurried out of the hall to the muffle of their voices.

"You and Walter aren't getting along," Thomas said sternly.

"What makes you think that, milord?"

"Because every time I come through here, I find you both nose to nose and steaming."

"He's an obstinate man and easily flustered. But I do enjoy his company." She shaved the quill tip to a fine point.

"Better than mine?"

"Far better, milord." She dipped the quill into the inkpot.

"Look at me when I'm addressing you, Mackenna."

She set the quill in the holder, folded her hands, and looked at him too placidly for truthful respect. "Aye, milord?"

"What is it about Walter's company that outstrips mine? Is he more considerate?"

"Nay, milord. He's . . ."

"More intelligent?"

" 'Tis just that he's . . ." She fluttered her fingers to aid in grasping her exact meaning. "Sir Walter is . . . smaller."

"He's *smaller?*" He reared back, scowling. "Bloody, bleeding hell! Walter's my secondary by a half-stone, no more!"

"That's not what I—"

"I'm a hair's breadth taller than he, yet you find my company less pleasing? Why? Do I crush you?"

"Nay, milord." Mackenna sighed. She had only meant that Walter wasn't such a huge presence in her life.

"Do I block the sunlight from your sky?" Montclaire opened arms that encompassed the world, and knocked over a candlestick.

"Not often, milord." Mackenna pinched off the flame before it could set fire to the stack of parchment.

"Have I gone to fat since becoming the lord of Fellhaven?"

"Nay, milord, I've not seen a dram of fat anywhere on you." She stumbled over the memory of a huge, naked warrior lowering himself into a steaming tub of water.

"Must I travel on my knees to gain your favor?"

She paused and stared. "Do you seek my favor, milord?"

Her aspect was so direct, he huffed and shouted, "Hell, no!"

"Then, milord, you needn't change a single thing about yourself." She patted his arm, then went back to her writing.

"I'll change whatever the bloody hell I want!"

"Mackennnnaaaaa!" Hock broke loose of his escort and scurried across the hall.

"Hock, what is it this time? Has there been another fire?"

"Cats, Mackenna!" Hock threw himself at her feet. "Cats got into the smoker and left nothing but bones!"

"Do stand, Hock!" She lifted him by the shoulders.

"How did a cat get into the smoke shed if you patched all the holes?"

"I patched most of them. Then there was Michaelmas day, and then—" He ticked his head twice toward Montclaire. "You know."

"You waste my time, Hock, and yours, and his lordship's. In the quarter day you'll have spent coming here, you could well have patched every hole ten times over."

"Patch the holes with what, Mackenna? His lordship's men have taken all the nails in the village."

She turned to Montclaire. "Well, milord?"

He spoke without loosening his glare from her. "Have your smithy make more nails, hostage."

Mackenna folded her arms. "He can't. You've stolen all the village iron."

"I see. Master Hock, you will have your nails. Squire!" Montclaire dropped his fist on the tabletop. Everything bounced once then dropped back into place, except the ink. Mackenna silently blotted up the ring of indigo flecks while Montclaire sent Hock with his squire to fetch the smithy.

"How many of my sheep did you steal, Mackenna?" Thomas asked quietly, setting aside the earlier part of their conversation in which she had sorely bent his pride. Damn the woman!

"I've stolen none, milord. Gilvane left a flock of 125. Walter says the sheep are yours."

"If that's what Walter says, then the sheep are mine. I want 125 sheep marked as mine and folded somewhere near the foot of the castle where I can see them."

"Yes, milord. Let me write that down. One-hundred twenty-five . . ." She smiled serenely, and painstakingly noted the amount while Montclaire observed. The other 655 sheep would now officially belong to the village. When Walter returned, she'd distract him with a good fight over pannage. She'd probably have to explain that pannage was the price paid to the lord for the village pigs foraging for acorns and beechnuts on the forest floor. With a bit of careful side-stepping she could make

up a good story to go along with the incriminating
evidence she'd so carefully scripted into the account
scrolls.

If only she could create another set of pages for all the
ones that pointed a damning finger at the village. One
page, one book, looked very much like another. She
kept spare wooden book covers, leather thongs, and
parchment in the millhouse. . . .

"That's it!" The words leaped out of her mouth before
she could catch them and draw them back.

"That's *what*?" Thomas had been watching the easy
flow of the quill under her hand and had seen nothing
in her script to warrant such an outburst.

"That's . . ." She stared at him, then jutted out her
chin. "That's the last time I have to think about those
bloody sheep. If you would sign your name here."

"Why?" Suspicion fretted his curl-tangled brow.

"So that I might set the page aside and consider the
matter complete." She watched him scrawl his large,
ungainly signature across the bottom of her figures. She
found the simple act oddly charming. Perhaps it was the
gentle, aching pleasure those big hands had wrought
the night before. She felt her face begin to heat. "Thank
you, milord."

"Who is John Cotes?" he'd asked suddenly. He drew
the bylaw book closer and sprawled out across the table,
his hands sun-darkened against the parchment. He
looked quite settled, like he planned to stay and study.

"John Cotes, milord?" Trying to sound nonchalant,
she peered over his arm. Had he found a discrepancy in
the fine levied upon Cotes earlier that spring? "Why do
you ask?"

"I ask because I am your lord."

"Ah, yes. I keep forgetting." She'd wanted to sneer at
him, but she couldn't seem to gather such defiant
energy.

"I want to know, Mackenna," he said evenly, his
brows drawn together in a humorless furrow. "Who is
John Cotes?"

"The cooper, milord."

"Ah," he said quietly, idly twisting the end of his moustache between his fingers. "And is he a strong man?"

"Aye, with the shoulders of a bear. Why?"

"It doesn't concern you."

"Lord Thomas! There's been a message delivered for you." The same freckled squire skittered into the hall and handed Montclaire a sealed letter, then darted away.

"Wait, Daniel." The squire skidded to a stop as Thomas turned the packet in his hand. The seal was Edward's. "Did the messenger stay for a reply?" he asked.

"Nay, my lord, he's off to Cockermouth and the coast."

"Did you feed him?"

"Aye, my lord. Gave him one of the village loaves."

"With or without rocks?" Montclaire cast Mackenna a teasing glance. She gave him a reluctant smile.

"Rocks, milord?" Daniel asked, scratching his ear.

Montclaire rose and turned to his squire with a lazy smile. "Never mind. Thank you, Daniel. You may go."

Montclaire stepped away to the hearth to read the message. Mackenna used his inattention to alter a passage in the accounts which would have revealed that Edwin and his stone cutters had uncovered a small vein of silver ore in a quarry above the mill. Such treasure was useless without a smelter, but it was treasure that belonged to the village, not to Montclaire. Now the record would read only that stones were cut for the churchyard wall.

Montclaire's letter had him muttering curses to himself when his blacksmith arrived. He ordered the man to the village forge with a cart full of iron, and sent Hock on his way with a bag of castle nails.

"Has her grace finished with her subjects?" Walter asked as he returned to the hall. Mackenna ignored him, and Thomas seemed engrossed in the contents of a letter. Walter lifted the broken seal dangling from the ribbon.

"Speaking of royalty," Walter said, dropping the seal, "what does this one want?"

Thomas looked up. "Me," he said, frowning. "Come, hostage. I have a need to see my village up close."

"Now? Why?" she asked, thoroughly shaken at his sudden change of mind.

"Bring parchment and quill." Montclaire handed the letter to Walter. "You'll have to do without my hostage."

"No, he can't!" Mackenna desperately needed to go to the village, but she couldn't allow Walter to continue his audit without her.

"He can't?" Montclaire looked at Walter and frowned.

"In truth, Thomas, I could use a break from these damn books." Walter waved his hand over the table as if to incant the offending objects into the netherworld. "My eyes are near crossing, and my head aches. Although the latter can be attributed directly to your hostage. She's—"

"I'm persistent." Mackenna carefully closed the by-law book. "Come with us to the village, Sir Walter."

"Aye, you might as well, Walter. My hostage prefers your company to mine."

Walter felt a sudden dampness across his brow. He hoped it didn't show. "Does she?" he said calmly.

"In truth, I prefer neither of you."

"Are you coming, Walter?" Thomas asked, wondering why the hell he had hauled the subject back into the light.

"Nay. I'm off to the training lists." He strapped on his sword belt. "Tonight, Mackenna. We can work until the moon is high. Thomas." Walter left the hall.

Mackenna breathed out a sigh of relief. It stopped abruptly when she found Montclaire looking down on her like a gargoyle.

"The ladies favor the man," Thomas said, wondering if he could allow Mackenna to sit with Walter beneath any moon.

"Has Walter never married?"

Thomas didn't like her question, didn't like it at all.

"Walter and I are of the same mind in the matter of marriage."

She turned to him, enormously curious. "And that is, milord?" She caught the corner of his gaze as he launched it from her face to a workman sitting bestride a rafter above them.

"We're against it." He glared down at her.

She laughed. "Against marriage? Altogether?"

"Against it for soldiers. No time for wives and children." He looked away again, presenting her a resolute chin.

"So, milord, you're one of those monkish knights who capture women just to sing to them? Is that why I remain unravished?"

The affront registered like a brand on his stormy face, from his levitated hairline to his jaw. She might well have told him that his mother was a flounder.

"I am neither monkish nor a ravisher of women. Were I either, Mackenna Hughes, believe me, you'd know it by now. Come, we're wasting the day."

"By all the saints! A giggling rosebush!" Mackenna dropped from her horse into the dusty lane. She lifted her eyes to Thomas and set her finger to her lips. "Do you suppose it was fashioned by the faeries, milord?"

The giggles came again, and whispering.

"Aye, Mistress Hughes, it was faeries." Thomas tugged on the corner of his moustache to hide his smile.

" 'Twas us, Mackenna! Us! We are the faeries!" Three little girls shrieked as they popped up from behind the bushy hedge and ran out to surround Mackenna.

Thomas kept a close rein on Baylor, fearing the brute would trample one of the little ones. The girls were fearless with joy. One grabbed the bridle of Mackenna's mare. Another pressed her cheek against Baylor's muzzle. The other stroked a dimpled hand along the length of his horse's sleek neck.

"Mackenna, what a beautiful horse! Is he yours? Is he?"

"No, Ellen. He belongs to—" Mackenna began.

"Who's the big man, Mackenna?"

"Berta, this is—" she tried again.

"Isn't he that mean old lord who lives up in the castle?"

Ellen ducked beneath the neck of Mackenna's mount and squinted up at Thomas. "He isn't old, Haitha, not very at least. But I do think he's the lord. Is he the lord, Mackenna?"

Mackenna glanced back at Montclaire. His eyes were large and his brows bemused. He was trying to look stern, but failing.

"Haitha, Ellen, Berta, this is Lord Montclaire."

"Hellooo!" the girls crooned in a chorus, jumping up and down like clockwork squirrels.

Berta thumped a dusty hand on Montclaire's boot. "Are you mean, then, sir?"

Ellen shoved herself in front of Berta and peered up at Thomas. "Nay, Berta, he's too handsome by far to be mean."

Thomas flushed beneath his beard. To be discussed like a bull at market was roundly embarrassing. He found Mackenna's laughing, unblinking gaze on him, and scowled at her.

"Ellen, Haitha, have you been at your studies?" she asked, enjoying Montclaire's stricken look.

The girls left him and swarmed around Mackenna, one draped through each of her arms, the youngest trapping her waist and squeezing hard enough to make her grunt.

"We can't learn when you're not here!" Ellen whined, adding a jumble of excuses that Mackenna denied with an emphatic snort.

"How can you grow up to be a reeve, like me, if you can't read or write or do sums?"

"I don't want to be a reeve, I want to marry Ned," Ellen said, looking with moon-eyes down the lane toward the village, where little Ned Falke lived with his widowed mother.

"Will you still be reeve when you marry?" Haitha asked.

Mackenna blushed as red as the rose hedge. She quickly headed Haitha away from the subject of marriage. She would make sure Montclaire never learned the truth about the circle he'd come upon that Michaelmas night. "I shall be reeve, Haitha, until the village votes me out. Now, off you go." She shrugged out of their arms and bunched the girls together by the side of the road.

"But we miss you. We love the stories you tell us."

"I miss you, too. But his lordship and I have important business. And winter's a'coming. You know what that means."

They jumped up and down again. "Christmas! Gingercakes!"

"Aye, my girls, that's what it means. Go on with you, now. Shoo!" Unshed tears stung her eyes as she watched the girls dance away in a surrender to childhood. She gripped her horse's reins beneath the bit and started off toward the center of the village, near dragging the poor beast behind her.

Thomas trotted Baylor even with her, then slid off to walk beside her. "I was hopelessly outnumbered, Mackenna. I thank you for coming to the rescue."

When she shot him a grin, Thomas noticed her scarlet-edged eyes, the threat of tears. He stopped her and tilted her chin with his thumb. "What's this?"

"Nothing." She pulled away and walked on. "Just—"

"Just what?" He followed.

"The girls don't remember the killing winters."

"And that saddens you?"

"Nay, it pleases me, milord. You can't know how much. They don't remember . . ." The sticklike bodies, the shed where the dead were kept from the wolves until the frozen earth would accept them. This man, this lord striding beside her had the means and the right to cause that same kind of sorrow.

"They don't remember what?"

"Mackenna, my love!" A young man came bounding across the stone bridge at a dead run and clasped Mackenna in a bear hug that spun them both in a circle.

"Witless cur! I've missed you!" Mackenna planted a noisy kiss on his stubbly cheek. He smelled of woodchips and ale. "I'm so happy to see you. Are you eating well?"

"I am, girl, now that you're not cooking for me!" He ran a raspy finger down the bridge of her nose. "Bryce was right; you look none the worse for his lordship's beatings."

"I haven't beaten her," Thomas said from behind her. He didn't know who the devil had his arms around his hostage, but he seemed far too friendly. And Mackenna seemed far too eager in her greeting. The young man flicked his quicksilver gaze from Mackenna and met Thomas' frown with a lively grin.

"Maybe not, my lord Montclaire, but I'll wager you've given more than one thought to paddling my sister's backside—"

"Cadell!" Mackenna swiped his cap from his head and sailed it into a gorse bush.

"You needn't chasten yourself for the thought, my lord." Cadell took both of Mackenna's hands in his. "She prickles the temper. But I warn you not to try a paddling; she's got a vicious set of knuckles," he kissed two of them, "and a knee that's pointed and direct, if you know what I mean."

"I shall keep that in mind, Master Hughes." Thomas found himself hugely relieved that this man was merely another of her brothers. He wondered if there was a lover somewhere in the village who had missed her laughter, who ached to have her smoky voice come round him like a vapor once again.

"Have you seen Bryce?" she asked, hoping Cadell wouldn't see that Montclaire had suddenly propped his hand against her waist.

"He . . . well. . . ." Cadell suddenly looked sheepish and let go Mackenna's hands. He scrubbed his palms together as he did when he wished he were two leagues from trouble.

"You can't save him by hiding him from me. What's he done?"

"Well, now, it wasn't his fault entirely. He just forgot—"

"He forgot to fix the pinion gear. It's Joelle, isn't it?"

"He's thoroughly besotted!" Cadell retrieved his cap from the gorse bush. "I've never seen him so."

"Where is he now?"

"At the mill, last I saw. He's sworn to have the stones grinding again by sunset. Go easy on him, 'Kenna." Cadell settled his cap over his untrimmed hair. " 'Tis all this talk of marriage that's got his sap stirring."

"You see what I mean, Montclaire. I cannot leave them alone for a day. I need to go to the mill. May I?"

Word of Mackenna's return had spread through the village like a wheat field afire in a summer wind. The church bell rang out, and a small group of villagers began to gather around them.

"May I?" she asked again.

"To the mill and nowhere else."

"My word of honor, Montclaire."

"Nay, Mackenna, my edict."

The moment Thomas stepped away from his hostage, the villagers surrounded her like bumblebees converging on new clover. He listened for a time while they asked her every conceivable question, and she issued orders with the self-possession of the king's vanguard commander.

He shouldn't trust her beyond his hearing, but he had business of his own. And a king to answer to.

Chapter 11

⌒ᕙᕙ⌒

"**H**e's quite a piece of handsome, is our new lord." Meg Bavitts planted herself in front of Mackenna just as she'd answered the last question and thought she could start off toward the mill. "Wouldn't you say that, Mackenna?"

Mackenna laughed. "Aye, Meg, some foul-smelling boars have their own particular beauty—but only to another boar."

"Ah, me, those dark eyes . . ."

"I'm sure I haven't noticed, Meg. I'm his hostage, not his paramour. I haven't time to talk. I've business at the mill."

"Did he kiss you?" Meg's sandy brows danced a saucy jig.

"Is your father at the ovens, Meg?"

"Aye, and I should be there too, but I had to talk to you."

"I've been thinking that he might be allowed to sell sweet cakes to the workmen and the soldiers."

"Mackenna, we've been friends since we were old enough to talk. Has his lordship kissed you?"

"Nay, Meg, Lord Montclaire hasn't kissed me—not really."

"Not really?" Meg clapped her hands together and laughed. "Either he has or he hasn't. Which? And was it wonderful?"

"I haven't time for this, Meg. I think we'll build

another oven in the quarry where it won't be found and taxed. Tell your father I'll come to see him after I've finished at the mill." Mackenna started away, but Meg grabbed her by the shoulder.

"Ow, Meg. Not so hard. I'm sore."

Meg gasped. "Then he's beaten you?"

"Nay, he hasn't beaten me."

Meg's eyes lit up. "Has he taken you to his bed?"

Mackenna blushed at the unarguable fact that they shared a bed, albeit a chaste one. It was none of Meg's business how she dealt with Montclaire. "Margaret Bavitts, you're a gossip. And I won't listen to you. Excuse me."

Undaunted, Meg skipped along sideways to keep pace with Mackenna. "Answer me, girl. Has his lordship had his way with you? We were all saying just last night that we'd none of us mind a heated moment 'neath his lordship's—"

"And who is *we*? Wait. You needn't tell me. Thea's ale was to be tasted last night. So you and the other women sat around speculating on what you know nothing about."

"We know the lord keeps you in his chamber." Meg was suddenly grave. "Does he know you chose him for a husband?"

"I did nothing of the sort. And I won't ennoble your gossip with an answer. Excuse me, Meg." Mackenna hitched up her skirts and started for the mill. "I have work to do."

She wondered where Montclaire was. Not that it mattered; he didn't know enough to cause much trouble. But he'd given her time enough to assign Garvey the job of woodward and to gather his lordship's sheep from the flocks hidden in the upper fields. She had mediated disagreements and listened to reports about the last of the winter planting.

Now she needed to see what had become of Bryce's repair work, and time was wasting.

* * *

Thomas stepped through the wide millhouse doorway. Inside, sunlight streamed in through unshuttered windows set high in the walls, striking the heavy web of timbers that supported the upper floors. The two millstones were still. Nothing stirred.

He was about to shout Mackenna's name when the floor thumped above him. As he looked up, a pair of slender legs popped out of the square hole in the ceiling, legs that were bare from the wriggling toes to the short braies threatening to expose an exquisite backside. Mackenna.

Her legs churned until her feet caught a step set into a supporting post. He watched in silence as she emerged from the ceiling and scrabbled down the ladder. A yard from the bottom, she dropped away from the post and landed facing him.

Mackenna screamed and was halfway back up the ladder before she realized the man was Montclaire. A fluted column of sunlight burned the floor behind him, its brightness keeping him in silhouette. But she knew the hulking figure, whether in darkness, shadow, or blinding daylight.

"What are you doing?" she demanded from her perch, her heart lodged somewhere up on Mickelfell.

"Standing in my mill. What are you doing?"

"*Fixing* your mill. As you can see."

Mackenna suddenly felt quite simple-minded, clinging to a pole ladder and chattering down at him like a squirrel. She descended to the floor and presented her most stubborn chin.

"Aye, I can see very well." He kept his gaze from lingering long on the shadows that teased the front of her linen shirt.

"Did you think I had taken off to hide in the fells?" she asked, thinking him much too smug at the moment.

" 'Twas possible."

"Not while I stand as hostage for my family and friends." She drew her fingers through her hair, dislodging the leather thong which had kept her plait knotted.

She reached down for her skirts but found only her bare legs.

"If you've a scrap of decency, you will turn your back."

"I've no decency at all, my dear." But Thomas obliged her modesty, amused that it should come after days and nights of close commerce. He listened to her stomp away toward the back of the mill. She returned quickly, wearing the sleek linen chemise and the woolen surcote she'd worn to the village. A bulging sack hung at her side, tangling with her skirts as she walked.

"What have you there, hostage? Your stock of weapons?"

"Aye, milord," Mackenna said, trying to appear nonchalant about the sack. "A pair of work boots, a warmer cloak and some personal things. Women's things." When his frown deepened, she continued, "Do you wish to inspect them?"

She began opening the sack, staging a ruse as old as time, praying he wouldn't look. He'd be more than suspicious about the blank parchment and the book bindings.

"Not necessary." He harrumphed. "Why were you wearing so very few clothes?"

"Safety, milord. Long sleeves and skirts get caught up in the gears. 'Tis an easy way to lose a limb—" Before she'd even finished her explanation, Montclaire yanked her away from the millstone and glared at it as if it were a wild animal.

"It won't bite, milord."

He cast his gaze upward across the snarl of machinery. "How do you manage to think with all the noise in here?"

"What noise is that, milord?"

"The everlasting groaning. It sounds like a hall filled with children, each attempting to squeeze music from a sackbut."

She laughed. "I don't notice it. 'Tis the heartbeat of my life, like breathing. And this noise is hushed and peaceful compared to the racket when all the gears are turning and both stones are grinding. Shall I show you how it works?"

"Please. The last hour has been a lesson in the trades."

"What have you been doing, milord?" She tried not to appear too suspicious.

"Touring my village."

"Then come tour your mill." Mackenna walked him through the threshing barn, demonstrated the winnowing sieves, skirted the pond full of trout at the foot of the millhouse, followed the power track from the wheel, and explained how the grain was finally ground into various grades of meal.

Having come full circle back to the millhouse, Mackenna opened a sack of barley. She held a grain in her palm and pointed proudly to the seed's shape and plumpness. "Our yield has increased from two bushels for every one planted, to four."

"Four? I know little about growing grain, but that does sound excessive. What is your secret? Witchery?"

"Fish."

Thomas laughed and leaned back against a millstone. He crossed his arms against his chest and prepared himself for a faerie story that would end in his having been the cave-blind fish caught in Mackenna's spellbinding net.

"Fish leavings sown with the crop. 'Twas an accident three springs ago, caused by a field flooded by a broken fish weir. 'Tis also the secret to the sweetness of our grain."

"That's quite a tale, hostage."

She laughed. "Taste for yourself, milord."

Mackenna reached up and offered him the barley seed pinched between her fingers. Montclaire hesitated, then smiled and closed his flawlessly fashioned mouth over both of her fingers. She lost her next breath. His lips were warm and supple and unyielding, his teeth a delicate entreaty to linger.

"Milord, I didn't mean . . ." She didn't know what she meant, only that she was suddenly a cloud and he the wind. He slipped his tongue between her fingers and took possession of the single grain of barley.

"Oh . . . my!" Her heart thrummed against her ears, muddling her thoughts. Her knees weakened to willow and she sagged a step toward him. She was about to chasten him when, with an aching slowness, he took hold of her wrist and withdrew her fingers from his mouth, past lips that tugged and tempted, and a tongue that begat images in her head too scandalous to be possible.

"Milord, you shouldn't—"

" 'Tis sweet, Mackenna."

"As I said," she whispered, as he kissed her fingertips.

"Aye, the barley is sweet, as well as you."

" 'Twas not my meaning, milord."

"But 'twas mine." Thomas drew open her fisted fingers one by one and smoothed his hand across her palm. Soft-skinned callouses bore witness to her devotion, evidence of the mill and the plow, indigo-stained and lightly scarred. " 'Tis a beautiful hand."

Mackenna watched in breathless awe as he lifted her hand toward his lips. She ought to stop him, but she caught herself wishing for his kiss. His moustache brushed her fingers, his breath caressed. Then his mouth touched her palm, and she closed her eyes to seize the sensation. When she finally looked up, his eyes were smiling down at her.

"Milord, you shouldn't. You are lord here, and I am—"

"Mine enemy, I know." He splayed his fingers through her hair and brought her face close. There was breath between them and nothing more.

"I do hate you, milord, and all your kind." She struggled to separate the man's radiant fire from the truth of who he was. She shouldn't be yearning for a kiss from the beast whose uncaring stride claimed the breadth of her life.

"As you tell me," Thomas breathed. He was sure that other kiss had been a misguided spark of blue lightning, which ought to have struck the top of Mickelfell instead of somewhere deep in his chest. He wondered if he could weather another.

"Then kiss me if you must, milord." She closed her eyes.

"If I must?"

"I'm not afraid."

"Not afraid?" He smiled against her temple. "Oh, but I am, Mackenna."

"You, Montclaire?" He smelled like the village: like baked bread and candlewax, iron and woodshavings, like home. "You're afraid of what?"

"Quicksand."

She opened her eyes and pushed away from him. "My kiss would be quicksand?"

"And certain madness," he said, picking up her sack. "Come. We've near lost the sunlight. 'Tis past time we leave."

"But I've not seen Bryce." She yanked the sack from him.

"I found him with the carpenter. Cort has the patterns from the last pinion gear he built. I told him to make a spare—at my cost, of course."

Mackenna gave him her best glare, incensed at his making a decision involving the mill. "I don't need your help, milord."

"'Tis my mill," he said, scanning the gears once again, looking quite satisfied with himself. "I do as I please. And that includes deciding what freedoms to grant you."

Mackenna halted the sharp comment that had formed on her tongue and asked calmly, "Freedoms, milord? Have you decided on any in particular?"

Thomas took leisurely measure of her mouth and eyes as he considered how far he could safely allow her to range. She would strain whatever boundaries he determined.

"You may travel anywhere within the castle walls. But

my edicts remain in force. Break one of them,
Mackenna, and the pit will be open for my guests."

"Then I must accept, milord. I'll do anything to keep
you from using that horrid pit again."

Mackenna lowered the ladder into the pit and climbed
into its dampness, lighting her way with a lantern. She'd
tried untold times in the last few days to free herself
from the interminable meetings between Montclaire,
Walter, and their craftsmen. When she wasn't scribing
for them, she was altering the bylaw records, leaving her
fingers permanently ink-stained.

In the light of the lantern, the differences in the pit's
walls were clear; the breeze came from behind a wall of
newer stone, lighter in color and larger. Armed with a
bag of mason's tools, she pushed and prodded at the
wall until she was able to shove a block through to the
other side. The air flowing through the hole was clean
and keenly scented with overripe blackberries.

She made an opening large enough to clamber
through with the lantern. The rough-hewn passage
beyond was lined with a dozen five-gallon barrels,
heavy and unwieldy. She pried open one of the lids and
found a stash of small sacks tied off and secured with a
lead seal. She lifted a sack and the contents clinked
together. Her hands shook with cold nerves as she slit
the sacking. A shower of silver pennies rolled out onto
the floor.

"Pennies?" Stunned, Mackenna knocked the chisel
against the sides of a few other barrels. "They're filled
with pennies! Hundreds of pounds sterling!"

What the devil could she do with all this silver?
Money was useless in the village, but she could think of
a hundred ways to spend it in a market town: a new
loom, dying vats, salt. She picked up the coins and
tossed all but a few back into the barrel, then replaced
the lid and sat down on top of it.

It must be Gilvane's money! Montclaire would claim it
if he knew. But it was village money, stolen and now
returned. If not the same pennies, then pennies held on

account. Famine turned to fortune, at a price no one should ever have to pay.

Wondering what other treasures might be hidden in the passage, she followed it downward through the mountain itself. The opening to the outside was obscured by a huge bramble of blackberries. Daylight showed through the yellowing leaves and she could see Montclaire's new sheep pen a few hundred yards further down the slope.

A doorway to the village and a cache of money! And both would be discovered if Montclaire ever used his pit again. From now on, she'd be careful to mind his edicts. She pushed the blocks back through the wall opening, repaired the hole she'd made, then climbed out of the pit.

Surely she'd been gone too long. Montclaire would be looking for her. She was supposed to be in the great hall preparing for the afternoon's court of review.

Whatever that was.

The hall was noisy with villagers. All of them, it seemed, for Montclaire's edict had demanded everyone attend. She had expected a mood of anger and foreboding, but Montclaire had promised a feast afterward and the tantalizing aromas from the kitchen stirred up a holiday mood. Musicians played as if it were a celebration instead of a court.

"What the devil is a court of review, milord?" Mackenna asked as she took her place at a table on the dais.

Montclaire dropped his foot on the bench beside her. "'Tis a review of justice. Righting the wrongs done in the name of the lord of Fellhaven."

"Justice has been done, milord. Village justice."

"But not *my* justice. Sit you quietly, and record what happens here, or I shall have you removed from the proceedings like a festered splinter, hostage. Where have you been?"

"Working."

"At what? Cleaning the undercrofts? You have cob-
webs in your hair." He plucked a clot of dusty webbing
off the top of her head and showed it to her.

"I was exploring. Looking for scrap iron, old hinges,
rusted nails. We're short of iron, as you know."

"We are, but we won't be for long. My bailiff and I are
going to the market at Carlisle."

"Carlisle? You're leaving?"

She didn't know what to make of her unsettling
disappointment. She ought to feel quite jubilant; instead, a peculiar ache hunkered down inside her chest.

"Have you ever been to Carlisle, Mackenna?" he
asked.

"I've not been beyond the valley. Did you say bailiff?"

"Aye. Fellhaven needs a bailiff, and I've found the
perfect person for the job."

"I'm sure you have." Another inexperienced outsider
to oversee the village. Just when she'd begun to train
Walter to her ways, another fool was to join him.

Montclaire chuckled at some private humor and
stepped off the dais to talk with Walter.

Her life was slipping out of control. The people she
had tried to protect now consorted with the enemy. At
least she had made great strides at setting the bylaw
records in order. They were spread out in front of her,
village and royal accounts, scrolls and books, and a
small strongbox she'd never seen before. She'd done the
best she could. Now she would try to pick up the pieces
as Montclaire shattered more of her dreams.

"Good people of Fellhaven," Montclaire shouted
from the dais, "welcome to my home."

Mackenna snorted and he looked back at her.

"Stand, Mistress Hughes, and come here."

When she made it clear that she would not, he
lowered a threatening glare at her and she remembered
the silver pennies in the pit. She stepped forward and
stood beside him, looking out over her friends and
family.

"Those of you who know my hostage must commend

me for my patience with her intolerable muleheadedness.'' Thomas was pleased to hear more than one snort
and a few muttered ''ayes.''

''Thank you, milord,'' Mackenna said between her
teeth.

''You've no doubt noticed that my assessors have not
yet come through the village to collect back taxes.''

The muttering died.

''I've not had time to do this. I was vexed to discover
the castle in sore need of supplies and in far worse repair
than had been reported. I know not who is to blame for
the severity of the damage, although I have my suspi-
cions.''

''Is this where you accuse, judge, and punish in one
stroke, Montclaire?'' Mackenna let her voice carry across
the hall.

''Silence yourself, hostage,'' he said, taking hold of
her elbow, ''lest I think you submit your defense too
quickly.''

''I did nothing to your castle—''

''Except to fire my bailey—''

''That's not why I—''

''If you'll listen for once in your arrogant life—''

''Me? Arrogant—''

''And shrewish, and dishonest and prideful. Shall I
continue? Your friends are listening. Why don't they
come to your defense, I wonder? Don't you wonder at
that, Mackenna?''

''You frighten them out of action, Montclaire.''

''Nay, Mackenna, look at them. They grin at my
courage.''

''They do not.'' Mackenna searched the crowd for
traces of fear but found poorly hidden amusement, and
waves of twittering gossip passing from the front rows
toward the back. She had always been called bull-
headed. 'Twas nothing new; but it galled her that
Montclaire should have the village agree with him.

He finally turned from her. ''I offer my village this
simple compromise: deal honestly with me and I shall
credit each household with four years' taxes.'' Thomas

saw shoulders rise and eyes widen in hope, heard hesitant murmurs of approval.

Mackenna snorted. "In exchange for what, milord? A month of love boons?" The fool hadn't the slightest idea what a love boon was, she could see that clearly in the cant of his brows.

Scowling at her, he continued, "In exchange for this year's tax of one shilling paid to the lord, in kind, from each croft. Due sometime between now and Epiphany. What say you?"

"Aye!" came a cry from the back of the hall. Its echo skipped around as others replied in kind.

"Now wait a minute, Montclaire!" Mackenna would never have given her assent so quickly. This was a bargain with the devil.

"Good, then. We shall call it done. Sit, hostage, and record this in your bylaws."

Mackenna gave him a frown and took her seat, knowing that he would study every word she wrote.

"Sir Walter, have you the list of who is not in attendance?"

Walter flicked a brow at Thomas and then cleared his throat. "Simon Roper," he called out.

Father Berton stepped forward. "Simon Roper is dying, my lord. I was in attendance this morning."

"Dying?" Thomas asked. "His ailment?"

"Age, my lord."

"Ah, and so his family is with him?"

"Nay, they are here, Montclaire," Mackenna said from the table. "As you demanded, milord."

Montclaire inspected Walter's list. "Roper's family is excused. See to his final comforts. My prayers go with you."

The family looked relieved as they left the hall, grateful for the favor granted by their lord. Beguile and conquer; he was far more dangerous than Gilvane.

"Anyone else not in attendance, Walter?"

"Mistress Hock requests his lordship's forgiveness. She was taken to her bed this morning with the pains of childbirth."

"Master Hock?" Montclaire asked, scanning the faces turned up at him. "I know you're here. I saw you."

Mackenna thumped the tabletop with her fist and hissed. "Hock has replaced the fish. There's no need to humiliate him."

"Hush, Mackenna," he said, not deigning to turn around.

"I am here, your lordship." Hock stepped hesitantly from among a group of men standing near the cold hearth. His face had lost its usual sun-scored ruddiness; his eyes were disks of coal.

"You are *here*." Montclaire folded his arms across his chest. "And where were you when this babe was conceived?"

"Your Grace?" Hock suddenly flushed brightly, and the silence in the hall broke into bright bits of laughter.

"You were eager enough to participate in the babe's conception. 'Tis time to complete your responsibility, Hock. Take yourself home to your wife."

Cadell locked his arm around Hock's shoulder. "They'll only throw him out, my lord. The midwife and her ladies won't let him anywhere near till after the babe comes."

"Tell them I sent him to fetch for them. Put the man to work. Go."

Hock flew out of the hall to the howling laughter of every woman in the crowd. Mackenna couldn't help but smile beneath her quill. She added madness to the list of Montclaire's faults.

"I'll hear the first case of review." Montclaire took a piece of parchment from the strongbox and handed it to Walter.

"John Cotes," Walter read.

"Me, your lordship?" Cotes had been lounging on a bench and jumped to his feet. "There's no suit pending against me."

"Come forward, Cotes."

Mackenna recoiled as Cotes planted himself in front of the dais, his thick legs rooted to the rush-covered floor like tree stumps. He was ham fisted, mutton shouldered, and there was a red cast to his pellet eyes that gleamed with rage. Montclaire had asked about the man a few days before; she could only wonder at his reasons for calling him forward.

"I don't know what this is about—"

"According to the bylaw record, last summer you beat your wife so severely that she couldn't work in the fields for three days. Is that true?"

"Aye, milord. It's sorry I am about it, too." Cotes passed a wink between Walter and Montclaire. "Cost me six shillings."

"What did she do to earn such a beating?" Montclaire asked.

"Don't rightly recall." Cotes lifted his arm and gave its pit a good scratching. "Talking back is what usually does it."

"And do your children talk back?"

"Sure they do." Cotes snickered and rocked back on his heels. "They're all whelps, aren't they?"

The hair rose on the back of Mackenna's neck. She'd seen and soothed his daughters' bruises. She'd held Berta while her little arm had been reset, and comforted the child until the pain had sent her into a deep sleep. Mackenna nurtured a hate for Cotes nearly the size of the one she held for Gilvane.

Montclaire stepped off the dais, dwarfing the man with more than his height, disabling the cooper's revoltingly smug smile. Mackenna prayed that Montclaire would strike him down.

Instead, his voice rolled like thunder through the hall. "When you beat your wife and your children, Cotes, you damage my property."

"Your property!" Mackenna bristled. Cotes backed away from Montclaire.

"I hadn't thought of it that way, your lordship."

"I think of it that way. When your wife or your children can't work, I lose money. Do you understand?"

Mackenna understood all too well. Disgusted, she set the quill to the parchment so fiercely she snapped the tip.

"I understand, your lordship. I shouldn't beat 'em so bad they can't work the fields."

Montclaire seized the cooper by the front of his tunic. "You'll not beat them at all, Cotes. Is that clear?"

Cotes nodded. "Aye, my lord."

Montclaire snarled and tossed him away. As he grabbed a handful of coins from the strongbox he looked up at Mackenna. Outrage had claimed his face. It seemed he wanted to say something to her, but he snarled again and turned back to Cotes.

The man had climbed to his knees, looking the worse for his landing. Montclaire stood over him, counted out six shillings, then dropped them on the floor in front of Cotes, letting the sounds ring out.

"What's this, my lord?" Cotes scrambled around, gathering up the coins.

"Six shillings. I do not accept the fine you paid me."

Cotes's face spasmed in his confusion. "You mean I don't owe his lordship anything?"

"Nay. You owe me, Cotes, and I always collect what is due me. Geoffrey, take Master Cotes to the bailey and see that he is flogged. Six stripes for six shillings."

Cotes gasped. "You can't!"

"I can, and I will." Montclaire looked out across the sea of stunned villagers. "And I will again, should another such case arise."

"Flogged, my lord," Cotes sputtered. "But why?"

"If you don't understand an eye for an eye, you soon will. Take him, Geoffrey." Montclaire turned from Cotes's pleading as Geoffrey dragged the odious man from the hall.

Mackenna wanted to applaud; instead, she dipped the quill into the inkpot and began to record the event. The beastly lord had his own wicked motivations for whipping Cotes, but the punishment was far more fitting than any she could have levied.

The whispering rose to chattering in the wake of Cotes's exit, then quickly became a roar until Montclaire raised his hand and the crowd quieted.

He reviewed other items, injustices and inquiries, taking a good part of the afternoon. Mackenna used up a pot of ink and two pieces of parchment, and was about to start on a third when he arrived at the final item on his list.

"One last name here," he said, smiling. "Ah, yes. Mackenna Hughes. Come up here, hostage."

Montclaire's smile seemed too expansive. Arranging her face in a mask of serenity, Mackenna approached him fearlessly.

"Mistress Hughes, you've done a commendable job as reeve."

"Thank you, milord," she said, flicking a piece of straw from her skirt, trying to hide her surprise at the compliment.

"Births, deaths, marriages, crop yields, fires, floods, famines, all tidily recorded. Yet I am curious about one thing."

"And that is?"

"My money," he said flatly.

"Your money?" The coins she'd just found in the pit! His spies were everywhere!

"You collected four years of fines and fees in the name of the lord of Fellhaven. Where is the lord's money, Mackenna?"

She gasped. "Do you accuse me of stealing?"

"I'm asking a simple question: where is my money?"

"Your money is in the ditch that drains the mill pond."

"You put my money into a ditch?"

"Aye, milord, and into the piers, and the fish weirs. It rebuilt the cart bridge over the Ullsbeck, and it put a slate roof on the tithe barn."

He folded his arms across his chest. "Are you saying, then, that you put *my* money back into *my* village?"

"That's right. I put *your* money into *your* village—" Mackenna stopped. She'd just said aloud what he'd wanted her to admit to him since his invasion began.

He hid his smile of triumph. "The village is mine,

Mackenna. No matter how the loaf is milled, baked, or eaten, it is owned by me. You've been working for me all these years, haven't you?''

"By all outward appearances, milord.''

"And you've done a splendid job. Now, Fellhaven needs a bailiff. And I have chosen you for the position.''

"Me?''

"You've been doing the job these many years; now you shall have the title.''

"I won't be your bailiff, Montclaire,'' Mackenna said, trying to outflank his stratagem. "I am perfectly happy being reeve.''

"Your happiness counts for nothing, hostage. You will be my bailiff.'' He bent to her to keep his threat between them. "I know you've been altering the bylaw records and the account rolls. I'm not half the fool you think me.''

"But you are a fool, Montclaire,'' she said too hastily.

"And you will be visiting your family in a very dark pit. The choice is yours.''

Mackenna corked her refusal while a strategy gained favor over her hasty objections. As bailiff, she would have more freedom, her orders would be followed. . . . She stalled long enough to make him think his coercion brought about her answer.

"Very well, milord, since I have no choice, I accept.''

And woe be to the man who had granted her the power.

Chapter 12

Montclaire insisted that Mackenna sit beside him at the feast he laid for the village after his court. She considered it a waste of precious winter stores—but he seemed to have made friends with everyone. When word came of the birth of Hock's daughter, he sent the child a silver penny and the mother a rose, drawing cheers for this most singular lord, this lord who gave when by rights he should be taking. He was a fool when it came to commerce, but who was she to instruct him? He only aided in her quest to secure the village's future against him.

And now he'd made her bailiff!

The tables had just been cleared and the dancing begun when Montclaire leaned over and whispered into her ear.

"Come with me." He took her hand and stood up.

"Come where?"

"I wish to partner you in a dance."

She yanked her hand out of his and folded it with the other into a bundle of trembling fingers. Heat raced down her cheeks to disappear beneath the neckline of her chemise.

"I don't think anyone should be dancing. This day has been wholly wasted with your crowing and strutting."

"This day was mine to waste. 'Tis none of your concern."

"It is if I'm to be the bailiff. I take my work seriously."

"Too seriously, my dear. There is a season for all things."

"I need an office, Montclaire. And my own lodgings. I cannot continue sleeping in your chamber. 'Tis unseemly."

"Have I made a single unseemly move toward you?" He wore an air of injury that didn't quite fit with his lazy smile.

" 'Tis not my point. Everyone in the village knows—"

"Knows what?"

"Or thinks they know . . ."

He grunted. "Where would this office be located?"

She paused in the face of his diversion. "You mean I may have one?"

" 'Tis a worthy idea, an office of your own."

" 'Twould be best located in my village."

" 'Twill be here in my castle."

"Too far from my work."

"Aye, but close enough to mine. Come, let's decide where this office shall be."

He took her hand and she was on her feet, his cape caressing her legs in its back-flying folds.

The evening wind swooped down off the mountains, autumn cold and cutting. She'd been swept from the warmth of the hall so quickly, she hadn't thought to bring her cloak. She shivered a bone-shaking, cheek-numbing shiver. Montclaire kept up his long stride all the way across the bailey, a torch held aloft lighting their way. She reached out for the hem of his cloak as it swirled and dipped in front of her. She caught it and hurried forward at the same time, drawing it around her shoulders.

Montclaire stopped abruptly at the door into the northeast tower. She ran into him, into that broad, warm back.

"Mackenna, what are you—" Thomas lifted his arm and looked behind him. He laughed. She'd slipped beneath his cloak and attached herself to his back.

" 'Tis cold, Montclaire. And I'd like to see this office you've promised me."

"Well, then. This is it." He opened the door and stepped into the empty room.

"This was to be Carson's office, milord. He won't be happy." But she would be. It was perfect: a window into the bailey to let in the daylight, a shutter to keep out prying eyes. The stone floor was even, the roof repaired. And best of all, the door in the rear of the room led down into the pit that sheltered the village coins.

"Carson will understand," Montclaire said. "He needs construction supplies and you will help purchase them for him."

She only half-listened to him as she paced across the room to judge its dimensions. "I'll need two worktables. Four benches will do for now. Shelves over there, I think, and there." She suddenly realized what he'd said. "How will I purchase supplies for your master carpenter?"

"My bailiff and I are going to Carlisle. Weren't you listening?"

"Your bailiff—" Mackenna knew she was staring at him. "I'm your bailiff. I'm to go with you?"

"Aye, Mackenna, and we leave the day after tomorrow."

"I can't." She couldn't go. She needed time alone in the village. There was so much to be done while he was gone: an oven to build in the forest, fish to smoke and hide.

"I'll have no argument about it. Time is critical. Repairs to the castle have fallen behind schedule."

"Then I should stay here and see to my duties as bailiff."

"Walter will stay."

"Walter knows nothing about running a manor. Winter fast approaches; this is no time to test his mettle. Starvation looms, I can smell it."

"Then your nose needs a change of air."

"I like the air here. And I'm a busy woman."

"You won't be if we run short on supplies. You're coming with me. That is an edict."

Mackenna opened her mouth to protest, but saw the

stubborn streak in his expression turn to determination. Then she remembered the pennies. What better place to spend the village's money than in the markets of Carlisle? She had to go with him!

"Bryce or Cadell?" he said. "Which would last longer in my pit?"

She sighed. "I'll go to Carlisle, milord."

"Peaceably?" He looked skeptical.

"As much as our personal war will allow."

Mackenna awakened before dawn to find Montclaire missing from the chamber. She dressed and went down to the bailey. She'd spent the previous day packing barrels of village goods for barter and sale. Hidden within each were small bags of coins she would use to purchase items for the village.

While she and Walter checked over the supply list and compared notes about what was to be done in her absence, Montclaire strode toward them with a determined gait. His shoulders were slightly rounded, his face long and serious.

"How is Roper, Thomas?" Walter asked, handing off a bulging saddlebag to a squire.

"He died not long after I arrived." Montclaire took the bag from his squire and started tying it to his saddle with large, rough movements.

Mackenna had liked Simon Roper. He'd been a good friend to her father. "How convenient, Lord Montclaire; you were in time to claim the first animal of their stock. They have a fine milk cow. Did you bring her with you?"

Montclaire seemed to finally notice her. He stopped tying knots and lowered his gaze. The weight of it nearly crushed her. His eyes were narrow and red-rimmed, and dark at their centers, a few long, sooty lashes damp and spiked together.

"Aye, Mackenna," he said quietly, "and I've sold off Roper's grandchildren to a slave trader that happened by." He held fast to her gaze while he tied off the saddlebag with a final yank. Then he brushed past her to the carts.

"I . . ." she began numbly. She should have followed him, but didn't know quite what to say. Were those half-dried tears? Had he wept for a man he hadn't even known? Where was she supposed to keep that kind of thought for a man who meant to do evil against her family and friends?

True to his noble station, Montclaire travelled with an ostentatious cortege of knights, men-at-arms, retainers and carts, his banners unfurled.

Mackenna rode sullenly all the way out the castle gate, made shy by the good wishes and fare-thee-wells of the garrison and the villagers. All too soon the caravan had advanced through the eastern pass that cleaved Shalefell from Ively Scree. The familiar and dear soon fell behind them. A part of her old life seemed to blow away like smoke. She twisted around in the saddle and saw the back side of Shalefell for the first time in her life. It was less craggy and softer shouldered on this side, with fewer trees and darker stone.

"You've never been away, have you?" Montclaire asked gently.

"You know I haven't." She turned in the saddle to stare at the road in front of her. The man hovered like a hawk inside her head, swooping down on her thoughts and shredding them.

" 'Tis no shame to admit to your melancholy."

" 'Tis not as if I'm leaving forever. If I thought that, I'd have hidden myself in the fells and you'd never have found me."

"I would find you, Mackenna. Make no mistake."

A cold, misty rain hung like a foul blanket over the entire day. Mackenna would have been soaked to the skin except for Montclaire's lambskin cloak that draped over her like a tent.

He was a hard man to travel with. When he wasn't joking with his men, he was humming a wastrel tune or smiling that smug, know-it-all smile that made her teeth ache. Twice she'd accidentally laughed at some little nothing he'd said. Not only had she laughed, but she had smiled as well. She didn't want to like his banter and refused to trust his easy ways. She wanted to hate him to the depth of his putrid soul, but, in truth, she was beginning to doubt there was quite so much darkness in him. A deep, grizzled gray, perhaps, but not the vile blackness she'd originally assumed.

Aye, and that was another problem altogether.

The caravan finally crowded into the courtyard of a substantial inn on the outskirts of town.

The common room was large and warm. It must have pleased the men, for they immediately sprawled out on the benches and made that groaning sound that all men make at the end of the day.

Mackenna followed Montclaire upstairs in the wake of the innkeeper. There was just one room, and it was offered to Montclaire and his "lady." Mackenna's protest was cut off by Montclaire's instructions to the innkeeper to limit the ale to two cups per man. The room was small, and smelled of ancient dust. The single window was shuttered against the cold rain.

Montclaire shuffled the innkeeper out the door, then stood in front of it.

"Since there is only this room, you and I will share it, as we have shared my chamber, without incident, for nearly two weeks. There is no other way." He threw open the door to a knock and took two small chests from one of his squires.

What could another night with the man hurt? she wondered. In truth, she hadn't even considered sleeping elsewhere until he'd brought up the possibility. All the images in her head of this ill-timed trip had included her in close company with Montclaire—riding in front of him on his horse, sharing a sweetcake in front of a brightly decked market stall, and feeling his breath ruffle her hair while he slept.

"Then I leave you to change out of your traveling clothes." He started out the door.

"Out of my traveling clothes, into what, milord?"

His study of her robes took only an instant. "Then

let's to supper before my men leave us nothing to eat but the rushes.''

The meal was substantial and wholesome: a lamb stew with chunks of sweet carrots, a bowl of crisp pears, and mountains of silky butter and fresh bread. The bread was good, but not as good as Fellhaven bread, and she was on this trip to open markets for her village.

''Excuse me, milord.'' When she stood up she found her wrist imprisoned by that big, pliant clamp that was Montclaire's hand.

''Are you so soon off to bed?'' he asked.

''To the stable, milord.'' She covered his capable fingers with her own and gave them a pat. ''Just for a moment.'' Her unconscious gesture brought her up short. She yanked her hand away and fled to the stable.

What had she been thinking? What would *he* think she was thinking? For the first time since meeting the man, she had enjoyed his company during a meal. Honest, uncomplicated, steadying conversation was shared between them.

Away from the constant reminders of the village and the castle, away from that balancing act that had become her life, Mackenna had discovered that Montclaire could be almost pleasant. Nay, he'd actually been entirely pleasant. And soothing. The deep, steady tones of his voice offered a steadfast comfort she hadn't felt since . . . well, never.

She took a handful of Fellhaven barley to the kitchen for the innkeeper's wife to taste. The woman was impressed with its sweetness and bought five barrels, to be delivered next month.

The deal complete, Mackenna sat down beside Montclaire and placidly folded her hands. His gaze was on her, his question unasked, but perched there on the sharpened arc of his brow.

''You didn't follow me, milord,'' she said.

''Did you miss me, then?'' He leaned back against the wall and took a sip from his tankard.

''As much as I would miss dancing barefoot in a patch

of nettles, milord." She cast him a tolerant smile. " 'Tis just that I've grown used to you ever watching me. I am suspicious when you're not there each time I lift my eyes."

"Though I prefer watching you myself, never forget that I have spies about."

"Ah, and did your spies tell you that I sold the innkeeper's wife five barrels of Fellhaven barley?"

He smiled. "Bravo. And did you get a good price?"

"That's not for you to know. The barley belongs to the village, traded fair and even for wood."

"I was merely curious as to what barley brings in Penrith."

"The same as in Fellhaven."

"Are you certain?" he asked. "A cup of ale in a London tavern is twice the price of the same in a village tavern."

"Truly, Montclaire?"

"Truly, Mackenna." Thomas watched the doubt slowly register on her face. A pouting frown, a drawn brow, then she aimed a fiery scowl toward the kitchen.

"Nay, milord, then I'm not certain at all." She stood up.

" 'Tis done, bailiff." He drew her back down beside him. "Did your price cover the costs of producing the grain?"

"Aye, even though we paid for it twice, thanks to you, milord. But that isn't the point. I might have gotten more. The woman was eager to buy; I was flattered—"

"Then consider it a lesson best learned on five barrels, not five hundred." He could tell by the way her jaw shifted that he'd struck a vein of truth.

"The next time . . ." she said.

He laughed. "The next time, you'll probably sell the woman her own shoes."

Lulled by the rumble of conversation, Mackenna soon found herself fighting off sleep while Montclaire and Hagan played at chess. She ought to go up to bed, but the night was so warm . . . so good smelling . . . so. . . .

She woke up sometime later, embarrassed to find her

head resting against Montclaire's solid shoulder and without a hint as to how long she'd been napping. His smile was far too generous for it to have been a short nap.

She excused herself and started up the stairs, not at all surprised to hear a familiar set of footsteps behind her. Once in the room, she stepped out of her surcote and in the next motion dropped face down on the crackling mattress. Montclaire bolted the door behind him, and settled a blanket over her.

"Thank you, milord," she whispered.

"Travel exhausts not only the flesh, but the soul. Especially the first time. At least, it did me."

"And when was that, milord?" She didn't even try to hold back her noisy yawn. The sounds of his undressing should have disturbed her, but she found an odd contentment in the familiar clank of his buckles against the back of the chair.

"I was nine," he said, dropping his boots on the floor. "My parents were dead. I had no family and possessed only a worthless title. I was miserable and very much alone." The mattress rasped with his weight as he lay down beside her. "I cried like a babe that first night."

It was difficult to imagine that the grown man lying next to her had ever been anything but a massively muscled warrior. But of course he'd been a child—a dark-eyed, homeless orphan. She caught herself feeling sorry for him.

"You have no family, milord? None at all?"

"None. The Montclaire family tree was felled by arrogance, betrayal, misfortune, shifting alliances, and royal writ. I am *the* Montclaire, the last, barren branch."

"Barren?" Laughing gently, Mackenna rolled over onto her elbow and looked at him. "Thomas Montclaire, how little you know about husbandry. The male cannot be barren."

Thomas had been staring up at the ceiling, his fingers laced across his chest. He turned and studied her face to see if she was taunting him; but he found the intoxicatingly patient expression of an indulgent teacher.

"A male can be barren, Mackenna. But I didn't say that *I* was. I merely stated that I have no heir. Nor is it likely that I will ever have one."

"None that you will claim, of a certain. But like all good men of the nobility, you've left dozens of children in your wake. Children of rape and seduction, forgotten children—hey!"

Montclaire was on top of her before her next blink, taking her wrists prisoner and her freedom along with them. She'd obviously struck a sore spot. She should have recognized the signs while she'd been listing his sins: that thick, pulsing vein that snaked swiftly across his forehead, the thin line of his usually generous mouth.

"Have I offended you, milord?" she asked, wondering why all his bound-up fury didn't frighten her anymore.

"Madam, you would offend the very angels!" he roared. "I have not strewn children across the fertile fields of Europe like so many weeds. I would not. Damnation!"

Thomas threw himself off the bed and unshuttered the window to the fresh air. Children. Flesh of his flesh. The only woman who had ever tempted him to fatherhood now made unsubstantiated claims against his character.

"Mackenna, you incite me to an anger I never knew I possessed. I am not a perfect man—"

"Honest with yourself, at least," she sniped.

When he turned to her, her eyes were wide. Her knees were tucked up to her chest, her arms locked round them as if they might have a life of their own. He set his foot against the edge of the bed and leaned down to her. "I will no longer defend my record to you. If my actions do not speak for my honor, if my words lack truth, the problem lies in your perception, not in me. It is, in fact, you who lack honor, Mackenna Hughes."

"Me? I lack honor?" She unfolded like a spring toy and popped to her knees.

"Your every promise is two-edged. You are unforgiving—"

"I am nothing of the sort!"

"You push until people can no longer push back, then you bend them without mercy. Grown men cower in your wake. Those bloody accounts that you keep in your head crowd out any compassion you might harbor toward we who are but mortal."

"Now I lack compassion, do I?"

"Oh, it's there inside you, Mackenna. You've just forgotten how to use it."

"Given your life of war and plunder, Montclaire, you're a fine one to talk about compassion."

"Soldiering is my profession. Yours has been to protect your village. Your tithe barn is well roofed and watertight, but you've certainly failed Mistress Cotes and her children."

"What have they to do with—"

"By Christ, Mackenna, you let Cotes beat his family!"

In the stark silence that followed his accusation, Mackenna scooted backward to the bedstead. "I didn't let him," she whispered.

"Mayhaps not, but you charged him six shillings for the privilege. How many bridges did his money buy?"

"It wasn't like that." She'd never seen him so enraged.

"What do you charge him when he beats little Haitha? Five shillings, four? The smaller the child, the smaller the fine?"

"You've no right to say that to me."

"I have every right, Mackenna. These are my people."

"And mine. I hate John Cotes. I've hidden his children from his rages. I've bound his wife's wounds. But I am one woman, Montclaire." Her outrage brought her back to her knees, stamped out her despair. "I cannot stop the cruelty by myself. He's not the only man with an unchecked temper and an iron hand—"

"Who else?" he demanded.

"Most of the men, at one time or another. Some are more violent than others, but women are chattel; you know that. You said so to Cotes. You called us your property."

"I was trying to make a point with a man who thinks that way. His head is hard." Thomas relented some. "By now he's discovered that flesh is tender, especially his."

"You saw him?"

"Aye, afterward. He was subdued."

"Thank you, milord." The betraying words skipped out before she could stop them. Now she might as well sink completely into a bog of indebtedness. "You gave him exactly what he deserved, which I could not. I'm grateful."

He nodded. "Mayhaps the next man who raises a hand will drop it when he remembers Cotes being dragged from the hall to the whipping post." A flicker of pain crossed his features as he sat down next to her. "These men with iron hands, Mackenna—have you escaped such punishment in your life?"

"So far, milord. My father was a gentle-tempered man. He raised four sons without a strap."

Thomas sighed. "And he raised a daughter with a pair of thick leather gloves." He took her hand and enveloped it in his. "Forgive me, Mackenna. I know you couldn't stop Cotes. I don't blame you. I truly don't." He tangled his fingers in the loosened tendrils of hair that bordered her face. "Indeed, my dear, I admire you."

Mackenna thought she might have to swallow her heart. "You do?"

"Aye, very much. 'Tis no great enterprise for a woman to be as beautiful as you. But you are a wonder to me."

He was so close his words brushed across her cheek. "Is that good?" she asked, waiting for his next breath to caress her.

"Aye, Mackenna. You are a challenge in my life that I've not only come to accept, but to—" Thomas stopped himself from saying "cherish." Once released between them, such a word might alter too many things that could never be changed.

"But to what, milord?"

"To enjoy." He smiled.

The spell he was weaving was perilous, and Mackenna entered it freely. On neutral ground. In an inn far from the village. "'Enjoy' is a strange word between us, considering the fact that we're enemies."

Her heart hammering in her ears, she lowered her eyes from his, from the purifying memory of Montclaire giving back the coins to Cotes. Something had changed forever in that moment of rare justice.

"Enemy is your word, Mackenna, not mine."

"It doesn't fit as well as it once did." She tucked a lock of hair behind his ear and followed its wavy length to his shoulder.

"Aye, we understand each other better than we did."

"Nay, milord. I don't understand you at all." She drew a finger across his collarbone above his tunic and wondered which battle had cost him the long, pale scar and the thickened knot of bone beneath.

"Do I not speak plainly enough?" Thomas could barely keep his thoughts in order, let alone his words. Her fingers were fire; flames licked at his chin.

"Aye, milord, you speak most plainly." Her lips bewitched him as she tried to hide her smile for the private jest he knew was coming. "That is . . . when you choose to speak English."

"Ah, Mackenna. . . . 'I wish you had kissed me.'"

Mackenna swallowed her heart again. "When—?"

"'Tis what you said to me to test my English." Thomas claimed the column of her neck as he had the very first time he touched her. This time his hand was quaking. "You remember."

"Uh . . ." Real words were difficult at the moment.

His eyes gleamed beneath his dark lashes. "Did you mean it then?" he asked. Unwilling to stop himself, Thomas tipped her chin with the end of his thumb as he had then.

"Nay, milord." Mackenna could hardly breathe.

His smile was lazy and lopsided. "Would you mean it *now*?" He drew his thumb across the rose arc of her lips. They were soft and damp, and might soon be his.

Mackenna measured her life's span against the inviolate simplicity of this moment. A tiny speck of time that no one would note but the two of them.

"Aye, milord, I would."

Montclaire's eyes glinted, and his mouth met hers, warm and worshiping. He was an enchantment; his dizzying elixir rippled through her, surrounded her heart, and roiled in her belly.

"Oh, my . . ." she breathed.

Thomas groaned against her words, shaken by her response, by the taste of her, by this simple kiss that should never be. He drew away slightly, hoping to find wariness in her eyes, but there was wonder and precariously banked passion ready to spill its heat all over them. He was breathing like a bull elephant, and she, like a hummingbird. Yet there must still be hope for him somewhere, a cooler place where a wise thought might prevail.

Then she moistened her lips with the tip of her pink tongue, and spoke with more honesty than he'd ever heard tumble out of her sweet mouth, "Milord, I wish you would kiss me . . . again."

She tasted the hurried heat of his kiss through the last of her words. His tongue was there, too, and his fingers, and hers. He kissed her palm and her brow, and that place where her temple met her eyelashes.

"Stop me, Mackenna."

His urgent whisper brushed past her ear, and made her toes curl up and the tips of her fingers tingle. Wherever his gaze touched, his mouth followed. He would light a kiss beneath her ear and then search out a more breathtaking place at the base of her neck. To stop him would be to stop the tides and the coming of spring.

"I've not the will, milord." Nay, not after he brushed away her hair and the ties of her chemise and nibbled a slow, disorienting path along the ridge of her shoulder; nor after he pulled her against him and placed kisses along her nape while his hand cradled the back of her head; and certainly not after she touched her mouth to his collarbone and tasted the salty scar that branded him a warrior and throbbed with the pulse of a man. She followed the course of the pulse up his neck, between the straining cords, kissing him, touching him, tasting him.

"Mackenna!" Thomas cupped her face with his trembling hands, kissed the corners of her mouth again, and then again. "Have mercy on a man of such imperfect flesh. Please."

She tried to answer, but his mouth covered each word as she spoke it. She reached out to the laces at the neck of his tunic. As her fingers grazed the down of curling hair, he growled and reared back.

He was still growling low in his throat when he lowered her to the pillow. And she was still drifting when the marvelous beast dipped his mouth to hers again and again. It was the only place he touched her; he was shelter and hovering warmth, but she wanted his arms around her and told him so.

"Nay, Mackenna. Sleep, Mackenna. Dream, Mackenna."

Then he was out the door.

She did dream, but she would never confess to anyone the source or the substance. Especially not to the subject of her dreams, who was now saddling his horse with grim concentration in the midst of the chaos of preparing to leave the innyard.

His hair hung in damp ringlets. She'd seen him earlier from the window of their chamber, scrubbing a towel through his hair as he returned from the shady creek behind the stable. She wondered where he'd slept the night. Not that she really wanted to know. He'd left her panting and too willing, and listening for his footfalls in the hallway. Once she had realized her door was guarded, she knew he'd not be returning, which had been all for the best. What good could come of remembering his kisses, or his intimate good humor?

"Your horse is ready, Mistress Mackenna."

She looked up into Francis' thin face. "Thank you, Francis." They started walking toward the knot of horseflesh. "What is his lordship's mood this morning?"

"I can't say, mistress."

"I'm glad you're not still angry with me, Francis."

"As I am. But I'm not a man to be fooled twice."

"I promise never to escape you again. I offer you my hand in token." Francis took the time to study her palm before he grabbed her hand and shook it.

Before they could break the clasp, a third hand, huge and gauntleted, covered theirs.

"Good morning, Mackenna. Francis." Montclaire's voice seemed a menacing cloud in the midst of a bright morning.

"Lord Thomas!" Francis knocked his heels together, then sped away as fast as his long legs could carry him.

"Good morning, Montclaire. Did you sleep well?" Mackenna arranged her face in a blank expression and declined to meet his gaze.

"I dreamed of you," he said just loud enough for her ears.

That made her look right at him. She almost confessed her own dreams of him, then caught herself. "I went right to sleep."

He laughed. "Not bloody likely."

Then she was sailing, without a warning or a by-your-leave, up into the saddle. Once astride, she beckoned to him with a finger and leaned down to his ear. "I do wish you would leave my backside alone, Montclaire!" she hissed.

"That's not what I would have guessed last night." He smiled too well, then turned away from her. "Mount up, men. 'Tis a long ride to Carlisle."

Chapter 13

A dreary morning drizzle turned to afternoon glory as Mackenna rode with Montclaire and his entourage through the town gates of Carlisle.

He'd been so bloody good-natured, she'd lost the spark of her anger and was now too busy to try to regain it. She was having trouble keeping him in sight as he spoke with the tower guards. People streamed in through the gates, eddying eagerly past her, shoving her deeper and deeper into the milling crowd. She kept a tight rein on her horse to keep from trampling a mob of children dodging in and out among the street stalls.

A tangle of baying hounds bounded in front of her, snarling over a leg of mutton. Her mare shied and backed into a peddler's wagon. She offered an apology, but the man had already shaken his fist at her and shoved his cart out into the traffic.

Never had she seen so many people all in one place, nor smelled so many smells. Plenty of ruddy-cheeked children causing commotion, knots of bawling and blustering townsmen, but not a familiar face in the crowd. Not Hagan's or Francis's or any one of the soldiers who'd been so agreeable and eager to please. Not even Montclaire's. She looked around for him, for those unmistakable shoulders, for that gleaming, dark hair that still needed trimming. He'd disappeared completely. She was a babe lost in a strange and dark woods, wrestling with a rising panic.

"Montclaire!" she called out, hearing the uncomfortable fear in her voice, but unable to mask it. The few faces that turned in her direction were those of strangers.

"I'm here, Mackenna." She felt his hand on her knee and looked down at him, expecting him to level a derisive comment against her fears. But he held out his arms and offered her a broad, absolving smile.

"Come, Mistress Mackenna," he said. "Carlisle awaits."

"Where are we going? Where are the others?" She didn't want to give in so abruptly. A little distance would contain the racing of her heart.

"I've given half of them leave to enjoy the remainder of the afternoon at their leisure."

"Letting your men loose on the citizens of Carlisle?" she asked as he easily dislodged her from the saddle. He held her too close and for too long, her feet dangling above the cobbles. She hid her smile until his own teased one out of her.

Francis was standing behind Montclaire, and cleared his throat. "I shall see to Mistress Mackenna's mare, Lord Thomas."

"Thank you, Francis," Mackenna said. "Please find a good stable, well out of the night chill. And have someone look after her right foreleg. She favored it some."

"Consider it done, mistress."

She caught the odd wink that Francis gave to his lord as he led her horse and his own into the river of people. Montclaire carried her well out of the current, and set her on her feet.

"What about the carts, milord? And the rest of your men?"

"They'll stable our horses, see to our lodgings."

"And where will that be?"

He stumbled over his explanation. She wouldn't be at all happy to learn their host was to be none other than the king of England. "I know of a place nearby." Indeed he could just see Edward's standards unfurled in the

wind buffeting the top of the red-stoned castle keep, a
sight not usually possible, but for a fire having recently
eaten away at the town.

"You've been to Carlisle before, milord?" When he
nodded, she asked, "And so you've stayed in these same
lodgings before?"

"The place is familiar to me."

"And the innkeeper knows you're to arrive today?"

"Aye, the . . . innkeeper knows. He's expecting us.
But he's not in residence and won't be back until
tomorrow."

"How do you know all that? We've only just arrived."

"The guard at the gate informed me." Edward and
most of his court were hunting in Geltsdale Forest and
weren't expected to return until the next afternoon.
Thomas hoped to find time enough before then to
prepare Mackenna for the king.

"Do the town guards keep track of the comings and
goings of this innkeeper friend of yours?"

"'Tis part of their duties."

"Then he must be a man of some influence in
Carlisle."

Thomas smiled with guilty pleasure at her assump-
tions. "Aye, Mackenna, he'd like to think he is." He
paused only long enough to redirect the conversation.
"Are you hungry?"

"'Tis a wonder you can't hear the grumblings of my
stomach."

"Then we'll sup on the very best. This is no ordinary
market day, Mackenna. 'Tis a sanctioned faire. Do you
smell the spices and perfume? The vendors will be
fighting for our coins."

"I have none to spare, milord." They would all be
used for the village, every one of them.

"You're here on my business, Mackenna. Your ex-
penses are mine. 'Tis the way of it when you're working
for me. Come."

She had no time to consider his statement; he took her
hand and plunged into the bustle and roar of the faire.

Overhead, the sky was a dazzling pageant of colors,

bright with standards and banners snapping furiously in the sharp wind. Music wandered the lanes, mixing with an assortment of smells—some pleasant and exotic, some nose-pinching and mean, and still another, overwhelming it all, the old-char stench of Fellhaven's own burned-out castle. But this was a faire, and everyone seemed to be wearing their best caps and cloaks. She looked like the country peasant she was.

The street narrowed and the overhanging upper floors of the buildings stretched out toward each other; and as the street narrowed the crowd thickened and then stopped entirely.

"What is it, milord?" She couldn't see a thing. Montclaire turned and lifted her up onto a shoulder. She was suddenly half-again as tall as anyone in Carlisle.

"Milord!" She looked down into his grinning face. The man was too handsome for her own good. And far too affable.

Thomas laughed at the surprise in her spice-flecked eyes. "Tell me what you see, Mackenna."

"A very strong warrior, milord." But she was still looking down at him.

"I mean ahead of you." He could see very well over the heads of the crowd, but he wanted her to enjoy the spectacle.

Mackenna looked away in time to see a circle widen in the midst of the multitude, giving room to three musicians and a strange little boy. The child's arms were exceedingly long and covered in shaggy, auburn hair. Indeed, his entire body was as hairy as a dog's. His ears were round and stuck out like small plates. He was hopping from one foot to the other in time with the tune that the musicians had struck up. He suddenly gave an ear-shattering screech, and climbed up the front of the tabor player as if the tall man were a pine tree.

"Well, Mackenna. What do you see?"

She bent down to Montclaire, still watching the odd display. "I haven't a notion, milord. At first I thought it an unfortunate boy, but now I think 'tis some kind of animal."

" 'Tis a monkey, Mackenna.''

"A monkey?'' She straightened again and studied the creature. "Are there many monkeys in Carlisle?''

"I can almost guarantee this is the only one.''

She laughed as the monkey leaped off the lute player's head onto the back of a soldier who had muscled his way through the circle. The victim bellowed and spun around and around trying to dislodge his attacker. The audience roared in delight, and Mackenna laughed along with them until the crowd finally folded in on the players.

She turned on Montclaire's shoulder to dismount him. He caught her against the length of him, holding her there, her chin just inches above his. He grinned like a fool.

"Have you ever tasted an orange?'' Montclaire asked.

"Nay, milord.''

" 'Tis time you do.'' The bright colors around him were muted next to the stunning smile she gave him.

He'd learned long ago how to maneuver in a crowd, and quickly had them skimming against the walls of the buildings. Mackenna had hold of his hand as if it were her only lifeline in a treacherous sea.

He stopped at a busy food stall and purchased two plump sausages. She held them while he crossed the street and returned with a crock of cider. Moments later his arms were laden with a block of cheese and a loaf of bread, and finally an orange.

She followed him up a short flight of stone steps in the remains of a burned out building. The landing overlooked a large, grassy expanse tenanted with dozens of stalls. Mackenna smiled at the commerce that had grown out of the ashes of the fire, thriving as her village now thrived after its own disaster.

She shared the meal with Montclaire and they watched the crowd from their perch, pointing out curiosities to each other, listening to the strolling minstrels, and admiring the jugglers and magicians as they enthralled their audiences.

"I'm looking forward to meeting your innkeeper

friend, milord." Mackenna offered him a smile and the last chunk of cheese. He took them both. "Such an influential man is bound to know the best places to purchase what we need for the castle, and the best markets for our goods."

"He knows the city well."

"But aren't we wasting time that could be used in the markets? This has been a pleasant diversion, milord, but—"

"There's no one to do business with today. The craftsmen are obliged by law not to sell from their shops during faires."

"Obliged by law? Why is that?"

"So the city receives its share of the revenue. There's a steep fee to set up a stall, and a tax on the goods sold."

"Not very good for commerce."

"But it brings in people from all over the countryside. New crafts, new ideas, new melodies—"

"New taxes." She shook her head. "I might have known."

"There's a town to rebuild here. And a cathedral. I'm surprised that Edward . . ."

"Surprised that he what, milord?"

But Thomas wasn't ready to comment on the fact that the king's entourage would burden the stricken countryside with its requirement of supplies. Carlisle was a military outpost, critical to keeping the peace along the Scottish border, and its people frequently endured raids and fires and sacrifice.

"I'm surprised that Edward didn't mention the extent of the destruction to the cathedral."

"Perhaps he hasn't seen it." She watched him peel the orange. The succulent skin sent sprays of citrus through the air.

"That smells wonderful, milord. 'Tis an orange?" She laughed. "A goodly name for such an orange-colored thing." The fruit broke apart easily with Montclaire's prying. He put a wedge to her lips and she took it between her teeth. The taste was so startling, she pulled the fruit back out and studied it.

" 'Tis sweet and sour at the same time." She bit down and delighted in the juicy coolness. "I do like it, milord, very much. Is it grown in Carlisle?"

"In Spain."

"On a tree?"

"Just like an apple." He parceled out the orange, giving Mackenna the lion's share. "Come, let us see what else the city of Carlisle has to offer." He took her hand and led her into the maze of eager vendors and elaborate stalls.

Thomas gave Mackenna the lead, following her through the market. Her interest was exuberant and contagious. She stopped to inspect an enamelled tile and smoothed her hands across its face. She cooed at its textures, and exclaimed at its serpentine design. Her questions about the tile's manufacture taxed the knowledge of the vendor and finally the man's patience.

Thomas urged her along to the ironmonger's stall, where they learned of a source for their considerable need for iron. Carpenters and toolmakers, grain merchants, weavers and dyers all received her promise to meet them at their shops in the next day or two. She stood by politely as Thomas engaged an armorer in a lively debate over breastplate design.

While she was busy learning the harnessmaker's trade, Thomas slipped into the dressmaker's stall across the lane. He doubted Mackenna would approve, but she needed suitable clothing if she were to survive Edward's court. He purchased four gowns of fine wool, two linen chemises, two of silk, four pair of stockings, and an assortment of head coverings—virtually the entire stock of samples—and received a promise of another two gowns which could be finished quickly. He pointed out Mackenna to the elated seamstress, ordered the dresses to be sized accordingly, and paid extra for the lot to be delivered to his rooms in the castle sometime before dawn.

As evening crept over the city, lights winked on everywhere. Still reluctant to engage Mackenna's wrath, which he was bound to do when she discovered the identity of the innkeeper, Thomas let the night wear on, dragging her from one wonder to the next until the sky opened up with a cold, drenching rain. Carlisle tucked itself indoors and snuffed out its lights.

"Time to see to our lodgings, Mistress Hughes."

Mackenna huddled beneath her cloak, her head bent as Montclaire hurried her through the streets toward the inn. The rain was brittle cold and blowing directly into her face.

The sound of horses' hooves clopping across wooden planks made her look out through the curtain of rain. Another city gate, it seemed. More guards and stone buildings. No one else was about in the storm. Montclaire finally took her up in his arms and she unashamedly burrowed deeper into his radiant heat.

Hagan met them at the castle guard room. Thomas followed him across the expanse of the inner bailey and up the stairs into an antechamber serving the great hall. He hoped Mackenna would keep her head buried beneath the folds of her cloak and remain unaware until they had gained some privacy.

The chamber was large and drafty despite the fire set in the grate. After promising to arrange delivery of two baths, Hagan left the room. When Thomas set Mackenna on her feet, her smile was wobbly.

"You look like a drowned rat, milord." A shiver wracked her to her bones.

"Then we are a pair." Thomas shook off the water running down his hauberk.

"I've never been so wet in all my life." She dropped her heavy cloak off her shoulders and hung it over a chair near the fire. She looked around at the substantial room and its well-fashioned features.

The bed was draped in fine green wool curtains, its pillows plumped and welcoming. A forest of beeswax candles burned in silver candleholders, scenting the air with smoky lavender. The windows were tall and glazed. There were two tables and three chairs, one large and comfortably padded. 'Twas the most elegant room she had ever seen.

"What's the name of this inn, milord? Heaven?"

Breathing a farewell to peace, he said, "Carlisle Castle."

She looked as if she hadn't heard him, but he knew by now that Mackenna Hughes only cocked her head to the right, chewed the inside of her cheek, and narrowed the outer corners of her eyes when she was carefully contemplating all the possible implications of a piece of displeasing news.

"'Tis what?" she asked too quietly.

"We are housed in apartments only a few steps from the great hall of Carlisle Castle." Thomas stripped off his boots and dropped them in front of the fire.

"Why?" Her fingers were splayed across her hips.

"Because, Mackenna, I am vassal to King Edward and you are vassal to me and that makes us both the guests of His Highness."

"Has His Highness now taken up the business of innkeeping?"

"The king has summoned a council of barons to consult with him before he meets with the Scottish lairds in Berwick. I am a member of Edward's council."

"Well, I'm not. And I will not take another breath inside this castle." Mackenna yanked her cloak off the chairback, dragging the chair with her as she headed for the door. But Montclaire was already resting in front of it like a stone wall.

"Then you'll soon be as blue as your lips, my dear, because you're staying here with me."

"Step aside, milord. I'll find a stable outside the city walls. There is not a soul in this world or the next who can persuade me to stay in the same city with the king, let alone stay in his castle as his guest, let alone with *you!*"

"You may well be my bailiff, Mackenna, but you remain my hostage, as well. You will stay."

"I cannot accept his hospitality."

"You accept mine."

"It seems I have no choice."

"Neither do I."

"You are a baron. You can do as you please."

"Tell that to Edward. I was commanded here by my king. Had I refused, believe me, he would have sent for me and housed me in a room not quite so hospitable as this one."

"In a pit, I suppose?"

"If I were lucky."

"You and your king are cut from the same cloth. 'Tis the reason I dislike you and all the others of your ilk. Stand aside." By now she couldn't keep her teeth from chattering. He wrested her wet cloak from her icy fingers and stood her in front of the fire.

"Even if I would consider letting you go—which I am not—you're in no shape to go anywhere. You must get out of these, Mackenna." Thomas unhooked the front of her gown and pushed it off her shoulders.

"And you must stop undressing me whenever my guard is low."

"And is it low?" He loosened the lacing of her chemise, wondering how he would get her out of it and into something dry without him giving in to his desire.

"Aye, milord. 'Tis too cold for rational thought. Even your hands quake."

Thomas was as warm as a summer day, and his hands quaked for an altogether different reason. "Stay here," he ordered.

Mackenna doubted she could gain the door before he noticed. Her muscles clamped her bones down tight and the fire was too good a companion on a night like this. He returned with her night dress and settled it over her head and shoulders.

"Excuse me," he said, trapping her eyes with his. He couldn't trust himself to do otherwise. Her silhouette was enough to send him over the edge. That and the memory of her soft mouth beneath his. "You won't be needing this anymore."

Before she could stop him, he tore the front of her wet chemise at the neck and tugged it off so that it fell to the floor alongside the hem of her night dress. Mackenna would have slapped him, but her arms were trapped inside her dry gown.

"What the bloody hell are you doing, sir?"

"Insuring that you don't freeze." He reached up into her empty sleeve, found her cold hand, and pulled it through.

"By tearing off my chemise? I've only got one other—"

"As I said before, you won't need it."

"Why? Are you going to keep me locked in your chamber? Because if you are, I am much obliged to you. I'll not be forced to look at King Edward, innkeeper of England, Wales, and Scotland, over my supper."

"He isn't here." Once he got her arms through both sleeves, he wrapped her from head to toe in a blanket, set her down in the padded chair, and moved her to the warmest part of the hearth.

At a rap on the door, he answered, "Come," and two pages trooped in carrying a large wooden tub. Mackenna ignored the parade as the tub was filled with steaming water and scented with mint and juniper berries. They were left alone in a silence broken only by the sound of Montclaire shucking off his clothes and lowering himself into the tub.

She glanced back at him when the water finally came to rest from his scrubbing. He lounged like a bear on a rock, with his head lolled against the edge of the tub, his eyes closed, his lips slightly parted. Those marvelously full lips, which curved like a flexed bow beneath his trimmed moustache. She remembered the taste of him, and thought she'd like to taste him again. When her heart thudded a warning, she looked quickly for his faults, but found only that his hair was sectioned in dripping tendrils and needed cutting.

"Where is he?" she asked.

Thomas didn't bother to open his eyes. He could think of nothing save the woman cocooned in the blanket across the room. "If you mean the king, he's hunting boar east of here."

"My best to the boar. When does the king return?"

"On the morrow. Time enough for us to make our rounds in town." She was silent for a while and he wondered where her thoughts roamed, down which treacherous path. God save Edward.

"Your hair needs a trim, milord."

"Then cut it."

"Me?" She had to laugh at that. "You don't trust me out of your sight; you can hardly trust me to cut your hair."

"Frankly, at the risk of my neck, I trust your sense of style over that of my barber's. There's a pair of shears in the chest, if you care to try your hand at trimming." The talk of cutting and shearing served as an effective damper to the arousal that had plagued him from the moment he'd carried her into the chamber. Using the refuge of the moment, he rose out of the tub and towelled himself dry as he walked over to his robe.

Mackenna knew her mouth was hanging agape. She barely got it shut before he turned around, cinching his robe at the waist.

"Are you warmed sufficiently, Mackenna?"

"Plenty, milord." She'd seen enough of him through the curtain of falling water to boil her bones to the marrow.

He scrubbed at his hair as he searched out the shears in the chest at the end of the bed. "And how are you with a razor?"

"Milord?"

"I dislike this beard." He tugged at the brush on his jaw. "It itches sometimes, like fire ants."

"I like your beard, milord. 'Tis soft and tickles . . ." She trailed off as he fixed her with a look that seared her ears.

"You shouldn't be telling me that, Mackenna."

"There is no secret between us, milord." Little drops of sweat had perched themselves like glistening confessions on her upper lip. She threw off the sweltering blanket and welcomed the rush of cooler air as she paced in front of the hearth, glad for the breeze passing through her night dress.

"The shape of you beneath that window of linen is no secret to me. Come away, before I do something we will both regret."

Regret? Her skin was afire. She might not regret anything at all, not in her current state of mind. The choice was the fireplace, or ten paces closer to him. Him, whom she'd very much like to kiss at the moment. Mother Mary, what wicked, wanton thoughts! When she dared look up at him again, he was holding the shears out toward her.

"Will you cut my hair?" he asked. She hesitated for what seemed an inordinately long time, then grabbed them as if they were a snake about to strike.

Arming his fiery-eyed bailiff with a pair of sharp shears was the only way to cool his desire, and even that ruse was beginning to lose its effectiveness. He threw himself into the chair and listened as she rooted around in the chest.

"What are you looking for?"

"A comb. Ah, here. Sit up, milord." He was nearly as tall sitting as she was standing. She could get through this, she told herself, by pretending he was just one of her brothers.

Just one of her brothers. Ha! She combed and clipped along the nape of his neck, trimming nearly two inches off the length. His hair was silky soft, and had a flirtatious way of curling around her fingers and refusing to let go after it had been cut. She worked her way up the back of his head, taking off the same two inches all over. When she was finished with the back, she stepped away to judge the results.

"Much better, milord." She brushed the spent curls off his shoulders, then stood in front of him. He hadn't said a word; his eyes had been closed most of the time. They were open now.

Thomas wondered if she knew she'd been humming. Such a blissful, intimate sound, so regular and right. It was as if she had cut his hair hundreds of times.

"Where did you sleep last night, milord?" She didn't know why she finally let that prying question slip out. "You left so abruptly, I thought you either ill or angry."

"I slept in the stable, in the hayloft." He smiled broadly.

"Why do you smile, milord?"

"I was thinking about the warm bit of fluff that slept upon me last night."

The blood drained from her fingers. They shook as she tried to make an even cut below his ear. "You needn't give me any details of your conquests."

" 'Twas an easy victory. And I can hardly be faulted for what happened in my sleep." Thomas was surprised to see spots of color brighten on her cheeks, surprised that she might care.

"In your sleep, Montclaire? I doubt that very m—"

The shears snipped with her next word and took a small bite out of his earlobe.

"Damnation!" He grabbed his ear and roared up out of the chair. "Bless me for a fool! You've bloodied me!"

Chapter 14

"I am sorry, milord!" Mackenna backed away from Montclaire, clutching the shears. "I didn't mean to cut you! I didn't!"

"Ballocks!"

"I wouldn't, milord!" He looked stricken. Feeling guilty for the pain she'd caused him, she climbed up onto the chair and balanced herself on the seat. "Let me see it."

"Nay!"

"Move your hand, please."

"And have you wound me again?"

"I slipped. I'm sorry. I surrender my weapon." She tossed the shears to the floor and pushed his hand away from his ear. "Do leave it be so I can tend to it, milord."

"'Tis bleeding!" He scowled and showed her the glistening red on his fingers.

"Yes, it is, and I'm sorry. Hold still." She took up the hem of her chemise and dabbed at the trickle of blood. He was so like a man, bristling with bravery until he raised a blister from a hot kettle, then bellowing and whining until it was kissed and made better. The cut was insignificant, but it did like to bleed. "Alas, milord, you'll live to fight another war."

"Not with you as my barber." Thomas clenched his hands together behind his back to keep from paddling her. The only thing that stopped him, besides Cadell's dire warning about her unerring aim, was that he was nearly convinced she hadn't meant to nip his ear.

"If I'd wanted to cut you, I'd have done it long ago."

He couldn't argue the point. She was in a position to do him bodily harm every minute of the day, but she hadn't. He was trapped by her logic as well as by her beauty. Her hair was a cinnamon halo, and her sleeves the drooping wings of a wayward angel. She was standing on the chair, her eyes level with his. Her delicate brows arched and dipped like twin meadow birds as she muttered to herself and tended his ear with seemingly unfeigned concern.

"There. All better. The bleeding has stopped." She dropped her hem and looked past him to the hearth, embarrassed suddenly when she remembered what had distracted her: that bit of fluff who'd shared his bed. Had it been the blonde girl who'd attended their table with such efficiency? And what did she care, anyway? Montclaire was a lord, and she the daughter of a miller. She would be married soon to a man from the village. She had no reason at all to care. And she didn't.

"Now you'll have another fine scar to show off to the next lady friend who seduces you in a hayloft."

"Mackenna." Thomas hooked the end of her nose with a bent finger and brought her gaze to him. Her eyes shifted to his chin and wouldn't budge. "It was a cat."

"What was a cat?"

"My companion was a cat. A big orange beast who came to me in the night and claimed my chest for her cot. Like you, she kept me warm; but unlike you, she kept her claws sheathed. Indeed, I received a kiss for my faithful service."

Her heart pounded with too much relief. He hadn't sought another woman. "And my kiss sent you dashing into the night?"

He should have let the invitation lie, but her waist was the span of his two hands and fit them with welcoming ease.

"Your kiss sent me into a very chilly stream."

"There to wash it off, I suppose?"

"To cool me, Mackenna. To bring me back to my senses."

He was looking at her in the way that scrubbed the reason right out of her head, and left her bare and sunning herself in his afternoon smile. "We both acted without sense last night, milord. It won't happen again—"

"Aye, it will." Thomas couldn't help it, didn't want to help it. He lifted her off the chair and lowered her until she claimed his mouth in a kiss that made her whimper and him growl. He held her against him and bent forward until her toes touched the hearthstone. Her urgent quest for purchase on his mouth made him laugh beneath her dauntless lips.

" 'Tis happening again, 'Kenna," he managed.

She mumbled something about ending this, but she laid each word down with another bedazzling kiss. Surely the passion she stirred in him must be evident through her flimsy linen chemise. His robe threatened to part and he let her go to secure his belt.

Mackenna whimpered at the loss. She let her fingers stray through his beard, caught at the excess and brought his face closer. Mother Mary, she oughtn't to be doing this, but he tasted of mint and sunshine.

"Sit down, milord," she suddenly breathed against his ear. She pushed him away and stared at him. "You are lopsided."

"I'm what?" He kept himself from glancing down the length of his robe. Did she think he had a condition that she could mend? If she reached for him . . .

She stood on her tiptoes and furiously combed her fingers through his hair. "Sit, milord. I've not yet finished cutting. One ear is lower than the other."

"Cutting, yes." Thomas sat down quickly. She was armed again with the shears. He tensed in anticipation of another wound. Yet merely being near her was enough to raise his needs beyond concealment. It seemed he'd not be able to regain his control until she was no longer a part of his life.

No longer a part of his life? A hollowness settled in his

shoulders and crystallized as it spread down his spine. It would happen one day. It must.

"Look at me, milord."

Her nose was inches from his, her eyes wide and hued with the fleeting colors of the sunrise. Her lashes swept the stars from the skies.

"Close your eyes, milord."

He obliged her and waited for her kiss. He grunted his disappointment when the cold metal of the shears rested on his forehead and then chomped its way along his brow. The hair tickled as it tumbled from the blades onto his cheeks.

"Done, milord." Mackenna puffed the circlets of fallen hair from his face and straightened. Her nerves were shredded, and her blood so heated from looking at him, and touching him, and feeling him—all of him—against her, she was sure her chemise would burst into flames.

"Thank you," he said. "I feel lighter by stones."

" 'Tis loss of blood, milord," she said wanly.

"Indeed."

She tried not to stare as he stood up and idly brushed off his robe. That lush, ruby robe which left so little to her relentless imagination. She wanted to grab it by the belt and fling it open and . . . well, she didn't know what she'd do then. She wanted him to hold her. She wanted most of all not to feel this way about him, out-of-control and careless and . . . caring.

The water for her bath must have been waiting outside. As soon as Montclaire gave the order, his bath was gone and hers steamed in the big tub. As always, he left her alone while she undressed, so strangely considerate for a lord, for a man. He moved the chair closer to the fire and settled into it with one of the mason's many lists of complaints, his long legs stuck out in front of the blazing hearth. His feet were bare, his soles flexed and catching the heat. He plucked at the ends of his moustache as he studied, his brows drawn down in concentration.

His expression set her to remembering the justice he

had dispensed, and that reminded her of all the people he had made happy at his court. She couldn't fault a single judgement. How could she, when he'd returned coins in exchange for promises that would be kept during course of the manor year? A new loom for Giles, a penny and a rose for a new mother and her daughter, a tear for a dying man. He wasn't a very good estate manager, this Thomas Montclaire, but maybe, just maybe, he was a good man.

Mackenna hoped he couldn't hear her thoughts; they were clearly unsuitable for her to think, and doubly dangerous for him to know. Her campaign against him was wavering.

She was looking at him through a gentle haze when she realized he was looking back at her from the hearth.

"Yes?" he asked when her vision focused.

"Mmmm." She tried to cover for her wayward thoughts. "I was just wondering if . . ."

"If . . . ?" He'd lifted a persistent eyebrow.

She searched her list of concerns for a suitable "if." "If I would have to meet the king." It was a thoroughly ridiculous question. The answer would be a resounding, "Of course not, Mackenna."

"Of a certainty, Mackenna." He returned to the business of feeding the fire with a clump of something that caused great billows of smoke to rise up into the chimney.

"Good. Because I've decided to stay in the castle, without further protest, as long as—What did you say?"

"You'll be presented to the king tomorrow night at dinner. You and dozens of other subjects."

"I won't do it."

"There is nothing to fear, Mackenna."

" 'Tis not fear that makes me refuse, Montclaire. 'Tis disgust. Give the king my regrets. I will not attend."

When he ignored her proclamation and continued poking at the foul-smelling mass in the fire grate, she dunked her head and scrubbed at her hair. She knew her cause was lost. In the end, Montclaire would drag her before the king no matter how much she objected. If she went kicking and screaming, she'd only add to the enjoyment of the nobles in attendance. *That* she wouldn't do.

Resigned to her fate, she stepped out of the tub onto the stone floor and threw a towel over her head. The fire had warmed the air and it reached out to caress her. Montclaire had returned to the chair, intent upon the parchment in his hand.

"What would I have to say to him?" she asked, trying to sound beneficent as she bent forward and spilled her hair out in front of her. The stray drops puddled on the floor.

Thomas smiled to himself and remained absorbed in the document. "To whom?"

"To the bloody king." She scrubbed the towel along the column of her hair.

"Probably nothing."

"Probably?"

"Edward has a changeable nature. I cannot warrant his moods. He may ask questions; he may nod and dismiss you."

If she was to give in this time, she planned to gain from it also. "The village needs two more boats."

Thomas would have scowled at her, but he couldn't be sure she'd covered herself yet. He needed no more inspiration. She was bold as brass, and as bare, and still bargaining with him as if she had the means.

"Two boats? Is that your price for obeying my edict?"

" 'Tis a fair one, milord."

"If the village needs boats, I'll provide them. You will present yourself to Edward either way." He returned to his work, unable to concentrate for the shifting silence.

"Where will you be when I'm dragged before the king?"

"Standing beside you."

"Truly?"

"As close as your shadow." His voice was steady and deep.

Warmed by his words, she drew her hair over a shoulder and towelled at it. 'Twas an odd and comforting feeling to hear him talk, one that had been with her from the first. He would protect her. She knew that. He was a man of unyielding principles. Even now, she had every faith that his eyes were politely averted—

He was looking right at her.

His eyes were bright and swept her skin like the heated breath from a bellows. The devil's leer she had once feared never came, nor did her shyness, nor shame. Where his gaze touched, she sensed tenderness and awe.

Thomas swallowed and slowly stood up. She was magnificent. One shoulder, bare and pink, the other draped to the waist with a cascade of damp, tumbled curls. The bared breast was small and high and perfect, tipped in deep rose and exposed to the gilding firelight. Its twin was tucked among the strands of copper, teasing him, taunting him.

"God's bones, Mackenna." His voice strained and cracked, then came up silent.

She was his dream come to stand before him, a glistening, unafraid Pandora. He'd been starved for the sight of her. He thirsted for the beads of water still caught on her thighs, for the taste of her shadows. She would be sweet and satisfying, and he would surely drown.

"You're no help to me, Mackenna."

"Meaning, milord?" Mackenna felt the towel slip through her fingers. It had been in her hand all along, as forgotten as her modesty.

"Meaning I'm not made of granite. Put your clothes on. Nay, don't move." In two strides he was in front of her, the snorting, fire-breathing beast whose hands trembled as he made a clumsy curtain of her hair.

"I need my sleeping gown, milord. Have you seen it?"

"To the bed with you." He turned her and nudged her toward the curtained bed. "Wear this."

Mackenna couldn't see for a moment while he pulled a garment down over her head and shoulders. It was leagues too big and smelled of cloves. She stuck out her arms and turned toward him.

"What is this?"

"My shirt. Your sleeping gown is unusable."

She wasn't going to argue. She liked the idea of sleeping in his shirt, and couldn't help her smile. "All right, milord. I'll go with you to meet the king."

"There was never any doubt in my mind."

He hoped she would as easily accept the fact that he had just sent all her clothes up the chimney in flames.

Early the next morning, Thomas came awake to the wide-spaced footsteps clomping down the hallway outside his chamber: merely hard heels on stone, but he knew their owner and could guess his purpose.

Mackenna had tucked herself against him, a captivating habit she'd developed in these two weeks: one warm hand on his bare chest, her head on his shoulder clouding his vision with coppery curls. He quickly disengaged himself from her embrace and settled her on the pillow.

The knock sounded as he closed the bed curtains.

"Thomas Montclaire! Come greet the sun, you cur!" The bellowing accompanied King Edward into the room.

"Your Grace!" Thomas finished tightening the belt of his robe. " 'Tis good to see you again, Edward."

"And you, Thomas!" Edward clasped Thomas against him and thumped him on the back. "You look fit, man!"

Mackenna yawned loudly and brushed aside the curtains. Montclaire slipped from her dreams into her waking. He was standing beside a man, a stranger. A loud and very rude one, who was staring openly at her.

"Well, well. . . . What is this, Thomas?" Montclaire's long-legged guest strode toward the bed, as imperious as a rooster on patrol in a barnyard. "Why, 'tis a beautiful young woman. In your bed, Thomas? I thought you'd sworn off fleshly pleasures. I see now that the mountain air has done you a great turn."

"Aye, it has, Your—"

"And 'tis a fine choice you've made, lad!" Edward beamed at him. "From a decade of monkishness to filling your bed with a stunning, bright-eyed beauty; you must tell me your secret."

Mackenna scowled at the man. No doubt he was one of Montclaire's loathsome friends let loose in the castle to badger the unwary. He looked as if he'd been awake all night drinking. He smelled of horse and rain. His grizzled beard needed tending, yet his clothes were well turned. She purposely held back the sharpest side of her tongue, because the man deserved to be ignored, not encouraged.

"Does she speak?" the man asked, peering at her as if she were a dancing monkey.

"Aye, she does. Too much at times."

Thomas came up beside Edward, praying for a miracle that would mute Mackenna. He returned her glare with one of silent warning to listen well. "This is Mackenna Hughes, my bailiff."

"Bailiff?" Edward turned to him and laughed broadly. "By the blood, Thomas, I've missed you! No man can cause me to laugh as you do. A woman bailiff!"

Thomas was one of the few men in all of Britain whose height allowed him to look the king directly in the eye. "I do not jest. Mistress Hughes is my bailiff."

Edward quieted and pursed his lips. "The devil you say!"

"Mackenna Hughes," Thomas continued, while he still had everyone's attention, "this is your king, Edward."

Mackenna sunk deeper into the covers. This tree-tall old man was the king? What was he doing in her chamber?

"What time is it?" she asked, puzzling out that she must have slept past noon, else the king and his party would not yet be in Carlisle. She'd overshot the best part of the market day.

"Time?" Edward raised his eyebrows to Thomas.

"Your Grace," Thomas began. This was not the kind of greeting to give a king, especially one with the conceit of Edward. "Please excuse Mistress Hughes's confusion—"

"If I seem confused, Montclaire," Mackenna hissed from the bed, "'tis because I've never had a king come calling in my chamber before dawn. Nor at any time, actually."

"Perhaps you'd rather wait to be presented in the hall—"

Thomas watched in horror as Mackenna wobbled to her feet on the mattress, wearing only the shirt he'd given her. Her unreadable intention pinked her cheeks, pouted her lips, and wrinkled her forehead.

"Mackenna," he began, casting an entreating glance at Edward. But the man was transfixed.

"Your Highness." Mackenna curtseyed and held the awkward pose as best she could, tangled as she was in the bedclothes. "I humbly beseech your forgiveness for any slight I may have given. None was intended. I am an insignificant village girl, and have no experience in royal greetings. If I have offended, I will endeavor to make amends."

"Dear girl, you do not offend me in the least. Do rise."

The king held out his hand and Mackenna rose out of her curtsey, caught her foot on the pillow, and fell forward on the bed into the pile of woolen blankets and linen sheets.

Edward hooted. "God's bones! The most engaging bailiff in all the realm. The bishop of Durham will want one of his own!"

"Well, he can't have mine." Thomas helped Mackenna settle back into the bedclothes.

"Why is he here, Montclaire?" she whispered.

"Quiet." Thomas drew the bed curtains closed in her face and turned to Edward. "You tired of the hunt, Ned?"

"How well you know me, Thomas. I tired of the chase, and the company, and came back alone when I learned you'd arrived. I have need of your advice. Those damnable lairds—"

Another knock sounded and his squire's voice followed. "Lord Thomas, there's a woman here, asking after you."

"Another, Thomas? And is this your sheriff?" Edward asked, his wiry eyebrows shooting into his hairline.

"'Tis my bailiff's dressmaker, Edward," Thomas whispered as he opened the door to tell his squire to bring the woman up. "They'll be wanting privacy."

"Damnation. 'Twould be a joy to watch, but the devil's own boredom to listen to. Dress yourself, Thomas, and join me in my chamber. If I'm asleep in my bath, toss a bucket of cold water on me. I've much to talk to you about before the others return."

The king was already striding down the hallway. Word of his arrival must have spread; he was met by three of his ministers before he reached the top of the stairs.

Mackenna was standing in the middle of the room, her fingers spread on her hips. "I'll give you a piece of my mind regarding the company you keep, milord, as soon as I'm out of your shirt and into my own dress. Have you seen my clothes?"

The woman was ever accurate in her targets, leaving him no choice but to draw and fire back. "I burned them."

"You—"

"So you'd have no excuse not to wear your new wardrobe."

"You burned my clothes?" Mackenna had no particular loyalty to her clothing, but they were *hers*. And he'd burned them!

"I've arranged for more suitable gowns."

"More suitable? What was wrong with my gowns?"

"Gown; you had *one*."

"'Tis all I need. It was perfectly good, nary a hole or a rip, made only last year."

"It was fine for the village, Mackenna."

"But I embarrass you here at court? Is that what you mean? You fear I will be a pea vine among the noble roses and so you decide to change my dress, thinking it will change who I am."

"Of all the things in the world I wish I could change, Mackenna, you are not one of them, whether in sack or silk." His dark eyes had taken on the same softness of the night before.

"So you burned my clothes?" she blurted against the cooling of her anger.

He heaved a huge sigh and opened the lid of the chest at the foot of the bed. "Walter was right," he said, shaking his head.

Suspicious of his pretense, Mackenna asked the question anyway. "Right about what?"

He wistfully pulled out a fresh tunic. "He tried to talk me out of bringing you with me. He said you'd be eaten alive by the poison-clawed she-cats at court."

"Did he?"

Then he turned his back and dropped his robe. He was bronzed muscle and heat as he stepped into a pair of long braies and tied them with string at the waist.

"I told him you could hold your own against them."

"What did Walter mean?" She watched his shirt hem fall from his shoulder to his knee, leaving the image of his flexing backside burned into the air in front of her eyes.

"The women at court have little to do with their time between feasts," he said easily. She couldn't bring herself to look away when he turned to her. "Some find pleasure in secret affairs, some do needlework, others hunt for prey like you."

"Like me? I am no one's prey, Montclaire."

"You would be, dressed as a peasant. These cats will tear you apart, leaving not a feather to drift in the breeze. I can defend you against any man with my title, my position, my sword; but I have little or no recourse upon another man's woman."

"All this because I do not dress as they do?"

"You are in my employ, dear hostage and bailiff, as much a soldier in my ranks as Francis. Consider your new wardrobe a cache of armor supplied by your commander. You'll need it."

"Armor?"

"That is an edict, Mackenna." Thomas stepped into his boots and donned his hauberk while he watched her consider his logic. It was ever a point with her: logic above all. He was learning.

"All right, milord." She crossed her arms, and her hands disappeared among the folds in her sleeves. "But where exactly do I find this armor that I am to wear?"

Thomas caught himself as he was about to heave a sigh of relief and changed it to a cough, then opened the door to the three women who were waiting outside.

Chattering among themselves, the seamstresses bustled Mackenna to the center of the room and drew off the shirt, leaving her once again bare to Montclaire's gaze. He smiled at her over the bobbing heads.

"How long will you be, milord?" she asked, as a heavenly soft chemise dropped over her head and obscured her vision.

"Only God and Edward know the future." He laughed as a pale green gown descended over her head. "Behave yourself, girl. And wait here for me."

When her head emerged, Montclaire was gone, leaving the seamstresses to pluck at the bodice of the gown and cluck over the hem. She missed him suddenly, feeling as if the sun had gone behind a cloud.

"Looks like a dream on you, my lady. His lordship chose colors to set off your hair. Very generous, he is."

Mackenna rolled the cloth between her fingers. It was softer and sleeker than any she had ever felt.

"What material is this?" she asked.

" 'Tis silk. From the Orient."

"I've heard of silk," Mackenna said. " 'Tis from the spinnings of a worm that lives upon the mulberry bush."

The two young assistants burst into laughter, then quieted abruptly when they were shushed by their mistress.

"What the lady says is true. The worms spin a single thread, and this thread is then used to make a very strong cloth."

Mackenna tried to correct the impression that she was a lady, but the women seemed not to listen to her. They hovered and discussed the fit and the folds. She turned when they asked her to, raised her arms, lowered them, walked forward and back, sat, stood, and performed for them like that poor little monkey with whom she was beginning to feel a close kinship.

Once the ladies were gone, and Mackenna was perfectly alone with her unorthodox armor, she finally gave in to a huge smile. The gowns were magnificent! And six of them! Never in her wildest dreams had she ever thought she might one day wear such sumptuous cloth, trimmed in intricate cording, underlaid by elegant chemises. Even the hosen were luxurious.

They'd left her wearing the most elaborate gown of all, unfit for a bailiff, and certain to make her a target for higher prices while she sought to make her purchases. She hung her new armor on clothes pegs, folded the undergarments, and changed into the simplest of the dresses and a soft linen chemise. The gown was the stormy blue of Dunmere lake just before a heavy snow. The bodice was drawn into pleats across her bosom and gathered just below her breasts with a doeskin belt dyed black. The sleeves were slit and showed the chemise beneath.

Montclaire had thought of everything, including a forest-green cloak, lush with folds and bordered in a fine fur she couldn't name. She wondered where he was just now. Sitting with his king, his brow furrowed in concern over some royal woe? She leaned out the casement and opened the hinged pane in the window.

The chamber overlooked a small chapel, and a portion of the bailey. Clouds scudded across the sky, leaving dark patches and light on the cobbles. Servants and pages came and went, anticipating the return of the royal hunting party.

She'd been watching for only a moment when Montclaire and the king came into view from around the keep and climbed the steps to the chapel. They were deep in conference, and unaware of the two well-dressed women who had stopped to stare at them.

It was Thomas Montclaire who drew the attention of the women. Mother Mary, but he grew more handsome

by the hour! His hard, wide shoulders, which dwarfed
his king's and could swing a broadsword with deadly
force, were her soft pillow at night. He was dark and
light, the sea and the shore. His whisper belied his
bellow. His kiss sought deeper than her skin, warmed
her inside, and tucked itself around her heart.

The wind whipped at his black hair, so recently
trimmed by her own hand. He held the chapel door
open for the king. She wanted him to look up and find
her in the window, but he unbelted his sword and
disappeared into the darkness.

Blessed Lady, she missed him!

To clear her head of the thought and the implication,
she turned her attention to the two women arguing
below her window. They must have finally decided
against following Montclaire into the chapel and hurried away. 'Twas a good thing. It saved her a trip into the
chapel to set them straight.

Walter was wrong about the cats. Given the right
armor, she could easily defend herself against their
poisoned claws. She smoothed her hands over her
skirts.

Aye, and now she was well armed.

Chapter 15

Mackenna didn't take well to waiting, and soon found herself studying the mountain of documents and planning her marketing strategy: which craftsman to see first, what price to charge for the village goods, and how to keep Montclaire from watching too closely as she bought extra supplies with her cache of coins.

Her nose caught the aroma of baked bread, and her stomach growled just as a knock sounded at her door.

"Mistress Mackenna, you must be hungry." It was Francis.

Thinking the man must have very good hearing, she opened the door to a basket of warm bread, a wedge of cheese, and an orange.

"From his lordship." Francis smiled, setting the basket on the table. "He sent me out to find the orange especially."

" 'Tis very thoughtful of both of you."

Francis beamed. "And I'm to give you a message that the king is, and I do quote here, 'long-winded and liable to drone on through the end of the century.' " Francis laughed at Montclaire's jest. "His lordship's asked me to aid you as you make your rounds through the town."

"Wonderful!"

They set out together through the streets of Carlisle, trailing carts full of Fellhaven wares behind them.

Mackenna negotiated a contract for smoked eel that

would keep three cotter families busy all year. Whenever the bargains favored the village, she bought extra with her bags of silver pennies and converted the figures in her account books with the ease of one of the jugglers she'd seen at the faire. The merchants seemed pleased to find a willing customer with plenty of coin. Francis had no idea what she was doing.

Hagan joined them, and soon nearly a dozen of Montclaire's men had affixed themselves to her party. Mackenna felt a bit foolish with her heavily armed escort, but she put up with them. They were an enjoyable lot and excellent for business. As her escort increased in size, so did the price she could charge for the village goods; and the prices she paid for supplies became markedly lower with every new man. A sample of sugar or fruit had to be enough for twelve, and her escort grew ever more jovial. They presented quite a wall in front of a trade shop.

"Would one of you please pass the rabbit pelt forward?" Mackenna bent over the counter at the tanner's, and smoothed out a length of weasel. She smiled at her customer and he smiled back. "You'll find the fur in Fellhaven to be exquisite, good sir. 'Tis the weather, I warrant."

When the pelt was not forthcoming, she turned and found herself looking up into Montclaire's eyes.

"Is this what you're looking for, Mistress Hughes?"

Resisting the urge to throw her arms around him, she plucked the pelt from his fingers. "Exactly, milord."

She quickly concluded a deal for a hundred each of rabbit skins and as many weasel as she could deliver. Her knot of tag-alongs made room for Montclaire as he took her hand and led them all away.

"Mistress Hughes," he said when they reached the market square, "you've more bodyguards than the king himself."

"Aye, milord. The very best in the land. And I thank them." The soldiers mumbled and kicked at phantom stones.

"I thank them as well. You're excused, gentlemen," he said, not surprised at their muttering disappointment.

When Thomas had finally shaken himself free of Edward, he'd immediately gone into town looking for Mackenna. Rumors of a beautiful lady and a horde of soldiers had made locating her easy. His men had looked like a band of little boys following after an indulgent nurse. Fascinated, he'd watched from the shadows, watched her win the hearts of his men and the shopkeepers and craftsmen, each falling to her silken blows like the oaks in his forest had fallen to her axmen. Like he was falling, himself.

" 'Tis a shame you sent them away, milord. They were very good for business."

"My men have work of their own to do, Mackenna."

"You have no sense of commerce, milord." She crooked a finger at the cart haulers and started off ahead of them, easing her hood over her hair to keep off the powdery ice pellets that had begun to texture the air.

He followed her, amused at her exasperated sigh. "No sense of commerce? Explain yourself, bailiff."

Mackenna turned into a narrow lane and the others followed. "Well, to begin with, you are far too generous, milord. Returning marriage fees and excusing taxes. How do you plan to make any money? You'll soon run out and then what will you do?"

"I live well enough."

"But for how long? Buying me silken armor was foolhardy."

"Nay, 'tis breathtaking."

"Aye, the money you spent takes my breath away."

"You'll learn, Mackenna, that appearance counts in the courts of kings—appearance and little else." Without missing a step, he lifted her over a shallow, cobbled ditch that ran down the middle of the street. She kept walking as her feet touched down. "Where are we going in such a rush, bailiff?"

"To see the tallow-chandler, two skinners, a draper,

and I promised Cadell I'd speak with a cartwright. And you have a list of mason's tools that needs filling." She handed the parchment to him. "I suggest we split up, milord; we'll make better time."

"Nay, we will finish the day together, bailiff. I want to know just where and how you are spending my coins."

"You don't trust me?" she asked, an innocent hand at her breast.

His laughter bounced off the close-set walls. "Not even while you sleep, my dear. Not even then."

Mackenna sat between Montclaire and his friend Lord Giffard at the long table on the king's dais. The enormous hall was lit by more candles than she'd seen in her entire life, and they were all burning at the same time. A band of minstrels played in a gallery above the ornately carved screens; so many sounds at once, from so many strange instruments, she could hardly make out the tune over the noise of the crowd.

When Montclaire wasn't hovering at her shoulder sharing a tale with Giffard, he was holding her hand, or had his foot caught up with hers. He was a conduit of energy and courage, and seemed to know everyone in the hall. A stream of knights and barons came to greet him, to share a jest. Ladies came in even greater numbers to touch his hand, to giggle and whisper some inane line of verse they had heard.

The women were obvious in their attentions. Montclaire was by far the most handsome man in the hall. Mackenna felt a jealous pride to know that he rarely let go of her hand, that he repeated each lady's verse to her, no matter that some made her blush and his eyebrows arch. She laughed along with Lord Giffard and his handsome lady wife, and gasped with them at the gossip that roared like wildfire through the castle.

Fellhaven Castle was plain-faced and unfurnished by comparison. The dinner plates here were made of silver. She had never eaten on a metal plate before, and thought the food suffered for the taste and the temperature. Though with all the sauces and succulent juices from the mountains of dishes that arrived by the minute, a single trencher of bread would have long ago turned to mush and washed over the edge of the table.

She was grateful for Lady Giffard's ceaseless stream of conversation; it kept her from having to look out at the long rows of tables in front of her. She felt as if something evil and life-ending lurked in the shadows near the rear of the hall. Smoke from a thousand candles and the roaring fires seemed to tumble and collect above it. Moonlike faces bobbed in and out of focus, never in enough light to sharpen to details.

"Is something wrong, Mackenna?" Montclaire whispered the question against her ear. He stayed too long and left a stray kiss that they both tried to ignore.

"Nay, milord. Why do you ask?"

His smile was too lazy, his mouth too near. "Because I wondered at the furrow here." He drew his fingers across her brow. "Tell me."

"Just a feeling . . . like someone walking across my grave."

He frowned fiercely. "No one can walk across your grave while you sit here with me. I won't allow it."

"Then I won't either." She smiled, but the chill remained.

A solemn-faced Edward appeared at Montclaire's side and leaned down to whisper something. Montclaire nodded, and Edward left the hall followed by a brace of wary-eyed lords.

"Mackenna, the king wants me to arbitrate a little exchange. Will you be all right?"

"Will you be long?" The hall seemed entirely too crowded all of a sudden, though half the men had left with the king.

"I can't say." He squeezed her hand. "But look around, sweet. There is Francis and a dozen other of my men. Just say the word if you should need them."

Lady Giffard fixed her arm around Mackenna's shoulder. "We'll take care of your lady, Thomas. Go see to the king."

"Go, milord," Mackenna said, feeling far less brave than she sounded. "I'll be fine."

Thomas smiled and nodded a bow to the ladies. He left the hall, assured that Mackenna would be safe with Lady Giffard.

"They say he's looking for a wife."

Mackenna spun around in her chair and found a stately woman in a robe of goldenrod standing behind her.

"Good evening, Lady Appleton," Lady Giffard said, sounding utterly bored. "Do sit down and tell us who you are speaking of."

The very thing Mackenna wanted to know. Was Montclaire searching for a wife? Her ears filled up with the beat of her heart. Her interest was strictly business. Montclaire's marriage would directly affect the village. If he married—nay, *when* he married—it must be to a kind woman who would understand how to run a manor. Her head swam a little at the thought, tightening a knot in her stomach.

"I speak of the king of course." Lady Appleton pulled out a chair and sat down beside Lady Giffard.

"The king is looking to marry again?" another woman asked. "You know that for certain?"

Lady Giffard cleared her throat. "Emlyn D'Arcy, don't encourage her. She speaks of things she knows nothing about."

Lady Emlyn sighed and shook her head so that her long hair spilled over her shoulders like a golden waterfall. "Whether Edward marries or not means naught to me. When Thomas Montclaire decides to take a wife, that's when I'll take notice."

"Alas, Emlyn," Lady Appleton said, "Lord Thomas will marry when the stars fall from the heavens."

"And what do you mean by that?" Emlyn's green eyes narrowed as she yanked a chair into place and sat beside Lady Appleton.

"Well, my father tells me that Lord Thomas took vows of celibacy some ten years ago."

"Celibacy?" Emlyn snorted and tore a dried fig in

half. "Our priest at Cliffrood took that same vow, and he fathers a bastard child every year to prove it."

"Lord Thomas's is not a priestly vow," Lady Appleton explained. "More like a vow against having children."

Mackenna felt her heart racing. She shouldn't be listening, but there were answers here, answers that might help her understand the man who fit himself against her each night, aroused and breathing unsteadily, yet never seducing her.

"Why would a man like Lord Thomas take such a vow?" Emlyn's cheeks had pinked and her chest rose and fell sharply.

Yes, why? Mackenna brushed crumbs from her skirts but listened with hearing that would cause an owl to envy her.

"'Twas some great tragedy, I hear," Lady Appleton said, touching her fingers to her mouth as if to filter the news.

"What sort of tragedy? A lost love?" Emlyn seemed to know Mackenna's questions and asked them for her.

"Father didn't know. I doubt anyone does. Such a waste." Lady Appleton sighed. "God fashioned that man to pleasure a woman's eyes. I can only dare imagine what he might be like in the heat of passion." She dropped a nutmeat into her mouth.

"You are a married woman!" Emlyn snorted and stood.

"Aye, but I can still imagine, can't I?" Lady Appleton pinned her gaze on Mackenna. "Who is your friend, Lady Giffard? I've not seen her at court before."

Mackenna braved her own introduction. "I am Mackenna Hughes, Lord Montclaire's bailiff."

Lady Appleton laughed and winked at Emlyn. "Is that what they call it where you live?"

"What do you mean?"

"My dear, in Kent, where I live, a woman who shares a man's bed without benefit of marriage is called his mistress."

Lady Giffard put her hand on Mackenna's elbow to warn her off an argument.

But Mackenna patted the cool hand and said, "Mistress to a celibate man, Lady Appleton? How is that possible?" She smiled sweetly at the woman.

Lady Appleton raised one eyebrow, then stood. "Come along, Emlyn. Isobel beckons. We wouldn't want to slight her."

Mackenna had been shamefully fascinated. She wanted to know everything about Thomas, yet if she asked him about his vow of celibacy, he'd know then that she had listened to idle gossip. Gossip was a terrible sin. And it might not be true. But chaste? Thomas Montclaire didn't seem terribly chaste to her.

"You did very well, Mackenna." Lady Giffard winked at her. "But then, I knew you would."

"Sir Walter called them she-cats."

Lady Giffard laughed. "Sir Walter has the right of it."

"I couldn't have done it without my armor."

"Your armor? Have you chain mail beneath your chemise?"

"Of a sort," Mackenna said with a smile. "Lord Montclaire insisted."

When the king returned to the hall with Montclaire and the rest of his lords, the tables were cleared and stored and the minstrels began to play a dance. It was intricate and teasing, and nothing like the village jigs she knew.

"Time to dance, Mackenna."

She looked up into Montclaire's face. He couldn't make her do this. "I don't know this one, milord."

"Neither do I, nor do half the people here, as you will see. The steps probably arrived from Normandy on the last tide. You're a quick study, Mackenna. You'll know it before I do."

"Let the lad take you to the floor. 'Tis all good fun," Lord Giffard said, coming up behind her. "See! Look at Edward!"

The king had turned the wrong direction and was backing up traffic in the circle of partners. The whole line of dancers broke down and fell to giggling. After a sharp-voiced young man untangled the jumble, the circle started moving again and Mackenna found herself a part of it.

Thomas delighted in her frown of concentration as she watched the feet of the other dancers. She forgave his boots tromping on her toes and finally taught him the way of the dance. She held his gaze as they passed shoulders. She was his music, a melody that left him strangely hopeful.

Hope. It was such a desperate emotion.

When the tune ended, another began. This time partners changed as the music progressed. As Mackenna wove her way through the line of partners, she would catch Montclaire's eye and his smile. He was never more than a glance away, until the line moved along and he disappeared entirely. She felt adrift in this sea of grasping hands and teasing glances.

A long-fingered hand claimed her waist, and another claimed her fingers. Mackenna gasped as if she'd been struck. The whip-strong arms sent her behind her new partner before she had a chance to look into his face. The man was lean-limbed and quick, and wherever he touched her he left a bone-cold chill. He was made of shadows and darkness. Then he was gone to another partner, a terrifying phantom without a face.

Mackenna stumbled and recovered. She moved through the rest of the dance without a thought for step or cadence until Montclaire found her as the music ended.

"Mackenna? You're as pale as milk."

His voice was a warm wind, filling her lungs with clean, clear air. He led her to a bench in a dimly lighted alcove and sat down beside her, clutching her hands.

"What is it, love?"

Quaking, she leaned against his warmth. "There was a man just now—"

"By God, did someone insult you? Show me who and I'll—"

She stayed his hand from his empty sword sheath. "Nay, milord. You are unarmed, and he did nothing."

"Who is this man who can do nothing and yet turn your rose cheeks to chalk? Tell me."

"In truth, I never saw his face. And he did nothing but partner me. He said nothing, he just made me feel cold inside."

"Do you see him now?" He pointed to the undulating wall of dancers, but she had seen no features, only shadows, no detail of clothing that would aid her.

"Nay, milord. Even if I could identify the man, I wouldn't point him out to you."

"Why the devil not?"

She finally found a smile that matched the fierceness of his frown. "Because I don't want to be responsible for you starting a row with a perfectly innocent man. Forget I said anything. I think I must be faint-headed from all the food I ate."

"May I claim a dance with your lady, Thomas?"

Thomas looked up at Giffard. 'Twould be a place of safety for Mackenna while he patrolled the hall for a man whose touch could turn his bold bailiff into a quaking damsel. "Please do, friend. But hold fast to her. She's had a fright."

Before Mackenna could reply, Lord Giffard led her toward the dancers arranging themselves for a new dance. She gave a pleading glance to Montclaire as the music started, but received an unrepentant grin in return.

"You are the talk of the castle, my dear." Giffard, for all his boulder stoutness, was an artful dancer. "The women are three shades of green and the men are inconsolable because they know you are Thomas's woman."

"I'm not his woman."

"You're not?"

"I'm his bailiff."

"Hmmm." Giffard's lips pursed beneath his drooping moustache.

"And his hostage. He hasn't told you this?"

"Thomas holds you hostage? Against what, pray tell?"

"He's afraid I'm plotting to steal from his village."

"And are you?"

She hesitated just a moment. "Yes."

"Good for you." He laughed.

Mackenna shared his smile. He had her father's straight nose, and the dark, stringy eyebrows that seemed to chase around on his forehead when he talked. Giffard and her father would have been of an age.

She looked past him and found Montclaire. His back was to her, one arm extended, his fingers splayed against a thick stone pillar. He was nodding and looking down, talking to someone. On the next turn, Mackenna found him again. Emlyn D'Arcy was gazing up at him as if he were honey and she a bear.

"The woman is Lady Emlyn D'Arcy."

"Yes, I know."

"A pleasant enough young woman, but not his sort at all."

Now Montclaire was gone and Emlyn, too. Mackenna could hardly hear for the ringing in her ears. They must be dancing. Must be. She craned her neck to find him, hoping to see those broad shoulders among the swirling partners. She wasn't tall enough to see well, but it was clear that he was no longer in the hall. He'd left her, had stolen into the shadows with Lady D'Arcy and her cascades of golden hair. The sudden desolation left her weak-kneed and weepy.

"He's over there," Giffard said, indicating with their clasped hands. "And, yes, he's dancing with her. Looks bored."

Mackenna couldn't risk a reply. She feared her voice would crack with relief. It wouldn't do for Giffard to hear it, and would only confirm to herself what she'd suspected for the last few days: she was a little taken with Montclaire. It was the only reason she could think of for the way she felt when he was near, and when he wasn't, and when he touched her. She knew her cheeks were flaming.

"I'm not one of you," she said as the dance ended,

and Giffard led her to a side table draped in green damask and laden with sugared sweet meats and wine cups.

"Not one of me? What do you mean?" He offered her a cup.

"No, thank you, Lord Giffard. I mean that I am a peasant, the daughter of a miller." She scanned the drifting mass of dancers for her lord. She tamped down her heart each time it tried to rise and animate her new-found streak of jealousy.

"And I am the great-grandson of a baker. So that makes me one of you. If the truth be known, we are none of us far removed from the croft. And there's a delegation of Scottish border lairds here tonight. The Lord knows they live in caves and call the goat their blood brother." He spoke this last overloud and near the ear of a rough-hewn man, who whirled on Giffard with blazing eyes and fists at the ready.

"If you'll step outside, Giffard, I'll be glad to give you a taste of your own teeth."

Then the two men butted chests like a pair of rutting rams, bellowed, and embraced like long-lost kinsmen.

"Giffard, you old saggin'-arsed boar!"

"You've not lost your charm, Dougal!"

Giffard introduced the Scotsman to Mackenna. She only half-listened to their raucous conversation. She wanted to find Montclaire—and Emlyn. Cursing her lack of height, she stepped up onto a stone bench and searched for them among the dancers.

She was nearly ready to give up when her stomach flipped and a wave of green-sick overtook her. A vile blackness blinded her for a moment. She forced herself to focus through the fog of memories, but after four years of erasing the features and eradicating the stench, he'd returned.

There, moving like a gray-green specter, was John Gilvane, dancing, smiling, nodding to his partner.

The devil incarnate, celebrating here in Carlisle!

Weaving on her feet, she closed her eyes and stepped

down from the bench, then stumbled out of the hall into the bailey.

The sleet hit her like tiny blades. She turned her face to the sky and scrubbed the bits of ice into her skin, pressing the heels of her hands against her eyes, trying to wash away the sight of him. But he was there still, behind her eyelids, cool and mocking. And a guest of the king.

Knowing she must get as far from Gilvane as she could, she started for the stables. Her knees failed her and she fell on the slippery, wet cobbles, gouging rocks into her palms. She got up again and willed herself forward.

She slipped into the stable unseen by the guards. Second row of stalls, fourth one down, on the left.

But a silken banner hung on the stall gate. Three thunderbolts slashing across a black sky: Gilvane's standard. She backed away as if it would strike her. The same blood-red bolts that had brought down her father and the children. A soft nicker from behind her made her turn. It was her mare, moved to a smaller stall to make room for Gilvane's beast. A thick, warm nose exhausted a familiar fume of oats into her hair.

"Good horse," she whispered. "True horse. We must go warn the village." Eschewing a saddle and a bridle, she opened the little gate and led the mare by the forelocks into the bailey.

The sleet fell harder now, driven by the wind. It collected in her hair and slid down into her face, into the front of her gown. The cobbles were slick and treacherous, and she dared not mount until she was on a firmer footing.

" 'Twill be fine, mare." The castle gate stood open on this wicked night to allow traffic into the feast, carts of food and drink. She would escape Gilvane, and the demons and devils who gave him sanctuary. She patted the horse's steaming neck, and grabbed hold of the mane to lift herself.

A huge, hot hand clamped down on hers, melting the sleet collecting between her fingers.

"You picked an enchanting night to escape me, hostage."

"Get away from me, Montclaire!" She launched her shoulder against him, then tried to heave herself onto the mare's back. But she hadn't the strength to fight the double weight of Montclaire's grip around her waist and the burden of her wet gown. "Let go! I'm leaving!"

"Nay, hostage, you're going back to the king's feast."

"I'm going home." Mackenna clung to the mane with both hands. Gilvane would find her and stop her from reaching the village if she didn't get away soon.

"You're going home? Like this? Are you mad?"

"You'll find me at the mill. I've got work to do. Now move so I can leave." She slapped at his arms, trying to shake him off. The mare stood her ground, an island of steaming flesh. If Montclaire would just leave her—

"You've work to do *here*, Mackenna. You're my bailiff."

"I quit, Montclaire!" She jabbed an elbow at him, but it caught in the folds of his robe. She stepped down on his foot, but her slippers were soaked through and her feet were frozen. "I'm going home and you can't stop me."

"I *have* stopped you, love. Here, now, let the stable lad take the horse." She fought him as he unballed her fists from the mane. He turned her in his arms and scrubbed the hair from her eyes. "What happened to send you out into this foul weather, with a damn fool idea about riding that poor animal home?"

"I don't need a horse. I'll walk home."

"You're staying here with me." He scooped her into his arms, and she stiffened as he turned back toward the hall.

"Don't take me back in there." Gilvane would be waiting for her. Panic seized her. "Please. I won't go. You can't make me. Please don't take me back in there. Please!"

She fought him with a strength born of terror, not anger. He finally stopped walking. They needed privacy. "To our chamber then."

"Nay. I want to go home. They need me there."

"I need you here."

"He'll hurt them."

"Who?" Her eyes were wide and bright even in the watery torchlight. She was terrified. "Tell me, Mackenna!"

"You knew he was here." They would protect each other, these base-born nobles. She beat her fist against his shoulder. "You knew, and you didn't tell me."

"Who are you talking about, Mackenna?"

"I felt him. And then I saw him."

"Damnation, Mackenna. This is not the time for a game of—"

"Gilvane." Her voice grew wispy. "He's here."

"Here? Gilvane's in Carlisle?" The news stunned him.

"Yes, and I have to go home now, milord."

Sleet matted her hair and sluiced down her face in wide rivulets. He kissed her temple and pressed her head against his neck. She was colder than the night itself.

"My chamber and an iron bolt will have to do for now." He started off across the bailey.

She stiffened again. "I can't go back into the castle."

"You can do anything you put your mind to, Mackenna Hughes. You've proved that to me a hundred times. You can't let a little man like John Gilvane do this to you."

"To me? Nay, let me go!" She fought him, plucking at his fingers. "Don't you understand, you dim-witted nobleman? Gilvane hanged my father!"

Thomas stopped mid-stride and looked down into a face frozen in fear. A scream was locked in her throat; he could see it working to free itself.

"Bloody hell!" he spat. He pulled her hard against him and left the bailey for their chamber.

"Bolt the door," she whispered, her frail voice rising just above the sleet snicking against the window panes.

"'Tis bolted, sweet." He tried to stand her on her feet near the hearth, but she clung to him, her arms locked around his neck. Thomas kissed her temple and met a patch of ice that caught in his moustache. "And you are wet through to your skin. Can you undress?"

"Sorry . . ." Her fingers were so cold, and laced together so tightly behind his head, that they had lost feeling. She was warm only where he touched her. "Can't . . ."

"Let me, then." Thomas managed to unfasten the tie at the back of the gown while she held on to him like an anchor. "I seem to be disrobing you again, Mackenna."

" 'Tis . . . all right . . . milord." Her breath was warm and shuddering against his neck. "Just don't let him . . ."

"He can't hurt you now." Thomas touched his lips to her forehead. "Can you let go for a moment?"

She did, and stepped out of the icy gown. Her chemise was wet and near transparent. He turned her to the fire and slipped it off over her head. She was wisp-thin in silhouette, clutching her arms across her chest and shivering. He wrapped her in a blanket.

"Hold me, please," she said. "Don't let him come."

"He won't." He surrounded her waifishness like another cloak. "You'd not have made it out of the city in this weather. You'd have died of cold; I wouldn't have liked that."

"I can't die, milord, not while he still lives. I have to warn them at home."

"Gilvane isn't going anywhere soon." Thomas towelled a drip running down the bridge of her nose. "Where did you see him?"

She heard a mad little giggle tumble out of her throat. "Dancing. . . . He was dancing, smiling. . . . He touched me. . . ."

Thomas took her face between his hands and turned it up to him, angry suddenly, a firebrand of disgust sparked to a blaze of outrage. "He touched you where, Mackenna?"

He'd kept her in his sight all night until he'd lost her in a turn of the dance. He had browsed the crowded floor with unapologetic rudeness, and then had trans-

ferred the sputtering Lady D'Arcy to the arms of a
young knight. When he hadn't found Mackenna in the
hall, a tightness had gathered in his chest.

"Gilvane touched you where?" he repeated. Her eyes
were fixed on his, but focused past him, into another
time.

"Dancing . . . before I danced with Giffard. I must
have seen him then. I didn't realize . . ." Her focus
returned and pinned Thomas with a sudden spark of
anger. "He was charged with treason and sentenced to
hang. Why is he here, Montclaire?"

"Any number of reasons—"

"Gilvane should be dead, not feasting with the king."
She turned away from him and stared into the fire.

"Grounds for treason change with the tides of politics. Edward must have forgiven him." Thomas took off
his sodden robe and dashed the ice from his hair, then
stood behind her. "Forgiveness is a valuable commodi-
ty. Perhaps Gilvane has paid for it to Edward's satisfaction."

"There is no forgiveness for murder, Montclaire."

"No, there isn't. When did it happen?" He lifted her
hair from its blanket prison and combed through it with
his fingers.

" 'Twas the night Gilvane set the castle ablaze. I found
Father's body in the bailey."

"In the bailey?" Thomas understood then; that damnable scaffolding had been a gallows. "Damn me for a
fool. I should have known. You told me it was the devil's
work, 'Kenna, and I put you into a dark pit for destroy-
ing it."

"I expected nothing more from you. You're one of
them."

"I'm not one of them." He turned her to him and
placed a kiss on her forehead.

"Then you must tell the king what Gilvane did."

"I promise I will." He didn't know how much good it
would do. Edward probably knew every blot on
Gilvane's record, and kept the books open to use against
the man.

"Please find the king and tell him tonight." She tugged at his arm with a fierceness that made him realize she would not be easily satisfied by mere promises.

He shook his head and tightened the blanket around her. "Edward is no doubt bedding that dark-haired young woman . . ."

"But Gilvane is here—"

"And he'll be here tomorrow." Thomas sat down in the chair opposite the hearth, then pulled her into his arms. "I'll speak with Edward then."

"You'll tell him to put Gilvane into the dungeon?"

"Mackenna, I can't *tell* Edward what to do. I can only advise him."

"Gilvane will be punished, 'tis all I want." She drew up her knees and wriggled until she was tucked comfortably in his arms. " 'Tis good that he'll be imprisoned, because I swear I won't run the next time I see him."

"Stay clear of the man, Mackenna. That's an edict." He had a sudden vision of Gilvane seeking her out in one of the dark corners of the castle where even the light didn't venture. He held her tighter. "Does he know you?"

"I don't think so. Father kept me out of Gilvane's way. I've changed a lot since then. We were starving, milord. I was bone-thin and young, not quite fifteen and . . ." She raised an eyebrow to him. "Undeveloped. If you understand my meaning."

Though filled with outrage that she should ever have suffered a moment for Gilvane's villainy, Thomas couldn't help his smile. "I understand. You're well past that stage now."

Her smile was shy and crooked and just a little hopeful.

A loud thumping on the door sent her into Thomas' embrace, her arms a vise around his neck, her cloud of hair smothering him.

"Don't open it," she hissed. "Please. It's Gilvane."

Chapter 16

Thomas carried Mackenna to the bed and pried her arms from around his neck. "Hide yourself in there, if you must."

"Be careful, milord." She kissed him then, a brief touch on the lips meant to boost her courage, but leaving her a little breathless. He yanked the bedcurtains closed.

"Thomas? Is that you, lad?"

"Giffard." Thomas threw open the door and drew the man inside. "What is it?"

"Is Mackenna all right? Have you seen her? She left the hall. She was there one moment and gone the next."

"Aye, she's been known to do that."

"Is she with you?" Giffard stopped when the bedcurtains moved. He scowled at Montclaire. "That better be her in there."

"Could be no other, Giffard." But Giffard peered deeper into the room. "Now, be a good friend and leave," Thomas said.

"Ah, yes, I see her dress there on the floor. I'm glad to know she's locked up safe. Have a good night, Thomas."

"You, as well." Thomas had the door nearly shut when Giffard stuck his boot in the jamb. "What now, Giffard?"

"Someone was asking after her, just before I left."

Thomas pushed Giffard into the hall and followed after him. "Someone, who?"

"Do you know that bastard, Gilvane? The one who held that tumbledown castle you're renovating for Edward."

"Yes, yes. Did you tell him anything about Mackenna?"

"I didn't even tell him her name. He was just one of many asking about her, and I told them all to ask you. After all, she's your hostage." Giffard chuckled and lifted his eyebrows.

"What's Gilvane doing here?"

"He's part of the delegation come to lend Edward a hand in setting Balliol on the Scottish throne. Arrived today."

"And Edward has allowed a man whom he, himself, charged with treason to set foot in his castle?"

"He did the same for your father, Thomas."

"That was a different matter altogether."

"I'm sure Edward didn't think so at the time, nor did his father. The baron's revolt failed, and your father would have been hanged if not for his ties to the royal family."

"You needn't remind me of the game, Giffard. I dislike it and play it as little as I can. Just keep an eye on Gilvane for me. I don't want him near Mackenna again."

"They know each other, then?"

" 'Tis a long story. And a long night, Giffard."

"Then sleep well, lad—if you get the chance." Giffard grinned and strode down the passage, whistling along with a tune that wound its way up from the great hall.

When Thomas peeked through the bedcurtains, he found Mackenna fast asleep on his side of the bed, her arms wrapped around his pillow.

"You're safe for another night, my love. From Gilvane and from me."

Mackenna stifled her panic when she awoke in the morning and realized Montclaire wasn't in the room. He wouldn't leave her unprotected. He'd promised her.

She found his note on top of a cup of fresh cider. He would see her at noon. If she needed anything, Francis was just outside in the corridor. As she opened the door, Francis's face loomed in the crack.

"Yes, mistress?"

"How long has his lordship been gone?"

"He left with the king at dawn."

"Left for where?"

"They didn't say, but it looked like falconing to me."

"You'd make a good spy, Francis. Would you like to come in for a game of chess after I've dressed?"

"I'd better not."

"If you don't, then I will become bored and try to escape. You wouldn't want that, would you?" When he scowled at her, she added, "Lord Montclaire won't mind."

"Get yourself dressed then." His frowning face disappeared.

Montclaire was probably even now speaking with the king about Gilvane's crime. Edward couldn't have learned of the hanging before this. Gilvane wouldn't have confessed to murder on his own. But once Edward knew the truth, Gilvane would be imprisoned and hanged.

She hated cowering in her room like a weepy old woman. She had bravely battled Gilvane for years when she was little more than a child. Now she was an adult; she shouldn't be afraid of him. With Montclaire at her side, Gilvane was no longer a threat.

Thomas Montclaire was Lord of Fellhaven now, and Gilvane was out of her life, if not yet out of her nightmares. Nightmares were fashioned of phantoms, and phantoms couldn't hurt her any more than a daydream could bring her happiness.

Francis had just lost his third game of chess when Mackenna decided that she had cowered too long. She had work to do in town, money to spend for the good of the village, and she was suddenly angry with herself for giving Gilvane the power to control her again.

"We're leaving, Francis." She pulled on her hard-soled boots while Francis sputtered.

"Nay, mistress. You're not going anywhere."

"What exactly were your orders?"

"Lord Montclaire made me promise not to let anyone in here."

"Good. Then neither of us will prick his lordship's temper. No one is coming in; we're both going out." She threw her cloak over her shoulders and left Francis standing in the middle of the room. Montclaire must have told the king everything by now; Gilvane was already counting the hours until his execution.

Francis caught up with her. "Lord Montclaire isn't going to like your gadding about the city. You've tricked me again."

"I didn't trick you, Francis. I convinced you."

He continued arguing all the way out the castle gate.

The morning hung gray and dark, and misted with blowing rain. Wind swept her new cloak out in front of her, flapping like a sail and hurrying her down the street. Undaunted by the weather, the shopkeepers were open for business, and even the stiffening wind couldn't scour out the riot of odors and aromas.

She returned to the lime seller to add another cartload to her order. In a bare hour, the village gained another three hand-looms, two carts of salt, a dozen sacks of seed grain, and ten new goats, all to be delivered a week after they had returned to the village so that Montclaire wouldn't notice the addition.

Francis had given up his campaign to hurry her back to the castle and was loaded down with sacks of sweet-scented herbs. As they neared the market square, a hard arm came around Mackenna's waist and she was scooped off the street. Suddenly she was sitting side-saddle. The stunt was so familiar, she wasn't at all surprised.

"Hello, Montclaire," she said, pulling her hood off her face just far enough to look up into his stony expression.

"You were to wait for me in the chamber." He didn't look at her, but straight ahead at some unfocused distance.

"You said nothing of the sort, Montclaire."

"I didn't think I had to, given our discussion last night. You'll notice, we are not alone here, Mackenna."

She peeked around her hood. Edward was staring at her.

"Good morning, Your Grace."

He nodded at her and smiled at Montclaire.

"What did the king say when you told him about Gilvane?" Mackenna whispered the question, knowing now that justice would be swiftly done.

"Gilvane is riding behind us and to your right." Thomas felt her stiffen, but didn't look down at her. He was always so damnably happy to see her, no matter what edict she had breached. He didn't need to be smiling at her when he ought to be scolding, when the morning had been so predictably unsuccessful.

Mackenna set her chin on Montclaire's collarbone and peered round his wind-tossed hair toward Gilvane. She fully expected to see a humiliated man, hands manacled draped in chains and, head bowed in supplicating shame.

But Gilvane was laughing with the knight riding beside him.

"You didn't tell him!" she hissed into Thomas's ear.

He tightened his grip around her waist. "Yes, Mackenna, I told him."

"And?"

"You and I will talk about it later."

"But—"

"I said later, Mackenna."

She stared up at his resolute chin and knew he would say no more. Justice turned slowly. She looked back at Gilvane. He was only a profile now, a blur of angular lines and ruddy skin.

If the king knew about his crime, then why was the man still free? It made no sense. Maybe Montclaire hadn't explained it correctly. He hadn't been there to see, and he didn't know the depths of Gilvane's evil. It was more than just the cold-blooded murder of her father; children had died because he hadn't cared that they were cold and starving! A simple peat fire and a small ration of the grain which they had worked to grow and harvest would have sufficed for the winter. But Gilvane's greed had been insurmountable. Nothing could change a man like that. He was no different today than he had been four years ago or ten years ago.

Yet for some reason that she would never understand, John Gilvane was still free.

"By the looks of these reports, Thomas, you've done quite well with the reconstruction." Edward hitched himself up in the chair and reached for a quill.

Thomas lounged on a bench opposite. The council had disbanded until after supper to cool a few tempers, Edward's especially, leaving them a moment to speak privately about the condition of Fellhaven.

" 'Tis a miracle anything has been done at all," he said. "It took a week to secure the drawbridge, and the road is still unsuitable. We lack lime and tools and enough men—"

Edward waved a hand in the air. "Yes, yes, you've told me. I don't know what I can do about it. I'm short of ready cash, as you well know. Carlisle needs all the attention I can give it. Have you seen the cathedral? A bloody ruin." He strode to a table and refilled his goblet.

"Ned, Fellhaven is your castle, not mine. You want it restored and garrisoned with trained men—"

"Trained as only you can train them, Thomas."

"Then why did you not send me as the garrison commander, and commission another of your barons to the job of managing the manor while the bloody castle is being raised?"

"You don't like being lord and master?"

"You know I don't. I have no experience and it shows."

Edward set his cup down. "They don't know, do they, these Fellhaven people? You didn't tell them you hold

the castle only temporarily, until I find another man to
hold it permanently."

"Nay, your idea was sound. They believe me as
permanent as those mountains of black slate. They
would have robbed me blind had they thought otherwise."

"I suggest you keep your silence on the matter."

"I intend to. But the people aren't the problem; they
are an asset. 'Tis my inexperience. I'm not prepared to
manage an estate. I'll never understand why you sent
me to do the job."

"You needed a change."

"I'm a soldier, Ned."

"My best, my most able. If you but say the word I'll
grant you land and an earldom, and a well-dowered
bride."

"Spare me, Ned. I want none of it." But he saw
himself standing knee-deep in sweet barley, helping
Mackenna and the village bring in the harvest. Her belly
was well-rounded with his child, and her joyous smile
was for him. He swabbed his brow to rid his head of the
costly image.

"You try my patience, Thomas. I'm getting older. I
want you settled on a substantial holding before I die.
My son will need your wisdom. If you have no land, you
will hold no sway among the other barons when I am
gone."

"I don't want land, Ned. At the risk of scraping at old
wounds, my father did not benefit from all his titles and
land."

"It needn't be Fellhaven. 'Tis an insignificant holding,
and I have others that need your lordship."

"With due respect, my liege, I like my life as it is. I
need nothing that ties me to false boundaries and sets
my days."

"You don't want family," Edward said too quietly.

Thomas shot him a glance, then looked away. "I've
made no secret of the fact."

"Your bailiff, does she know?"

The question dug deeply. "That I want no family?"

"Nay, Thomas. Does she know that you'll give over the holding to me as soon as the castle is complete? That another man will hold it?"

"She would lead the rebellion if she knew. 'Tis she I fear most of all."

"A bit of a girl like that?"

"One who adds long columns of numbers in her head; who learned to read and write French, Latin, and English when she was five; and who has the devil's own gift for piracy."

"A dangerous woman, Thomas. Take care."

A sharp knock came. "Mistress Hughes, Your Grace."

"Come!" Edward cast Thomas a steely look. "I'll say nothing about your stewardship of Fellhaven."

"Nor will I, Ned."

The king's guard opened the door and motioned for Mackenna to enter. She did, her knees shaking. The king stood in the center of the opulent room, his blue woolen robes shimmering in the sharp candlelight. A rail of boldly patterned curtains insulated the walls. The room smelled of camphor and candle smoke, and hinted at cloves.

"Your Grace," she said as she dipped into a curtsey, executed with far more dignity than her first had been. He smiled and raised his cup to her.

"Lord Montclaire." She nodded to Thomas and was nearly leveled by the tenderness in his smile, the splendor in his eyes. It was a moment before she heard the king's question.

"Oh, aye, Your Grace. I am enjoying my stay at Carlisle."

"'Tis a pleasure to serve Lord Thomas' beautiful bailiff."

Mackenna fought the need to lower her eyes as she remembered Lady Appleton's comment about her title.

Thomas smiled. "Did you have a restful afternoon, bailiff?"

"I've been in the solar, with the ladies." She enjoyed

the look on his face—the arched brows, and the twitch of confusion that dropped the corner of his mouth.

"And did the ladies behave themselves?" Edward asked. " 'Tis a trial I'd not long endure."

"No blood was drawn. Though they were armed with needles and scissors, goose quill is my weapon of choice."

" 'Tis a good thing, too, Ned. She's dangerous with a pair of scissors."

Mackenna turned three shades of red and set down her folio on the table to cover her embarrassment.

"I stand warned, Thomas." The king followed her to the table. "I'm told you're also good with numbers."

"I have some knowledge of them."

"Never hide your light from your king, Mistress Hughes. He needs to count every brilliance among his assets." He motioned Mackenna to sit beside him at the table. "These reports are your doing?" he asked her.

"Aye, most of them, compiled with Sir Walter."

"Do show me," he commanded.

Mackenna spent the next half-hour explaining the reports, supporting Thomas' recommendations with facts and figures. The king seemed fascinated by the increases she'd managed in wool production and in her use of fish to fertilize the fields, though he dismissed the last as her fancy. All the while, she kept her temper in check, holding back the seething questions she wanted to ask him about murder and justice.

A particularly pointed question was about to pop out when a knock sounded at the door.

"Come," Edward said.

Thomas wouldn't have given a thought as to who might be behind the door, if Edward hadn't turned an expression of challenge on him, a suspicious fusing of amusement and warning.

"Lord Gilvane, Your Grace."

"Damn you, Ned!" Thomas couldn't prevent the oath. Edward was ever one for pitting one man against another then sitting back to enjoy the sport. He'd not leave Mackenna to suffer Edward's games. He took a step toward her.

"Leave it be, Thomas." Edward raised a hand and Thomas halted, his eyes fixed on Mackenna. She lacked the cowering fear that had brought her to confess her hatred of the man. Her mouth was set in a line, her chin tilted toward the door.

Gilvane strode into the room, a man of refinement and falsehoods. Cold hatred settled into Mackenna's chest. She forced herself to breathe evenly, looked past the man's congenial smile to the rising anger in Montclaire's face.

"Gilvane, you know Montclaire, of course," Edward was saying. His gesture was grand as he turned toward Mackenna. "And this lovely young woman is Mistress Mackenna Hughes."

"Ah, yes, Mistress Hughes." Gilvane nodded in her direction, his eyes glossy with interest. " 'Tis a pleasure to meet you again . . . at last."

Mackenna couldn't even manage the man's name for the taste of bile rising in her throat. She could feel Montclaire's eyes on her. He had matched Gilvane's steps in her direction, steps taken against his king, who even now grinned as he watched the drama being played out before him.

She gathered her courage and nodded at Gilvane.

"John," Edward said, "good of you to come so quickly."

"Ever your servant, my liege."

"Of course. It seems I have need of your counsel. 'Tis Harwood. He's not convinced that Balliol should have the throne. Wine, John?"

"Thank you, Your Grace," Gilvane said, taking the poured cup. He put the vessel to his mouth, tipped it, but didn't drink, a gesture only Mackenna could see. "Delightful," he said, running the tip of his tongue over his lower lip.

"From my vineyards in Gascony. There is no better wine, as you well know."

Thomas sat down on the edge of the table nearest Mackenna, within an arm's reach should she need him. Her chest rose and fell evenly as she stifled an anger only he could see.

"I fear Harwood is stubborn," Gilvane continued. "English to the core, but with a leaning toward his new Scottish wife."

"I care not which way the man leans, only that I expect him to fall my way, Gilvane." Edward tapped his ring of state on the bowl of his cup, a dull clunk that made Mackenna think of the ever-expanding circles that follow a stone tossed into a pond.

"He will, my liege. I know this for a certes."

"For a certes? You can deliver Harwood's support to Balliol?" Edward paused, to make sure that his point was understood. "And you will deliver it then to *me*?"

"Harwood will not bend either way until the council meets next week in Berwick. But I know his mind. Your offer in exchange for his support has sweetened his disposition, despite what you might have sensed to the contrary."

"I should hope it has, for his sake. He needn't be reminded that no matter whose backside warms the Scottish throne, I remain Scotland's rightful overlord. Harwood and his peers pledged fealty to me at Norham last year."

"Aye, Your Grace. No one is more aware of your authority than Harwood . . . unless it be me."

"Good. I hope your stay here reminds you also of my great generosity, the benefits of staying on my . . . sunny side."

"It has been a distinct honor, my liege, to accept your hospitality. I am humbled by your mercy and by your trust—"

"My trust, Gilvane?" Edward snorted. "You take me wrong. I can hardly trust a man I've so recently pardoned for treason."

Mackenna's heart thumped against her chest. This was it! The king would now throw the accusation at

Gilvane. She glanced at Montclaire, but couldn't judge his mood. His attention was hard on Edward.

"Wouldn't you agree, Thomas?" Edward refilled Thomas' cup with wine and handed it to him. Thomas took it and scowled at Edward's toying smile.

"Aye, my lord king," he said, curtly. "Trust lies at the heart of every great alliance. Whether it be between king and baron, lord and villein, or man and woman."

"By the blood, Thomas! You have grown poetic on me! I approve the sentiment, fervently approve. You might learn well from it, Gilvane. Take it to your heart the next time you think to send good English silver to France."

Mackenna watched Gilvane's face drain of its ruddy health. Whatever the meaning of Edward's words, the message seemed clear to his vassal. Gilvane drank this time, a loud gulp that seemed the only sound in the room. She waited for Edward to level the other charge against him, the charge of murder.

"My folly is my shame, my liege. I seek your trust again, and will bring you Harwood's support in token and pledge." Gilvane's color grew with each word, surpassing his natural ruddiness and causing his hands to shake in suppressed outrage.

"Wise of you, Gilvane. One of my illustrious grand-sires, though I don't recall which one, had a most effective deterrent to men who counterfeited the coins of the realm."

"And that was, my liege?" Gilvane's voice betrayed his deep indignity.

"Had their ballocks clipped off!" Edward drained his cup.

Thomas cleared his throat.

Gilvane straightened his shoulders. "A most effective deterrent, my liege."

"Aye. 'Twould be for me!" Edward laughed and made a great show of noticing Mackenna. "Ah! I beg your indulgence for the coarseness of my words, Mistress Hughes."

"'Tis unnecessary, Your Grace." Mackenna said no more than that and received Edward's nod of acknowledgment. Indeed, she enjoyed bearing witness to Gilvane's predicament. It was no substitute for true justice, but it gave her hope of its coming.

"And, now, if you'll excuse us, Gilvane." Edward indicated the door.

That's it, Mackenna wanted to shout. What about the murder of Randolph Hughes?

"By your leave, my liege," Gilvane said, setting his cup on the table. He nodded toward Mackenna and smiled, then gave Edward a truncated bow and swept out of the chamber.

"Charming fellow," Edward said, dashing the contents of Gilvane's cup into the fire. Some of the liquid missed and spattered red on the marble facing.

"What was your point in that display, Ned? To humiliate Gilvane or to distress my bailiff?"

"I'm not distressed," Mackenna said, stuffing the sheaf of documents into the folio. "Surprised is all."

"You are gracious, my dear," Edward said. "Though I did not mean to burden you."

"Your point in this, Ned?" Thomas repeated impatiently.

"To make it clear to Mistress Hughes why John Gilvane cannot be charged in the murder of her father."

"And is it clear to you, Mackenna?" Thomas asked, knowing full well that it couldn't be. It was barely clear to him, and he'd studied Edward's logic for years.

Mackenna could only shake her head.

"To put it in heartless terms, my dear, Gilvane's crime of dispatching silver coins to my enemies in France was by far more heinous than the simple murder of a village reeve."

"More heinous than hanging my father?" Mackenna stopped when Montclaire frowned a warning at her.

"'Tis a matter of degrees and changing times," the king continued. "As you must realize from my parley with Gilvane, he holds a certain power over a block of influence among the Scots."

"Why wasn't Gilvane punished four years ago, Ned?"
Thomas asked the question, hoping to check the imprudent comment he knew was forming on Mackenna's
tongue.

"The vile bastard disappeared. Into Gascony, if you
can imagine the insult! Into my own province at the very
time I was there!" Edward sat down on the edge of the
chest and laced his knuckles together. "A charge of
treason and a death warrant means nothing without a
man to hang. Believe me, I tried. Then this business
between Bruce and Balliol was thrust at me, and who
did I find among the barons of Scotland but Gilvane, so
festered among them that I cannot tweeze him out.
Balliol himself talked me into pardoning the man. You
understand. I am sorry, my dear."

Mackenna took a breath and opened her mouth, but
Thomas intercepted her. "I'm sure Mackenna thanks
you for your time, Ned, and I add my own. A great
mystery has been solved."

"Good. Good." Edward clapped his hands together
and stood. "'Tis time to sup. You'll join me, of course."
Edward put a hand to Mackenna's back and guided
them from the chamber.

Chapter 17

"**W**hat about justice, Montclaire?"

Mackenna had kept her peace throughout the feast. Edward had been jovial and talkative, and once the dancing began, he'd often sought her as a partner. Unable to keep up the pretense of lightheartedness, she'd finally excused herself, and Montclaire had followed her to their chamber.

"Sometimes justice can't be had, Mackenna."

"Not by a peasant, you mean. If my father had murdered Lord Gilvane, royal justice would have been done, and swiftly."

"Aye. Randolph Hughes would have hanged for it. And in most cases I would hang for the same crime. But the moment for punishing Gilvane has passed. Greater issues have arisen."

"Greater issues than the death of an innocent man?"

"Mackenna." He held her shoulders to force her look at him. "For now it is finished. How can I make you understand that?"

"You can't. Ever! 'Tis the difference between us, between lord and peasant. You proclaim your edicts, and we obey, kind sir. Grateful for the privilege to serve you."

"That will be the day, Mackenna Hughes—when you obey me, or anyone else, at anything but your pleasure. Count yourself among the few who have ever gained an explanation from our king."

" 'Tis a wicked game he plays with people's lives."

"No more than you play in the village."

"You compare *me* to *him!*" Mackenna threw off her cloak.

"Think on it, Mackenna. You abhor John Cotes for the crimes he has committed against his family."

"I hate him!"

"And yet who makes the barrels that hold your grain?"

Mackenna didn't want to answer, looking for a reason that would explain her commerce with the man. "Cotes does, but—"

"And the barrels which keep the rats from the apples?"

"Cotes," she said quietly.

"Your decisions don't fill as large a kettle as Edward's, but they have the same flavor." Thomas came to her side. "You didn't know Gilvane was here until two days ago. You thought justice was as impossible to grasp as a vapor."

"I thought justice had been done. I thought he was dead, or at least rotting in a dungeon."

"Discovering otherwise hasn't changed the outcome."

"But he's alive, and my father isn't." She stared into the fire, her eyes red-rimmed but dry. She sniffed back tears that weren't there.

" 'Tis no shame to weep, Mackenna. I do it myself, after every battle. Whether we win or lose."

She looked at him to see if he were grinning. He wasn't.

"And I rarely lose," he added, lifting a curtain of hair over her shoulder.

She looked away from him. "I have no need for tears. I haven't wept since before my father was murdered. You needn't make up stories."

"Suit yourself, Mackenna." He left her to shuck off his boots. "But 'tis no story. I've never been able to stop myself. 'Tis contagious, too. My men seem to join me straightaway. A sight to behold: hundreds of grown men, covered with blood and guts and mud, sweating in the blazing sun, and all of us blubbering like babes. Feels right good after it's over."

The idea of succumbing to tears on such a grand scale frightened the life out of her. "Why do you allow yourself to do such a thing?"

"Because, my dear, 'tis safer than weeping during the battle. Tears may be transparent, but I cannot see through them to swing a sword."

"But why do you weep at all? You're a soldier. These men you battle are your sworn enemies." The idea of a courageous warrior like Thomas Montclaire loosing his grief in huge bouts of weeping reached inside and tore at her heart.

"Dear God, how can I take a man's life and not feel his pain reach up through my sword like lightning? I weep for his children who need him, and his wife who mayhap adores him, for his parents who raised him up to be more than a vessel for my weapon. Killing is a heathen business."

"If you hate soldiering so much, why do you continue?"

"Edward needs my sword. I'm very good at it, and . . . I don't really know how to do much else."

"You're an excellent and honorable justiciar. The king could learn much from you."

Thomas smiled. "That's high praise coming from you."

"I don't withhold praise when it's due."

"Except from me."

"You're a lord. I judge you on a different scale."

"Oh? And what else do you approve of, Mackenna?"

She felt suddenly shy, declaring her approval of the man she had once so roundly despised. "Well . . . I like the way you divide the work among your commanders, and they among their men. And I like the way you listen to your advisors as if their opinions held great worth."

"They do."

"You've trained your men to be respectful, and helpful. I like that, too. And your justice with the village. I was . . ." She hesitated to confess it. "I was moved by your generosity."

"And are you as moved by my singing?" He looked very serious.

Her laughter caught in her throat but spilled out anyway. "I think I'll just say that I like your enthusiasm immensely." She sat down on the edge of the bed.

"Walter says he prefers to listen to a swine giving birth."

"Then, come the spring, we shall give him the opportunity."

"Have any of my other traits earned your approval?"

Mackenna fell backward onto the mattress and threw her hand across her eyes. "I can't think of a single one, milord."

The mattress dipped with his weight.

"Not even my kiss?"

His breath brushed against her cheek and the back of her hand. "Uhmmm . . ." she mused.

He watched as she drew her lips together to gnaw on them as if she were considering a long-forgotten and insignificant event. Her mouth reformed into a glistening smile.

"Well?" Thomas was sure she could hear his heart slamming against his chest.

"Your kiss? I'm sorry, milord, but I just don't remember."

"Ah, well." It took every bit of his will to leave her sprawled across the bed. "I can't remember a particular quality to your kiss, either." When he glanced back at her she was staring at him, her mouth open to speak, her brows raised.

"You can't remember?" she asked as he stopped at the door.

"Nay, love, I remember all too well," he said, reminding himself that he must learn to forget—else he would die a lonely, unhappy man.

"Where are you going, milord?"

"For a walk in the bailey."

"But 'tis raining. You'll get cold."

" 'Tis the idea, Mackenna. If you're not asleep when I return, please pretend to be."

It was more than she could fathom, this feeling she harbored for his lordship. She understood longing; she felt it for her father a dozen times a day, and for the mother she remembered only through his stories. She longed to see her brothers again, the four men she loved most in the world. She missed them and worried about them. She longed for the sun that lit the surface of Dunmere, and for the dots of sheep on the high meadows. She longed for the wreath of smells and sounds that were Fellhaven.

But more than all of these, she longed for the man sleeping in the bed beside her.

She'd awakened from the chill. Montclaire had rolled onto his back and stolen the covers, leaving her with a corner of the sheet. He was turned to her, the portrait of a man at peace. No lines of worry, no fretted creases. His hair was sleep-rumpled and swept off his high forehead. His even breathing ruffled the soft hair of his moustache. She liked the pattern of his beard, cheeks clean shaven, cropped deeply toward his jaw, and below his bottom lip. She tried to avoid focusing on his mouth, but his lips were parted and damp; and her longing for him surged.

If she kissed him while he slept, she could study the effects without having to worry about what he might think of her. Light kisses shouldn't wake him, and with enough of them, she might become bored and the longing would go away—like an itch dispelled by a good scratching, or eating an entire bucket of honey and never wanting another taste of it as long as she lived.

Thomas was dreaming the most unbelievably arousing dream he'd had since he'd first discovered the fair sex. He was trapped inside the burnished copper tent of Mackenna's hair, the scent of violets all around him. She was straddling his hips with her knees, and his shoulders with her arms, and settling kisses on his mouth, this one planted a bit more to the left than the one just before it. And in this peerless dream, she drew a warm fingertip across the rise of his lower lip, then placed another honey-warm kiss where her finger had strayed.

He opened his eyes.

"You're awake," she whispered against his mouth.

Good Christ, he wasn't dreaming!

"How long have you been doing this?" he asked, setting a finger against her lips to stop the next. She gently brushed his hand aside and continued her study.

"This one," she said, stroking the tip of her tongue along the enticing place where his upper lip arched and met in the center. She'd have set a kiss where her tongue had been, but he groaned and drew his knees up. His thighs met her backside.

"Mackenna!"

"That would have made ten, milord. I was hoping to grow bored with it by now."

"Bored with this?" He tried to sit up, but she put a finger in the center of his forehead and pushed him back down, her lips seeking still another site on his mouth. He groaned again.

"I won't be much longer, milord. But you must lie quietly until I am finished. Go back to sleep."

She must be mad. There was nothing but a chemise of fine linen between his arousal and her belly. His breathing was ragged, and his skin sizzled with a fever.

"My God, woman. I can neither lie here quietly nor go back to sleep with you lounging atop me, putting your lips wherever you please." Thomas rolled her onto her back. He brushed the cloud of hair from her face and cupped her chin with his fingers. "Do you think me a marble statue?"

"Nay, milord." The longing now coursed through her blood like a river slipping its banks. "I know you're made of flesh. I feel it quicken against me."

Thomas shuddered in a white-hot burst of physical

desire for the woman trapped beneath him. "Damnation, Mackenna. I saved you from Gilvane. I can't save you from me too, all in the same week. I haven't the strength—"

And then he covered her mouth with his, tasting and teasing. Her tongue found his and played until he groaned and clutched her shoulders, and drove her further into the pillow with the depth of his kiss. He couldn't still his hands; they caressed her face, her neck, and the soft rise of her breasts. His fingers loved her mouth and her hair, and met her hands in the wild spray of copper above her head.

"Oh, my!" Mackenna stretched out beneath his wandering hands and wondered when the horrible beast had become prince and protector. Scant weeks ago she couldn't stand the sight of him; but now she couldn't take her eyes off him, watching the way his lips parted before they touched hers, the way his lashes dusted his cheekbones, the play of passion across his brow.

"Are you bored yet?" he asked roughly, looking up from a kiss below her chin. He hoped to hell she said yes.

"Not yet, milord."

The end of his nose touched the end of hers. "I'm afraid I'm not either. Do tell me when it happens."

She smiled at him. "I will, Montclaire."

"Bloody hell, girl." He rose up on his elbow, trying to control the gravel in his voice. "Do you, by any chance, recall my Christian name?"

"Aye, milord."

"Then use it when I'm kissing you."

"Thomas." She was grinning. "There. Now, Thomas, kiss me as you would kiss Lady Emlyn D'Arcy."

He narrowed his eyes and rose above her on his hands. "As I would kiss Lady D'Arcy? Are you sure?"

"Aye. Show me how you would kiss her."

"As you command, my lady." He played at a yawn, stretched, then rolled away from her, his breathing every bit as ragged as it had been before. His arms ached for the want of her.

"What are you doing?" she asked when it became obvious that he wasn't going to move.

"I'm ignoring you, Lady D'Arcy." He fisted the pillow and blew out a sigh that was anything but soothing.

"Why would you do that, Thomas?"

"Because, Lady D'Arcy, I don't want to kiss you now, or tomorrow, or at any time in the future."

Mackenna ran her hand along his bare shoulder. "She wanted to kiss you," she said quietly.

"I can't help that."

"*I* want to kiss you."

"Aye, so you've proven."

"But now you're bored?"

"Far from it." He'd begun to growl between breaths.

She wanted him to turn back to her, but she wouldn't beg. Mother Mary, she shouldn't be kissing him at all.

"I'm glad you didn't shave off your beard. 'Tis very soft."

"Good night, Mackenna."

She sighed and turned her back to him. "God keep you safe, Thomas Montclaire."

"And you Mackenna Hughes." Thomas listened to her unsteady breathing for a time and knew she was wide awake, and wanting. He turned and fit her against his chest. She settled her arm over his at her waist, her breathing ruffling the hair at his wrist. She felt so good, so right. And so very impossible.

He was a soldier and wanted nothing to complicate his life. Strike swiftly, cleanly, and ride on to the next battle. Villages were royal booty. Fields fed armies on the move. Land meant nothing but shifting boundaries and unquenchable royal tempers. His father had been a man of influence, wealth, and titles, but he'd risked it all on politics, and it had cost him everything. He had died broken, humiliated, impoverished. Thomas had learned well. A man without family, without property, could obey his own conscience, could choose his battles and move on. No one suffered, save himself.

Aye, he lived a fine and satisfying life.

Until he'd ridden into the tidy village of Fellhaven.

Now his life was tangled and painful, and challenged by the woman who lay awake in his embrace. She had taught him to value the beauty of the steep fells and the high meadows, had made him heed the cycle of the harvest, laugh with the children, and understand the intricate weave of life.

He was shaken to his soul. Looking ahead seemed as bleak and lonely as looking backward. The only moment that seemed right and real was this one. He fumbled with the curls at her temple, left a kiss there, and tightened his embrace. The aching in his chest made his hands quake and his voice unsteady.

" 'Tis for a husband to sleep beside you, Mackenna, no other." The words tumbled out of some other man's life. A man who wanted a wife and children and a home—not a soldier, not him.

His whispered words cut into her like a rusted knife. Husband. She never should have touched him the night he'd first ridden into her life. She was glad she had never told him about the purpose of the circle. She'd chosen him for a husband. Someday, very soon, she'd have to choose another. She had promised.

She slipped out of Thomas's bed and wrapped herself in a blanket, then settled into the chair in front of the hearth.

"Good night, milord."

The bed creaked as he left it. His good night came from above and behind her. He stood there while she watched the flickering faces in the flames. Some were haunting, others frightening, and still others called her to her dreams.

She awoke in Thomas's bed.

They spent the following morning arranging for more supplies and transportation back to Fellhaven. Edward and his entourage were packing for the great assembly at Berwick, where the Scottish lairds would choose between Balliol and Bruce.

Mackenna was eager to return home, where she knew

the rules, and the players, and how the pieces moved: where everything was as it should be. Her brothers would run the mill and the cart shop, she would run the village, the castle would lie in ruins forever—and Thomas Montclaire would never have come striding into her life.

She once believed he sought only her destruction; now she knew better. He sought truth and compromise, and had uncovered a measure of compassion she had forgotten in herself. He'd kissed her sparingly last night, holding back his passion but not his tenderness.

And now what? She was leaving a place of upheaval, and returning home to despair and emptiness, where Montclaire would live in the castle and she would take up her real life as a wife and mother in the village below. She had promised her brothers that she would marry as soon as she had eliminated the threat to the village. The threat had evaporated. Thomas himself, in his goodness, had seen to that. Fellhaven would always be safe in the hands of its honorable lord. He would never forsake the people she loved, because he loved them well himself. No man in all the world had a finer sense of right and justice. She no longer feared that another Gilvane would ride through the village and dispense his horror. That would be solace enough. It would have to be.

She said her farewells to the Giffards. Edward was his blustery self and gave her a bone-cracking embrace. And their caravan, now longer by two dozen carts, finally creaked into motion and began the lengthy trip home.

She spent the final night on the road clinging to Thomas, wrapped in his irresistible embrace. She hadn't moved to kiss him since leaving the castle, and he had seemed reluctant to do the same. But he was never far from her. His touch was a comfort and a heartache.

And as the valley broke open before her, revealing Mickelfell and the glassy glints of Dunmere, her heart sank to the lowest depths it had seen since her father died. Today she must break her bond with Thomas, for good and for all.

Everyone in Fellhaven turned out for the return of the lord and his entourage. Mackenna stood alone as her people bustled back and forth, each busy with a task. No one stopped to ask her questions; no one stopped to complain. There were smiles and greetings for her, but not a single request for advice.

A swarm of people had gathered around Thomas. His smile was so inclusive, from the widow Falke with her new wool combs, to the children he delighted with the oranges he'd brought for them. But the man who brought them hope had brought Mackenna despair.

She turned to the nearest cart and took over its unpacking, sending her legion of young helpers scurrying across the village with their deliveries. When nothing was left but the goods bound for the castle, Mackenna carried a box of vellum toward the rectory, hoping to avoid Father Berton. She had much to confess, but little courage. For the same reason, she would avoid her brothers for a time. Even as the thought spent itself, her reprieve ended.

"Welcome home, sister!" Galen embraced her fiercely. "I missed you, love. I truly did."

Cadell pushed Galen away and gave Mackenna a noisy kiss on her cheek. "Rumor has it you met the king! Did you, 'Kenna?"

"Aye, Cadell," she said, grunting as Bryce gave her a squeeze and passed her to Addis for another. "King Edward has all the charm of a rampaging bear. Reminds me of Galen."

Addis whooped. "Then you did meet the king! I told you she did, Galen! You owe me a crock of ale."

"And Mackenna owes us a husband," Galen said, the old irritation back in his voice like a death sentence.

She felt suddenly exposed and alone. "I haven't forgotten, Galen."

"Yet you've tarnished your reputation by taking up with his lordship—"

"I've taken up nothing!" Mackenna hoped her anger would disguise her blush of embarrassment. "Lord Montclaire and his bailiff visited Carlisle on castle business. I did very well by the village. I'll say nothing more on the matter, except that if none of my grooms are willing to take me to wife—"

Cadell snorted. "They are willing, and eager to know when you'll do your choosing."

"Are you still bent on your blasphemy, Mackenna?" Father Berton had slipped unseen between Addis and Bryce, and now stood frowning at her, his arms embracing a sagging sack of raisins.

Galen rounded on him sharply. "Your pardon, Father, but 'tis family business. Our sister promised to choose a husband when the village was safe. This Montclaire has proved himself a just and generous lord. Hasn't he, Mackenna?"

"Aye, Galen, he has." No one knew this better than Mackenna. To say differently would be a mortal sin.

"And so you'll be choosing when?" Galen prodded, crossing his arms against his chest.

Mackenna sighed, and said the first thing that came to her mind. "Three days from now." She didn't want to think any further ahead than that, and she wanted to choose and be done with it. "And I'll not make the same mistake again, Father. We'll meet at the mill, in private. As to right now—"

"Meeting in private, bailiff?"

Thomas. Cloaked in leather and cloves and dear memories, he whispered low against her ear, "Do you renew your rebellion against me?"

She heard the gentle teasing in his voice. He would be smiling, but she hadn't the courage to look him in the face. He thought her honest and brave. Her brothers shuffled uneasily, thankfully quelled by his presence.

"Nay, milord, 'tis no rebellion," she answered, hoping to lead the conversation toward the schedule for the mill and away from her coming marriage. "We were discussing dull and ordinary village business."

"Family business," Galen said, casting another glare

toward Father Berton, who seemed too pleased to see Thomas.

"Speaking of such," Mackenna said, quickly finding a new subject to explore, "how did you fare in Furness? You kept all your limbs, I see; are you money to the good?"

Addis preened. "We made you proud, 'Kenna. You'll see!"

Thomas clamped his hand on Mackenna's shoulder. "And as you see, I've returned your sister safe and sound."

"If not slightly used!" Galen's face paled even as the words escaped him. "I mean—"

Thomas lowered his brow and his volume. "I know what you meant, Master Hughes, but you needn't worry that I have taken advantage. I have not."

"I told them so, milord," Mackenna said, blushing, and impatient to be away. She stuffed her load of vellum between Father Berton's chin and his sack of raisins. "We should leave for the castle, milord, else the carts will take all day—"

Feeling like a thief as she pulled her gaze away from Thomas, she started past him. Another moment or two and she'd be away from Galen's questions. She would tell Thomas tonight.

"What about the banns, Mackenna?" Father Berton's words stopped her beside Thomas. "Will you be wanting them said *this* Sunday?"

A moth doomed to the flame, Mackenna looked up into Thomas's midnight eyes.

Thomas wasn't sure he'd heard right, but his stomach twisted anyway. "Banns?"

Mackenna wanted to run from the confusion in his eyes.

"Then she hasn't told you of her promise to her brothers, my lord?" Father Berton asked. "Mackenna is to be married soon."

"Married?" Thomas thought the world was tilting. He'd believed he'd sealed up the part of himself that wanted to stay and keep Mackenna forever. When the time came to leave the castle to the next lord, he would wish Mackenna great happiness and depart Fellhaven with a clear heart. But this news had run him through. "Mackenna?"

His voice broke, crowding her with the silence that followed. She couldn't move, couldn't speak.

"You didn't tell me," he whispered so quietly she barely heard him. "Do you marry for love?"

"For love?" She closed her eyes to escape the hollowed-out intimacy of the moment. But he lifted her chin with his thumb, and she was looking into a terrible darkness.

"Do you marry for love?" he repeated, his voice grown raspy and stern.

She swallowed the lump lodged in her throat. Even in anger, his touch was gentle. "In the village, milord, we often wed for circumstances, for our families, for property . . ."

"Those are your reasons?" His brows came together in an even deeper scowl.

"'Tis the way of it, Thomas. Do barons wed from the heart?"

He was so close his breath feathered her eyelashes. "For me . . . it will be the *only* reason."

"Then," she whispered, fighting the desire to gentle the lines on his brow, "I hope you will be boundlessly happy."

He ripped his gaze from hers and glared at the priest and her brothers. "Excuse me, Father Berton. Gentlemen."

Without a glance at Mackenna, he started away, then stopped. "You shall accompany the carts to the castle, bailiff. I'll be going ahead."

Mackenna couldn't see his face, but she knew he was waiting for her to say something.

"As you please, milord," was all she could manage.

His black-maned head dipped for an instant, then he stalked off toward the market square.

She'd been right all along: the new lord of Fellhaven had stolen everything from her, and filled her life with sorrow.

Chapter 18

"Good to see you, Thomas." Walter met Thomas in the inner courtyard before he'd even dismounted. Baylor huffled and snorted, clattering his teeth against his bit. Thomas looked thunderous. "Was the trip a success?"

"It was a bloody triumph." Thomas dropped from Baylor.

"Excellent. Did Edward promise more supplies?"

"Aye, some."

"Then tonight we shall celebrate!" Walter had only been jesting, but Thomas turned a slow, charring glare on him, then stalked off toward the stables, hauling Baylor behind him. Unwilling to give Thomas the peace he so obviously desired, Walter followed. "What happened in Carlisle?"

Thomas threw the reins to the stableman. "Nothing of lasting significance. How have things been here?"

"Very well, considering."

"Show me."

"Aye, Thomas." Walter led him across the bailey and into Mackenna's new office.

Thomas tried to concentrate on Walter's reports, but every mention of castle business recalled some bit of negotiating he and Mackenna had done together in Carlisle. Even the parchment betrayed him with her violet scent.

"Damnation!" Thomas slammed the quill into the ink

pot and yanked his fingers through his hair, which reminded him of the haircut she'd given him, and of her soul-melting kisses. Overriding the chaos of anger inside his head was the delectable melody that she hummed as she worked, and the huskiness of her voice, and the fall of her laughter in the night shadows.

"We formed a right fine alliance in Carlisle. We made purchases for the castle, for the village. We danced. We—"

"Save me from the details."

"There are no *details*, just . . . Who will Edward send when I've rebuilt his castle?" Thomas leaned against the door jamb, watching the bustle of activity in the bailey. Mackenna would be another hour with the carts—a very long hour, in which he would struggle with himself not to bolt down the trail to meet her.

"I shouldn't think it would matter."

Thomas pinned a dark glare on Walter. "It matters to me."

Walter trod carefully. "Because it matters to Mackenna? I understand completely. I'd make her my wife in a moment, if I thought—" Walter found his speech suddenly cut short by Thomas's fist twisted up in the neck of his tunic.

"That's enough, Walter! Not even in jest." Startled at his own outburst, Thomas quickly dropped his hold but couldn't shake his anger.

"I don't jest where Mackenna's concerned." Walter righted his tunic. "I'll thank you to remember you've no claim on her."

"And you do?"

"I make no claim but to that of wanting her. I've suffered having to stand beside her and discuss the carter's schedule while she swaddles me in springtime; or having that glorious mane of hers lifted by the lake breeze to brush my cheek, my hands—"

"You'd best stop now, Walter." In the wild days of their youth, they had made sport of their exploits with women. Maturity had brought discretion, but never jealousy—until now. It burned Thomas to the quick.

"You can stop marking the walls with your scent. I understand the way she makes you feel."

"She makes me feel bloody angry." Thomas slammed the bailey door and leafed, unseeing, through one of Mackenna's flawless account books. "I don't know when she was planning to tell me about it—" Thomas stopped as the image of Mackenna, grown large with another man's child, filled the space between him and Walter. "Bloody hell, Walter, Mackenna's to be married!"

"Married?" Walter sat down on the bench, his spirit suddenly withered. "Married to whom?"

Thomas opened his mouth to answer, then frowned. "I don't know. I don't want to know. Some damned promise she made to those worthless brothers of hers."

"Forbid the marriage, Thomas. 'Tis within your legal rights as lord. Or send her brothers to a tin mine in Cornwall."

"I haven't the right, Walter. Not the moral right. I am not lord here. I am a nursemaid."

Walter cleared his throat and asked quietly, "And if you were lord here, Thomas? If this holding belonged to you?"

Walter watched the thunder clear from Thomas' brow, swept away by the pure light of heaven. The man was in love.

"If Fellhaven were mine . . ." His face clouded as suddenly as it had brightened. "I would soon be a madman."

"So what *are* you going to do, Thomas?"

"Do?" That brought Thomas up short. His choices faded even as he thought them. He threw open the scrolled plans of the chapel. "I'll do whatever it takes. Now, show me where we stand. The sooner this castle is finished, the sooner I can leave it to Edward and his accursed bailiff."

Mackenna supervised the unloading of the carts in the bailey, glad for something to take her mind off her misery. Her bones ached to be back in Carlisle, back in that horrible place with those horrible people, where, in the midst of her heartache, she had found tenderness and goodness.

" 'Tis good to have you back, Mistress Mackenna," the cook said, peeking into the sack she had handed him.

"Spices, Master Skeat, from the orient." Mackenna caught his smile and nodded. "And I brought you four sacks full of cinnamon and cloves, pepper, turmeric, and—"

"Thank you, gal! I'll be right back with my assistant." Skeat ran off toward the keep.

Mackenna stopped to compare her list against the carpenter's, and then allowed the man to carry off his new tools. There were leather goods and steel and rivets for the armorer, and mason's tools, and two carts full of lime for the walls, with more to be delivered within the week.

She had spent nearly all of the purloined coins and no one had suspected a thing. Gilvane's hoarded treasure was already bringing joy to her village. Thomas had been right—sometimes justice had to be postponed.

Thomas . . . Nay, she didn't want to think about him. A clean break. It was the only way. She couldn't live here in the castle. Seeing him in the early morning as he began his day, falling asleep every night knowing that he was somewhere nearby, trying not to pretend that her life would always be as sweet. Working as his bailiff would be heartache enough. Telling him now while her courage was high would be the easiest.

But finding him was like seeking his shadow. She finally gave up and decided to peek in at her new office.

Thomas was bent over a drawing and looked up as the door squeaked open. She stood trapped in the doorway, feeling cold and uninvited. He'd lost color and his shoulders drooped. The wind whipping at her skirts was the only sound.

"I've finished with the carts, milord. I'll be going now."

"Going where?"

She stepped inside the office and closed the door. "I'm going home to the village, milord. 'Tis where I live."

"You live here at the castle." His words might have been born deep inside the mountain. His mouth bowed downward in a course she'd never seen before.

"You forget, milord: the village is my home." Her courage faltered in his silence. Thomas made it worse with his staring. "I should have told you—"

"When, Mackenna?"

"When?"

He rose and took his time stepping around the table. A jangle of spurs, creaking leather, his deliberate tread—the man's music would always haunt her. He came to rest a yard from her, the span of his arm and a lifetime.

"When did you and your . . . groom decide upon this match?"

"Decide?" He still didn't know. She closed off a laugh and touched her throat to keep the tears at bay. His eyes grew darker then, if it were possible, and she rushed forward with her defense. "Nothing has been settled, milord."

"I asked you that first night if you had a husband."

"I didn't then; I still don't. I had only a promise to my family. Then you caught me, and I was your hostage." Her cheeks grew hot in a blaze of anger for his part in this absurdity. "I wasn't about to divulge my secrets to you. Not then."

"And later? While you accepted my kisses and gave me your own, while you bathed in my chamber—"

"You gave me no choice, milord!"

He shook his head and his voice thickened, softened. "The choice was there all along, Mackenna. It was yours to make. You know me well enough, knew me well enough then. If you belonged to another man, by promise or otherwise, I would never have touched you. Never. And yet, you said nothing."

"Habit, Thomas."

"Habit!" he barked.

"I was your hostage," she hissed. "I am still."

"I release you." He lifted his palms as if he'd let go a robin into the sky. "You may travel the manor as you like."

And like that robin, she'd lost her way. "I can go home?"

"Aye, whenever you wish. But you sleep in the castle."

"In your chamber, I suppose?" she snapped, wanting his conscience to pierce him.

Thomas hesitated. "Nay. In your own chamber."

She snorted. "And you claim I am not still your hostage?"

"You're my bailiff."

She hugged herself and drew away from him to the opposite end of the table. " 'Tis not wise, to keep me so close, milord. Because . . . I do confess to a great longing for you."

Thomas closed his eyes. He didn't need to hear this. "A longing?"

"Aye, milord, and it needs breaking."

"Does it?" When he opened his eyes she was looking at him with a steady, clear-eyed resolve that made his heart ache.

"I'll fight you no more, Lord Thomas. We'll work together as proper lord and bailiff, for the good of all. The castle will be repaired. We'll prosper together—"

"Damn it, Mackenna!" The curse roared up out of his chest and he turned from her. She talked of longing as if it might wither instead of grow more vital with every breath. He wanted to know who the man was, this husband who would claim her, but he feared the knowledge. Would he beat the man senseless? Would he banish him? Would he act the beastly lord she'd always accused him of being? She'd robbed him of every defense and left him ready to surrender everything else he valued.

"Forgive me, Thomas." She dare not touch him. A brush of his hand and she would be in his arms. "You're

not the beast I once fashioned you. You're not a murder-
er or a thief. I denied the goodness I saw in you. I was
wrong. I'm sorry."

"Aye," he said quietly. "So am I."

She didn't know what else to say. "I'll gather my
things." When he didn't move, she started for the door.

"Mackenna." When she turned, he wrapped her in a
gaze that was as flinty as any cliffside on Mickelfell.
"You'll live in the castle, until I say otherwise."

"Aye, milord. Until then."

"Lord Thomas, you have a visitor."

Thomas winced as a careless young soldier was
knocked from the quintain to the rocky ground. "Who is
it, Daniel?"

"Father Berton. He waits in the solar."

"Excellent. Excuse me, gentlemen." Thomas left his
officers and hurried from the training area into the keep.
He put out his hand as he entered the solar.

"Good afternoon, Father. Good of you to come so
quickly."

"My pleasure." The priest's handshake was firm and
fervent. "You've worked miracles since last I was here."

Thomas looked around at the restoration. "The gla-
ziers finished the windows only yesterday," he said.

" 'Tis a very pleasant room. I sense Mackenna's hand
in it."

"You sense rightly. Her hand is in much of the castle."

"As it is in the village. But 'tis been good for her to
have something else on her mind for a change. She's
been the heart of the village for so many years, we'd
forgotten how to live on our own, or even that we
could."

"Mackenna does take hold of a cause and not let go."
Thomas offered a bench to Father Berton and the priest
sat down.

"Aye. That was her father, too. A good and wise man,
but stubborn and outspoken. It cost him dearly, and
Mackenna, as well. I didn't know her mother, but I
understand she was a beauty. Died of childbed fever

after birthing Mackenna. Hughes never remarried. As soon as she was old enough to speak, Mackenna started raising her elder brothers, if you can imagine."

"I can. She has her own opinions."

"You are kind, Lord Thomas." Father Berton smiled too slyly. "But then, I would expect that of a man in love."

Thomas looked down at his boottops, then back at the priest. Confession was confession, whether it be spoken in a solar or in a chapel. "Aye, that you would," he said, feeling the shyness of youth and a sudden, very adult exaltation as his words gave life to the declaration of his heart. "Father, I've a question to ask. 'Tis about the village and its marriage rites. My duties as the lord—"

"You want to know about Mackenna and her plans to choose a husband tomorrow evening."

"Her plans to . . ." Thomas held his breath, then expelled it in a rush as his heart kicked at his ribs. "She's *choosing* a husband? You mean she hasn't already? I thought—"

"My lord," Father Berton said as he stood and folded his hands, "I am a cleric, not a gossip. But before Mackenna makes another mistake, I suggest you remind her of her first choosing. Ask her about last Michaelmas eve."

"The night of Mackenna's rebellion? We've thrashed that night about, and the dust has nearly settled."

"I don't speak of her rebellion. I speak of her choosing."

"Her choosing?"

Father Berton canted his head. "Did you ever wonder what she was doing blindfolded in the middle of that circle of men?"

Thomas had often wondered. He'd never found the courage to ask. "She was dancing—"

"Was she?" The priest smiled.

"Or playing some village game?"

"Ask Mackenna. I'll say no more, except that you are a wise man who knows what must be done." He clapped Thomas on the back. "Now, I'd like to see your new chapel. It needs consecrating if there's to be a wedding soon."

Mackenna watched Father Berton take his leave of Thomas and stride across the inner bailey toward the main gate. Thomas was going in the opposite direction. They'd been together for a very long time, and had parted with unreadable expressions. Like a thief, she had hung back in the shadows.

Father Berton had been smug since her Michaelmas disaster. He'd been right to try and dissuade her from choosing a husband from a circle of men, but now he'd been pressing her to tell Thomas of her folly, to confess that she'd chosen the lord of Fellhaven for a husband. What good would that do? None that she could see. Thomas would laugh at her foolishness; worse than that, he'd lose even more respect for her than he had already. They were lord and villein, and nothing in this world could change the fact.

But she had to know what they'd talked about. Clutching her cloak around her, she started off after Thomas. She caught up with him as he was lifting a breast plate from a wooden rack set into the armory wall.

"Polished to perfection, Cleavon. Very well done." He held the shiny metal above his head. "Polished well enough to see a beautiful woman approaching from behind."

Mackenna stood behind Thomas, peering up into the burnished plate. "Beautiful? Is that how I appear to you, milord? It makes my nose look overlong."

"I was speaking of beauty 'neath the skin, my dear."

Cleavon and his assistants climbed over each other with compliments on the color of Mackenna's hair and the brightness of her smile and the rose of her cheeks, until they realized that Thomas was frowning at them. Cleavon scattered his men with a wave of his dark-stained hands.

"How is Father Berton, milord?" she asked, trying to appear as breezy as the November day.

"He seemed in a very good humor."

"What did you and he talk about?"

"He wanted to see the new chapel. He thought it very fine."

"And, milord?"

"And I wonder why you never told me the name of the man you plan to marry."

"His name?" Her heart thumped around inside her head.

"Nay, don't look away from me, Mackenna. I know there is no man to name, because you're to choose one tomorrow evening."

" 'Tis a village custom." Or would be as soon as she did it. "What else did you talk about?"

He studied her for a moment, then shrugged as if he were bored. "I confessed a sin or two," he said, setting the breast plate back onto its peg.

"You didn't!" She was suddenly mortified. If Thomas had confessed his sins, then surely Father Berton had learned of Carlisle and Penrith and . . .

Mackenna grabbed his arm and hauled him out of the suddenly stifling armory into the windswept bailey. "Tell me what you said to him!"

"I will not! Confession is a private matter."

"Not when it concerns me!" she hissed.

"What makes you think I said anything about you?"

"Because I've been involved in half the sins you've committed since you arrived here."

Thomas smiled down at her upturned face. "Then you and I disagree about the nature of sin, my dear. But it may soothe you to know that I said nothing that he didn't already know."

She frowned. "What does that mean?"

"Father Berton is a very perceptive man. Outside of suggesting a rather steep penance for my sins, he told me to remind you of something."

"And that was . . . ?"

He leaned closer, prepared for a well-danced jig around the truth. "He said to remind you of your first choosing."

"He said *that?*" Mackenna swallowed. But she didn't want Thomas ever to learn of her folly. That night, it had been a weapon he might have used against her schemes; today it would lay waste to her heart.

"What did he mean, Mackenna?" Whatever she was hiding from him, he would know before he let her out of his sight again.

A whirlwind whipped around the corner of the building and tossed up a cloud of leaves and straw. She coughed as the dust rose up into her face. He took her by the hand and guided her up the new stone steps into the chapel.

"Here, now," Thomas said, plucking a length of straw out of her hair. "We're away from the wind and prying eyes."

"Aye, but I should be leaving." She took a short step backward, into a stone wall. The wall in front of her was just as impenetrable, and pinned her with his demand.

"First, you'll tell me what Father Berton meant."

"He meant . . . well . . . I don't know, milord. Unless . . ." She sorted through plausible answers for something that Thomas might believe. Truth was the only thing he seemed to recognize anymore, and she couldn't very well tell him that. She had been such a fool! Trying to choose a husband from a circle of men, then mauling the lord of Fellhaven instead.

"Unless what, Mackenna?"

"Well . . . unless he meant . . ." Shades of the truth would have to do. She looked up at him, setting her brow earnestly to make her half-truth appear whole.

"Yes?" His eyes were half-lidded with suspicion, as if he knew each word would be a falsehood.

"He said that I've been unwise in choosing to have a longing for you . . ."

Thomas towered above her, his eyes becoming narrower and glinting brighter, as he leaned down and down until his nose was nearly touching hers.

"I don't think he meant that at all, Mackenna Hughes."

"Well . . . then, I don't know."

He was wearing that almost-smile again, the one he wore when he was about to kiss her, when his lips would part and she would watch them, fascinated. Closer, and his moustache brushed her cheek; his breath warmed it.

"Nay, Mackenna, one cannot *choose* to have a longing, never one such as ours." He cupped her chin, laying his fingers aside her mouth.

Then he kissed her, softly, tenderly. He was warm, and threaded his fingers through her hair, cradled the back of her head in his large hand, protecting her against the stone.

"I have . . ." she breathed against his mouth, wondering when her fingers had strayed to the curls at his nape.

"You have what, love?" He brushed his kiss against each corner of her mouth, and drew in a sharp breath when the tip of her tongue caught the arc of his lip and invited him in.

He was shaking with the banked fires of his near-spent temperance. He didn't know the day or the year, or even his own name, but he knew Mackenna was warm and melting against him. She tasted of brook-water, clean and honeyed with sunlight. Her tongue stroked his, and he held back the ferocity of his desire for her. It would break them. It would frighten her just as it frightened him. The sweet perfume of pine and fresh mortar blended with her erotic violet scent in the chilled air of the chapel. Outside, the wind tore at the new glazing.

And they were an island of fire and surety.

"I have . . . what, milord?" Mackenna sighed, having forgotten the subject they'd been discussing.

Thomas stepped closer and imprisoned her against the arch, his face buried in her hair, his arm still cradling her from the cold, hard stone. He lifted her hair, nuzzled that vulnerable place behind her ear, and set her to whimpering with his impossible courting. And all the time, he whispered his wonder to her, called out her name in a voice raw with emotion.

She drew him closer, arched against his length, felt the fullness of his passion against her belly, and the tingling ache in her palms when she imagined touching him there. Each breath drew in more of his scent, drove more of him to her core. She wanted him inside her, to live within her heart, to be her pulse. She wanted to receive his touch as he stroked Baylor or peeled an orange or gripped his sword in battle. When she married and grew large with another man's child and lived a separate life in the village, she wanted to be in his eyes as he walked the ramparts of the castle, his dark mane lashed by the harvest wind that rose up from the valley.

Her eyes began to burn with tears, tears that would consume her. "Nay, my lord," she whispered against his ear. But she hadn't the strength of will to push him away. He was her conscience and her code. If he would have her here in the chapel, she would give herself, gladly, wantonly. But he wouldn't. This man of honor and courage would stop them from defiling God's dwelling.

A groan rumbled out of him and into her as he pulled her from the stone pillar and held her in a fierce embrace. He kissed her hair and her face and her neck, the rise of skin at her breast, branding her with his mouth and hands as if he would bind himself to her.

"Sweet, tell me what he meant," he whispered, dashing his breath against her eyelids. "Tell me about that Michaelmas eve."

The truth contained her hopes and an aching irony. It was the difference between them: the lord and the miller's daughter. Now he held her face between his huge, hot hands, his gaze never shifting from hers, though she would look away if she could.

"You'll think me foolish, milord."

"Arrogant and stubborn, but never foolish, love." He kissed her too tenderly, and she lowered her gaze.

"You thought I played at a game that night."

"Blindfolded and dancing in a circle of men; I remember."

She knew their world would change. He would find her pagan and laughable. She looked up at him. " 'Twas no game, Thomas.''

"So Father Berton hinted. What was it then, Mackenna?''

She swallowed. "I was to choose a husband from among them.''

He straightened.

"I was to marry the first man I touched.''

She'd never seen his brows drawn so completely together. He leaned closer, as if he hadn't fully understood.

"The first man? But you touched . . . *me*, Mackenna.''

"Aye, milord. I did.''

The cold hit her like a wall of ice as Thomas stepped away from her. His chest heaved like a buck brought down by a feathered bolt. His face was a mask, shadowed and foreign. The wind chattered at the loose panes of glazing; it thumped at the door as if seeking permission to whisk her from his sight.

"You chose *me*,'' he said, so sharply that his words made her flinch like the slamming of a door.

"You shouldn't have been standing there, milord,'' she said quietly. She waited for his anger, for anything but his stony silence. "You're not one of us, milord.''

When he looked down at her, his face had hardened to granite.

"God help us both, if I were.''

Before she could reply, he dropped her hand and left through the chapel door.

Mackenna sighed. This wasn't the same Thomas who'd left her standing in the chapel the day before. He was looking at her in the same intoxicating way he'd done when he'd come whistling into the hall at midmorning, full of himself and famished. Now that the afternoon was nearly spent, he seemed even more jovial. He'd become heartlessly good-natured.

"Yes, milord?'' she asked him finally. He'd found her here in her office, placed a sweetcake in front of her, then had sat down across from her at the table as if he had all the time in the world. "Were you going to ask me something, milord?"

"What? Oh, nay, my dear. Just gathering wool." He caught a length of her hair that dangled on the table and curled it around his finger.

"Speaking of wool, milord, I have a confession to make."

"Another one?"

Not trusting his mood, she disentangled her hair from his teasing. "A confession I forgot about until just now."

"And that is?"

"I stole 655 sheep from you." He didn't seem to care, just sat loosely on the bench, his back against the stone wall. "Thomas? Did you hear me?"

"Aye, and have you given these sheep back to me?"

"Not yet, but I will." She rose and put another scrap of firewood into the small hearth—any excuse to be away from his vigilant gaze.

"When?" he asked. "As your wedding present to me?"

Mackenna looked up at him. He might as well have struck her with a stick, and he knew it. He obviously didn't care.

"Milord. They are your sheep. I cannot give them to you, if they are yours already." She stabbed at the fire.

"Do you like your new chamber?"

"'Tis grander than a bailiff deserves."

"Do you sleep well? Are you warm enough?"

"My bed's not been warm enough since you left it." Her pulse rattled when she realized what she said. His smile was far too wicked, and brought with it a flood of memories. "I should be staying in the village. I will be, when I'm married."

"I miss you, Mackenna," he said too quietly.

She turned on him. "Milord, don't you have something to be doing? Training your men, or hovering over the plasterers? I thank you for the sweetcake, but I am very busy."

"And very beautiful."

"Milord!" Surprised at his persistence, she presented a stiff frown and kept it there.

"Your pardon, Madame Bailiff." He smiled and rose from his lazy sprawl. "I know when I'm not wanted."

"Nay, milord. I don't think you do." She caught herself and covered her mouth with two fingers. "I mean—"

"No offense taken, Mackenna. You think me a beast. I've learned to live with your disapproval."

"I don't disapprove."

"Ah, then you haven't broken yourself of that disagreeable longing for me?" He wore that indolent half-smile again.

"I'm working on it." But she couldn't look away.

His laughter was low, and traveled along his fingertip as he traced her jaw. "Choose your husband well, Mackenna. You'll not get another chance this time."

He teased her mouth with a quick kiss, then left her dreading the coming evening.

Chapter 19

It was Michaelmas night all over again. Mackenna's head was spinning, and her bridegrooms stood gaping at her. This time, she was standing on a grinding stone in the mill, watching Galen pace imperiously in front of her suitors.

"There will be no game of chance tonight," he said, casting a challenge toward her. "And, God willing, no interruptions."

"Then let's get on with it!" Owyn brayed. He'd grown a beard, a wiry thing that crawled down his neck into his shirt. The man might as well go back to his smithy, for all his chances. Richard had his fingers laced together as if he were praying; Kyle stared shyly at his shoes; Lucas winked whenever she glanced his way.

Aye, 'twas just as it had been on Michaelmas night. Nothing had changed—nothing but her heart and all her hopes. She told herself not to look for Thomas; he wouldn't come. He would have no interest, save a lord's, in village life.

Father Berton stood nearby, peering past her toward the mill doors, a frown stiffening his brow. He spared her a glance, then went back to his watching.

" 'Tis time to choose, Mackenna." Galen motioned her forward, and she felt a surge of resentment toward him and everyone else in the room.

"I know that, Galen," she snapped.

"Then do it."

Addis squeezed her hand and whispered, "If this husband isn't good to you, 'Kenna, he'll have me to reckon with."

Good to her? She nearly laughed. How could she measure any man against Lord Thomas Montclaire's goodness? They had met in the exquisite breach between two unforgiving worlds; 'twas time for her to return home where she belonged.

"Come, Mackenna," Bryce whispered. "Have you decided?"

"Have I . . ." Decided? In all her ramblings and denials, she hadn't given a single thought toward this night's choosing! She swallowed the lump in her throat.

"Well, of course I have, Bryce." Fighting down an oppressive panic, she quickly scanned the room to remind herself of her choices.

Robbie? Too young. Lucas?

"Well?" Galen hissed. She scowled at him. She wouldn't let him hurry her last moments of happiness.

"After careful consideration," she began. "Well, uh . . . I've chosen . . ."

Richard? Garvey?

"You've already chosen, bailiff."

The rumble of Thomas's voice drew Mackenna like the shore draws the tide; hope and despair turned her toward the door.

He was dressed for battle in his padded leather gambeson, a wine-red cloak, tall black boots, and heavy, steel-studded gauntlets. He wore no helm; he needed none to assert his station. He was lord of Fellhaven and, damn the man, he'd obviously come to disrupt and delay.

"Go away, milord," she said, sensing her cheeks growing more and more crimson. She wanted it to be over quickly, mercifully. Another two heartbeats and it would have been done.

"Lord Montclaire, this is your village," Father Berton said smoothly, almost grandly, as if he'd spent the night rehearsing. "'Tis your right to be here."

"'Tis my right, indeed." One step sounded in the

silence, a metal-clad heel and the jangle of mail. "And I do claim my rights, Mackenna."

"You have none in this, milord," she said, in a throat-scratching growl, closing her eyes against her pounding heart and head. What the devil did he think he was doing?

"Look at me when I am talking to you, Mackenna."

She didn't; she lifted her gaze to the great, silent water wheel. "Go back to your castle, Lord Montclaire, and leave us to the business of the village."

Thomas's spurs clanked as they struck the stone floor. She could see him at the edge of her vision. She could feel him staring at her, willing her to look at him. She would not.

"You chose *me*," he said finally.

No one breathed. No one moved.

"As I explained before, milord, you were not invited into the circle," Mackenna said evenly.

Thomas snorted. "Unmarried and prosperous. I'm told these were what you required. I am both!"

"But you are *not* one of us, Lord Montclaire," she said, her jaw aching from the tears of outrage gathering in the back of her throat. "You can never be!"

"*I* was the first man you touched, Mackenna. Is there a person among you who can gainsay me?" Thomas turned and scanned the silent room. He snorted. "I thought not."

"Don't do this to me, Thomas!"

"Don't do what, Mackenna? Don't marry you?"

A rippling murmur rolled over the crowd.

Thomas frowned at her. She'd gone as pale as if he'd just threatened to hang all her brothers one by one, instead of offering marriage to her. He caught Walter's unsubtle grin from across the mill, adjusted his stance and his sword belt, then continued.

"Answer me, bailiff!"

"Thomas," she said, and looked him full in the face. "I can't marry *you*!"

"Can't?" he asked, finally impatient with her resistance. "You've no choice in the matter, Mackenna."

She drew herself up suddenly, her eyes narrowed at him.

"I've no choice, Lord Thomas?" Her challenge was low and guttural. "You're telling me that I *have* to marry you? Is that what you're saying?"

He nodded once. "That's what I'm saying."

Braving the fire in her glare, Thomas took her by the hand and broke through the crowd, past her brothers and the men whose dreams he had just dashed.

Mackenna finally found her voice as he lifted her onto a horse. "You've lost your senses, Montclaire! There can be no marriage between us. Not now, nor in the future."

Thomas took a long breath to steady his control. "Name one of your reasons."

"If I married a lord, then would I not be a lady?"

He'd been taken in by her logic too many times to grant her any point without study. "Aye . . . that's the way of it."

"And once a lady, I would then be a noblewoman. And I will *never* stoop to being noble."

"John Gilvane is no example, Mackenna."

"Aye, he is a good example, and a vile memory I live with daily. But 'tis much more than that. Having spent a week among them, I am convinced of the iniquity of their lives. People who think nothing of taking favors for plundering the lives and property of innocent peasants—"

"You know me better than that, Mackenna."

"But you allow your king to manipulate your life. You hang on his words as if he granted you your every breath."

Judging by the rock-strewn trail her reasoning was traveling, now was not the time to tell her he had just that morning sent word to Edward asserting his claim to Fellhaven. The king would be pleased. The writ would be granted, but to tell Mackenna about it now would only invite trouble.

"We'll talk about this later, love. Walter, take her home."

"I'm not going anywhere!" She tried to slide off the

horse, but Thomas's ever-present hand had clamped around her knee.

"If she gives you cause, Walter, tie her to the saddle."

Mackenna leaned down to Walter. "You wouldn't dare!" But his scowl told her that he would. "So I am hostage again?"

Ignoring her, Thomas handed the reins to Walter. "When you get to the castle, stand over her until I return. I've some business to settle with her brothers."

He glanced over his shoulder at Mackenna's family. They looked stunned.

"Don't listen to him, Galen!" she shouted.

Thomas wound his fist in her plait and reeled her to him. "I've not forgotten the pit, Mackenna. Have you?"

"Pit or no, I can't marry you, Lord Montclaire!"

Thomas growled and dropped her plait. "Take her away!"

He closed his ears to her curses and strode back toward the mill. Bargaining for Mackenna's hand with her brothers would be simple commerce—not the pitched battle that would greet him when he got home.

"I won't marry him, Walter." Mackenna stood at the open window in Thomas's chamber.

"He loves you."

She didn't need to hear that. "Hearts don't matter in this business between castle and village. Common sense matters."

"I've known Thomas since we squired together for the king. He's not loved any other woman in all that time."

The admission warmed Mackenna, but she drew in a huge breath of cold air to dispel the comfort.

"You can't know all he gives up for you."

"He needn't give up anything. Let him stay in his castle and leave me to the village. That should be the way of it—"

The heavy door slammed open.

"Well, my dear, your fit of temper cost me a year's rent on the mill and a new house for two of your brothers."

Thomas was huge and breathing hard.

"Excuse us, Walter," he said through an inhospitable smile.

But Walter had already let himself out. They were alone, and Mackenna wasn't about to leave the safety of the casement.

"You never were very good at bargaining, milord."

"Remind me next time to ask your help," he said, throwing off his cloak.

"Thomas, you can't be serious about this . . . this—"

"This marriage between us?" He'd reached the casement in his long, slow strides. "I've never been more serious about anything in my life."

"We are not the same kind of people, Thomas. Ours would be a marriage between noble and peasant—"

"Between good and evil? Is that what you mean? We are not all monsters, Mackenna. You've met Lord Giffard—"

"Aye, a charming man who sent his sons away to be raised by strangers." She left the casement and Thomas's heated gaze for the impartial warmth of the hearth.

"Hugh and Garth were sent to Prince Edmund's household to live among their Lancaster kin, where they've grown up to be well-favored men among the king's own family."

"They were boys of five and six when they were stolen from their mother."

"Not stolen, Mackenna!"

"I will not have my sons taken from me. I will nurse them myself, raise them in *my* home, in *my* village—"

"Where they would have no advantage—"

"None but what comes of love and belonging. That is another difference between us. I would love our children fiercely—"

"As *I* would—"

"But you would send them away! One day they are small enough to comfort on my lap, and the next, they are torn from me and made adult strangers."

Thomas caught up a strand of her hair and lifted it to

his lips. "Is that what you fear, my love? That I would send away our children?"

Mackenna nodded, fearing her voice would catch and betray her. He brought her chin up, forced her to look at him.

"You have my word, Mackenna. Our boys will be gray old men before they leave our home. And only then if you allow it. And as for our daughters . . ." Thomas suddenly felt protective of his unborn children. "Let any man step foot in our home to take them from me, and I promise you he'll pay the price with his life."

She wanted to believe his bluster, but she knew better, and pulled away from him, going to the bed. "Why do you talk of children? You don't want any. Why should you care what happens to them?"

He followed her. "Where did you get such a fool idea?"

"From—" She couldn't tell him about the sinful gossiping, her sin of listening. She fluffed up his pillow, then hugged it. "You told me so in Penrith. 'Tis why you have not strewn your seeds across the fields of Europe. You don't want children."

"I save my seed to plant only in my wife's garden, where I may watch it grow." Thomas tossed the pillow across the room. "Bear my children, Mackenna, and I will love them as I love you."

A smile trembled on her lips. He wondered if a kiss would coax it from her. As he leaned down to bestow it, she shoved him away and put a chair between them.

"Nay, I'll not have you kissing me, Thomas Montclaire."

His smile grew lazy and lopsided again, the very worst thing he could do at the very moment she was most vulnerable. "What's the matter, Mackenna?" he whispered, advancing on her as she was caught in the glare of his gaze. "Have you grown bored with my kisses at last? Is your longing finally spent?"

"You . . . you're a thief."

"Nay, I'm nothing of the sort, love. You chose me. I'll not be denied my right to be enslaved by you."

"You're a baron. I'd have to live in the castle."

"You already do. Sweet 'Kenna, I'm a simple man who wants only to be a husband to you." He laughed ruefully. "One of many, it would seem. There was quite a knot of bridegrooms in that circle, as I recall. A hundred, was it?" He teased a reluctant smile from her at last, one that vanished as quickly as it had appeared, but the sort that left him wanting more.

"There were twelve men, milord. 'Tis prophetic that you made thirteen."

He frowned. "You think me a Judas?"

She looked away in answer.

"I'll not betray you or the village."

She nodded, unable to deny it. She trusted him with her village. That was a formidable endorsement, and coming from her own heart, it could hardly be denied. But there was something else that troubled her about him. Something that her ever-reliable memory had forgotten. Did it conspire against her too? He was standing behind her, his mouth warm against her ear.

"Come, be my wife. I'll not fail either of you."

Her pulse rose at his touch, at the directness of his pledge. She had already bequeathed him her home because she trusted him, why not her heart?

"Thomas, I am a common woman—"

"As uncommon as the stars that light the night sky."

"I'm a miller's daughter."

"My grandmother was the daughter of a lucky stable-man who happened to save the life of a prince."

"I don't want to live in a castle, Thomas—"

"But do you want to live with *me?*"

A moan escaped her. "That isn't . . ." She struggled to catch her breath. "Thomas, I . . ."

He turned her in his arms and studied her face. "Do you want to live with me as my wife, to let me be a husband to you and a father to our children? 'Tis what I want, more than my life."

She opened her mouth to say yes, but couldn't yet. Too much had happened too quickly. And he was far too wonderful. "I must have time to think on it."

He straightened. "You have until midnight."

"I'll take 'til March, milord."

"I'll give you 'til tomorrow."

"Epiphany."

"Next week."

"Christmas Eve."

"The banns will be read three times," he said evenly. "You can decide at the third reading."

"And you'll accept my decision?" When he nodded, she said, "Very well, Thomas."

She ventured a smile, and he bent from his great height to kiss her. She tilted her head to be kissed, and whimpered when he stopped just short of her mouth.

"Mmmm. I'd best not, love."

"Why not?" Her mouth was tucked just beneath his moustache, aching for his coming.

"I am nocked and ready to let fly. We can't start our life together making noisy and joyful love in our chamber with Father Berton awaiting us in the hall."

"Really?"

"He wouldn't understand."

It wasn't a kiss, but his clove-scented breath against her lips left her as light-headed as his kisses did. Mackenna thought she might die of his nearness.

"Come, love," he whispered, "We've a wedding to plan."

"She's driving me mad, Walter."

"You'll get no sympathy from me, Thomas." Walter followed Thomas' gaze over the ramparts. The lake and the village seemed closer now than they had when Thomas had first unfurled his banner over the skies of Fellhaven. "Have you heard from Edward?"

"Not yet." Thomas picked up a shard of stone and threw it as hard as he could into the brilliant morning sky. It disappeared into the azure brightness before beginning its arc downward toward the foot of the mountain.

"Nearly three weeks and no word from him. Perhaps you should go to him, Thomas. Tell him the situation."

"Tell him that I'm to marry without his consent, and want Fellhaven to secure my bride's acceptance?" Thomas snorted. "Think what kind of hell that would bring down upon us all."

"Waiting until after the fact won't make him any happier."

"Nay, but the deed will be done." Thomas looked out again at the distant peaks, feeling a part of the valley. A guilt-ridden melancholy plucked at him. "Am I cheating her, Walter? Without a true hold on Fellhaven, how can I hold her? Do I dare bind her to me by marriage? If Edward refuses my claim, I must take her away from here, away from her family and the village. She mistrusts the barony as it is. If I leave Fellhaven to the whims of another lord, she'd never forgive me. I cannot live with that. Nor can I leave her to another husband."

"And you cannot live with her in the village. Not while another lord sits up here, wondering what trouble you are brewing among his people: unseated by a king, husband to a known rebel."

"Nor can I give her up. I need her, Walter, as I need air."

"'Tis a problem that would grieve good King Solomon."

"Look there." Thomas laughed suddenly, and pointed to a rivulet of sheep moving across an autumn-stubbled field. "Mackenna admitted to hiding over six hundred of the beasts in one of the upper fields. Apparently, she's found time to return them to me."

"I told you to watch your flanks, Thomas."

"I am as blind and as dense as this stone where that woman is concerned."

"And as immovable."

Marry Thomas? Mackenna's heart raced every time she let the idea filter through her thoughts. She listened for dread and found only joy. She'd even brought Meg to stay with her and help make ready for the wedding.

A wedding that Mackenna had yet to agree to—a point which she mentioned to Thomas each time they

ended another panting embrace. He would smile and
nod, and then walk off whistling.

She allowed herself to be dragged up to her chamber
for a fitting. If the wedding actually took place, she'd
rather have been wed in one of the gowns Thomas had
given her. But she couldn't refuse him when he
presented her with a fine length of silk he'd bought for
her in Carlisle.

Now she was standing on a stool, a mere two days
from a decision that everyone but she thought was
already final. She wasn't at all certain this was a good
idea. Marrying the lord of the castle seemed a blasphemy against her father.

"A beautiful bride, a beautiful wedding."

Mackenna wondered how Mistress Bedlor could talk
so clearly with her mouth prickly with pins.

"Ah, he's a fine man, he is."

Meg winked at Mackenna. "Who do you mean,
Mistress Bedlor?"

The woman laughed and blushed. "Why, his lordship,
of course! Your mother would be proud, 'Kenna."

"Aye, but what about my father?" She hadn't meant
to ask the question aloud. "What would he think of his
daughter marrying the lord who lives in this castle?"

Mistress Bedlor plucked the pins from her mouth and
rose to her feet with a groan. She frowned and glared up
at Mackenna.

"Mackenna Hughes, if your father were alive, I believe that he would be downstairs right now beating his
lordship—" she grinned, "In another game of chess."

Mackenna sighed. "Aye, Father would approve of
Thomas. But he'd be as stunned as I am."

"Nonsense, girl. You've been lady of this valley for
years. 'Tis long past time you married yourself a lord."

Mackenna let them turn her, and tuck her, and they
finally finished just before dark. She needed to think, to
be alone. A nearly impossible feat these days, with
Thomas's men come to aid her at every turn and Meg
attached to her hip. The only time she was alone was in
the privy, and even then there was usually some impa-

tient person talking with her through the door or the
screen.

No one would think to look for her in the granary loft.
The structure was three stories of stone and wood, built
to house enough grain for a year-long siege. So close to
suppertime, the yard was deserted. She climbed to the
third floor, spread her cloak on a pile of sweet-smelling
sheaves, and then wrapped herself in it to think about
Thomas and his proposal.

The moon was low and bent its brightness through
the glazed windows, closed now against the coming
winter. But it was surprisingly warm in the loft, warm
and lazy. She fell asleep not thinking at all, but dreaming of Thomas.

She awakened in the dark to footfalls on the planking.
She bounded to her feet and backed to the window, her
heart slamming against her chest as if it meant to leave
the granary before her.

"Who's there?" she demanded. "And what the devil
are you doing up here?"

His low laughter slipped around her like an embrace.
"Trying to escape you, my love. It didn't work."

Mackenna giggled then hicoughed. "Hello, Thomas."

"My God, you're beautiful, Mackenna," he said. "Oh,
moonlight, you are shamed."

Thomas's nerves were flayed and raw. He hadn't
made a move for fear of setting the sheaves afire with his
need of her. He saw her smile as she touched the
window glass with a shy fingertip.

Mackenna's pulse throbbed to the beat of his steady
footfalls across the planks. The moonlight silvered his
brow and nose first, shadowed his eyes, then set them a-
glitter. His mouth opened softly as he lowered his head
and breathed her name, then pressed his lips against
hers.

Her sigh became an animal-like growl that surprised
her, and sent him rearing back.

"I shouldn't, Mackenna." His breath burned his
throat.

She laughed low in her chest. "Shouldn't kiss me?"

"I don't know if I can stop." His head grew light, his vision blurred as she plucked at the laces of his tunic. He pressed her hand against his chest, stilling her intoxicating motion.

"Sir, I am betrothed to you. Have been, it seems, since Michaelmas night. I have the right to undress you."

"Not here, love."

"Where then?"

"In our chamber, on our wedding night."

The ghostly objection to taking Thomas to husband flitted past her, unnamed. But the more she struggled to unmask it, the more it eluded her. She knew only that it was an incompatibility that she could never endure. "I haven't agreed to this wedding, *Lord* Montclaire."

"You will." He laughed and swept his fingers into her hair. He kissed her mouth and held her to him as he lowered her to the sheaves. "Ah, the prospect of making love to you each night—"

"Only at night?" She thought the question a valid one, but Thomas groaned and buried his breath against her neck, smoothing kisses there and making her gasp. He finally looked up at her, his eyes glinting with his ill-timed restraint. She drew her fingertips across his lip. "I should think that a swim in a creek and an afternoon of love-making among the mosses would be a fine way to spend a summer day."

"You make it hard for me, my lady."

"Nay, milord, it seems to do that all by itself." She touched his hip and he caught her hand and held his breath.

"I hope you'll be gentle with me come our wedding night, my wanton, unruly bride."

"You're the one with experience, milord."

"But you, my love, are blessed with an imagination that will surely slay me in our marriage bed." He flicked open the clasp at the top of her gown. He hadn't the slightest idea what he was planning to do, where he was going, or when he would stop. He toyed with the ribbon that fastened her chemise, tugging gently, his pulse thrashing against every part of him. "Shall I untie this simple ribbon?" He kissed the valley below her lip.

"Oh, I think, milord—" Then he kissed her chin and the soft place beneath it.

"You think what?" He trailed his mouth, then his tongue, down her throat. She tasted of honeyed violets.

"I think you should." She sighed as the ribbon came loose and her chemise opened at the neckline. She felt the tremble of his fingers, the heat of his breath, as he parted the fabric.

"Ah, sweet woman." Thomas loved her smell, loved the feel of her ragged, warm breath in his hair. He touched the underside of her breast through the linen, cradled it, brought its weight to his mouth. She caught her breath and rose up to meet his hand. He laughed softly then, and lifted her to her knees, near-drowning in her whimper.

"Thomas?"

"Yes, my lady?" He slipped his dagger from its sheath and nicked the seam that stopped the neck slit from fraying.

"What are you . . ." She'd been so taken with watching his hands, feeling them brush against her, she hadn't realized what he was doing until she heard the sound of the linen ripping.

"I want to kiss you here, my lady." He lifted aside the fabric and cradled a bare breast, then took the splendid, silky peak into his mouth. Hot and sweet and roused, she called out his name.

"Shhh, love," he whispered against the morsel in his mouth. "You're all the company I want."

Mother Mary! She feared she was going to faint for the pleasure ripping through her. She moaned and arched toward his tugging and tasting.

"And you, Thomas, I want no other but you." Hot honey flowed through her limbs toward her belly, toward the place between her legs that she hadn't given much thought to till this man had first whispered his fancy into her ear. She wanted his hand there, tangled in her curls, to soothe her longing for him.

"Touch me, Thomas. Please." She was a budding rose and he the sun, and she wanted his warmth against her.

But he gave a groan and lifted his magnificent head, breathing like his horse after a hard ride. "Two days, my love," he said finally, his chest heaving in his efforts to regain a steady breath. "We'll marry in two days."

"'Tis blackmail, my lord."

"'Tis love and honor, 'Kenna," he said, returning her chemise to her shoulders. "And worth the wait. I promise you."

Chapter 20

"Mackenna Hughes, what the devil happened to your chemise?" Meg stood amid the jumble of wedding day chaos, holding up the chemise Thomas had shredded. "'Tis split from throat to gullet—oh, I see! My, how you blush!"

"I'll forgive you your pointy nose, Meg."

"You've never been able to hide your leering at his lordship. But when the two of you walked into the hall the night before last, disheveled and straw-covered, as well as late for supper, you were looking at him as if he were formed of sugar and you had thought of a brand new use for your tongue."

"Mind your business, Meg, lest someone mind it for you. Have the boughs been brought up from the forest for the hall?"

"Aye, Sir Francis carried them for me, and stayed to help me . . . bind them." Meg seemed too shy of a sudden.

"You needn't pretend, Meg. I've seen you *leering* at him."

"I'm sure I don't know what you mean." Meg broke off a length of thread and tried to stick the end through the eye of a needle with nervous fingers.

"Then I'm sure you don't care to know that Francis likes three scrapings of cinnamon in his wine." Meg looked up at Mackenna over the needle. Her smile said she cared very much.

"He kissed me, Mackenna. Kissed me very well."

"Shy Francis? He must fancy you. Did you kiss him back?"

"I did. He's asked to sit with me at the wedding supper tonight."

"Ah, is there another wedding in the wind?"

"Mackenna, Francis is a knight. He'd never marry the daughter of a baker."

Mackenna felt suddenly faint-hearted. "Nor should a lord marry the daughter of a miller."

Feeling adrift on a treacherous sea, Mackenna let Meg help her into her wedding dress. The fabric seemed to take on weight from the air. She was a miller's daughter, not a lady. Thomas was a lord, a soldier, a warrior. He'd never settle peaceably in her village. He'd grow bored and leave her for his wars. His wars! She was about to marry a *soldier!* Dear God, no!

A sharp knock sounded on the door and Meg leaped over a basket to open it. Galen stood there, dressed in his new robes. He was beaming like a lord.

"His lordship awaits you, Mackenna." He held out his hand.

She sat down on the linen chest. "I've not said I would."

Galen frowned and stepped into the room. "You're going to marry his lordship, and you'll do it today."

"I can't." She wanted Thomas with all her heart, would lay down her life for him, but he was a soldier. The most unreconcilable difference between them. Why hadn't she realized it before she'd fallen in love with him?

"Come, sister."

"I'm not going, Galen. Tell him I said no."

"He told me this might happen. He said I'm to warn you of a dark, damp pit."

Mackenna would miss Galen, but, right now, he deserved the pit. "Tell his lordship I'm no longer impressed by his threats."

Galen had no more than slammed the door behind him, when it burst open again. Thomas filled the doorway. He looked magnificent in his soldier's garb, his gold buckles glinting, his boots polished, his robes full and trimmed in fox.

"I never said I'd marry you, Thomas. Not even yesterday when the banns were read for the last time; I never agreed."

He said nothing, but came straight toward her. She thought he was going to kiss her again, but he lifted her onto his shoulder as if she were a butt of wine.

"Brute force won't convince me otherwise, milord."

She didn't kick or claw, because she didn't want to hurt the lout. But she did curse him roundly all the way through the great hall and out into the guest-crowded bailey.

Father Berton awaited them on the church steps and exchanged a suspicious smile with Thomas. "A lovely day for a wedding, isn't it my lord?"

"Indeed, Father." Thomas set Mackenna on her feet and held fast to her shoulders. She was beautiful and frightened, and he wondered how he could ever have considered a life without her. "Now, stand here, Mackenna. We'll marry today, or else."

Father Berton raised his hands above them. "Most worshipful friends and family, we come together this day to witness the wedding of Lord Thomas Montclaire and our own Mackenna—"

"You can't force me to wed without my consent, Father."

The priest frowned. "Hush, Mackenna. 'Tis God's plan."

"'Tis his lordship's plan. And not a very good one!"

Thomas bent to her. "I love you, Mackenna."

"I love you, too, Thomas, which is a problem because you're a soldier," she whispered intensely. "You'll ride off to war!"

"When I must."

The fact confirmed, Mackenna turned to leave, but her feet left the ground and she found herself encased in Thomas' arms and facing Father Berton.

"Proceed, Father," Thomas said.

"I'm a selfish woman, Thomas," she explained without preamble. "Once I possess something, I want to keep it safe forever."

"That isn't possible, Mackenna."

"Then neither is our marriage."

He turned her inside the circle of his arms. "I'll keep my vows and never stray. If I'm alive, my love, I'll swim the deepest ocean and cross the harshest desert to return to you."

"*If* you're alive." She bowed her head. "You don't understand, Thomas. I waited each night of my life for my brothers to come home, could sleep only when they were all tucked in and sleeping. Even now I watch for Francis and the craftsmen and the laborers and all the others I've come to care for to settle into safety." She looked up at him, her cinnamon eyes dark with earnest worry. "So you see why I can't marry you."

He shook his head. "I don't see the connection at all, Mackenna." He turned back to Father Berton. "Continue, please."

"Aye, my lord. With what do you endow your bride?"

"A grist mill—"

"Damn you, Thomas!"

"Six-hundred fifty-five head of sheep—"

"Listen to me!" She shook him by the sleeves. "You'll leave me one day and ride off to do Edward's fighting for him; you'll be gone for years and years. I'll not spend my heart waiting by the door for you to return from your damnable wars!"

"And I'll not spend mine waiting outside our chamber door while you bring our children into the world, Mackenna."

"It isn't the same, Thomas."

"It is, my love. I've sat up through the night with many a friend while the screams of their wives pierced stone walls fifteen feet thick. The anguish near brought me to my knees, and I had no stake in the matter but friendship."

"Men don't belong in a birth room."

He fixed her with a glittering gaze. "Make no mistake about it, woman. *I* will be there beside you when our children are born, as surely as I will be there when they are conceived."

She was more shocked by the vehemence of his statement than by his bellowing it in front of all these people, who were staring at them again.

He loved her. He'd become the beating of her heart.

"Then I'll go to war with you, Thomas. You'll not stop me."

"Not unless you take up the sword, my love. I draw the line there." He smiled and took her hand between his.

"I warn you, Thomas, once you have me, I'll never let you out of my sight. I'll be your shadow and your shade."

"Then I take thee, Mackenna, to my wedded wife," Thomas said through his wide grin, "to have you, and to hold you from this day forward. You see, love, 'tis there in my vow, and so 'tis here in my heart."

His heart beat steadily beneath her hand. She prayed it would beat forever. "I'll marry you, Thomas. Not because I'm brave; I do it because I love you."

The air seemed suddenly sweeter, the sunlight brighter, as Thomas slipped his ring onto Mackenna's finger. A cheer rose up around them. He closed her hand in his and set a kiss to the golden band.

Then he turned to her there on the chapel steps and made love to her mouth until she was whimpering and unable to walk.

"'Tis done?" she asked, unbelieving, though his kiss still heated her mouth and the crowd still whooped around them.

"Aye, my sweet wife. My Lady Montclaire."

"Lady Montclaire?" Mackenna looked out over the pandemonium: Thomas's brazen banners flapping on the battlements, his garrison of soldiers glad-handing the villagers, her brothers handsome and smiling in their new robes.

Then Thomas gathered her into his arms and kissed her again till she was dizzy.

Whatever would her father have said?

Thomas led her into the great hall to a roaring tumult. He had wisely hired jugglers and troubadours to entertain while he and Mackenna had celebrated their private wedding mass.

Now wine flowed as water, and the feast would have fed the village for a year when times were bad. But Mackenna kept her worries to herself, and held fast to her new husband.

"My turn, Thomas," Walter said, taking Mackenna's hand and leading her toward the dancing that had begun at the center of the hall. "Come, Lady Montclaire."

Thomas blew his bride a kiss and looked down to find little Haitha tugging at his sleeve. Her hands were stained with blackberries. She crooked her finger, and he bent to her.

"Will you dance with me, Lord Montclaire?" she asked.

Thomas knew he was grinning like a fool. "I'd be most honored, Mistress Cotes."

Haitha's two sisters claimed him next, and then he managed to snag Mackenna from her line of partners.

"Sorry, gentlemen, she's mine now."

"And forever, my lord husband." She kissed his thumb, brushing the tip with her tongue.

Thomas groaned. "'Tis time, Mackenna," he whispered, as he turned her in step with the tune.

"'Tis past time, husband," she said as he turned her again.

The music parted them, then brought them together. "They'll want to see us well bedded," he whispered, thankful not to be at court where Edward would surely see their marriage underway with the greatest amount of embarrassment.

She frowned and shook her head. "I want you alone, Thomas."

"As I want you. And so I have a plan. So bold, so daring . . ." He scooped her into his arms and left the dancing.

The dancers parted for them, smiling, bantering. A roar began as Thomas started up the stairs with his bride. As the surging sea reached the bottom step, he turned and stopped the them with the strength of his glare.

"If you'll pardon us, honored guests. 'Tis time my bride and I retire for the evening. Please enjoy our hospitality: drink our wine, eat our sweetmeats and venison; dance; sing if you like. But, on pain of death and dismemberment, do *not* disturb Lady Mackenna and me. She's a light sleeper and I need my rest, as well."

The laughter roared up the staircase after them and accompanied them down the hall toward their chamber. But no one followed. Walter and Francis would see that they didn't.

Thomas set his bride on her feet only long enough to gather her against him and thread his fingers through her hair. He looked down into eyes of shimmering cinnamon. Never strangers, he'd known her all his life, this unimaginably significant rebel. He'd been the hostage all along.

"Do you know that I love you, Lady Montclaire?"

"Aye, my heart, and I love you."

His wonderful mouth was suddenly everywhere. She loved it when he touched her face. And 'lady' did sound like an honor when he said it. She kissed him, held his face still, so she could get enough of him. Nay, never enough, but some purchase on him. His hands were huge and warm even through her gown as he ran them the length of her back, cupped her backside, and pulled her against his hardness.

"You're very forceful, my lord."

"Am I hurting you?" He loosened his embrace, but she tightened hers.

"I mean that you sent our revelers away with the very

sound of your voice." There was the smell of mulled
wine and pine bough, and always Thomas and his
cloves.

" 'Twas our only defense. I've known bridal reveries
that kept the groom from his marital duties well into the
next day."

"The poor bride. Sitting alone in her chamber, waiting for the man she loved to—"

"Rarely loved, my sweet. And never as I love you. I
daresay some brides would willingly wait uncomplain-
ing, for a year or ten, for their groom to be thrown into
their bed."

"Waiting would be worse. 'Tis best to get it over and
done with." She looked toward the bed. It was draped in
fine linen and plumped with down; the rushes were
gone from the stone floor, in their place a carpet of furs
and braided mats. Scented steam rose from a tub set
near the hearth.

"Done with? Is that what you think?"

" 'Tis what I've been told by some."

"And by others?"

"They say 'tis best if one's groom tarries at his task."

"So says the woman who would have torn my clothes
off two nights ago in the granary had I not . . . tarried."

"I only know that we are married and I'm still reeling
from the idea. I cannot imagine what you will do with
me tonight."

"I plan to make you moan and sigh and howl my
name as you did in the granary—"

"I howled? When?"

He laughed. "When I did this to you."

She watched him dip his head to her naked breast and
caught back the howl in her throat. The sound erupted
into a kind of mad laughter. "You've taken my clothes
from me, my husband!"

"Only your gown and these ties that hold your
chemise. How is this? 'Tis slit clear down to your naval.
Not by my doing, for it is hemmed this time." He looked
up into her smiling eyes.

"Fashioned especially for you by my own hands. You

seem hard on my undergowns. Will you be as hard in my hands as well?"

Her gaze was smoky and direct.

"When I have strength enough to allow it."

She smiled. "I should like to bathe, my husband, in that steaming tub. I've danced 'til my muscles are sore."

He guided her to the tub, and kissed her neck and shoulders as the silken chemise crumpled to the floor. He slid his hands down her sides, to her small waist, where he knew there was no belt to tie her hose. He'd seen the turn of her ankle in the chapel when she'd knelt to accept communion. It had been bare, nothing between his hand and her heat but the draping of her wedding gown and chemise. How his palms had burned each time his thoughts had wandered up his bride's skirts!

He lifted her now into the bath, and turned one last time from her nakedness. He wouldn't again, but the last thing he needed was more prompting. He didn't want to go off like a Chinese fire display. This night belonged to Mackenna, and he would give her pleasure until dawn pinked the sky.

While she hummed and splashed, he busied himself with the chalices of wine and lit a candle on the wall above their bed.

"Will you join me, Thomas?"

"Aye, my bride, but not in there." He slipped off his robe and started to remove his tunic.

"Nay, husband." In a great whoosh of water she stood up and ran to him. Her hair was loose and dry and hung round her in a curtain, while the rest of her dripped water as if she were a fountain.

"Nay, what?" he asked.

"Allow me," she said, unclasping the gold buckle that held his tunic together across his chest.

Thomas stood by silently, while his wife unlaced the tunic and unbuckled his belt.

"Now off with it, husband. Over your head."

He did as she bade and then stood transfixed by the touch of her hands, the rise and fall of her brows as she

studied him in his shirt and chausses. If she wished to
lead, he would try to let her. He would try.

"You are recklessly handsome, my lord husband, and
I want to maul you once again. Yet I want this night to
last for all time." She felt his laughter rumble under her
fingers as she unlaced the tie that held his linen shirt
closed. The sleeves were loose and cuffed, and the
shirttails hung down to the middle of his thigh where
his muscles shifted beneath his hosen.

"The shirt, too, Thomas." She crossed her arms across
her chest and tried to look stern. "Off with it!"

"Aye, my lady, wife," Thomas said as he obliged her.

Mackenna watched muscles stir across bone, sinew
made for war and for love. The cords of his stomach
rippled and made her want to touch him. His chest was
bronzed and lightly haired, and she settled her cheek
and her palms where his heart beat. "You are real, my
lord. I wondered all day if I were not dreaming."

"Aye, my sweet, we were wed today." He held her,
stroked her hair, while her breath played against his
chest. "There is naught can change that now. Not fire
nor flood nor royal writ. That is, if we plan to consummate this marriage."

Mackenna smiled up at him. "I do."

"So do I, eventually." He strained against his braies
and her belly from desire for the dark points of her
breasts pressed against his ribs. He would sup there, but
later.

"Mmmm," she said, moving her palms over his hips
and around to his backside. She spread her fingers and
kneaded his flesh and the taut muscles beneath his
braies. "You are hard here as well. These, too, must go."

His groan was mighty when she fingered the strings
that held up his hosen. They operated much like her
own, hung from the waist of his braies. With a tug, the
four strings loosened and his chausses slumped. Thomas bent and hauled them off, managing to kiss her
through it all.

Now she was left to remove his braies. Her cheeks
burned as she cast her gaze down the length of his chest

toward the dark swath of hair that plunged below the linen. The garment was slung so low on his hips that his manhood strained against the tie. How would she ever find the nerve to touch him there? She wanted to, yearned to, but how would she find the nerve? She reached out with her fingers and captured one end of the string.

" 'Tis very . . . crowded down here." She looked up at her husband, into a face so impassioned she thought he might uncoil at any moment. And she must do something before this wondrous, throbbing part of him quit working.

"You're killing me, my love. Boiling my brain." When his bride tugged on the string, stood back, and gave an awed little gasp, Thomas decided he'd taken all he could of the too-glorious moment. He set her from him, turned his back, shucked off his braies, and dropped into the cooling water of the tub she had deserted. He closed his eyes, and tried to transport himself back to one of the punishing treks through Gascony in the heat of summer. Not possible. He was in his wedding chamber.

And his extraordinary bride was standing at the end of the tub grinning at him.

Chapter 21

"I would have gotten your braies off you, eventually, milord. You were too eager. Give me your foot, please." He didn't and she smiled. "Just your foot, husband, not your manhood. I'm willing wait for that till you're ready."

"Mark me well, love, I am more than ready. But, my foot?" When she didn't answer, he reluctantly lifted one out of the water and balanced his heel on the edge of the tub.

He sighed loudly as she began massaging his toes, pushing at the ball of his foot, digging her thumbs into his arch. The harder she twisted and pressed, the more he liked it, the more he moaned as if he were in mortal ecstacy. He hadn't known his feet were aching until she'd started this marvelous treatment. He gladly changed feet and let her work on the other.

"Where did you learn this, Mackenna?" He pulled his foot beneath the cold water and looked at her out of one eye, suddenly interested in what other man might have received such attention.

"Just now. It seemed the thing to do." Mackenna reached into the water and brought his foot back. "And this . . ." She kissed the underside of his heel, his arch, drew her tongue over the ball, but when she closed her mouth over his toes she lost her grip on his foot as it disappeared under the water and Thomas rose up, roaring and behemothlike out of the sea.

He stalked to the casement and threw open the window, standing naked and freezing in the wind. Snow had begun to fall in huge flakes, drifting into the room and melting in the warm air before they landed.

"'Tis cold, Thomas." She came up behind him and used his back as a shield against the cold. Heat poured off him as off a brazier.

"'Tis the only way I'll last with you tugging and licking and . . . Damnation, woman. I feel like I've run from here to London and back."

"Come away from the window, Thomas. You'll catch your death. I can't have that."

"And I can't have you so willing, if I'm to last long enough to satisfy my bride." He heard her teeth start to chatter.

"I'm very satisfied right now."

His laugh was more of a snort. "Believe me, you've not been satisfied at all. 'Tis for the best if you stand over here." He walked her to the fire, settled a blanket over her shoulders, and left her there to stand at the window again.

"My lord husband, I don't know if standing soaking wet in a cold wind is truly cooling you down, but the sight of you at the window quite naked is heating me to my ears."

He snorted and turned his back to her. "Is that better?"

"Nay, milord. Your backside is nearly as intriguing as your front side." She sighed when he closed the window. "You are a wonder, my husband, my warrior." She smiled. "My lord."

Her voice reached out to him, wrapped his icy-damp skin in her warmth. She dropped the blanket and took a step toward him. Her hair swayed, its curling ends tangled in the shadow at the cleaving of her thighs.

She was Eve. And he would live here in Eden for the rest of his days.

"Thomas." He was that beast from her dreams, forge-cured and hard, his blade risen in mystery from an intoxicating darkness, her warrior husband whose eyes smoldered when he looked at her. She reached out to him and he came to her then, lifted her hair from her shoulders and draped it behind her.

"Ah, beauty," he said, stepping away to look, his eyes always rising back to hers after heating her. His breath was her blanket. He touched her cheek, then followed the ridges and hollows to her breasts, cradled them, loved them; slid his hands to her waist, to shape her hips and thighs; then he was on his knees, holding her against him, his mouth beneath her breast and on the flat of her belly. She felt her skin meld with his where they touched; and where she ached, he gave delight. He enfolded her with a reserve that made her love him even more.

This was enough for any man, he thought. If he died now, struck down by a stray arrow from the bailey, he would have known bliss that few men can claim. But the moment was slipping from him, this moment of intimate wonder as her textures first engaged his; her silk against his grit; her pliancy, his rigidity; feather and stone. Reverence and awe had banked his appetite; those same heady passions now sparked and blazed.

He slid his mouth along her belly to the gentle slope beside the patch of sweet-scented curls. She cried out his name and arched against him, held onto his shoulders as she pushed her hips toward his mouth. He left only a sigh there, and looked up at her. Her eyes were wide and bright; her breathing equalled his for its roughness.

"Thomas!" She bent her knees and slid down the front of him to her knees. "Do you plan to kiss me there?"

"Do you want me to?" He smiled as she nodded and flushed. He lifted her into his arms and carried her to the bed. Ever contrary, she scrabbled to her knees, leaving him to stand.

"Thomas, is that a place where a wife might kiss a husband, too?" She touched his hip with her open hand.

Not trusting himself to speak, he nodded.

She smiled, looking very pleased.

Every measure of zealously hoarded reserve finally broke open and surged through him. He sought her with his mouth and hands, and bent her to the embankment of pillows. He slung his leg between hers, and she opened to him like a flower, her legs parted, her thighs lush and welcoming. She mewled and sighed and arched as he suckled a breast, rolling the budded peak of its twin between his fingertips. She gasped and pulled him closer, her fingers twined in his hair.

"Husband," she whispered. The word alone now meant Thomas Montclaire, this wondrous man who wrought these ecstacies, who made sense of her life and loved her village. He nibbled on her neck and left a trail down her breast, where he drew in her nipple, caught it between his tongue and his teeth, and caused her to cry out again, "Husband!"

"Yes, my lady wife?"

He rose on his knees above her, a silly grin on his face, looking very much as if he'd been head-first in the honey crock. He was the wonders of the earth to her, seed and sod, sky and rain, the cycle of the seasons, the father of her children.

"I love the sound of the word 'husband,' because it is you." She held his gaze, then slid her eyes downward along the ridges of his torso to the dark concentration of fleece above his flexing thighs, to the sleek and consuming rise of his flesh. The sight of him heightened the ache between her own legs, the opposite part of him, where she could imagine their meeting when she welcomed him inside of her.

"I want to touch you here," she said, rising up onto her elbow and reaching for him.

Before Thomas knew her purpose, Mackenna had put her cheek against his hip and nuzzled him, was reaching for him, was opening her lips to hold him when he pushed her back against the pillows. He pinned her hands above her head and closed his eyes to escape the dawning pleasure in her eyes.

"I can't let you, Mackenna. Not yet." When he opened his eyes again, she was grinning.

"But soon, Thomas. For I do ache to take you to me." She brought his hand to her belly and slid it to the place of such deep aching. "Here, my husband." And she sighed into his ear.

He closed his eyes again, his breath blending with her moans as he flexed his fingers and combed through the curls there.

"Heaven bless me!" he whispered. He buried his face in the side of her neck but couldn't still his fingers. He explored her mouth with his tongue, parting her lips, even as he parted the petals of slippery dampness for his fingers.

She called out his name, and the name of three saints.

"These are carnal pleasures, Thomas? Sins?" She rose into his hand, seeking his closeness, wanting him to plunge deeper and swifter. But her husband seemed terribly content and determined to be leisurely where she would be frantic.

"We are wed to one another, love. One flesh." He mastered his breathing and focused his attentions on his squirming wife. " 'Tis the only way I know to make children."

"Surely not with fingers and lips and—"

"Aye, and tongues, Mackenna."

She heard herself howl this time, as he knelt between her legs and flicked his tongue where his fingers had just been, and were again, sliding, teasing.

"Oh, I need you, Thomas! Right away, or I shall explode."

"Need me, love? You have me."

"Will you make me beg? If so, I will, sir. Please!" Then he plunged deeper, but only with his fingers, two now. And she watched his eyes whenever she could keep hers from rolling back in her head. He would study her, then lean to her and kiss her mouth or a breast, or some other place of mystery, and all the while his hand was giving her pleasure, stroking her thighs, touching, plunging, holding.

She was liquid and sighing, and ready. And he was near breaking. Kneeling between her thighs, his hands holding his weight off her, he searched her face for lucidity. "You know I will hurt you, love."

"Not possible, husband."

"Aye, sweet, when your maidenhead yields to me." He rested his hand at her cleaving, dipped his fingers into her honey.

"I've heard so, Thomas. A man sunders a woman's soft flesh when he first enters." She sat up and kissed him. "But that is not hurt, husband. You cannot hurt me here." She covered his hand with hers where his fingers had paused inside her. "Hurt would have come if we had never met, if you had been the demon lord I accused you of being, if you had given up on me, if you'd not rescued me . . . My love!" She threw her head back as he lifted his hand and hers and took her to his mouth. His tongue caused riots and comet tails, and shot her upward toward some dream that stayed just out of her reach, a paradise kept from her through his purpose and plan.

Then he was at her ear. "If I give you pain, my love, cry out and I will stop. I swear on the lives of our children, and theirs, that I will try to stop."

She nodded and felt it then, a thick point of heat. The urge to impale herself on him, to fill up on his mystery was almost stronger than her will.

"Wait, husband!" She pushed at his chest and he sat back on his heels, startlement and dread in his eyes.

"What? Did I hurt you already?" He looked for panic and saw none.

"Nay, Thomas. I would see what you bring to me. I know your hands and your fingers, but this other part of your flesh you've kept well hidden from me. Though it sought me out of its own accord often enough." She rose up on her heels and moved toward him. "Thomas Montclaire, you are blushing!"

"I'm not. But *you* should be."

She laughed. "Your cheeks are cherry-stained, milord.

I only ask for your indulgence—a touch only, no kissing, I promise. Not this time, at least. But it is my right."

He would have refused, but her hands were close, and then holding him. She was sighing into his ear and fondling the sack that had tightened to an orb as she grazed the wiry hair. The sensation was deep and binding, and drew great rattling breaths from him; but when she bent to his shaft and held him and stroked him, all the while telling him how very stirring and dangerous she found him, he finally clasped her to him and carried her back to the pillows.

"You've had enough, wife, and so have I."

She looked suddenly wise. "That wasn't so bad, was it?"

His smile was wicked; his breath and mouth brushed at both her temples. "Aye, it was very bad. And I liked it very much. Now I wonder if you'll like becoming my wife in body."

"If 'tis anything so beautiful as becoming your wife in soul, then bury me in one of the high meadows come morning, for I will surely die of it tonight."

She spread her hands above her head, tangling her fingers in her hair, feeling like a meadow flower ready for his sunlight. His gaze played like a rising melody across her face as he kissed her mouth and her breasts and her brow.

"When, Thomas?" Then her hand was there between them, holding him, offering a shattering caress before guiding him through the petals. "'Tis the last I have to give to you." She tilted her hips out of instinct, and opened to him as he lingered, his heat an exquisite urgency.

"The last?"

"I gave you my village."

He groaned and held her hips quiet. "*My* village."

"Aye, the village is yours now. And the pressure is sweet."

"And you are ready for me, but it will hurt, love. Cry

if you must." Her resistance was internal and tight. Her arms were around his neck, drawing him to her kisses. He held her hips to the mattress, to keep her from lurching and shattering his control. The restriction only made her arch upward, brushing the hard points of her breasts against his chest. And still her hips moved, circling, wanting more of the building urgency. He didn't want to hurt her, but he knew no other way.

"Just come to me, Thomas."

"I love you, Mackenna."

"Please!"

"Dear love . . ." He locked his fingers with hers above her head. "Don't look away, Mackenna. Let me see you."

Her eyes glittered cinnamon and flecks of fire. "I love you, Thomas."

His growl was guttural and shattering, and carried him all the way into her sheath. She gasped, then stilled beneath him as he held her close, fighting the drowning waves that wanted to draw him out to sea, to dash himself against her again and again. He tried to calm the tremors that shook him, but failed. He wanted her, wanted to lose himself in the pounding waves.

"Are you hurting, wife?"

"Nay, Thomas."

Then he supported his extraordinary, possessive weight on his elbows, groaning as if in pain, blowing out great gusts of breath as he rained his mouth down on her temples and eyelids. He was quaking, still in need of something she hoped she could give him. She prayed that a child would come of this night. She held his face between her hands and kissed him. "You and I are one, now. There is no hurt in that. Only love and promise."

He smiled, a drunken, happy expression that made her circle her hips against his. He groaned, still breathing like a horse raced too hard. The tension was still there inside her, caused by her husband's splendor still buried there, unmoving, but sheathed so tightly she could feel his pulse. The thought made her light-headed. This feeling of waiting for something else would soon be dispelled by sleep. But the deed was done. It was over, and she had liked the rising passion. And felt only a little disappointment that such potential would end by sliding them back together to a breezy calm. But she had given Thomas her virtue, and had done so gladly.

" 'Tis done now, husband." She sighed and tightened her arms around his huge shoulders, kissed the side of his nose. "But you needn't leave me yet. I like to have you here inside me."

He fixed her with a look of surprise. "What is done?"

He was panting harder than he had been just after he'd claimed her. And each time he took another noisy, ragged breath, he moved a bit inside her and she trembled a little herself.

"The consummation, Thomas. We are one, in the flesh."

He smiled and touched her lips with his mouth.

"We may be one in the flesh, sweet wife, but 'tis not complete until we are one in spent passion."

He touched his fingers to his lips, then to hers, then combed through the hair at their joining til he found the nub that his tongue had teased to near-distraction. She gasped and tightened her knees around his hips. What was he talking about? If he didn't let her rest, she would surely die.

"Spent, how?" she asked, drawing the words through her teeth as he stroked her.

He smiled again. "How would you like?" He started to pull himself out, but she gripped his backside and tilted her hips to take him deeper inside.

"Don't go, Thomas."

"I won't. Not completely."

"If you promise . . ." She could feel his heart raging inside his chest. He lifted off her with his arms extended. His brow glistened with the same dampness that filmed his chest and arms.

"Believe me, love, I'll not leave you long."

His eyelids sagged, his brow dipped, but a dark light

sparkled from his eyes as he refilled her tingling depths. Her hunger for him, for his closeness, grew each time he drew himself out of her, and each time she gasped and insisted upon his return. His movements were slow and deliberate, and accompanied by a quaking that shook his voice and tore at his breathing.

"You are too sweet, my love. I cannot last."

When he took an aching nipple into his mouth, Mackenna felt it at their joining. The power shook her, made her lock her ankles around his backside.

She took up his rhythm, his breathing; abandoned her thoughts as he stroked her and crooned her name. He was her sky again, his dark eyes glinting above her as he carried her upward and upward, leaving her and returning, telling her the secrets of his heart and watching her, ever smiling down on her.

And he was with her when the stars exploded, when she strained with him, when pleasure and desire shattered into hot fragments of love and hope and dreams and molten honey.

Thomas saw the bliss unfocus her eyes, the half-lidded ecstasy. With his last shred of control, he let her climax ripple along the base of him, wanting to feel her most secret caresses before he abandoned himself to his raging desire.

"Husband, I pledge you my life . . ."

Her words of faith, whispered against his mouth, ripped ten years of control from him and sent him roaring into her, deeply, hotly.

"Sweet wife—oh, God . . ." The sound caught in his throat and became a long, low groan that finally convulsed him.

"Thomas!" His magnificent fullness stiffened and arched within her, sending her soaring again. He swabbed her hair aside and kissed her, pumping and plunging, the sudden, intoxicating pulse of him lifting her again to another release, more gently this time, a brief companion to his passion. He whispered her name, pledging his love as he spilled his searing seed into her and flooded her with life.

"Mackenna . . . my wife . . ." He clung to her mouth, drained, yet yearning for more. His throat ached with unspoken emotion.

Mackenna held him with unstrung muscles, the descent from his skies as lilting and peaceful as the rise had been fierce and unbridled. "I do believe we are well spent, husband."

"Aye, and well married, wife." He cupped her cheek.

"And well pleased." She moved her hips beneath him.

"Twice, my love?" He smiled at her confusion, and struggled to catch his breath. "Pleasured twice the first time?"

Mackenna grinned. "Is that unusual?"

"I'm told so. 'Tis not in my experience."

"Then I have married an unusual man. But I knew that, long before this night."

"You weren't afraid of this? Not ever?"

"Curious and uninformed." She sniffed the air. "The fragrance . . . is it always that way?"

"I don't recall. I was but a callow youth then, and rarely took time to notice such things."

"I have a confession, Thomas."

"A long-held, dark secret?"

"Nay, a recent sin that took place in Carlisle."

He rose on an elbow, an eyebrow held aloft. "And that was?"

"The sin of gossip. I listened when the ladies were talking about you."

"Me?"

"And while I was committing the sin of listening to gossip, Lady Appleton hinted that you denied yourself fleshly pleasures because of some tragedy in your past. And I shouldn't have listened, but I am curious about your life. So, you don't have to tell me, if you—"

He cut off her string of confessions and apologies with a kiss. "You need only have asked me."

"Then I'm asking."

He settled the blanket over them, protecting them from the chill. "When I was a young man, I was as randy as any lad let loose at court. I was ruled by my lusts, bedding one young woman one night and another the following night. Until . . . 'twas shortly before I took my knighthood, more than ten years ago. We were at Shrewsbury. I lay with a young kitchen maid who I knew had become quite enamored of me. She was willing, and I was such a piggish clod, I didn't notice I had taken her virtue until after it was over and I saw her maiden's blood on her clothes."

"You were not always the considerate lover you are now?"

"I appreciate the compliment, sweet. But no—though I wasn't entirely bent upon my own pleasure. But I was a piggish clod, nonetheless."

"Insensitive, Thomas. But that's no tragedy."

"No. But one came of it. I didn't love the kitchen maid, but I liked her fine enough. She was fair of face and baked a delicious gingerbread, and she was willing to meet me wherever I would have her. And . . . I got her with child."

"You did?"

"There was no other man but me. She was in love. I was . . ."

"Piggish."

"Aye, and she hid the pregnancy from me until I could see it for myself." He could see it still, the belly beginning to round. "I was so shaken by the idea of my babe growing inside her, I couldn't touch her. Twice I tried to bed her, but I had no passion for it. I didn't love her, but I instantly loved the babe. I would lift her skirts and stare, and stroke the roundness. In sad truth, I hardly remember the young woman's face, but I remember the quickening beneath my hand and the tremendous feeling of immortality and awe."

Mackenna felt the loss as he slipped from her and spread his hand over her belly. He was silent in his memories. His heart hammered against her ribs. She threaded her fingers through his hair, drawing a sigh from him. She kissed the top of his head.

"I watched her from afar, watched her skirts begin to strain across her belly. I had spoken to Edward. I would claim the child and support it, see that it was raised at court. Of course, I hadn't told this to the girl. I was not only piggish, but shy and arrogant. A destructive but customary combination in men. Then one morning I noticed the girl wasn't serving in the hall. I was told she'd been taken ill. I found her in the village at her mother's house."

"Was it the babe?"

He nodded. "It had come months too early. It was wrapped in a linen shroud, like a small loaf of bread, and it lay in a basket by the door, not yet buried. My child, Mackenna. I stared at this bundle of still-steaming cloth that cradled my flesh, and I wept." He swallowed. "I sat down on the dirt floor of that cottage, and wept until I realized where I was, and staggered out the door. I stayed outdoors that night, trying to count all the women I had lain with, wondering how many children I had fathered and lost, either by death or by never knowing they existed. I was reeling by the time I stumbled back into the castle the following dawn."

"I'm so very sorry, Thomas." She felt a scalding wetness on her breast. Aching for the man in her arms, she touched her lips to his temple. "What happened to the babe's mother?"

"A week later she died of childbed fever. I sent money to her mother; I still do—guilt money for taking her daughter from her. I watched the funeral mass from afar, but I was too ashamed to reach beyond that barrier of class and grief. I vowed it would never happen again. And I knew of only one way to ensure that it wouldn't." His eyes were glistening, his lashes damp as he look steadily at her.

"You are a very good man, Thomas Montclaire. And I love you for it. I have only one question, sir. If you were callow and unskilled as a youth, and celibate all these years of your adulthood, where did you learn to so please a wife?" Her brows were slanted and suspicious.

He rolled her on top of him. "There be dozens of ways to find pleasure with a woman without spilling seed into her."

"Thomas!"

"I took no priestly vow, Mackenna." She looked shocked and rose up on her elbows. "I made no regular thing of it, love. In truth, the temptation to break my oath was too powerful and best left unapproached. But I occasionally spent myself with a lady in other ways. And I make no apology for it."

"I don't ask for one. 'Tis just that . . ."

He feathered her ear with his lips. "I expect you will find my education especially useful during your flux."

"'Tis a sin to partake of carnal pleasure during—"

"Nay, 'tis an excuse for a man to seek another woman. I will have you whenever you want me. And while you carry our child in your womb, I will visit the babe gently and often, so it will never doubt its father's love. And I understand that pleasure eases birth pangs." He slid his fingers into her warmth. She was still moist from him, and from her yearning.

"Thomas!" She lifted her hips to be closer to his touch.

"Yes, love?"

When she found her breath again, she glared at him under passion-leaden eyelids. "I might agree to your company in the birth room, but I will not allow you to pleasure me with a midwife looking on."

He delved again and whispered into her ear. "Then I will send the crone away and catch our babe myself." He moved atop her and replaced his fingers with his fullness, sheathing himself to the hilt.

"Aye, my lord husband, whatever you say." Her release came with his first stroke, and came again minutes later when he teased the straining tip of her breast past his tongue and teeth, and again an hour later when he poured himself into her.

Sated and submerged in her comfort, Thomas settled his head between her breasts, cradling the fullness of one with his hand. "You are most incredible, my love. If

I didn't know better, I'd think you the one with the experience."

"Imagination, remember?"

Chapter 22

Thomas expected to hear from Edward any day. The royal court was to spend Christmas at New-castle, and after Twelfth Night would travel to Westmin-ster. But another week of silence slid into two and then three, and finally Christmas Eve came with no reply to his missive. He sent another, adding to it the news that he and Mackenna had married, that he wanted to settle down. He held his concern from Mackenna, uncomfort-able with his deception. She had given over the care of Fellhaven because she trusted him; he would make it right.

On Christmas Eve the Yule log was carried into the hall and set into the giant hearth with great ceremony and celebration. Greenery hung from every rafter— holly and pine, ivy and laurel. The forest scent was sweetened by the ginger and cinnamon that spiced the food paraded from the kitchen.

As he held Mackenna's hand, Thomas wondered how he ever could have preferred the solitary life of a soldier. Here was his family now: the children and the elders, the maidens and their young men, hundreds of lives tied to his through Mackenna. She'd known this intoxicating sense of belonging all her life. It was what had made her so determined to protect her people.

"Lord and Lady Montclaire!" Bryce had found the Christmas bean in his wastel loaf and had been declared "king of the bean." He now presided over the ceremonies, wearing a brightly colored cap festooned in holly and gold ribbons. "If it pleases your graces, we have commissioned your herald to retell the wondrous tale of your courting."

The herald had recruited villagers to act the parts while he told the tale. Mackenna and Thomas watched in delight as their meeting and the other events surrounding their relationship were presented in great exaggeration, but smoking with truth. By the end of it, the hall was hooting and Thomas and Mackenna were laughing hardest of all.

Thomas gave out gifts of food and privileges to the villagers, gifts of robes and saddles to his castlemen. Every woman and girl received a length of ribbon, every man a flint. Mackenna watched her husband as he grinned and laughed and handed out his favors. He was a very generous man, such a good and honest man. How could she ever have thought otherwise? The truth was there in his eyes; she had just refused to see it. Mother Mary, how he had changed her life!

He finally sat down next to her, smiling like a boy who'd just won a foot race. He took her hand and kissed her.

"My sweet wife, I hope I can get through the next dance without whisking you up the stairs and into our room."

"Thomas, I heard something very distressing tonight."

A chill settled across his shoulders. "And that was?"

She leaned against him and spoke in a voice shadowed in conspiracy. "The widow Sawyer asked me if you and I were sleeping in separate chambers during Advent."

His relief escaped in a burst of laughter. "Why the devil did she ask that?"

" 'Twas my question to her as well. She told me that if she had a husband as handsome and as attentive as I, she'd be hard pressed to stay away from his bed during Advent." Mackenna glanced at her husband out of the corner of her eye. He was silent, waiting for her to continue. "I didn't dare tell her we sinned nightly, most often more than once."

"Neither the widow Sawyer, nor anyone else, has any business in our chamber. God cares not a whit about when or how often a husband and wife take pleasure in each other."

" 'Tis love that binds us, Thomas. And trust. A more holy union cannot be granted on earth."

Thomas restrained himself from hauling her into his arms and kissing her. If he did, the widow Sawyer would know for certes they'd not been abstaining. Instead, he let himself burn for her, let his passion fill his limbs with its spirits. His hauberk was heavy and would mask his lust from any but his perceptive wife. He led her into the midst of the dancing and lost himself in her seduction.

With the New Year come and gone, and Epiphany approaching, Thomas knew that Edward's silence was more than just the neglect of a king engaged in holiday revels: it was a condemnation. Had Edward taken umbrage at his marriage?

Thomas lost a good dirk to Walter in a protracted game of dice. For the first time since their marriage, Thomas had lingered below while Mackenna took her bath. He felt every inch the liar, the cheat, dangling on a wire, while the block of ice was melting out from under his boots.

"What are you going to do about Edward's silence?" Walter asked.

"I must go see him."

"He'll be gone from Newcastle soon after tomorrow."

"I'll find him, but I must first discover his mood."

"How do you plan to do this? Sorcery?"

"A quick visit to Giffard. He'll know, and can advise me. I can be there and back in the space of one day."

"Aye, if you kill your horse and yourself in the bargain."

"I cannot leave Mackenna alone."

"You still don't trust her, Thomas? After all this time?"

"Bloody hell, Walter, I trust her with my life. I love the woman, and I don't want to leave her so soon after we've married."

Walter laughed.

"You needn't be so smug."

"Nay, I am most pleased for you. You both have chosen well. I shall do whatever you wish to keep Edward from spoiling it."

"Thank you. Barring bad weather, I'll leave here long before dawn the day after tomorrow. See that Mackenna doesn't worry. Keep her busy. Now, I must tell her my plans—without revealing my reasons. Pray for me, Walter."

Thomas's bath was waiting and Mackenna was asleep, his angel tangled in the bedclothes, clutching his pillow to her breast. He slipped out of his clothes and lowered himself into the warmth and stayed until it was cold. He left the tub and donned a robe, then fell into the chair in front of the hearth. The flames drew his imagination: daggers dripping blood, jagged mouths opened in silent screams, demons, lost souls condemned for far lesser crimes than his.

A silhouette blocked his view of the flames—impeccably rounded hips, a pair of shapely thighs, and a sprig of shadowy curls between them.

"You look quite solemn, Thomas." Mackenna knelt and folded her arms on his bare thighs.

He leaned back and sighed. "I love you, Mackenna."

"And that makes you solemn?"

"It makes me altogether defenseless." He laced his fingers through hers. "'Tis difficult for a soldier to accept: unarmed and without armor in the midst of a pitched battle."

Mackenna felt her world tilt. "Thomas, are you sorry you married me?"

"Sorry? Dear God, no!" He rose and gathered her into his arms. "Never for a moment, my love. Never."

"Good, because I'm not sorry, either."

Her heart was gallumping beneath his palm, the panic of a doe dashing from a hunter's bolt. Guilt plagued him, truth protested in his ear.

"You feel wondrously alive to me, love," he whispered, trailing his tongue along the ridge of her shoulder. "And these." He kissed the standing points of her breasts, one and then the other. She arched toward his mouth and cooed as he rolled one between his tongue and teeth.

"Oh, my!" His smile broke against the straining peak and she cooed again. "Thomas?"

"Mmmmm?"

She slid her palms over the angular ridges of his chest and around to his taut backside. "'Tis been thirty-six days."

"Thirty-six . . . ?" He lifted her hair and draped it over his arms and shoulders, a breathtaking curtain of delight. She was looking up into his eyes, teasing her upper lip with the tip of her tongue to tease him. "Thirty-six what?"

"We've been married thirty-six days, and still you've not allowed me to kiss you . . ." She parted his robe, brought her hands to the front of his thighs and slid them to his knees.

"Kiss me? Ah." He drew a ragged breath when he realized what kind of kiss she meant.

"Here."

He gasped as she measured him with her hands, gentle explorers that cupped him and held him, and then left him to stroke his inner thighs.

"Mackenna." He sighed through his teeth as she slid to her knees, her breath breaking hot against his belly. Her fingertips were feathers, skimming the back of his knees, his ankles.

"You are handsome everywhere, husband."

Mackenna had to hold his hips to keep him close after she left a kiss in the still-damp curls where his brawny flesh pulsed like a burnished blade, heated and eager to thrust. She brushed her cheek against the length of him, and was filled with a heady sense of power as he moaned and bent forward to grab her shoulders.

"Hard and soft at the same time, husband?" Her lips danced near him while she spoke, nipped the curling hair. His knees seemed to buckle and wobble with each steaming breath she took of his feral fragrance, an intoxicating blend of soap and oak moss, fire, and the wind.

"Sweet, I'll not live through our thirty-sixth day." His words seem to strangle out of his chest in the wrong direction.

"I think you'll want to live to a thirty-seventh." Her mouth was a breath's distance from the head of his rising. "Do you want me to kiss you here?"

"God, yes!"

He made a choked sound in his throat as she wove her fingers through the hair at the base of him. The curls were so springy, and his shape and textures so absorbing; a thick sword of shimmering silk, webbed with sturdy veins. It took all her resistance not to capture him right then. He was so expert at teasing her until she cried out his name and begged for him, she would do the same for him. He was quaking already. Her warm lips brushed past him, a breath only, but it drew his body as taut as a Welsh longbow.

"Dear wife . . ." Thomas staggered backward a step, knocked his heel on the tub, and sat down on its edge. It was the powerless anticipation that incited him, that made his head spin.

Mackenna followed her husband like a stalking tiger, sliding her hands along the coarse-haired insides of his thighs, drawn to the dark nest and its standard. She knelt down between his spread thighs, and as she dipped her head to taste him, he caught her chin with his fingers. His gaze was as heated as his flesh, seeking a communion of the soul.

"Need to touch you, love," he whispered as he slanted his mouth over hers. "Need you." Then his hand was between her legs, his fingers finding her moist and aching for him.

His palm was as shattering as his kissing. She whimpered as her tongue danced with his, and she pressed herself into the heel of his hand. He filled her senses, the fragrance of his passion familiar and stirring, his enchantment nearly swaying her from her purpose.

"You can't distract me, Thomas." She took him into both hands, gripped him like a distaff. A groan ripped from him. He threw his head back and grasped the edges of the tub behind him. She held his measure in her hands, ringed him with her fingers, practiced the pulsing pressure that matched the flexing of her own muscles when she held him within her body.

"My sweet wife." His breath came and left his chest like a storm. Somewhere in his youth a woman had done this to him, a skillful woman he'd paid handsomely for his delight; but he hadn't ached like this, his arms hadn't hurt with the loss of the woman's embrace. This was Mackenna, loving him, learning him, wanting him as he'd allowed no other in all those years.

"Let me, husband."

Her words steamed against his navel, her chin a soft pressure alongside his staff. Her fingers tantalized the hair 'neath his taut sack of jewels, a delicious torment that near stopped his heart. He leaned back further and gave himself over to the astounding pleasure of having his wife at his loins.

And then she took him into her mouth.

"Sweet Jesu, Mackenna—" He lurched forward and grabbed her shoulders, quaking, offering prayers of thanksgiving and calling out her name. Her mouth was hot and pouting; her tongue flickered fire along his ridges. She drew him into her mouth, and he lifted his hips.

"You are delicious, my lord husband." She licked him then, as she'd once taken sugar from his fingers. She buried her fingers in the hair at the root of him, fondled his knees, then his ankles, then she was holding him again. All the while her hands wandered; her lips tugged at him; her tongue slid along his shaft; her mouth left scorching kisses.

A sudden, blinding fire shot through him, a need to plunge, to enfold her, to lose himself inside his wife.

"Come, love." He lifted her, and in one motion sat her on his lap. Her thighs fell open to his hands and his eyes. "Guide me, Mackenna. Bring me to you."

"I was not finished, husband," she murmured, tracing the arc of his lips with the end of her tongue. He took in a sharp breath as she found him again with her hands.

"You nearly finished me. Come to me, love. I miss you fiercely." He wrapped her in his arms, and laid down kisses along the curling margins of her temples.

"I've been here all along. I'm surprised you hadn't noticed." Her gaze was languid as she stroked him and held him with hands that pulsed and guided him, and made his breath thunder out of his throat.

"I noticed. Aye, you were there, my love, and everywhere else." She was hot and slick and open wide to him. He held her bottom, and watched her eyes as he inclined his hips and eased into her. He wanted to plunge, but the sensation of her closing around him was sweet and sultry and to be savored. Until the last, as her sheath contracted with her groan, and she drove him to the hilt, where his bluntness touched the deepest part of her.

She rode him, holding his hips as he held hers. She locked her gazed with his and held him there, too. This was what he had missed: her eyes, molten cinnamon, flecks of gold, colors dancing in her hair, a sheen of sweat gilding her skin, and always the passion in her gaze, seeking him in their morning bed, and from across the bailey.

"Oh, Thomas!" His seed rushed into her, as he huffed and seized her against his grinding hips. He growled and made new noises that made her giggle and nibble at his shoulder.

Mackenna had managed to hook her feet on the edge

of the tub behind him. Her last thrust was so strong, she sent Thomas off balance and he toppled backward into the tub, carrying her with him. The landing drove him further into her, a final meeting that left them both breathless and laughing.

Thomas brushed the tangle of hair out of her face, and kissed her mouth. Her laughter rippled in rings along the length of him. "Tossing water on a pair of mating dogs does cool their ardor, my love, but it causes me to want you more."

"And I, you, my water dog." Mackenna leaned against him, kissing the drops of salty-sweet water off his chest and neck. "Sir, you have left me unstrung."

"I pray I have left a babe growing."

"As I do. But my flux came shortly after our wedding."

"And did I not tend you well then?"

"Aye, you did." Mackenna felt herself blushing at the vivid memory of his cure for the low back pain that accompanied her moon-month bleeding. His touch that raised her passion, had soothed the tightness, as well. "Far better than any balm."

Thomas rose out of the water and stepped across the flooded rushes to the bed. He towelled her dry and then himself, then settled into the pillows, his wife tucked safely in his arms.

"Shall we stay abed until Lammastide?"

"I'd like nothing better, my love, but I must leave for Giffard's castle well before dawn the day after to-morrow."

"Leaving? Why and for how long?"

Thomas thought Mackenna looked charmingly possessive of him. He liked that in a wife. "I go to counsel with Giffard. I'll only be gone for the day; I shall be back before midnight."

"Good, I haven't see Lady Giffard since Carlisle."

"Nay, I'm going alone. 'Tis faster that way."

"You're going with me. Your shadow, remember?"

"This isn't a war, Mackenna. I go alone."

"You'll take at least three men, or I'll follow you myself."

Thomas considered the threat and relented. "Then I'll take three men. But you must stay here. I leave you in charge."

She laughed to conceal her dark fears for his safe return. "I'll protect your castle, my lord Thomas. By my life I will."

Mackenna watched Thomas ride out of the bailey with his three knights on his heels, feeling as horrible as she knew she would. Blessed Lady, he was just riding to a neighbor; how would she bear up when he was riding off to war? There was so little moon, and the sun wouldn't rise for hours. He had turned to look at her at the last, and threw a kiss to her through the darkness. She caught it and kept it close, and told herself he would come back to her.

"Lady Montclaire!" Francis stood loose-limbed at her office door. He looked stricken, his cheeks pale but mottled with crimson. Fear shot through her.

Her chair fell backwards as she left it and clutched his sleeves. "God, no, Francis. Tell me it isn't Thomas."

"Nay." He took a breath, meant to say more but couldn't.

"What is it, then? Has someone been hurt?"

"No one. 'Tis—at the drawbridge . . ."

"Don't coddle me, Francis!" She brushed past him and headed toward the main gate. If Thomas and her brothers were safe, then no adversity on earth could be so devastating that she couldn't face it straight on. She could hear his footsteps following quickly behind her.

Low-hanging clouds had moved in from the west, darkening the afternoon, promising snow. Thomas would have a dangerous time coming home in the dark. As she hurried down the slope toward the drawbridge, she prayed he would stay the night at Giffard's.

A crowd of soldiers were gathered around the gate. In

the gray afternoon light, their faces seemed too solemn; the eyes that found hers shifted too quickly. They let her through with a whisper of encouragement, as though they, too, thought her incapable of handling whatever awaited her on the drawbridge.

"Walter?" she asked. He was standing among the guards blocking the entrance. His smile grew tight when he saw her.

"Mackenna . . . Lady Montclaire," he said, as grimly as she'd ever heard him. "We've some trouble."

"Trouble?"

Walter stepped aside, and she saw him.

John Gilvane.

His dark robes rippled in the updraft, the feather in his hat lurching madly. His smile was easy and feigned.

"Good day, Lady Montclaire." He nodded a courtly bow toward her; his spurs made a hollow sound on the drawbridge, a sound that echoed into the chasm below. " 'Tis good to see you again."

"You're not welcome in my husband's castle, Gilvane." She wanted to run past him to the village and sound the alarm.

Gilvane examined her as he stripped off his gauntlets. "Your husband chose well, Lady Montclaire. 'Tis too bad you don't come with the castle."

Walter took a sharp step toward the man, but Mackenna restrained him with a hand on his arm. She had right on her side, and all of her husband's might. She had seen Gilvane denounced by the king himself.

"I suggest you turn your men around and leave this valley before Lord Montclaire returns."

Gilvane shifted his eyes to the dozen men standing behind him and shared his amusement with them. "And I suggest you look at this." He slipped a scroll from the sleeve of his robe and thrust it at her as if it were a broadsword.

Mackenna folded her arms across her chest. "The only thing I intend to look at, Gilvane, is your scrawny backside in retreat." The muted laughter from behind her gave her strength.

Gilvane's eyes narrowed. "Read it, Lady Montclaire. 'Tis from King Edward."

"So you've become a royal messenger?" she asked. "A right well-paying job, I am certain."

"'Tis a writ, Lady Montclaire. Addressed to your husband. Mayhaps I should hold it until he returns."

Something dark and sure in his tone unnerved her. With far more bluster than she felt, she grabbed the scroll out of Gilvane's hand and turned her back on him.

Her hands were shaking, her fingers frozen in fear and loathing. She tugged, and the royal seal popped open, leaving the ribbon to flutter. She tried to unroll the stiff parchment but it curled around her thumbs, fighting her efforts.

"Let me, 'Kenna." Walter caught one edge and held it.

The Latin words shimmered in front of her eyes, blurred by the wind and unread in the uneasiness that hovered like a fog. Something about Fellhaven . . . the castle . . . the village. . . .

"I can't read it," she whispered to Walter. But Gilvane must have heard her fear.

"I assure you the writ is in order, Lady Montclaire. Fellhaven belongs to me!"

Chapter 23

⟨~∽◯◯∽~⟩

Gilvane's words slammed into her back, making her stumble forward a step.

"Did you hear me, Lady Montclaire?" The voice was sharp with impatience.

Mackenna swallowed the bile rising in her throat and whipped around to glare at him.

"I heard you fine, Gilvane," she said in a voice propped by her outrage. "And you are a liar."

His entourage shifted behind him, their leather and iron creaking in the tense silence.

Gilvane took an easy step forward. "The writ states that Lord Montclaire is to vacate his holding immediately."

"'Tis a forgery." Mackenna threw the scroll at his feet.

"'Tis no forgery, Lady Montclaire. The castle is mine, and the garrison, and of course, the village." At a nod from Gilvane, the man beside him retrieved the scroll. "Now, if you will move aside—"

Mackenna yanked Walter's dirk from its sheath and thrust it forward to block Gilvane's approach. "Another step, Gilvane, and I'll consider your advance an attack on my husband's castle." Mackenna heard the slow rasp of swords behind her, the clink of mail, the scrape of boot heels against stone—battle sounds that rallied her.

"You are a wild young thing. Wherever did Thomas find you?"

"Take your filthy writ, and leave this valley."

"I stay."

The laugh she heard from her own throat was barbed and foreign. "Take him, Walter," she demanded, "and his men."

"Mackenna," Walter said quietly, turning her from Gilvane and motioning for his guard to watch the party as he pulled her into the shelter of his arm. "You can't do this. You can't imprison a lord of the realm without severe consequences."

"Imprison him? I want him dead. Christ, Walter, he hanged my father! He starved my family. I will not give him the castle. I will not give him my village."

"And if the writ is genuine?"

"Genuine!" Her throat ached. "Thomas Montclaire is lord of Fellhaven! If I gave over his holding to John Gilvane, he would never forgive me. Thomas loves his land as much as I do."

"Until we know, until Thomas decides how best to handle this matter, you must treat Gilvane as your guest. You *must!*"

"My guest!" she spat. "I will not!"

"Think of the village, Mackenna."

"I *am* thinking of them, and only them. He must leave."

"Nay, Mackenna. Let his men stay here, inside the castle walls where we can contain them. I recognize some of these knights. I'd not trust a one to guard my back in a battle. They take no prisoners, unless they be women to defile."

Her chest felt hollow, her heart a drumbeat that echoed off Mickelfell and slid into the valley. Her brothers were in the village, hot-headed and brimming with arrogance at their new status. And what of the three Cotes girls—saved from their father to be sacrifice to the pleasure of Gilvane's demons?

"I'll take care of it, Mackenna," Walter offered, his voice a gentle wedge into her reason. "I'll see that no man is let out through the gate once it is closed."

She had no choice but to invite the viper into her home. Mackenna said nothing for a long minute, then nodded. He started to hand her to Francis, but she jerked out of his grasp and turned to Gilvane.

"As my husband is vassal to King Edward, I open these gates to you as a guest. But know that when Lord Montclaire returns tonight, he will deal rightly with you: turn you out into the cold, and bar you from his land forever."

Not leaving a second for Gilvane to reply, Mackenna turned and strode through Thomas's wall of faithful soldiers. They were grinning now as if she were one of them. And she was. None could guard her people better than she, none except her husband.

Mackenna smiled all the way to the bailey, delighting in the thought of Thomas's anger at learning that Gilvane was trying to claim Fellhaven. Foolish arrogance. She wondered how the man thought he could get away with such an obvious falsehood. She would stand beside her husband in the bailey and watch Gilvane recoil from Thomas's scorn, watch her enemy grovel and beg for mercy. Then she'd watch Thomas's soldiers escort the writhing serpent down the castle road and out of the valley.

Mackenna focused on her work in her office with a ferocity and sense of purpose that surprised even her, making plans and diagrams for the raised planting beds that would support the castle gardens and come to bloom in the spring. She looked up when the door opened, and noticed that night had fallen. Walter came through and shut the door against the wind.

"Does our guest like his accommodations?" she asked, feeling more and more smug as the time for Gilvane's humiliation neared. "I hope he's allergic to horse dung."

"I've put Gilvane in the solar."

With the studied calm that comes after a blow, she put her quill into the holder. "Why?" she asked quietly.

"'Tis his rank. Barons do not sleep in a barracks,

whatever one's opinion of them. Gilvane and his officers will be eating in the hall. I assumed you would not be joining them."

"You assumed incorrectly, Walter. I'll be there. Gilvane will not frighten me out of my own hall."

"Please don't do anything rash, Mackenna."

"You mean like poisoning Gilvane's wine?"

He smiled some. "That, and doing anything that might put Thomas in a position to have to defend you."

She hadn't considered that: Gilvane complaining to Edward of an insult, and then the king devising some trial for Thomas, merely to serve the royal humor.

"Aye, Walter. I shall be on my best behavior. In the meantime, I'll be in here. Do send someone for me."

Walter started to leave than turned back. "He doesn't remember you, Mackenna."

"Who doesn't? Gilvane? He does. He mentioned Carlisle."

"That's not my meaning. He doesn't know you were Randolph Hughes's daughter. He's made no connection to your past."

A cold memory crawled down her back. "I don't doubt it, Walter. We were a village of gray skeletons the last he saw us."

Walter dropped his gaze. "Christ, Mackenna, I'm sorry." His voice cracked. "I'm so sorry."

" 'Tis done, Walter. It happened a lifetime ago. Thomas will be back in a few hours and he'll put it all to rights. I trust him in all things. You must learn to do so, as well."

The meal was brief, the music strained, and conversations never strayed from the confines of the cloistered sets of diners. Mackenna avoided looking at Gilvane, but felt his attention on her too often. His eyes were a cold, blue light as he appraised her over the top of his goblet.

Mackenna felt entirely safe. Flanked by Walter and Francis, she seemed to have gained the power to attract Thomas' men like iron filings to a rasp. Three had been waiting for her outside her office. Walter had other men watching Gilvane, and had ordered additional guards at the gates and the towers. For once, she was glad that Thomas was a soldier.

Gilvane had only twenty men with him. They were as she remembered: not the faces, but the resemblance to unholy beasts disguising their devil's heritage in human clothing. Walter had been right: the village was safe tonight only because Gilvane's men were locked inside the castle gates.

After presiding over the uncomfortable meal, Mackenna retreated to her chamber. Tonight, she was perfectly happy to have her door well guarded. She took a hot bath and had another readied for Thomas. The covered kettles steamed on the hearth while she sat at the casement window to wait for him. Sleep would be impossible until he had put Gilvane off their land, and she could rest in her husband's arms.

No matter how hard she tried, she couldn't make the notched candle burn any faster between the hours as she waited for her soldier to return. Ten and then eleven, and twelve, and then half-gone twelve. Snow had fallen, just enough to whiten the landscape, and catch the moon's light on its soft blanket.

She was about to despair of his return tonight when she heard a distant but utterly familiar shout that carried over the curtain wall, across the outer bailey, up the castle walls and into her chamber window.

"Thomas!" She put on her slippers and her cloak and raced down the stairs and through the hall. She ran across the carpet of snow, toward the muffled clatter of hooves coming through the gate.

He was home!

Thomas was off his horse as soon as he saw Mackenna—his moon-kissed wife, with her hair streaming behind her and her arms outstretched to him. She threw herself into his embrace, and he held her and hugged her and soaked up the warmth of her mouth on his frosted cheeks and forehead.

"Thomas!" Mackenna couldn't get enough of him,

couldn't hold him tightly enough. He smelled of alder smoke and ice and cloves. His cheek was raspy. "You've come home!"

He lifted her into his arms and started across the bailey. "Did you ever doubt it?"

"I could never doubt you, husband. Ever! Did you miss me?" she asked, grinning so hard her cheeks hurt in the cold.

"I missed you more than any husband ought to miss his wife." She hugged him closer and gifted him with a dozen more kisses, until he was laughing again. "Mmm . . . but with such a rousing reception, I think I ought to leave you more often—"

"Nay, Thomas! Never say that!" She pressed her cheek to his, clamping her hands against the back of his head.

"Sweet, it was a jest." He would have smiled, but she was holding his face now and searching for something in his eyes. "Mackenna? What is it?"

"Thomas. He's here," she whispered. "He's come back."

"Who has?" As he climbed the steps to the keep, he looked up into Walter's stony face. "What's happened?"

"Lord Gilvane," Mackenna breathed against his cheek. "I told him you'd throw him out when you got home."

Thomas held back his curse. "Gilvane is here? In the castle? Why?" He looked at Walter as the man joined them, and Walter nodded silently. Thomas stopped in the antechamber and set Mackenna on her feet. He tried to lighten his voice, tried to soothe her with his humor.

"Where did you put the bastard, Mackenna? In the garderobe? 'Tis a shame I never had that dungeon finished."

"I didn't want him to stay, Thomas. But Walter thought it best to put him in the solar and treat him like a lord."

"He carries a writ, Thomas." Walter's tone was leaden.

Deep down inside her, a murky blackness stirred,

jostled by the shuttered look that her husband shared with Walter. The taint of Gilvane—she sensed it everywhere, even where it couldn't possibly be.

"I keep telling Walter the writ's a forgery. *You* are the lord of Fellhaven, Thomas. I gave you the village myself."

"Take Mackenna to our chamber." Thomas put her hand into Walter's. "I'll have a private word with Gilvane."

She wrenched out of Walter's grasp and caught up to her husband before he reached the hall. "I'll stay, Thomas."

"This is my business, Mackenna."

"'Tis mine, as well. Gilvane is *my* devil!"

"And I will deal with him," he said calmly.

Fear tumbled around in her stomach, knocking against her courage and her trust. Walter wouldn't look at her.

"Thomas! Promise me you won't do anything foolish."

"Nay, wife. Nothing more foolish than I've already done."

Gilvane was standing at the hearth among a knot of his soldiers, drinking ale brewed in the village, warming their flanks with hard-hewn firewood. A possessive rage blazed inside Thomas.

"Gilvane!" Thomas called out from the center of the hall.

"Ah, Lord Thomas, you have returned." Gilvane broke away from the hearth and crossed the floor. "My men and I were just enjoying some ale. Care for any?"

"I will speak with you in private."

"Turn him out, Thomas," Mackenna hissed from beside him.

"Your wife and I didn't start off on the right foot—"

"Leave us, Mackenna." Thomas said evenly.

When she started to object, he turned blazing eyes on her and she backed down. *Trust me, Mackenna*, he seemed to be saying. *Trust me*. Thomas would deal with

Gilvane as harshly as she would, but in his own way. There were formalities among the nobility that she didn't yet comprehend. Honor to be saved. If it would make it easier for Thomas, she would do as he wished.

"Aye, my lord. I'll leave the hall." Trust was all she had to hold onto, with her husband standing opposite the man she hated more than the devil. She followed Walter to her chamber door, and thanked him for standing by her through the long day.

"'Tis for your own peace, Mackenna," Walter said, before she closed the door.

Mackenna listened to his footsteps as he walked away. She quietly swung the panel open, waiting until his footfalls finally met the stone stairs and started down. She left the chamber and held back at the top of the landing, shielded by the stone wall. Voices were muffled. She peered around the corner.

The hall was empty but for Thomas and Walter standing together near the hearth, and Gilvane sitting lazily in a chair. Thomas was reading the forged writ; the edges of the parchment were crumpled hard in his fists.

"Your wife thinks the document's false, Lord Thomas." Gilvane pried his dagger blade into the seam of a walnut shell. "'Twas not my business to press the truth."

Mackenna waited for Thomas to call Gilvane a liar; waited for him to summon his guards. She waited for him to order the evil baron down the mountain.

Thomas calmly handed the scroll to Walter.

"When did you get this, Gilvane?" Thomas asked. For a man ready to throw an enemy out of his castle, her husband was remarkably cool-headed and polite.

"On New Year's Eve. 'Twas quite an honor."

"And a surprise?"

"Ah, you are perceptive, Lord Thomas. In truth I had been hoping. Even then in Carlisle, when the king brought us together in conference, I thought it was to transfer Fellhaven."

"You were disappointed."

"I had not yet delivered Balliol."

"And now that you have?"

"I've been well rewarded. I always did love it here."

Thomas touched the hilt of his dagger. "Was that why you razed it before you left?"

"I was angry at Edward. But we've settled our differences."

"My God, Thomas!" Mackenna shouted, no longer able to tamp down her anger. "Throw him out of our home! Make him go!"

Thomas looked up at his wife. She was on the landing, gripping the railing. He needn't wonder what she had heard of the conversation; its effects were scribed upon her face.

"I can't do that, Mackenna." He faltered under her look of horror and disgust.

"You can't? Well, I can!" Mackenna ran down a few steps, and with a nod, Thomas sent Walter to stop her.

"Send him away, Thomas!" she screamed. Then Walter's arm was a vice around her waist. "Let me go!"

"Don't, Mackenna," he said against her ear, his hand across her mouth. "I am sorry, girl. 'Tis for your own good."

She struggled and tried to bite him, but he was too strong.

"The rebuilding is progressing well," Thomas was saying as if discussing the weather.

"As I've seen. And I was well pleased with the village. It was in appalling shape the last I saw of it. But what can one expect of lazy, free-loading peasants?"

Thomas wanted to slam the man against the wall and beat the life out of him. But he stayed his hands. His resistance might cost him his wife's trust and perhaps her love, but it was the only action that would save her from Gilvane.

Thomas nodded. "Then, Lord Gilvane, as the writ seems to be in order, I relinquish Fellhaven to you: its village, the castle and the people it serves. We shall be gone by noon."

"Come, wife." When Thomas reached for Mackenna, she flung herself out of Walter's arms and backed up against the railing.

"Don't touch me!" He'd become a stranger to her. The same tainted beast who had invaded her village, who had wooed her trust and gained her love, who had promised to protect and defend her village, had just coldly and calmly betrayed her to the enemy.

"We've not time for this, Mackenna." Thomas pulled her against him with one arm and started up the stairs. "Walter, see that the men are packed and ready to move out come morning. I'll meet you in the gate tower as soon as I finish with this. Send a guard to my chamber immediately."

Mackenna beat against him, but he released her only after they were inside the chamber. She darted across the room.

"Bastard!" she hissed. Her breathing matched Baylor's in full gallop. Her hands were raised from her sides; she hunched forward as if she were ready to launch herself at him. Her face was pale and stony. But it was the naked despair in her eyes that made him hate himself.

"Aye, that I am, love."

Francis appeared behind him in the hall. Thomas gave orders that Mackenna wasn't to leave the chamber, then he closed the door and turned to her.

"'Tis time to pack, Mackenna." He strode purposefully to the stack of trunks in the corner.

"You can't mean to deliver the village to the devil?"

Thomas threw open a chest and rummaged around looking for his battle kit. "Gilvane has a writ from the king."

"To hell with the king. How can he do this? How can *you* do it? How can you walk out on me and my village?"

He looked up at her. "I haven't."

Hope flickered then, her frown muted, her brow smoothed. Her faith in him rising again, she asked softly, "Then you're not leaving? You're staying here to fight Gilvane?"

Thomas felt corrupt and unworthy. He knew what

she wanted him to say. But that kind of promise lay beyond him at the moment. "Fellhaven belongs to Gilvane. The writ is blindingly Edward's. I have no choice but to leave." –

"No choice? How can you let Edward steal your holding and give it to someone else?"

Thomas knew his confession would seal her hatred, would leave her trust and his honor tattered.

"Fellhaven is not mine, Mackenna."

"Not yours?"

"It never was. I came only to train the garrison and to oversee the repairs to the castle." He lifted him palms in supplication. "I never meant to stay here."

The silence shifted, a sky-born fog turned to bog-born blackdamp. It chilled her heart and hardened her marrow.

"Never meant to stay?" The loss ripped through her, a bolt of despair that tore at her strength and her will.

"I was born to the saddle, Mackenna, not to the manor. You said so yourself. I'm a soldier. I thought myself destined to roam from one bleak and bloody battlefield to the next. I was proud and blissfully happy to claim no more land than the three-square feet upon which I stood." He gave out a short, self-mocking laugh. "I've never had such a bed before, Mackenna, never slept in one place for so long." He lifted his near-black eyes and wrapped her in his ruthless devotion. "Nor have I ever been loved so well."

His gaze was so deeply honest, she hated him all the more. "You deceived me from the start."

"I deceived myself. I thought I was immune from wanting a wife and a home. God forgive me; I didn't know you, then."

"But I knew you, didn't I?" She backed away from him to the casement; his words turned too easily on his tongue. "Begat of a noble evil, practiced in the art of deceit and seduction. You courted the village as you courted me. You gave us hope and justice and, damn you, Thomas, we learned to trust you. I gave you my village! I wouldn't have married you if I'd known—"

"Don't you think I know that?" Swift and sharp, his words seemed to injure him as he spoke them. "I couldn't let you marry another man, I couldn't leave you, and yet I knew there was a chance that Edward would not grant me Fellhaven. Can you imagine how much I loathe myself for the lie?"

"Not near as much as I loathe you. Now go back to your unholy king and his unholy games. I will be glad to see you go. And when you leave, Montclaire, be sure to look west; I shall be waving from the top of Mickelfell."

He sighed, and his sagging shoulders lifted to their usual squareness of authority. "Nay, Mackenna. You are my wife; we are one and will always be. Hate me or no, you'll come with me."

"And forsake my village? Leave it defenseless as you have done? I will not. You've laid us bare, Thomas. You've made us weak. Our food stores are exposed for any to take; we've grown dependent on the lord's favors; and our children have lost the fear that would hide them from the soldiers. You should have been openly cruel, Montclaire, honorably evil, just as Gilvane was. And you should have let me marry someone else."

"Should I?" He walked toward her, a slow and determined gait. He took her chin in his inescapably gentle fingers. "Be assured of one thing, my love: you and I were bound to each other from the moment you first touched me."

She pulled free of him. "And you used that, too. Twisted our customs, and left me reeling. Aye, you were clever, Thomas: make the girl love me, and she'll never notice that I prepare her home for a blood sacrifice to the noble gods of the royal court."

"That is not the way of it, Mackenna."

"But my village will not suffer. I will play the game *my* way from now on. And in the end, I will kill Gilvane before I let him steal a single grain of barley!"

"Listen to me, love." He caught her near the hearth, gripped her shoulders. His fingers should have hurt, but he wounded her always with his blessed tenderness. "When I came here Fellhaven was a burden, a favor I owed to Edward. I had decided to do the job as quickly as I could and be done with it. I would find another war, the sooner the better."

"Why then didn't you just leave?"

"Because I was met by surly villagers, a well-ordered village, a castle in near ruins, and a young woman whose ability to deceive me was exceeded only by her courage. And I loved you from the first, Mackenna. From the very first."

"Stop it." She resisted when he pulled her against him, and held her head to his chest. She didn't want to hear his heart, didn't want to take in his scent. She closed her ears to the ragged intake of his breath as he spent his sweet endearments against her hair.

"Please let me go, Thomas."

"I never meant to hurt you."

"But you always meant to leave me."

"Not after that first night when you began to teach me."

"Stop—"

"You made me see Fellhaven through your eyes when I'd rather have remained blind and indifferent. 'Twas on the battlements, against the stunning skies, when I realized that I'd never seen such a blue before. 'Twas then I understood why you fought me."

"And now I must fight another." She shrugged out of his embrace and put the bed between them. "I will stay, Montclaire."

He sighed again. "You'll come with me."

"Not while I have a breath in me."

" 'Til death parts us, Mackenna. I will have no wife but you." He moved past her to the door.

"Where are you going?" she demanded.

"To talk to my men. I suggest you pack, Mackenna."

And he was gone, the door echoing her dread. She listened at the panel, and heard Thomas reiterate his orders to Francis.

If he wouldn't let her go, she would just have to escape. She yanked the mattress off the bed and went to work on the grid of rope beneath. With every pull of the rope, she prayed Thomas would stay with his men long enough for her plan to succeed.

Thomas. Her arms felt leaden, and she sat down on the wobbly webbing. Her heart ached. He'd lied to her, deceived her, and made her love him. And now he was deserting her. Nay, she mustn't think of it.

The rope came free as Francis tapped on the door. "Do you need help with your packing, my lady?"

She grunted as the last of the rope came through the hole. "Nay, Francis. I thank you."

"If you promise not to overpower me, I'll give you a hand."

"Nay, Francis!" Mackenna ran to the door to keep him from opening it. "I'm not decently dressed."

"Oh! Sorry, your ladyship." Mackenna heard him straighten, and imagined him primly crossing his long arms against his chest. She would miss Francis. And Walter. Mother Mary, she would miss Thomas! Nay, she mustn't think of it.

She secured one end of the rope to the iron sconce ring imbedded in the wall nearest the window. There was far more than a hundred feet of rope, and no more than fifty feet to the ground. She quickly made triple knots every two feet and piled the tangle on the floor.

Her own clothes were too light in color and too cumbersome. She donned a pair of Thomas's dark green braies and woolen hosen, and overlaid it with his blackest shirt and tunic. They were miles too large for her and required extra belting. And they wore his scent. Nay, she mustn't think of it.

She bound her cloak in a bundle and secured the ties around her waist, leaving it to hang over her backside. She tugged on a pair of heavy gloves and her boots, and then began her watch.

She'd seen Thomas cross the bailey and enter the guard tower carrying an armload of items he'd taken from his trunk. Timing would be everything in her escape. Timing and patience.

A half hour later, Thomas started back across the bailey with Walter. She stood in the shadows of the casement, waiting for them to enter the keep below. He hung back on the steps, and she feared something else would draw him away. But he pointed toward the row of craft workshops, said something to Walter, and then they both disappeared inside the keep.

Once the bailey was empty, Mackenna dropped the knotted rope out the window, then lowered herself over the side. The air was numbingly cold. The knots supported her feet and gave her hands purchase as she clambered down the rope. One hosen came loose of its ties and slid down to her ankle. Grabbing for it, she slammed into the stone, and nearly screamed as it tore open her knee. The pain stunned her, causing her to hang in place for a moment to regain her breath. The bitter wind quickly numbed the agony and made it bearable.

She tried to picture Thomas in the great hall, snagged by a dozen other questions that needed answers. Anything to keep him out of their chamber. The sight of the unstrung bed would give her away in a heartbeat. He'd know and then come after her, and then . . .

Nay, she must not think of it. She must go on.

She looked up at the window sill that grew further and further away, and knew her feet would soon find the cobbles.

A body's length from the ground, her heel connected with something solid. Before she could look down, a pair of strong hands gripped her ankles and turned her out to the bailey.

She knew the hands only too well.

"Let me go, husband!"

Chapter 24

"Damnation, Mackenna! Are you trying to kill yourself?"

"I'm trying to get away."

"I can see that, love. We all do."

Still dangling above her husband, Mackenna finally spared a glance at the bailey. Though the moon had descended, the cobbles were filled with men staring up at her. Most were grinning, some wore frowns of concern; Francis was frowning hardest of all. Francis, who should have been guarding her chamber door.

"I won't go with you, Montclaire!" she shouted and kicked.

"You were fast on your way to the angels." He gave a gentle tug on the rope, and the whole thing came loose from above.

Mackenna screamed and dropped into her husband's arms, while the rope coiled around her neck and shoulders like a mythical snake. She bucked and tried to get away from Thomas, but he ignored her and walked toward the steps of the keep.

"I'm not leaving with you," Mackenna growled into his ear. "I'm not! I'm not! I'm not!"

He ignored her still as they passed through the great hall and up the stairs to their chamber. He stopped only when he'd closed the door behind them, then let her scramble away from him. Two guards had followed them up and were now posted in the corridor. The window had been shuttered and locked.

"That was quite a spectacle, love. My enchanting wife, dangling from our chamber window against the wall of the keep, her braies—excuse me—*my* braies barely covering her perfectly rounded bottom, exposed for all my men to see."

"I'll get away from you."

"Only when one of us dies, Mackenna. And I pray that I be the first, for I doubt I could live without you."

"You've made it impossible to live *together*, Thomas."

He stood over the webless bedframe and lifted the corner of the mattress with his boot. "You've certainly made it impossible for us to sleep in this bed tonight."

"I'll not sleep beside you ever again, Thomas. I cannot."

"I love you, Mackenna, and I seek redemption. Tomorrow we leave for court where I will plead my case with Edward. I will bow and grovel and do whatever is necessary in order that I may give you back your village."

Mackenna stood there, not believing his words could possibly mean what she prayed they did. "Don't give me false hopes, Thomas. I've had enough of those for a lifetime."

"I lost your home for you; I will recover it."

"You didn't lose it. You never had it."

"But I had you, and it seems that I cannot have one without the other." Thomas stripped out of his traveling clothes, then stood in the tub and washed. Her eyes never left him, and though her gaze was chilled, it aroused him all the same. "Excuse my state of interest, love, but 'tis where my thoughts were ranging until they were waylaid by Edward's game."

Supple bronze and heat: she wanted to touch him, to warm the chill from her hands and her heart. But she could only watch him scrub the towel over his body and don a clean shirt and hosen.

"Good night, Mackenna." He slid the mattress away from the frame and lay down on it, covering himself

with the blankets. She lay down beside him, wrapped in
another blanket. Her knee hurt like fire, her leg was
sticky with blood and needed tending, but she wouldn't
give him the satisfaction of knowing she'd hurt herself
while trying to escape him.

"By the way," he said, his voice slurring with sleep,
"I've five men posted on the wall walk above, and three
below the window, not to mention the two outside our
door. So scuttle any ideas about leaving this room
without me."

She balled herself up in the blankets, fully intending
to lie awake with her plotting, but she awoke during the
night in dreamy splendor. Thomas was warm against
her, his knees tucked behind hers. He was asleep,
blowing his slumber-soft breath into her hair, entwined
as they had done their first night together.

His grand plans to placate Edward would come to
naught. There would always be another game, and
another. And she couldn't let Gilvane loose on the
village, no matter how quickly Thomas might return
with his sword drawn against the villain. It took but a
single match and a gentle breeze to raze the village and
fields, and bring on another killing winter.

She would escape to the fells tomorrow.

When she awakened again, Thomas was tapping on
her foot.

"Get up, Mackenna. And dress in your warmest."

Placidly and without comment, she did as she was
told. "What are you leaving with Gilvane? What records?"

"All of them. They are no good to me."

"They are evidence of gain, Thomas. He'll use them
as you didn't. May I confiscate some of the records from
the office?"

He stared at her for a very long time. "You're coming
with me, Mackenna. Your word on it."

She nodded falsely. "My word on it."

"All right, then. Take Francis with you to the office.
Bring what you can carry in your saddlebag."

"I love you, Thomas." The declaration slipped out and she clamped her hand over her mouth. Shame washed across his face.

"Aye, love, and you know how I feel." He left the chamber.

Drowning in melancholy for what might have been and for what she was about to do, Mackenna finished her packing, tended her knee as best she could, then went down to the hall.

"'Tis a tragedy, my lady," Francis said, closing her office door and setting her saddlebags on the table.

"Aye, Francis. It is. And what about Meg? What are you going to do about her?"

He smiled shyly. "I'm sending for her as soon as we're settled somewhere with his lordship. I plan to marry her!"

She bit off her comment about a snowball in hell. "I'm happy for you both, Francis."

Ready with her next plan of escape, Mackenna moaned and swiped her hands across her face as she stumbled to a chair.

"Dear Jesu, are you all right?"

"I'm very hot all of a sudden, like I walked past a blazing hearth. It'll pass, Francis."

"Are you sick? Can you make such a journey?"

"Nay, I'm not sick, I'm . . . Dear Francis, my husband doesn't know this yet, but I think I'm carrying his babe." Mackenna glanced up at Francis and found him grinning widely. It was a lie, a terrible lie. There was no babe. Her flux was due any day, and she felt as she always did just before it came. But she'd gained the sympathy from Francis that would set him up for her deception, and that was all that mattered.

"You've not told Lord Thomas?" Francis looked scandalized. "And you've told me?"

"I was going to last night; then . . . well, we had other things to talk about and—" She stood up and straightened her skirts. "There. The feeling has passed.

Now, we must quickly sort through these records for the most incriminating.''

Francis looked skeptical. "But you'll tell his lordship about his babe just as soon as you see him?''

"I will, Francis." Mackenna answered his grin with a painful one of her own. She found the books she wanted. Gilvane would use the accounts to guide his raiding parties, so she'd burn them as soon as she got the chance.

Ten minutes later the bags were packed, and she was ready to complete her deception. Thomas would be in the outer bailey with the last of the wagons. She and Francis were to meet him there. She needed time to get away.

"The saddlebag is heavy, Francis," Mackenna said, picking up the leather bag. She sighed suddenly, and clutched her head.

"My lady?" He stood there dumbly transfixed. "What's wrong?''

"I'm going to faint . . .'' Mackenna moaned and tee-tered. "Go get my husband!''

"Mother of God!" he shouted, his face gone dramatically white in the space of a breath. "Blood!''

She thought he'd gone mad as he pointed at her skirts. "Blood?'' She looked down the length of her pale blue gown and saw a stark smear of deep red in the middle of the skirt.

"The babe," he wailed.

"Sweet Mary!" she cried, suddenly frightened to death until she remembered her knee. She'd been scrambling around looking through reports, and hadn't noticed the wound leaking. Francis gasped as she brought her hand out from under her gown. He was clay-faced. "Nay, Francis. 'Tis not what you think!''

"My lady—" He swayed, then toppled over like a tree, knocking the back of his head on the bench as he fell. He landed on the stone floor with a sickening thud.

"Francis!" she yelped as she went to his side. The dear man was out cold! But at least he was breathing. And hard-headed; there wasn't a scratch on him. Mother Mary! She hadn't expected Francis to hurt himself, hadn't planned to use her own blood. But 'twas what she deserved for pretending to be with child!

Francis moaned and his eyes fluttered. "My lady?" He looked up at her, gasped, then his eyes fell shut again.

Francis would live. She kissed his forehead.

If she left now, Thomas would think she had clunked Francis on the head and left him for dead, when all she had wanted was for Francis to chase after Thomas and give her time to escape. She ought to stay and let Francis know that she was well, but then he wouldn't leave her . . .

Francis moaned again and stirred. Time was her only ally. She had no choice but to escape.

Hefting the saddlebag over her shoulder, she opened the office door, closed it carefully behind her, and descended into the wicked darkness toward the pit. The heavy trapdoor squealed as she opened it. She had never told Thomas about the pit and the corridor. There had never been a reason to. The coins had been spent and distributed to the merchants in Carlisle: they were tied up in the village economy. Nay, she admitted to herself, she hadn't told him about the pit, because she never really believed that her dream of peace and comfort could last.

"Goodbye, Thomas, my love, my heart."

The drop to the floor of the pit without the aid of a ladder was ankle-stunting, but it worked and she found the saddlebags in the dark. She scrabbled over the rubble, and felt her way along the passage until the breeze and the light became her beacons. The trip took five minutes, no more. The brambles still hid the opening, but they were moveable as a clump and she eased out of the dimness into the bitter, winter landscape.

Snow had drifted to calf high in places, causing her to wish she'd worn her boots. Her leg was streaked with new blood from her knee. She wondered if Francis had been found. Poor Francis.

There was a sheep fold in the first of the upper fields. She would spend the rest of the day there, then slip into the village as soon as the moon set, as soon as she knew that Thomas was well gone from the valley. Dear Thomas.

Nay, she mustn't think of him.

"Mackenna lost what?" Thomas felt his throat constrict.

"Did she come here to you, Lord Thomas?" Francis asked, gray and swaying on his feet. "Have you seen her?"

"I've not seen my wife since I left her in your care."

"Then—" Francis looked as if he were going to weep.

"Then where is she, Francis?" Thomas gave him a single shake. "Where did you last see my wife?"

Now Francis *was* weeping. "In the office . . . she . . . Jesu, forgive me . . . she's lost her babe—"

"Babe?" Every muscle in him turned to stone.

"It happened and . . . I must have fainted—"

"*What* happened, damn you? What babe?"

"And now I can't find her! There was blood—"

"Blood! Francis, tell me what happened!" Thomas could barely hear for the pulse pounding in his ears.

"She didn't feel well . . . and then she was fine. Then there was blood . . . on her fingers and on her dress—"

Thomas grabbed the nearest horse and headed for the bailey. He didn't know whether to find Gilvane first and kill him now, or to find his wife and help her. His child, *their* child. Nay, he would go to Mackenna.

The office was empty. Books strewn across the table . . .

"Where are you, Mackenna!"

He ran up the stairs to their chamber. A padded chair he'd never seen before sat near the window, as if someone had been watching, enjoying the tragedy in the bailey below. Gilvane—the parasite. Had he seen Mackenna and followed her?

"Have you lost something, Lord Montcl—"

Thomas threw the punch before Gilvane finished the sentence. He left the swine in a moaning heap, sprawled against the wall.

Walter caught up with him coming down the stairs. "Thomas. I heard. Christ, I'm sorry. Have you found her?"

"Nay. She could have crawled into any corner. We'll find her even if I have to tear down this castle stone by stone."

By noon, Thomas had begun to wonder if Mackenna had tried to walk home to her brothers. Betrayed by her king, by her husband, and now by her own womb, she was quite possibly not thinking wisely. Especially if she'd lost a great deal of blood.

While the search continued in the castle, Thomas ordered the wagons to roll out. He rode on toward the village, leaving the groaning caravan to struggle behind him over the frozen roadbed.

He'd done a thousand things wrong in his life, and only one thing right: he loved Mackenna. And he loved this child who'd come too early, and the one lost so long ago, and he would love all their children. Now he needed to find Mackenna and make it right.

The snow began as he reached the section of road that followed the base of the mountain. He scanned one side of the track, then the other, looking for footprints, cursing the heavy flakes that would cover her trail within an hour.

He almost missed the footprints as they crossed the road; most were obscured by the imprint of something trailing behind. A sack, or a saddlebag.

Thomas leaped off Baylor and examined the trail.

Blood. Spots of red leaking into her right footprint. She was still bleeding, the sweet little fool.

"Mackenna." His eyes stinging with unshed tears, he followed the trail, leading Baylor between trees where the snow sometimes gave way to fallen leaves and twigs, and bare creepers. She wasn't following the road to the village; the trail had begun to rise into the steep, rock-strewn fells. He ought to tell someone where he was, but he might miss her. She might be lying unconscious just over the next drift.

She had stopped rarely, but wherever she did, fresh blood collected and sickened him to the core. He was afraid to call out her name, fearing she would hide from him. He left Baylor at the edge of a meadow and kept climbing.

The sun was setting behind Mickelfell in its winter light, blanketed by snow clouds. Flakes fell in showers, but Mackenna's tracks were getting fresher; he was getting closer.

As full dark threatened, he gained a copse and found himself looking at an expanse of meadow. A hundred head of sheep huddled around a small stone building; pale light yellowed the inside.

Probably only a shepherd, but Mackenna may have stopped for help. He said nothing as he approached, letting the sheep part for him. Cold with dread, he peered through the opening and found the most agonizingly beautiful sight he'd ever seen.

Mackenna was seated sideways on a wide bench built into the walls. She was huddled inside her cloak and hood, shivering, her feet tucked under her. The rush light was weak, could serve only to warm her hands. But she was there, and alive.

"Mackenna?"

She looked up at the whispered entreaty and froze. Thomas filled up the doorway. Broad, heaving shoulders; gloved hands gripping the stone doorframe hard enough to dislodge the tiny shower of mortar that rained down on his boot; familiar and dear features were rendered strangers because he shouldn't be here. Even in the soft amber of rush light, his face was as gray and hard as the slate he clutched and crumbled.

"Thomas—" His name scratched her throat. He'd tracked her here to this sheep vault after she'd promised him she wouldn't run—she'd promised. Her reasons for defiance were a litany; he'd heard them a thousand times. How could he believe she'd ever abandon her village without a fight to the death?

"Thomas, I—"

"Sweet Jesu." He dropped to his knees and held her as if he'd been away at war. "I'm sorry, love. Forgive me."

Mackenna was confused, but nuzzled him for his comforting scent and held him because she missed him as she would miss breathing. He should be blazing with anger; he had every right. He must have spent all day searching for her. He'd tracked her through snow drifts, and now that he'd found her he was . . . apologizing? Nay, this was a trick, one of his damnable lessons.

"Thomas?" She pulled out of his arms, ready to scold him. But tears welled in his eyes. Fear shot through her. Her brothers. One of them must have been hurt, or—

"I found you," he said fiercely. "You're alive and that's all that matters." His fragile smile forced tears to spill from his eyes. "Oh, my love, I didn't know . . ."

"Didn't know?" She was suddenly afraid. This was no trick, no confession of misunderstanding.

"Francis told me what happened."

"Francis?" A chill settled against her heart like a stone. "Is he all right?"

"His head aches, and he's nearly as shaken as I am." He held her face and kissed her eyes, and her cheeks. "Our child, Mackenna. Can you ever forgive me?"

"Forgive you? I . . . dear God, Francis told you—!" Thomas thought she had lost his babe! Just like his nameless girl had so long ago. "I didn't mean to—"

"I should have been with you, Mackenna."

"Nay, Thomas, I—"

"Shhh." He gathered his cloak around her and rocked her. "You need rest, love. I don't know how you made it this far. You're cold as ice."

Mother Mary, all day long he'd been mourning a child who had never been, and searching for a willful wife he thought was in mortal danger. When he learned the truth, his anger would be cataclysmic. *Tell him. Tell him there was no child.*

"You left a trail of blood in the snow."

"Blood?" Her knee. The wound had broken open and

bled with every step. She had finally staunched it with a clump of moss.

He lifted a handful of her dark-stained skirt. "Has the bleeding stopped?"

She could only nod at his expression of self-loathing, and mete out some of her own.

"Should you see someone before we leave, 'Kenna? A midwife?"

"Nay! I'll be all right." In all her plans, she'd never considered how Francis's panic would affect Thomas. It had seemed such a simple deception! Thomas should have returned to the office, discovered her missing, and realized she had tricked Francis once again. If she had been carrying a child, not even a Viking raid would have stopped her from telling Thomas about it.

"Rest then for awhile. I can't lose you." He slid onto the bench behind her and wrapped her in his cloak. "I'm afraid I lost my temper with Gilvane. When I couldn't find you, I punched him. I didn't stay to see how he fared."

"But still, you're leaving the castle to him." That was, after all, why she was in this dilemma.

"For now, love. I have no choice. And neither have you." He spoke the last with his jaw set. "Can you travel?"

"Whether I can or not, it doesn't matter. You don't seem to understand that I won't leave the village unprotected—"

"Mackenna, I've posted guards."

"Gilvane will find them—"

He twined a curl around the tip of his finger. "Nay, my love, he'll merely find that most of the families in Fellhaven have gained a strapping son, or an uncle—"

"Your men?" she asked in sudden wonder at his care and resourcefulness.

"Aye, 'tis what I was arranging when I found my wife dangling from the keep."

"Thomas, how can a village of disguised guards help? Gilvane has a whole garrison of trained soldiers—"

"Trained by me, Mackenna, and devoted to you.

Gilvane's loyal men are few, and will be easily disabled by mine."

"The peace won't last long."

"It needs only last long enough. 'Tis why I am anxious to leave. The sooner I change Edward's mind, the sooner we can relieve Gilvane of his ill-gotten holding. Edward has his price. But I won't know what that is until I confront him. And I cannot confront him, until I find him—"

"And you cannot find him if you're forever chasing me all over creation." Chastened and aching, she covered his hand with hers, finding it in its warm nest below her breast. "I'm sorry."

He tightened his embrace and caught her ear with his lips. His whisper was lazy and timeless, and stretched out over their lives. "Ah, my love, I'd follow you to the very ends of the earth."

Trust him. He offered her village the kind of protection she could never match with her plans to bury and hide and pilfer. Once again, he'd thought of everything. She could do no better for her village than to trust her husband.

"Take me with you, Thomas," she whispered.

"Truly?"

When she nodded, he turned her in his arms and held her.

She might have cried then, let go of the molten grief that seared the backs of her eyes. But this was not the end. Her father's death was still on Gilvane's hands, and Thomas thought another babe had slipped through his arms.

"If you're sure you can travel . . ."

"I'm very sure, Thomas. Take me with you."

Chapter 25

Thomas had insisted Mackenna ride in a wagon, deepening her feelings of guilt. When he saw the treacherous wound on her knee, he tended it himself with a poultice and bindings, never questioning its origin. Where he had once been a teasing and gallant husband, now his attentions were profound and encompassing. He often held her as if he thought her a vapor.

Walter and Francis were no better, treating her as if she would break in two if a strong wind came round the bend.

After two days of travel, they found Edward's hunting party in the stony dale of the river Tees, a few miles from the royal hunting lodge. Massive islands, thick with trees, rode a great sea of gray moors; the winter-grim landscape offered little color save a speckling of bright blue tents pitched on a rise.

Edward rode up to meet them, his blue-black horse blowing frost clouds into the cold air, sending a halo around the king's head as he leaped from his saddle.

"Well, Thomas, you came."

"Did you think I wouldn't?"

Edward took a long moment to assess Thomas. "Frankly I don't know what to think anymore." He turned abruptly toward Mackenna. "And Lady Montclaire."

He stretched his arms up and took her from the

saddle. Thomas was out of his and at her side in an instant.

"Ease off, Thomas," Edward said, setting Mackenna on her feet. "My lady, you've grown even more beautiful, if that were possible. Was your wedding exquisite?"

"It was, Your Grace," Mackenna said, knowing full well she was being led into deep waters, that the king wasn't speaking to her, but to her husband.

"Since I wasn't invited, I had to ask."

Thomas frowned. "I have ever stated, my liege, that if I ever married, it would be for love and nothing else."

"And 'tis what you did, it seems. And 'tis what you got: nothing else."

"It grieves me that you believe that I meant it to be an affront to you. I thought you would be happy for me."

Edward looked at Thomas as if he were a stranger. "And I thought you a loyal vassal."

Before Thomas could respond, Edward took Mackenna's arm and started across the frosted field toward the tents.

Walter fell into step beside Thomas. "There's more to this than a monarch thwarted in his matchmaking."

"Much more, I fear."

Thomas was glad to see Lady Giffard sitting by a brazier in the tent, tending her embroidery. He wanted to give his wife all his attention, but Edward would require enough for a regiment.

"We lost a babe the day before yesterday," he said quietly to Lady Giffard, as he settled Mackenna into a chair beside her.

"My dears, I am so sorry." She put her soft hand on Mackenna's forehead. "How are you feeling?"

"Tired is all." Mackenna held tightly to Thomas's hand, wondering if he would stay with her when he discovered she had woven so grievous a lie.

"Any fever would have set in quickly. I do hate to sound callous, but there will be many other babies. I lost one of my own before I'd even known I carried it. Thomas, I believe this is woman's business. Go play with Edward."

"Mackenna?" He looked down into her eyes.

"Go, Thomas. You need to talk with Edward."

"If you're sure, my love." He bent down and kissed her forehead, then cupped her chin and kissed her mouth so tenderly she wanted to cry and confess, because the waiting was so painful, because he deserved better.

Lady Giffard sighed as Thomas strode away. "Tell me, Lady Montclaire, do those kisses taste as good as they look?"

Mackenna had to smile. "Better."

"Ah, you are a lucky woman."

Mackenna looked away from her friend's honesty. They were alone but for pages and musicians and a portly knight snoring in a corner. The huge blue tent was well lighted with thick tapers; a wall of braziers warded off the frosty air that seeped beneath the canvas. There was food aplenty, rich and unappetizing, and Mackenna's stomach tumbled when the aromas floated past her.

Lady Giffard asked questions about the wedding, claiming only to have heard Thomas's version, and asserting her dismay over not being there to see it herself.

"I know he seems quite upset about losing this child," Lady Giffard said kindly. "But he doesn't blame you, dear."

"Aye, but he should." She had to tell someone, make someone understand. So far from home, Lady Giffard was her only friend.

"'Tis God's will, Mackenna. It cannot be helped."

"Lady Giffard," she said too abruptly. "I did not lose a babe. I'm not with child now, and I wasn't then."

The lady took Mackenna's hand. "What are you saying, my dear?"

Mackenna told her about how her escape had gone so terribly wrong. "I thought Thomas would see through my scheme, like he always has. Instead—"

"Dear girl, what a mess you've made."

"I've ruined his life." Cold to the bone, Mackenna lifted out of her chair and held her hands over the brazier. "Thomas should have rebuilt the castle, trained the men, and then left for his wars. He was perfectly happy being a soldier."

"Nay, Mackenna, he wasn't happy. He was lonely."

"But he wasn't miserable."

"You'll have to tell him the truth sometime. He's a man of great heart. Don't sell him short. Dear, are you all right?"

The air had gotten thin, and Mackenna caught hold of a tent post to keep from pitching over. Her skin flushed cold and damp. The tent pitched about; then the spinning in her head stopped as abruptly as it had come.

"I'm very tired, Lady Giffard," Mackenna said, suddenly weary. She wrapped her cloak around herself and sat down in the chair beside Lady Giffard.

"Are you hungry?"

The thought made her stomach roll. "Please. No food."

"Really? Mmmm . . . then tell me more about your wedding, Mackenna. I'm leaving for Darlington this afternoon to visit my sister, and I must hear everything before I leave." Lady Giffard smiled and picked up her embroidery.

When the skies threatened snow, Mackenna and Lady Giffard were escorted to the king's hunting lodge. The building was enormous, a palace to anyone but a nobleman. She left Lady Giffard in the great hall and arranged for their bedding and clothes to be brought up to their small chamber. She made up the bed herself, undressed to her skin and slipped beneath the clove-scented sheets to wait for Thomas. But sleep claimed her in the midst of her prayer for his safety.

The afternoon had played more like a game of cat and mouse than a hunt. Edward had been in splendid form, his temper short and regal, especially where Thomas was concerned. The king was obviously going to take

his own time, would lay out his line and wait for the
perfect moment to spring his trap.

It was near dark when the hunting party rode into the
courtyard. Mackenna was sleeping deeply when Thomas found her in their chamber. He prayed that her
weariness was no more than the difficult ride and the
emotional strain of the miscarriage. She had been
keeping little food in her stomach, a sure sign of a fever,
yet her skin remained cool and dry.

He smoothed a finger across her cheek and she moved
in her sleep, nudging his hand, entreating him to touch
her again.

"Dear love," he whispered, "what have I done to
you?" He'd never been so frightened, nor cared so
deeply.

Seeing the blood on Mackenna's skirt that day in the
sheep fold had brought it all back to him. Guilt had
become a part of his breathing again. Images he'd
buried long ago intruded without a breath of warning,
causing him to stammer and stall until he could finally
focus past the memories: past the tiny, linen-shrouded
bundle, the bloodied towels piled on the dirt floor, past
his molten grief.

The small fireplace was unlit, and the air chilled
enough for his breath to collect in a cloud. He brought
up a fire and washed quickly in the small tub. He dried
off, then leaned down to her on the bed, watching his
astonishing wife. He found himself smiling stupidly. He
was a lucky fool.

There would be other children, just as Lady Giffard
had promised. It wasn't a cruelty to think that. 'Twas the
cycle of life: sow, then reap. Mackenna had taught him
that.

She opened her eyes when he kissed her. He nuzzled
her ear and whispered, "Good evening, wife. I missed
you."

"And I adore you. Have you been standing in the rain,
husband?" He looked untamed, overhanging her like a
great lion with its paws planted on either side of her

head. She whisked her fingers through his mane, and tiny drops of water fell on her cheeks and forehead. She tucked away her misery and gave herself over to kissing her husband.

"May I join you under the bedclothes, my love? 'Tis cold out here and I've not a stitch to cover my backside."

"Come, let me warm it for you." She lifted the blanket and opened her arms. His skin was cool and coarse-furred beneath her hands. "I've missed you, Thomas. May we stay thus all night?"

"That would be paradise, love. But we must dress soon for Edward's feast. There will be game and sweet-meats aplenty. As I passed through the hall I could smell—"

Mackenna's stomach lurched up her throat. "The privy—"

She made it as far as the hearth before she was on her knees in the rushes, sweating and trembling with a clenching stomach that had no food to give up. He swabbed her forehead and the back of her neck, ran the cooling cloth over her nakedness. By the time he was finished and the wave had passed over her, she felt oddly rested and hungry, and safely wrapped in his arms.

He kissed her forehead. "You're not feverish."

She knew that she couldn't be, at least not for the reason her poor husband thought. Now was the time to tell him.

"I've not felt well for a few days."

"Perhaps that's why you lost the babe."

Tell him you didn't lose anything. "Thomas, I can't go on like this."

"But you can. We'll have other children." He sat cross-legged on the rushes, rocking her in his lap. "Ah, love, after so much time . . . I'd settled in my mind that I'd have no children. Trouble they are, and noisy. But the longer I knew you, the more I saw you as my wife, overripe with my child, and suckling another, and I saw little ones perched on my shoulders and four others using us for a Maypole dance. And the noise turned to gladness, and the trouble turned to stuff that family legends spring from. I am a man of great good fortune."

Salt-thick tears burned behind her eyes. This was Gilvane's doing. All of her sorrow, all the misery in her life flowed from him. All of her happiness was tainted with his poison. She would shed no tears until he was vanquished.

She turned clear eyes on her husband. "Will you make love to me, Thomas? Plant another seed?"

He cocked his head. "Ought we? So soon after—"

Staving off the intrusion of her deception, she put her fingers to his lips. "You have amazing curative powers."

He looked skeptical, with that wilful eyebrow arched and his eyes narrowed. She kissed his shoulder. He'd grown warm and tasted of her own violet-scented soap. "I want you, Thomas."

His gaze was like a summer day as he carried her to the bed. "If I'm to plant my seed, I must first prepare your furrow with care."

Her guilt lost ground to the glint in his eyes. "Oh, and what is your scheme, sir plowman?"

" 'Tis too complicated to explain. Better that I show you." Never losing her gaze, he flicked his tongue along the ridge of her jaw, making her wriggle and sigh.

"Aye, 'tis a fine scheme, Thomas." She gasped as his fingers led his mouth in a sweep across the rise of her breast to the pulsing tip that puckered for him. He teased there; a tiny, quick pressure with his lips, then a boyish smile that made her heart run wild inside her chest; a flick of his amazing tongue, then a rowdy sucking that made him moan and close his eyes and grind his hips into her belly. And all the while he tantalized the other breast with a steadfast, pulsating pleasure.

"You tremble, my love. Are you in mortal pain?"

She tried to talk, but his fingers wandered ever further down her hip, and she was left only enough breath to sigh.

"I take that to mean you are not." He laughed. "I promise to wield a gentle plow—"

"Not too gentle, I pray." She'd have opened to him, but he'd trapped her legs closed with his, and only rested there between them, twining his fingers in her curls, teasing, watching her whimper and writhe. And so he teased and talked in his deep tones about hunting for eager game in the royal forests until he drove her to the brink with his fondling.

Mackenna reached for him, but he imprisoned her hand above her head. "Sweet, I cannot plant another seed if you wield the plow with your own hand and cause me to spill the lot before I reach your field."

She giggled. "You are not so negligent a plowman."

"Nay, but I am a hungry one." He entered her swiftly, but not deeply. His restraint played across his face, beading sweat on his brow, tightening his lips. "I don't want to hurt you."

"You can't, Thomas. You've proved that a thousand times." She held his face and rained kisses over it. There would be no bright flashes of fulfillment for her tonight. She was trembling with her need of him, but the melancholy of guilt made absolute pleasure seem a falsehood. She would give pleasure to him.

Thomas tried to hold back for her, but her passion had waned and he knew the cause. It wasn't pain; she was trying to draw him deeper than he ought to go. When she slid her fingers between their bellies, his cause was lost, blinding him to all but the place of their joining, and he spilled into her. She hadn't been with him this time and his pleasure was fleeting, though his muscles still shuddered with spent passion.

"Forgive me, Mackenna. I will tend this babe with far more wisdom than the last."

"Don't, Thomas."

She bound him with legs and arms of forged steel, and seemed in no great hurry to let him go. He smiled against her cheek and let her have her way with him, this jailer of silk. He was well trapped and well loved; and lying abed with Mackenna till all the seas ran dry seemed a wondrous thing to do. His heart finally fell to resting and his breathing eased.

He stroked her hair and took in her scent, and she was asleep again in a minute. He dipped to kiss her, but a sharp rap on the door stopped him. He covered Mackenna and donned a clean shirt before he opened the door.

Giffard's frown was locked fiercely beneath his moustache.

"Before you speak, Giffard, remember to keep your voice down. I want Mackenna to sleep for as long as possible. She's not been feeling well."

Giffard peered at the bed. "Aye, my lady told me. The devil take you, Thomas, you did pluck a wild beauty. But then, I expected as much. Soon as I saw you together in Carlisle, I thought to myself, 'Edrick, old boy, those two will love each other till the sun goes dark.'"

"I wish you'd mentioned such to me then; we might have been saved all this madness." Thomas pulled on his braies and fastened his hosen.

"Edward does have a burr 'neath his saddle about you, lad. I can't get two words out of him about it." Giffard lowered himself into a chair.

"He says I was disloyal to marry without his leave."

"'Tis more than that. 'Tis something to do with that rotter Gilvane. Once you left the court, he hung at the king's ear like a moorish ring. When word of your marriage reached him, Edward took to using your name in vain."

"Bloody hell!" Feeling as if he were suddenly dressing for battle, Thomas slipped his tunic over his head and buckled on his sword belt. "I'll not have Mackenna suffer another moment of Ned's temper. She's lost a child and her home. I'll not wake her for another of Edward's feasts. Come, Giffard."

Thomas touched Mackenna's cheek with his lips. "I'll make it right, my love." He closed the door behind them.

Mackenna opened her eyes in time to see the latch fall into place. She'd awakened when Giffard had come into the room, and all the while she had pretended to sleep, too ashamed to face Thomas. If she had any honor she

would have confessed to him in the sheep fold. She
would have thrown herself on her knees and begged his
forgiveness for letting him grieve, and for not trusting
him to protect her village.

She'd become a helpless fool, still too angry to cry,
and too frightened of the price of confessing her deception. She had given over her life to Thomas and to
Gilvane and the king. Her father wouldn't have. He'd
have confessed, suffered his rebuke, then he'd have
risen from the aftermath to fight again.

She sat up, surprised that her stomach was settled and
her head was clear. As soon as the feast ended, she'd tell
Thomas. Let him rail and call her a liar. At least it would
be done.

She dressed in the gown she'd been married in,
settled a silken coif over her hair and a circlet of ribbon,
and left for the feast.

Thomas saw Mackenna the moment she walked into
the hall, a delight for his sore eyes. He met her below
the tables.

"Love, you are a vision." He kissed her temple. "But I
left you, thinking you needed sleep."

"I've had entirely too much of that lately. Thomas, I
must speak with you when this is done. 'Tis very
important."

"I hope you'll speak with me during the feast, into
this ear, with your teeth and tongue. I shall try to behave
myself."

"Thomas, this is a serious matter."

"Aye, *very* serious." He guided her to her chair and sat
down beside her. "For I love you with all my heart."

Through the meal, he held her hand as if he thought
she might float away. She ate only bread and apple-
sauce, fearing a return of the queasiness.

Thomas kept an eye on his liege lord. Edward had
been overloud in his celebrating, but had not drunk
much at all. A weathervane of trouble on the horizon.
The king liked his wine, but eschewed it for cider before
an important event.

Locking glances with Thomas, Edward suddenly rose.

"Lords and ladies, we drink a toast to Thomas Mont-claire and his new bride, the Lady Mackenna."

Thunderous stomping and thumping of fists bounced off the stone walls, as pages poured wine into cups and goblets all around.

"I don't like this, Thomas," Giffard said amid the noise. "Look at that smile. Cold as glass."

"Neither do I like it, but we will bear it. In truth, the waiting was laying me low."

"Thomas, what's happening?" Mackenna asked, sud-denly frightened by the muscles that had gone rigid in his arm.

"We'll know soon enough, love." He closed his hand over hers. "Whether he denounces me or our marriage, whether he banishes me or imprisons me, I vow that I will return Fellhaven to you within the week."

"Imprisons you?" Imprison Thomas? He wouldn't!"

"My lords!" Edward raised his bulky goblet high over the table, spilling some of the liquid onto his hand. It ran down his wrist into his cuff. "To Lord Thomas Montclaire and his remarkable lady. May they be blessed with many healthy children, and may they prosper in their new lives so they no longer find it necessary to steal from the royal treasury."

Thomas shot to his feet. "You accuse me of stealing?"

"I've not finished my toast, Thomas."

"My liege, I would hear the proof of this charge."

Edward reached over his plate and held aloft a small leather bag. "Is this proof enough?" He shook the leather pouch and it sounded of coins.

"Proof of what? How can I defend my honor when I do not know the charge?"

Edward tossed the sack the length of the table. "This reminder should be enough."

Thomas snagged the sack midair and pulled out a handful of coins. Snorting, he looked up at Edward. "Silver pennies?"

"Exactly!" Edward exclaimed, crossing his long arms across his chest.

"Exactly *what*, Your Grace? I know nothing of these coins."

"Nothing?" As Edward started toward Thomas, the knights and ladies sitting in his way scooted back in their chairs, felling them and stumbling in their haste. "These coins were struck in Newcastle seven years ago and never circulated, because they were underweight. The lot of silver was recalled and new coins were struck. All but a dozen barrels of the old were accounted for. They were stolen before they ever left the silversmith. Where have these coins been, Thomas?"

Thomas held out his palm. Two coins rolled off into Mackenna's plate. "Buried, by the looks of the tarnish. More than that, Your Grace, I cannot tell you."

"I can," Edward said. "Gilvane confessed that they had been among the hoard he'd stolen and hidden in his castle. They'd been readied for shipment to Normandy when he abandoned his holding."

"And?"

"And a large quantity of these coins were spent in Carlisle to purchase arms and armory."

Thomas snorted. "And is your charge that I have a stockpile of arms hidden somewhere, purchased with stolen silver? To what purpose, my liege? Do you think me a man standing in rebellion?"

"Rebellion takes many guises."

"If this charge did not spring from the mouth of John Gilvane, I would consider it a threat. Your Grace, I have never seen these coins."

"But I have, Thomas." Mackenna stood up, placing herself between the two men. She knew the coins very well.

"Sit down, Mackenna," Thomas hissed into her ear. "I'll handle this."

"You cannot, Thomas. 'Tis my doing." She turned to the king, braving his fury. "Your Grace, I am your thief."

The crowded hall erupted for a moment, then quieted to the shushing of those who loved a scandal.

Thomas pulled her against his chest. "Say not another word."

"I stole these coins from you, Thomas, and spent them in Carlisle." She couldn't let Edward think Thomas had anything to do with this. He was innocent. The crime was hers.

"You couldn't have, my love. My coins are with the rest of my treasury—held safely with the Templars in York."

Edward straightened. "You've money with the Templars?"

"Mackenna, love, I've never seen these coins before. They're not mine."

"Nay, Thomas, they belong to our king. Please, Your Grace, I didn't know they were yours. I thought Fellhaven belonged to Thomas. I thought I was stealing from him."

"Only stealing from your husband? This is your defense?"

"Nay, Your Grace. 'Tis my explanation."

Thomas turned her in his arms and held her chin up. "Mackenna, you needn't cover for me—"

" 'Tis the truth, Thomas. I found barrels of silver pennies in a sealed corridor leading off the pit."

"Off the pit? You mean the dungeon? When?"

" 'Twas soon after you imprisoned me."

"You imprisoned your wife, Thomas?" Edward looked shocked.

"She wasn't my wife then."

"And that is *your* defense? What did she do?"

"I tried to burn down his castle . . . *your* castle—"

"Mackenna, you found coins, and you never told me?"

"By the time I would have dared, I'd spent them all." She looked up at Thomas and found his brow deeply furrowed. She'd betrayed him once again, another deception come to haunt her. "Didn't you wonder how your money went so far in Carlisle?"

Neither Edward nor Thomas said anything; they only stared.

"Thomas?" she said. He was clearly ready to paddle her.

Walter's head was in his hands.

"Is there anything else you've not told me, wife?"

She had confessed her theft in front of the entire hall of gaping courtiers. They now awaited her answer just as her husband did, just as the king did. She couldn't tell Thomas about the babe; not now with an audience looking on. Her knees had been wobbling and watery since she'd stood up.

"Aye, Thomas. But I cannot tell you here," she said, not sure that her lips had actually moved. His face had begun to swim, his features blurred. "I think I'm going to—"

"Mackenna!" Thomas caught her as her legs gave out beneath her. His heart was struck from his chest. Others might think this fainting spell a ruse, but he'd seen her eyelids flutter and her eyes roll back. "Excuse me, Edward." He lifted her and moved from the table.

"One moment, Thomas."

"Your Grace?" Expecting sympathy, Thomas was surprised to find a tic of anger jumping out at Edward's temple.

"When you are finished, Lord Montclaire, I'll want to know of this treasure you have stockpiled with the Templars, and why you never told me of it."

Thomas nodded curtly and left the hall with his ungovernable wife a dead weight in his arms.

"Mackenna, my little thief, wake up!" She was stirring by the time Thomas lowered her onto the bed. He loosened the ties at her throat, determined to call a midwife into the room. His hands quaked as he laid a cold cloth to her brow.

"What!" Mackenna gained her senses immediately and recoiled from him, taking refuge behind a pillow. "How did I get here?"

She'd been in the midst of a terrible dream; she'd told Thomas about the baby and he'd put her in his pit.

"You fainted and I carried you. How are you feeling?"

"Did I say anything?"

"Other than confessing to raiding Edward's trea-

sury—nay." He sat down on the edge of the bed and felt
her cheek. "I'm going to find a midwife to look in on
you."

"Mother Mary, what have I done?" She bit at her
knuckles. "I don't need a midwife, Thomas."

"You do—"

"Is the king terribly angry? I would have told you
about the coins, Thomas, but they were gone by the
time it mattered. I have it all written down, every penny
accounted for."

"Ah, yes, the coins. I no doubt you've accounted for
them better than the royal exchequer would. The king's
anger doesn't matter. This is a severe offense, whether
you knew the owner of the silver or not."

"Every penny went back into your village."

"Your good intentions are admirable, but your lack of
sense has cost us valuable time in reclaiming your
village. Edward didn't know the Templars hold money
and other treasures for me."

"What will he do?"

"Your little game of rob and plunder has seriously
damaged my power to bargain. I might have gotten
away with paying him treble what you stole in silver
pennies. Now that he knows I have a treasury, he'll
want every morsel for himself."

"I'm sorry, Thomas." She held his warm hand against
her cheek.

"Be sorry for Fellhaven, Mackenna. I don't know
when I'll be able to reclaim the holding. If I open the
doors to my treasury and let Edward have all, in exchange for allowing me to keep Fellhaven, the next time
he levies another of his war aids I'll have nothing to
give, and he'll dangle eviction in our faces until I do as
he bids: ride to war, strongarm a minister, side with him
in a dispute with the other barons. He has fixed his dice
and, unfortunately, Fellhaven will suffer."

"Because of me."

"You've sown a row of weeds this time." He leaned
down and kissed her. "Have you told me everything,
Mackenna? When I'm standing face to face with the

king, is he going to surprise me with another of your
follies? Have you been smuggling wool out of the port at
Ravensglass without paying Edward's export duty?"

She shook her head. "Nothing like that, Thomas."

"Nothing like that . . . but there *is* something. You
told me so in the hall. 'Tis time to tell me everything."

She drew her knees against her chest. The shortness
of breath and the grinding in her stomach wasn't illness
this time; it was fear and shame. Her mouth was dry, the
words bitter.

"What is it, sweet?"

" 'Tis unthinkable, Thomas."

"Unthinkable?" He absorbed the fist of fear that
struck his gut. Adultery was unthinkable . . . Nay, not
Mackenna. For all her willfulness, she was faithful unto
death.

"Thomas." She scooted toward him and took his
hand. "I went too far this time."

"Too far?" he asked evenly.

"I was ever honest with you in stating that I would
protect my village, no matter the cost to me. That I
would do anything—"

"You always made that potently clear to me. What
have you done, Mackenna?"

"I've hurt you, Thomas."

He studied her for a clue, but found none. "You've
annoyed me, love, and angered me to the quick. This
matter with the silver pennies has put a strain on my
charity, but—"

"Nay, Thomas, it has nothing to do with Edward.
This is between you and me. I didn't mean it to happen,
but—"

He released her hand and straightened. "This is
beginning to sound like something I might not want to
hear."

"Please, Thomas. 'Twas something I caused in my last
bid for freedom. Something that will hurt you deeply."

"Then stop twisting the knife, Mackenna. Is it someone else? Have you been with another man?"

She scrambled to her knees. "How dare you think that!"

"Christ, woman, what am I to think?" He clasped her chin between his hands. "Just tell me straight out."

There was no other way. "I didn't lose our babe, Thomas."

He canted his head as if he wanted to hear the words again. "You didn't . . . ?"

The light of hope in his eyes made her look away from him. "I wasn't carrying a child."

"And you thought you were?" He knelt beside the bed, her head still caught between his hands, his careworn thumbs stroking her cheeks. "The blood—was it your flux?"

"Nay, Thomas. 'Twas a terrible mistake. I was sure you'd realize that I had deceived Francis again to escape you—"

"Deceived him? What's he to do with . . . ?"

Mackenna watched the terrible shadows of understanding cloud his eyes, and felt her world crumbling.

When he spoke again, his words seemed clotted. "Francis thought you'd miscarried, because . . . you wanted him to."

"I meant only to frighten him into leaving me alone to fetch you, so that I could escape the castle. I only told him I was dizzy. But he saw blood on my gown from my knee. He assumed I'd lost the baby, then fainted and hit his head on a chair. I never meant him to see any blood. I know I promised to go with you, but I couldn't leave the village unprotected. I had no choice but to escape. No other choice! I thought you would know that!"

"And I thought I knew you, Mackenna," he said, too quietly. A cold muscle moved inside his cheek.

"You do know me, Thomas! Better than anyone, better than I know myself."

"Well, at least we both know what price you'll pay for your damned village." He stood up. "'Tis more costly than I had expected, but I do understand now."

"Nay, Thomas, you don't. I never meant for you to

think I'd lost our child. I couldn't do that to you. Not after . . . I know how you feel about—" She couldn't look at him any longer. He was a frightened, grief-stricken young man again.

"Then why keep it from me, Mackenna?" he asked evenly.

"I tried to tell you in the sheep fold—"

"Stop it!" His face as lifeless as a statue, he started for the door.

"Thomas, please stay a moment. Hear me out."

He stopped, one hand on the latch, the other hanging loose at his side. "You had fully two days to explain yourself, wife. What more could you possibly say in the space of a moment?"

The door slammed behind him.

Chapter 26

"**T**homas?" Mackenna whispered. She touched the smoothly planed door with her fingertips and rested her cheek against its coolness. "Thomas . . . I'm sorry."

But he was gone, his footsteps retreating.

He was grand-hearted and forgiving, blessed with a seemingly endless store of mercy. She had wounded him; she'd wounded that great big warrior who wept after each battle. She'd never felt so wicked in all her life. She had committed crimes against him that would have caused a lesser man to leave her to the wolves. But he'd stayed through her rebellion and loved her; she'd lied to him and stolen from him, and still he loved her . . . until she'd used his phantom child to make good her escape.

An innocent child . . . Mother Mary, what had she done?

A knock sounded at the door. Mackenna ran to it, expecting to see Thomas standing there, too blazingly angry to talk, but standing there all the same. She flung open the door.

"Francis? What—?"

"Your pardon, my lady, I've been told that you must pack."

Mackenna clutched at the door frame. "Pack? Francis, why?"

"You're to leave on the morrow with Lord Giffard."

353

"I'm to leave?" Mackenna staggered backward into the room as if he'd had struck her. Thomas was sending her away.

"I'm going with you, my lady, to Giffard's castle."

"Until when?"

Francis hung his head and fiddled with his cuff. "Lord Thomas didn't say. And, if you don't mind, my lady, I think his lordship is overangry. You didn't mean to spend the king's money. 'Twas a mistake. I was there. You bought anvils and looms, not arms. And I told the king so—"

"Francis, you stood up for me to the king?"

His face reddened. "I don't know what came over me. Lord Thomas stopped me from saying more. That's when he told me—"

"That he was sending me away." She sagged into a chair. "Please don't blame him, Francis. 'Tis not pennies that have torn us apart, 'tis my selfishness. But there's nothing to be done now."

"Shall I help you pack?"

"Nay, Francis. I'll do it."

"As you wish, my lady." Francis grabbed her hand and pressed a kiss to the back of it, then hurried out of the chamber. An unseen bolt slid into place.

It was done, then. Her marriage was over.

She'd never lied about her devotion to the village, and Thomas had been as good a lord as he knew how to be. They both had done their best, but truth had been secondary in their alliance. She was of the village, and he of the nobility.

And so they would remain.

"We'll be home by tomorrow noon," Giffard said, stepping aside as Mackenna's trunk was carried from the chamber.

"He's truly sending me away, Lord Giffard?" Mackenna asked pathetically, folding Thomas's tunic.

"For a time, only for a time. My home is near Penrith, and 'tis quite comfortable. And my lady wife will be returning there within the week. You can sew and chat, and in no time, your groom will come for you. Mark me, he will." He slipped her cloak over her shoulders and fastened it at the collar.

"May I say goodbye to him at least?"

Giffard shook his head, diverting his gaze. "He's gone with the king. They left the lodge together late last night."

"They left? To go where?"

"To Barnard Castle. I know not why. Perhaps to wait out the report from the Templars. 'Tis Balliol's castle; perhaps Edward had business there."

She had squandered Thomas's chance to claim Fellhaven; no amount of talking or money would change Edward's mind. Besides, Thomas was no longer concerned about the holding; his treasure was threatened. She was on her own again. She had managed without him before, she would manage again.

"Did Thomas leave me a message?"

"None that I know of, sweet. I'm sorry. Come, 'tis nearly time to leave for home."

"Nay, my lord. 'Tis long past time."

Mackenna was ravenously hungry by the time they stopped for the night at a comfortable inn. She sat with Giffard and Francis in the common room and eagerly downed a meat pie: a fat, greasy meal that yesterday would have brought up her morning cider.

She would travel with them as far as Giffard's castle, then she would set out for Fellhaven. But first she had to convince her escort that she was hell-bent to return to Thomas. It was a simple matter to look forlorn; she was that and more.

"What's wrong, lass?" Giffard asked.

"I want to go back to Thomas. Please take me to him." Her eyes were dry, but her voice quavered of its own accord. "If I could just see him, I could convince him—"

"Now, I don't know what it is you're spatting over,

but if Thomas has sent you away, he's got a good reason. He's quite busy minding the king and his temper."

"But he needs me. I shouldn't have let him send me away."

"You had no choice in the matter, my lady," Francis said.

"I chose to leave with you. Now I choose to return to the hunting lodge." Stuffing the remainder of the meat pie into her mouth, she started toward the door. She got all the way outside before Francis caught her arm.

"You're not going anywhere, my lady." Francis was scowling as Giffard came up beside them.

"You can't stop me!" She hid her eyes and cried her barren tears.

"Take care, Lord Giffard," Francis said, "I've been tricked by this woman more times than I will ever admit."

Giffard laughed until she resisted his entreaty to return to the inn, dragging her heels and trying to pull away. He deposited her in her room and put a guard at her door. Pleased that they'd taken her bait, Mackenna fell asleep and awakened a few hours later feeling better rested than she had in a week.

By the time they rode into Giffard's bailey, she was hemmed in on four sides by mounted guards, her slippers were stuffed into Giffard's saddlebags, and her hands were tied behind her back. But she escaped the castle in the dead of night, clothed in the long braies, tunic, and close-fitting cap of the lad who tended the great hearths of Castle Giffard. He'd come to her chamber with a load of kindling. She had apologized as she bound and gagged him, and had blushed along with him as she stripped him of his clothes. Couldn't be helped. Her village needed her.

'Twas over, her life among the nobles. Good riddance to them all. She would live out her life in the woods that surrounded the village. She'd be their guardian and protect them from whomever Edward would send to replace Gilvane. For the man would not be lord for much longer. 'Twas the only way.

Justice must be done.

Thomas's head ached. His heart was shredded. He stopped Baylor on the edge of a wooded copse, and gazed unseeing into the understory of leafless bracken.

These were the longest two days of his life. Sitting out Edward's black temper had been simple, a recurring theme in his long history with the man. Awaiting the accounting from the Templars in York was nerve-wracking but endurable, even with Edward constantly examining his motives for not telling him about the funds he held in cash, funds that Edward would have tapped for any one of a dozen campaigns in the years past.

These were merely annoyances compared to his crisis with Mackenna. He closed his eyes against hearing her words shoot through him again. God's blood, he'd confessed his guilt and sorrow over the death of his first child; how could she have thought he'd feel any different with another?

She had played expertly on his heart, letting him think she had lost a child that they had created in love. She'd let him think he'd been responsible. He had damned himself a thousand times, had tried to scrub the sight of her blood from his memory, just as he'd tried so long ago.

And she'd used this false child to escape him and run off to her damnable village. A false child. A false marriage.

His anger insisted that her love had also been false, but he knew at the center of him that she loved him. Mackenna loved with a ferocity that drove her to act imprudently in defense of those lucky enough to be loved by her.

And he loved her because of it.

He wondered if she'd gotten the missive he'd sent to Giffard's the night she had left the lodge. Had she searched his words for forgiveness and realized it was still locked inside him? He'd sent her with Giffard to put a distance between them, unable to deal with Edward and Mackenna at the same time. If he wanted to keep Mackenna and her damn village, he needed to tend to Edward first.

Edward rode up beside him. "If you miss her so much, why don't you send for her?"

"I can't just now." He turned Baylor and started down the copse toward Walter. Edward followed.

"He once told me he was as dense as shale where his wife was concerned," Walter said, slanting Thomas a cutting glare as he approached. "It seems he was right."

"Bring her back, lad. She's got a devilish sense of duty to that damnable village; loyal to a fault, but I've forgiven her."

"I have not."

Walter blocked the path with his horse, forcing Thomas to look at him. "They were only silver pennies, Thomas. She was buying iron for hinges and pots, not for arms."

Edward penned Thomas in from the rear. "Aye, that doesn't excuse the debt, but it does excuse the motive."

"'Tis something else. A personal matter."

"Infidelity?" Edward asked.

Thomas laughed. "Nay, she's as constant as the sun."

"Then what? Does she have a shrewish tongue? Does she keep you from her bed? She's a delight to speak with. And it cannot be her scent—"

"Mackenna betrayed me. I never thought she would, never imagined she could." Thomas watched a hundred emotions play across Walter's face. He didn't know the truth; no one did but he and Mackenna.

Edward snorted. "Betrayed how, Thomas, if you say she is constant?"

The king was the last man he wanted to confess his problems to, but he was near at hand, and Walter, too, a friend of long-standing faith.

"In my misguided wife's last bid to protect the village,

she escaped the guard I'd set on her by pretending she miscarried."

"Pretending?" Walter gasped.

Thomas hung his head, uncomfortable airing this very dirty linen. "I tracked her into the hills, and she let me believe the babe had been lost due to my harsh treatment."

"She said those words?" the king asked suspiciously.

"Nay, she implied it by her silence. For two days I believed that my history had followed me into my new life. I believed that I had failed her."

"And you have, Thomas," Walter said with a growl. There was banked fire in his friend's eyes.

"Meaning?"

"She swallowed her pride and allowed Gilvane into her home, because she knew you would protect it when you returned. Then you walked away and left everything she loved in the hands of her greatest enemy. *You* failed *her*, Thomas!"

"Forced out by a royal writ," Thomas said sharply. "I had no choice in the matter." He turned to Edward. "By your leave, my liege."

"'Tis the truth of it," Edward said with a shrug. "But I think you're the source of your own troubles, Thomas. If your tales are true, your wife has made a practice of deception in the name of her village. And yet you believed she had conveniently lost a babe when you knew how badly she wanted to escape."

"She should have told me it wasn't so."

Walter reined in beside Thomas. "Mayhaps the thought of disappointing you was more frightening than letting you mourn. She knows you, Thomas. She was doomed to keep her secret from you from the moment you caught up with her. I can't imagine she enjoyed it."

Thomas sighed and looked up through the canopy of barren limbs to the heavy gray skies. "Nor can I."

Edward pulled up on his other flank. "If you mean to abandon her, Thomas, I know any number of barons who would take her off your hands."

The threat struck Thomas like a death blow to his newfound dreams. "I'm not bloody hell going to abandon my wife to *any* man! She's mine—thorns, falsehoods, and all."

"If she were mine," Edward said, sending a satisfied smile toward Walter, "I'd go get her myself."

"You're the king, Ned; you can do most anything you please."

Edward sighed. "Except that I can't give you Fellhaven. 'Tis Gilvane's. He paid me well for it, bringing Balliol to the throne. If I revoke his grant, I'll have northern barons and border lairds snapping at me for decades. I need them."

"Then will you negotiate a settlement between Gilvane and me? I don't care the cost. I'll purchase his grant and see him settled in another holding. I'll buy off the good will of your barons—"

"You have that much in your treasury, Thomas?"

"We'll know soon, won't we?"

Mackenna hoped no one would question the new musician beating upon the tambor in the loft at Fellhaven. She had dressed herself in Addis's clothes—dark, homespun braies, a tunic and short surcote. She was still bone-tired, hungry all the time, and every other thought strayed to Thomas and near dropped her in her tracks. At least she was safe in her disguise. The village had learned long ago to keep its secrets, and to listen to the tales that spilled down off the castle walls.

She watched Gilvane and his men in the great hall below, listening to Colin's tales of terror. 'Twas nothing that she hadn't heard and seen already since she'd returned two days before. Fear and misery, a hopelessness so palpable it thickened the air: the winter stores were gone, carted up here for the lord's table. Firewood, fleece, fodder: all of it stolen from the village barns and transferred to the castle.

There was just one way to reclaim it.

Gilvane's men were soon drink-sodden and loud. The soldiers trained by Thomas sat straight-backed and ate with eyes downcast—not cowed, but outraged. She could see it in the set of their shoulders, in the way they would look to each other for silent comment on their new lord and his men. The soldiers Thomas had left in the village were security against harm, but not against the pillaging. Besides, they would be gone soon, recalled by their commander to other battlefields.

She forced her tears to retreat.

Finally, the figure she'd been watching for entered the hall from the screen directly below her. Meg. Every step was marked by terror; the platters of bread shook in her hands. She'd been taken from the bakery that morning to work in the castle kitchen. Meg's father had been ready to storm the castle himself, but Mackenna had made him realize that she could easily get Meg out without arousing suspicion.

Disguised as a working lad, Mackenna had slipped in and out of the castle gates carrying a bushel of apples or leading a goat. She slept in the granary at night and left when the gates opened in the morning. But tonight she would make use of the passage that led from the pit.

She watched as one of Gilvane's men grabbed a platter out of Meg's hand and crushed her against him. The other platter of bread tipped and spilled its load into the rushes, rousing a pack of hounds to a scuffle for the booty.

"After dinner, Roderick," Gilvane shouted. "Let the girl finish serving." As quick as a doe, Meg broke out of the man's arms and skittered back toward the kitchen.

"Later," Gilvane had promised. A temporary reprieve.

Mackenna left the loft as the tune ended and ducked into the buttery. When Meg came through the passage again, she snagged her by the elbow and brought her inside. The girl's mouth was open to scream, but her terror was too large to fit through.

"'Tis Mackenna, Meg. If you scream, I'll pinch you."

Meg nearly swooned in relief. "Am I happy to see you!"

"Good, then follow me."

They went through the chapel, and kept to the perimeter of the bailey until Mackenna found her old office. The door fell open against a crate. Her worktables were gone, and her scrolls. It didn't matter anymore.

She lit a rushlight and led Meg down the stairs. She handed Meg down through the opening in the floor, and then followed her. Half way down the passage, she noticed a branching of the tunnel that hadn't been there before—not ten feet deep, but its walls were rough and the floor littered with the dark rubble of digging. Picks and shovels leaned against the walls, buckets were stacked in columns waiting for work to begin again.

"What is this, Mackenna?"

"I don't know. 'Tis strange. This new tunnel slants back up into the mountain, toward the castle, not away. Mother Mary!" She handed Meg the rushlight and examined a sampling of rock. " 'Tis lead, laced with silver ore. Gilvane is mining silver! The bastard."

Meg grabbed Mackenna's elbow. "Shhh, 'Kenna! I just heard something move."

Mackenna heard it, too. She shoved Meg behind her and raised the pick over her head. "Stop there. Who are you?"

The shape shifted and stepped into the watery cloud of light. "You tricked Giffard—"

"Francis?" Mackenna said, dropping the pick.

"But you didn't trick me, Lady Montclaire. Not this time!"

Meg handed Mackenna the rush light with a cry of joy and pushed past her. Francis caught Meg and held her, and Mackenna heard kissing noises in the dimness. She closed her eyes and leaned against the cold wall, longing for her lost husband, for the strength of his arms.

Francis finally set Meg on her feet, his suspicious nature returned. "What are you both doing down here?"

"One of Gilvane's men took a fancy to your Meg, Francis, and stole her from the village."

"Bloody bastard! Are you hurt, Meg?" He threw his arms around her again, caught her face in his hands.

"Mackenna saved me."

"She did?" He looked at Mackenna with renewed appreciation.

"And look what we found in the process. I know this passage well. These are new earth works. Silver ore! And I'll lay odds that the king knows nothing of it. This is why Gilvane returned to Fellhaven. He's known about the silver all along."

"I'll be damned—"

"Meg, you must hide in the village, but not with your family. Go to the mill. Francis, you must rejoin the garrison. There's such confusion in the ranks, Gilvane's officers won't notice a new man. And after tomorrow night, it won't matter anyway."

"Why won't it matter?" Francis asked.

"Because Gilvane will be gone, and he won't be coming back."

Giffard and his men rode lathered horses into the courtyard of Barnard Castle just as Thomas was leaving the stables.

"Thomas, I can explain!"

"Giffard, what is it? Is Mackenna ill? What are you doing here?" Thomas grabbed the reins of the blustering horse.

Giffard's wind-reddened complexion blanched. "Blessed Mother of God, she's not with you?" He slid off his mount.

Thomas went cold to his marrow. "What the hell do you mean, Giffard? Where is my wife?"

"Have you lost that woman again, Thomas?" Edward joined them, his humor as unwelcome as a swat from a bear.

"Where is she?" Thomas yanked Giffard up by the shoulders.

Giffard gasped to gain his breath. "She was in her chamber the night before last, locked in, the door guarded. She beaned my hearth boy, and left him trussed and naked in her bed."

Edward slapped Thomas on the back. "Constant, eh, Thomas?"

"Shut up, Your Grace." Thomas would have withdrawn his disloyal retort, but the king deserved it—and by his sheepish look, knew very well that he'd crossed a line. "Why the hell did you come looking for her here, Giffard?"

"Where else would she go? All she could talk about for the entire trip was you. She kept begging us to bring her back here. She escaped and headed this way as often as my back was turned. She said she missed you— wanted to make it up to you."

"Christ on the cross, Giffard! That was what she wanted you to think. My wife is on her way to Fellhaven."

"But she said—"

"She has said a thousand things and done the opposite."

"Then Francis was right. He told me she wouldn't come back here, that she would go home to her village. I insisted he come with me; and he followed for a while. Yesterday afternoon, he turned his horse without a by-your-leave and headed back toward Fellhaven."

"Aye, Francis is dead right. Mackenna's gone home. She'll lead a pitchfork assault on the castle and get herself killed! Excuse me, Your Grace. I have a wife to look after."

In the short hour it took Thomas to gather his men and equipment, he gained a writ of search from Edward. It would ensure him access to the castle and the village until Mackenna's mess was straightened out. By the time he arrived in Fellhaven, she would have at least four days' lead on him.

He prayed without hope she wouldn't do anything foolish.

Mackenna sat in the gallery with the musicians and watched the scroll as it passed from Gilvane's steward to Gilvane himself. He set aside the scroll and turned to speak with the man sitting beside him at the table. They laughed and drank a toast to each other.

"Read it, damn you," she said under her breath. But

instead of reading the scroll, Gilvane stabbed a mutton chop and chewed out the center. The man beside him picked up the scroll, and Gilvane grabbed it out of his hand. Lounging against the back of the chair, he unrolled it as he read it.

If she'd been closer to the dais, she could have seen the flicker of dread that crossed his face, and heard the sudden thumping of his black heart against the inside of his chest. But fear had a stench of its own, and she could smell it from the gallery.

Gilvane looked over the top of the scroll and found his neighbor's eyes on him, awaiting a comment. Cool as ice, Gilvane stuck the scroll into his sleeve and said something. When the man burst out laughing, Gilvane clapped him on the back and shared the laughter, but his eyes lifted from the game and scanned the crowded hall.

Before his gaze could reach the musician's gallery, Mackenna disappeared behind Colin, then made her way back to the village.

The terror would end tonight.

Chapter 27

Mackenna waited at the well in the market square. Matins had rung, and it was time for Gilvane to meet his blackmailer.

> Your plans for mining beneath the castle are known by one who has much to gain from the information. Come alone and unarmed to the well in the village at matins. Should you disobey this summons, or should harm come to the one you meet, a messenger is poised to send word and proof to King Edward.

That would smoke out the devil. He would underestimate his blackmailer and would come alone, or with but a few of his men. Pride and a need for secrecy would force him into the open.

Snow hadn't fallen for a day, leaving the market square frozen, dry, and rock-strewn. Mackenna was cloaked in her darkest clothing, sitting on the wellhead and leaning against the great cog Thomas's engineers had constructed. Dear Thomas. Days of fighting off her powerful memories of him had left her weary and wanting him more than ever. But she'd made her choice now, and so had he.

In the distance, she heard the faint clip of iron-shod hooves against stone shards. She could easily imagine the devil approaching, invisible save for the unearthly glow of red where his eyes ought to be.

Gilvane dismounted at the edge of the square, his form separating from his mount's in a cloud of dark fabric.

Mackenna lowered her voice and spoke through a gravelly whisper. "Do you come alone?"

As he shifted his feet, the rocks chattered his position. "As you demanded . . . sir."

She knew he couldn't see her; she hadn't moved, and would seem only a dark shape against more darkness. "Step forward, Gilvane. I would have you closer. This is private business—though you, more than I, would be loathe to make it public."

Rocks crunched beneath his boots as Gilvane slowly ate up the distance between them. He was careful to keep the well between himself and his blackmailer.

"So you think you know something of silver?" he asked easily.

"There is a vein of it beneath the castle. It's been worked quite recently by your trolls."

He snickered and stepped closer. "Who are you?"

"One who knows your past . . . and your future." She could smell the camphor, the dankness. Not a sound stirred but the whisper of his cloak.

"I'd be concerned for your own future, lad. You don't really think I am stupid enough to come here alone and unarmed."

She mocked his laughter. "Nay, Gilvane, 'tis not your way."

"Guards!" he shouted, lifting a dirk from inside his cloak.

The silence was sweet and frosty.

"Guards!" he shouted again, sparing a glance behind him.

"You don't really think I'd be stupid enough not to have your men bound and gagged by now, do you, Gilvane?"

"You dare lay a hand on my guards? I'll have your head for this—" He lunged for her and she moved aside.

Bryce and Galen threw their weight into him from

behind, and Addis sprang out of the well. Gilvane's dirk clattered to the ground as Bryce landed a bruising punch to his jaw. Her brothers imprisoned Gilvane's arms, and hauled him upright.

"There," Mackenna said, brushing off her hands. "That was simple. We should have done it fifteen years ago."

"What the devil is this mockery?" Gilvane shouted.

Torchlights flared, surging forward like a fiery wave from every part of the market square. Faces appeared beneath them, familiar faces, damp with courage and determination.

Mackenna let her cowl fall and stood in front of the cowering man. She smiled as he recognized her.

"Lady Montclaire? This is an outrage!"

" 'Tis justice, Gilvane, for the man who hanged my father."

He looked quizzical. "I don't even know your father."

"You knew him."

"You are mistaken, lass. I've hanged no one," Gilvane blustered. Mackenna could see his mind paddling backwards in time, trying to recall a man he might have hanged.

"His name was Randolph Hughes," she said, watching a heavy bead of sweat bridge a path along the furrows of Gilvane's brow and drip into his eyes. "You left him swinging in the firewind, in the bailey of yonder castle."

"I remember no such man." He flinched as she flipped his cloak latch open with his own dirk.

"I'm the one you should have hanged, Gilvane. My father was kind. I am not. Bryce, bring me the rope."

"Rope?" Gilvane gave a laugh that rang of disbelief. "Do you hold me for ransom?"

"Ransom? You're not worth the air you breathe." Mackenna held the knife at Gilvane's chin, while Bryce ripped aside the cloak and tied the man's hands behind his back.

"Let me go and I will reward you handsomely. I've got money and great influence at court."

"You've got only one thing that I desire, Gilvane."

"Tell me and 'tis yours."

"I want your life."

"My life?" He stammered and then swallowed. "You're going to kill me? Here? In front of all these witnesses?"

Gilvane stared out at the crowd of villagers, his face twitching with fear. He would find no hope in what he saw. Only anger and outrage, and relief that it would soon be over.

Mackenna shrugged. "I'll probably be hanged for killing a member of the nobility, but that is the price I must pay. Bring him, Addis."

As she started for the green, the crowd parted for the small procession. They jeered at Gilvane, calling down curses on his bared head.

A barrel waited beneath an overhanging limb of a huge oak. Above it, a thick rope with a noose dangling from the end swung slightly in the wind.

Gilvane dug his heels into the ground. "You can't do this, Lady Montclaire! For God's sake, turn me over to the king. I'll take his justice over this."

"Royal justice is unreliable. Nay, this time the justice is ours." She slipped the noose around Gilvane's neck, wedging it hard against his bobbing Adam's apple.

"You're all mad! Every last one of you!"

"Lift him," she said as she backed away.

"Stop this! I demand it!" Gilvane bleated as Bryce and Addis lifted him to the top of the barrel. Cadell drew the rope taut as the man teetered. Addis tied his feet together, then cut the rope that bound his hands. Gilvane reached for the noose, but stopped as Cadell drew it tighter.

"Why look here, Gilvane!" Mackenna pointed at the barrel beneath his boots. "Your soldiers missed this one. 'Tis a pity. The oversight will cost you your life."

"Lady Montclaire, be reasonable."

"But I am being reasonable. Your life for my father's. And for Nabon's wife and his two children; for the entire Styles family who perished for lack of a fire to

warm them; for Malcomb and Druella, and Cody's three
sisters; for Meg's mother, and Anne's and Kyle's; and
for the babies that never lived to suckle. Your life for all
these and so many others. You are nothing, Gilvane.
Your life is dust." Mackenna's stomach lurched.

"I remember none of this. I am no monster. Starvation is the way of the world. I'm not the cause."

"Tie it off, Addis."

Addis looped the rope around a gnarled root. He
stood back and brushed off his hands. Gilvane had to
stand unwavering on his toes to keep from choking.

"Stop this! I command that you . . ." His words faded
as she neared the barrel. He watched her with a wild,
wary eye. Mackenna could feel his terror. Her stomach
fluttered again. She searched her heart for triumph, and
found it empty. She wanted Thomas. She wanted
Gilvane to disappear.

"Does the king know of the vein of silver that runs
below the castle?" She gave the barrel a tap with the toe
of her boot. It teetered, and he drew himself up like a
sentry. "Remember, if you lie, you will die sooner rather
than later."

"Nay, the king knows nothing of the silver mine."

"Of course not. And you've begun to extract the ore.
Haven't you?" She growled the last and sped his reply.

"Aye, Lady Montclaire."

"Unless I missed my mark, it's bound for smelters
beyond the Scottish border. And to your support of
Balliol's rival, Robert Bruce."

"Aye, but there's plenty of silver for you and all these
good people, if you'll only—"

"Let you purchase your life with a promise of great
wealth?" She laughed, and its coldness startled her.
"Now who is mad?"

"I remember your father now. Randolph Hughes. Yes.
A clever man, but he knew too much, and—"

"And so you hanged him."

"'Twas nothing personal, Lady Montclaire. 'Twas
business."

"Business!" Mackenna felt sick again. Her hands were shaking, so she hid them.

"Aye, and if you think your husband will leave this commerce unscathed, you are naive. A husband must atone for his wife's sins. Thomas Montclaire will surely hang, if you hang me."

A chill nearly dropped her to her knees. "Leave my husband out of this."

"You've brought him into it, yourself, Lady Montclaire." Gilvane's voice slid into a studied seduction. "He'll hang alongside you. Can you live with that knowledge?"

Mackenna closed off his argument with the barest of excuses. "The king will know this is my act of justice, mine alone."

"My lady, I'll have this silver worked by the good people of my village. Together we will labor to bring great wealth to Fellhaven. No one needs to know but us."

"I'd rather be executed for hanging you, than for a charge of treason. Are you ready, Gilvane?"

Sweat glistened on his brow, slick in the torchlight. His lips were drawn tightly; his eyes watered with his frantic efforts at remaining on this earth for a few moments longer. How precious those final moments must seem . . .

"Hang him, Mackenna!" Nabon's voice was raw with the moment, a gentle soul persuaded to the supreme act of violence.

Could she close the circle? Could she hang the man who hanged her father? She had always been a coward. Too cowardly to choose a husband like an honorable woman, too cowardly to keep the one she loved. Was she too much the coward to hang a devil?

Just a few steps forward, a nudge with her foot, and John Gilvane would be gone forever. The consequences would be swift and sure. She would be outlawed and spend her days in the fells, leading her raids on the next lord. But the circle would be closed.

"Let me kick over the bleedin' barrel, 'Kenna!" Garvey pushed forward, but Mackenna stopped him.

"I'm the reeve, as was my father. I'll close the circle."

Gilvane's fear had silenced him, but his twisted face spoke his confession. She had brought him to justice when no one else would. 'Twas the only way to put her father to rest, the only way to ensure that Gilvane would come no more.

Just a nudge, that's all it would take.

"Oh, my love, you haven't got it in you."

His voice bathed her in warm honey and made her turn.

"Thomas?"

He was there at the edge of the circle.

"Cut him down, Mackenna."

Tears stung her eyes, foreign, hot, thick with salt. "Nay, I cannot." She turned away from the ravaging gentleness in his eyes to stare up at the creature quivering on the edge of doom. The barrel canted slightly as Gilvane tried to shift his weight.

"If you hang him, Mackenna, I'll lose you forever."

"If I don't, he'll destroy everything that I love."

Thomas's steady steps were the only sounds in the night air.

"I heard his confession, sweet. He's signed his own death warrant. But his life isn't yours to take. It belongs to God and to the king."

"To forgive and release as he pleases."

"God may reprieve Gilvane this time, but Edward will not."

"I don't believe you or your noble friends, and their noble games. Life is cheap."

"Even the babe you're carrying?" His arms came round her shoulders, and his mouth was at her temple, making his words more tender for their heat.

Mackenna hung her head. "There was no babe, Thomas."

"Aye, love, it was there all along." No one could hear him but Mackenna; these were private words. "You were just too busy with your rebellion to realize it."

"I'm not—" she whispered.

"Dizzy, and sick at your stomach, sleeping all the time." He turned her in his arms, and whispered. "Aye, you're carrying our babe, Mackenna. You must be."

Her flux had never come. She put her hand to her stomach, and gazed up and up into his flashing dark eyes. "Thomas . . ." She'd hurt him so terribly. "I'm so sorry. I know you can never forgive me, but—"

" 'Tis done, my love. Can you forgive *me*?"

He smelled wonderful; he was worn and wind-blown, but he was her sky, and her salvation made flesh.

"Mackenna, I lied to you from the beginning to make it easier to control this valley. I used you to influence the villagers. I kissed you when I knew I shouldn't. I used my authority to rid me of the rival for your hand. I married you, knowing that I had no right to accept the care of the village from you, because the holding wasn't mine, because I would have to take you from your home if I wasn't granted the holding. I did all this out of my selfish and consuming love for you. And when you lied about losing our babe, in order to save the village that I had lost for you, I couldn't see the parallel. I accused you of the very sins I'd been committing against you."

" 'Tis not the same at all."

"It is, and I was wrong. And I was piggish and blind, and I let the past become part of our present. Forgive me, love. I've offered Edward a handsome price for Fellhaven. When he learns of Gilvane's treason, he'll have no choice but to give it to me. Fellhaven is safe. You needn't carry out this hanging."

She stepped away. "But Gilvane hanged my father."

He followed her. "Is it vengeance you seek for your gentle father? Ask yourself what he would do. If he were standing here instead of you, could Randolph Hughes hang the man?"

The answer was clear.

"Nay, Thomas, he could never hang anyone." She measured her life by her father's creed. "Nor can I."

"He'd be very proud of you, Mackenna. Proud as any man can be. Proud as I am. I love you, wife." He lifted her into his arms and held her against him, rocking her, kissing the salty tears from her lips.

"I love you, Thomas. And I love our babe." Mackenna clung to him, kissed him, pressed her cheek against his bristly face.

"You'll pay for this, Montclaire!" Gilvane screeched. He was gasping for breath, his anger returned with the reprieve.

"Cut him down and tie him, Cadell," Thomas said.

"I'd not be so quick, Thomas." The familiar voice broke out of the darkness, and a tall figure moved into the circle.

"Edward! Welcome to Fellhaven." Thomas set Mackenna on her feet, but held fast to her, covering her hand where it rested on her stomach. A murmur grew and spread through the crowd. A king, visiting Fellhaven?

"My liege—" Gilvane squealed like a pig.

Edward peered up at Gilvane as though sizing up an oddity he'd paid a half-penny to see at a market faire.

"I wouldn't speak if I were you, Gilvane. You've said enough to send yourself to the gallows. Another word and I'll have you drawn and quartered." Edward turned to Thomas and Mackenna.

Mackenna offered a deep curtsey. "My lord king, I ask your pardon for the many wrongs I have done you."

He lifted her chin and chuckled. "Lady Montclaire, you've snared my favorite as your husband, and forced him to accept the lordship of this valley." He stopped to give Thomas a wink, then looked back down at Mackenna. "I underestimated you."

"I meant only to keep my village safe."

"Would that my ministers were all as clever as you. As for him—" He waved his hand toward Gilvane, gone still as a statue. "He'll not be bothering you, or anyone ever again. Thomas, I give this holding to you, for the price you offered. Now that I know the worth of your treasury, I shall know where to come for my next campaign."

Thomas smiled wryly. "Thank you, my liege."

"And Lady Montclaire, to reward your persistence and to encourage such loyalty and successful commerce, I grant the town of Fellhaven to you, to hold in trust to your descendants, separate from the castle holding."

"To me? I don't understand."

Thomas leaned down to her. "You've been granted a town charter, my love."

She thought the two men had gone a bit mad. "But I don't want to own a town—"

"You've owned us for years, 'Kenna," Cadell said, strutting forward with the rest of her brothers. "Why not make it official?"

The market square erupted in laughter.

"But—" she began, her face hot, her head spinning.

Thomas glared down at her, his brows drawn fiercely. "'Tis at an end, Mackenna. Just stop where you are and be happy. Your father is at peace. We're home now, the village belongs to you, our babe is growing 'neath your heart—"

"And 'tis all because of you, Thomas Montclaire. My love, my husband."

"Because of me? 'Tis your schemes that brought it all about. I merely sat back and loved you."

Mackenna had forgotten how hot tears could be. They scalded as they burst their dams and slid down her cheeks. She held Thomas tightly, raining kisses down on him.

He smiled that heart-stealing half-smile. "I missed you, love, fiercely, like a husband shouldn't miss his wife."

"And I missed you. I wasn't sure I'd ever see you again."

"'Til death parts us." He'd had all the kisses from her he could take and still remain civilized. "We need to be alone just now, wife, else I will make a fool of myself here in your market square." He lifted her into his arms and carried her to the edge of the circle. "If Your Grace would excuse us . . ."

"Take your time, Thomas."

But his wife was nibbling on his ear, and whispering

what she planned to do to him as soon as they were alone. "That, my liege, might be difficult. My lady wife is the most stubborn and impatient woman I've ever met."

Mackenna giggled as Thomas carried her out of the circle and across the market square. "I may be stubborn and impatient, my lord. But I do know how to choose a husband."

Avon Romances—
the best in exceptional authors and unforgettable novels!

WICKED AT HEART
    Danelle Harmon
78004-6/ $5.50 US/ $7.50 Can

SOMEONE LIKE YOU
    Susan Sawyer
78478-5/ $5.50 US/ $7.50 Can

MIDNIGHT BANDIT
    Marlene Suson
78429-7/ $5.50 US/ $7.50 Can

PROUD WOLF'S WOMAN
    Karen Kay
77997-8/ $5.50 US/ $7.50 Can

THE HEART AND THE HOLLY
    Nancy Richards-Akers
78002-X/ $5.50 US/ $7.50 Can

ALICE AND THE GUNFIGHTER
    Ann Carberry
77882-3/ $5.50 US/ $7.50 Can

THE MACKENZIES: LUKE
    Ana Leigh
78098-4/ $5.50 US/ $7.50 Can

FOREVER BELOVED
    Joan Van Nuys
78118-2/ $5.50 US/ $7.50 Can

INSIDE PARADISE
    Elizabeth Turner
77372-4/ $5.50 US/ $7.50 Can

CAPTIVATED
    Colleen Corbet
78027-5/ $5.50 US/ $7.50 Can

Avon Romantic Treasures

*Unforgettable, enthralling love stories,
sparkling with passion and adventure
from Romance's bestselling authors*

SUNDANCER'S WOMAN *by Judith E. French*
77706-1/$5.99 US/$7.99 Can

JUST ONE KISS *by Samantha James*
77549-2/$5.99 US/$7.99 Can

HEARTS RUN WILD *by Shelly Thacker*
78119-0/$5.99 US/$7.99 Can

DREAM CATCHER *by Kathleen Harrington*
77835-1/$5.99 US/$7.99 Can

THE MACKINNON'S BRIDE *by Tanya Anne Crosby*
77682-0/$5.99 US/$7.99 Can

PHANTOM IN TIME *by Eugenia Riley*
77158-6/$5.99 US/$7.99 Can

RUNAWAY MAGIC *by Deborah Gordon*
78452-1/$5.99 US/$7.99 Can

YOU AND NO OTHER *by Cathy Maxwell*
78716-4/$5.99 US/$7.99 Can